NO
ROAD
HOME

ALSO BY JOHN FRAM

The Bright Lands

NO
ROAD
HOME

A NOVEL

JOHN FRAM

ATRIA BOOKS

New York   London   Toronto   Sydney   New Delhi

ATRIA
BOOKS

An Imprint of Simon & Schuster, LLC
1230 Avenue of the Americas
New York, NY 10020

First Atria Books hardcover edition July 2024

ATRIA B O O K S and colophon are trademarks of Simon & Schuster, LLC

Simon & Schuster: Celebrating 100 Years of Publishing in 2024

For information about special discounts for bulk purchases, please contact Simon & Schuster Special Sales at 1-866-506-1949 or business@simonandschuster.com.

The Simon & Schuster Speakers Bureau can bring authors to your live event. For more information or to book an event, contact the Simon & Schuster Speakers Bureau at 1-866-248-3049 or visit our website at www.simonspeakers.com.

Interior design by Erika R. Genova

Manufactured in the United States of America

1 3 5 7 9 10 8 6 4 2

Library of Congress Cataloging-in-Publication Data is available.

ISBN 978-1-6680-3144-5
ISBN 978-1-6680-3146-9 (ebook)

For my father,
who showed me how good a man can be

God loves you,
But not enough to save you.

—Ethel Cain

Ask, and you will receive; search, and you will find.
—Matthew 7:7

THE WRIGHTS WHO MATTER

JEROME JEREMIAH WRIGHT — Prophet, Patriarch and CEO of Two Creeks Ministries

ABIGAIL WRIGHT — His wife (deceased)

CORAH WRIGHT — His sister

SARAH NELLA WRIGHT — Jerome's older daughter, COO of Two Creeks Ministries and Head of Ramorah (House and Grounds)

RUTH WRIGHT — Jerome's younger daughter, Head of Congregational Development

HUGO WRIGHT — Her husband, Director of Praise and Worship

GINGER WRIGHT — Ruth and Hugo's older daughter

MATTHIAS WRIGHT — Ginger's son

RICHARD WRIGHT — Ruth and Hugo's son, Director of Future Ministry

KASSANDRA WRIGHT — Richard's wife

ALYSSA WRIGHT — Ruth and Hugo's younger daughter

TOBIAS ("TOBY") TUCKER — Her husband, the newest addition to the family

LUCA TUCKER — Toby's son

STAFF AT RAMORAH:

MARIE AND JULIAN — Hired help

YE BROOD OF VIPERS

JEROME

THE KNIFE SLIDES FREE, the door clicks closed and here, at last, is the rain. A cold drop strikes his eye, another, but Jerome doesn't blink. He can't. The knife has seen to that.

Jerome warned his family this storm was coming. They've been warned all year. They've been "enjoined to repent," as the old translations say, harried in word and deed these past ten months, but will they finally listen, now the thunder is rolling in over the black grounds, the water pooling around his head?

Who is he kidding?

Jerome watches the stars. He lies bleeding in the night, staring at a sky rapidly shrouding itself in cloud, and knows there will be no more messages from that quarter, no more revelations. Lethal Scorpio, pious Anuradha, the dim and terrible shapes of the ancient Akkadian constellations, their names long since lost to dust: light-years of fate and fire are all vanishing above him, a foot at a time. Billions of years ago, the Lord sent a stray scrap of rock drifting through the void so that here, now, on a rooftop in the middle of nowhere, this dying old man can watch a comet, brilliant as a phosphorous needle, thread its way through blackest velvet. His brother would have gasped.

Regular viewers of Jerome's television program would be surprised to learn how widely the old man has read. More than a few of the folks at home would probably run screaming if they'd seen the contents of their favorite preacher's shelves these last few months. But even before his tastes turned to the esoteric (or the heretical, as any honest man would admit), Jerome once read that the Lord's sole consolation to the dying is the way the brain begins to fizz as it chokes for air. They say that old memories surface. That life flashes before the dimming eyes.

As has been the case for most of his life, Jerome now finds the Lord lacking.

As the stars vanish above him, one by one, Jerome's mind shows him none of the things he's hoped (prayed, begged, pleaded) to see one last time, the memories he's worked all his life to reclaim.

Instead, as Jerome Jeremiah Wright breathes his last, he thinks of the man his granddaughter introduced to the family today. Tobias. Goes by Toby. Jerome thinks of Toby and of Toby's son, and in a flash of horror he realizes that Toby and his boy are in even graver danger than Jerome could have ever imagined. Jerome understands the meaning of an omen that has haunted him for days.

And Jerome realizes it's already too late.

A sharp breeze blows over the roof. There might be a rushed whisper in that breeze, a still small voice, or it might merely be the storm. Rainwater pools on Jerome's black eyes. The light of Aquarius is reflected there, pouring out his cup of disaster before he, too, is lost to the clouds and all of Ramorah dwells in darkness.

Quiet bodies move in the house below. Blood dries on a long blade.

And from the shadowy corner of a lonely room, a hand reaches out for a small ankle in the dark.

It is midnight: the appointed time, the witching hour.

TOBY

Twelve Hours Earlier

THE LAKE SEEMED TO spring up out of nowhere. It unrolled beneath them in a great green sheet, water as far as the eye could see, so huge and jarring Toby's first thought was that his family had stumbled onto some undiscovered ocean. They'd left Austin two hours ago—like everything else in their relationship, his new wife had covered a terrifying amount of distance at a blistering speed—and in that time they'd driven through nothing but brown plains, yellow scrubland, the occasional withered cedar practically crying out for water.

And now here was this lush, miserly lake that fed nothing but a tiny town and a few lucky pines.

"I've never seen water that color before," Toby said.

"Grandma loved it," Alyssa said. "She said it looked like money."

Toby's wife was right. The distant waves did indeed have the emerald tinge of a dollar bill, but there was more to them than that. Once, long ago, Toby's sister would have spent ages trying to work out the precise name for every shade framed by the windshield of Alyssa's Mercedes. Cyan. Evergreen. Envy.

And then, with a *slam* so loud Toby was almost surprised no one else in the car heard it, he closed a door in his mind and turned its key with a brilliant *click*, sealing away all thought of his sister.

It was better not to think about Willow this weekend. Safer. A few seconds' work and she was buried so deep Toby could almost forget she'd ever existed at all.

"I'm sorry there won't be any swimming this trip, buddy." Alyssa spoke to the rearview mirror. "The house is nowhere near the shore."

Luca, Toby's son, looked up from his coloring in the back seat. "That's okay. I can't swim."

Alyssa shot Toby a look: *He can't?*

Toby only shrugged, embarrassed. He'd spent the last seven years providing a home for his son by working as many jobs as he could cram into a day. When was he supposed to teach the boy how to do something as frivolous as swim?

Wasn't it funny, though: all the things Toby and Alyssa still didn't know about each other's families?

Toby's new wife brought them to a stop outside a dusty Cracker Barrel that overlooked the lake. Alyssa somehow took up three parking spaces with her single black Mercedes. "They still make Cracker Barrels?" Toby said.

"They do outside of Los Angeles. Time for a comportment check."

"A what?"

"Can you imagine if my family saw me with this hair?"

Toby liked a lot about Alyssa: her work ethic, her laugh, her astonishing eyes. "I like your hair," he said.

"You're not my family." She swung open the door, glanced back with a wince. "Sorry."

As they crossed the parking lot, Toby held out his hand for Luca. His son acquiesced with a roll of his eyes. "All right, *Tobias.*" To Luca, Toby was never, ever Dad.

Except when they neared the door to the store, Luca gave Toby's hand a tight squeeze: *I'm here.*

Toby squeezed back: *I know.*

The inside of the Cracker Barrel was blurry with dust. Toby felt like he was viewing it through the tube of a dim cathode ray. The restaurant in back was empty and dark. The store, too, was practically abandoned. In a distant aisle, Alyssa plucked up a can of hair spray and waved to him on her way to the bathroom. "Mind taking care of this for me?"

Toby was surprised she didn't just steal it. His wife might have been made of money, but he'd seen her rob stores blind. He'd even helped her once or twice, the two of them giggling like kids as they scampered into her Mercedes.

There wasn't another woman in the world like Alyssa. That was probably for the best.

Luca slipped free of Toby's hand and trudged toward the other bathroom, the string of glass beads braided into his long hair chiming a perfect C-sharp.

A round old woman smiled at Toby from behind the cash register. She kept smiling for a few seconds longer than he would have liked. When they were alone, she said, "It's good to see Miss Alyssa looking so happy."

"Yes."

"Are you . . . Tobias?"

He gave her his most gracious smile. "Toby is fine, thank you."

The old woman had a name tag pinned to her generous chest: HI I'M LOTTIE. "Goodness. Lucky me. None of us around here even knew Miss Alyssa was *engaged* until we saw the wedding announcement last week. You're even more handsome than in the picture."

Alyssa had warned Toby about this. The little town of Hebron, Texas, apparently tracked the minutiae of her family's life the way another town would follow its local football team. Toby couldn't blame them: judging by the faded state of this store, Alyssa's family had the only decent business going around here.

"We moved fast." Toby gave old Miss Lottie another smile. If he could do one thing, it was smile. "We knew what we wanted."

With her long neck and narrow head and plump cylinder of a body, old Miss Lottie of the Cracker Barrel almost resembled an enema poking from the neck of a pale blue muumuu. "Your daughter's precious, by the way."

"My son, actually," Toby said, though the word had never meant much in his house. Luca was whoever he wanted to be. For now, he wore his hair long and dressed in lots of pink and mauve and called himself a boy, which was fine with Toby. If Luca ever decided to change that, Toby would adjust accordingly. It really wasn't rocket science.

But still Toby added, "Thank you."

Miss Lottie had already forgotten what she'd said. She was gazing at Toby with the distant, dazed look he'd endured from strangers almost from the day he'd hit puberty. He was thirty now, but he looked like a brooding twenty-five, blessed (if that was the word for it) with the hard cheeks and pointed jaw and deep-set eyes that photographers dreamed of. Toby knew from long experience that he looked both desirable and utterly opaque, like the cover boy of a romance novel or the face of a new cologne.

Indeed, Toby had lived on his looks for about as long as he could stomach the modeling industry, and then a little longer. Mere days after he graduated high school, Toby and his sister, Willow, lost their uncle Ezra to a heart attack (the sweaty bastard always found a way to escape an obligation), leaving them little choice but to pack their bags and fuel up the car and light out to LA the way they'd always joked about doing. Even in his worst moments in California, Toby had never looked back on Texas fondly.

For a few years after they'd arrived in Los Angeles, it seemed as if his sister's painting career would take off at any moment. It just needed a little more of Toby's support, and then a little more. But the Smoldering Factory (as Toby used to call the modeling business) really was as vapid and mercenary as everyone believed, so much so that he was almost relieved when he aged out of it. His sister's art career had long since imploded by then, anyway.

Slam. Click. Toby closed the door on Willow again and gave himself a little shake. What was his sister doing here again, popping up in his mind after he'd sealed her away not fifteen minutes ago? It didn't bode well for the weekend if his mental defenses were already this faulty.

The old lady at the Cracker Barrel noticed none of Toby's anxiety. She was still staring at the man like he'd caught her in a thrall. Toby knew from long experience that the woman's fascination with his face would pass on its own, like a stomach virus. He just had to wait. In the meantime, he adopted a distant, benevolent expression, staring past the old woman's shoulder, looking at the sign over the counter (KEYS CUT HERE) and the rows of dusty crosses on display, at the massive lake blazing with emeralds through a dingy window. He held Alyssa's black Amex between two fingers, waiting to pay for that hair spray. He smiled.

But when Toby looked back at Miss Lottie, her expression was changed. The old woman's gaze had wandered from his face. It had drifted down his chest and over his arms, halting at the single fault in his looks that had always prevented him from modeling in the big leagues. Miss Lottie's eyes went wide.

"Son—let me see that scar of yours."

The sudden fear in her voice sent a sliver of ice rolling down Toby's neck. He flipped his right arm over. For as long as he could remember, a thick shaft of white scar tissue had stretched from his wrist to just below his elbow, where it ended in a wide half loop. The scar looked almost like a comet, or a shepherd's crook, or—

"A fishhook." The old woman seemed barely brave enough to say the word aloud. She shook her head, a thin lip bobbing in shock. "Oh my dear Jesus. It's you."

BARRING A FEW SUNDAY ads for defunct department stores and the wedding announcement he shared with Alyssa, Toby had only appeared in the newspapers once in his life. MIRACLE CHILDREN SURVIVE DEADLY HIGHWAY CRASH, the article had been titled. (And don't forget the second header: BOTH PARENTS SLAIN.)

The article had run in a local rag up near Dallas when Toby was six, though he hadn't seen it until years later, when he'd discovered the story lining a drawer full of cat food in his uncle's mildewed house. He'd read the article twice, committed it to memory, and then burned it in a trash can out back, even though it had contained perhaps the only photographs of his mother and father still in existence at the time. *An autopsy revealed the blood of both parents contained several times the legal limit of alcohol*, read the photo's caption.

They were probably better off as ash.

Now, two decades and a hundred miles away, as Toby stood bewildered in that dusty Cracker Barrel, he briefly wondered if old Miss Lottie recognized his scar from that newspaper article. Toby had a remarkable memory—he'd spent so much of his life keeping his mind under lock and key, it was rare for him to forget anything by accident—and after a few moments of consideration, he felt confident that the article from twenty-four years ago had made no mention of the scar.

But if that was the case, how in the hell did this old woman know who he was?

"He told me you were coming today. By the Lord Jesus, he did."

Miss Lottie swept a shaky hand at a row of books stacked at the end of her counter. The books bore titles like *The Plan He Has for You*; *Led into Your Promised Land*; *The Seven Sacred Secrets to Knowing—and CLAIMING!—the Wonders God Has in Your Future*. A trim, tan old man with capped teeth beamed from every cover. The man looked smooth and tailored and perfectly well-rested (which was to say, incredibly rich), and he possessed the most remarkable eyes Toby had ever seen. They were a deep, deep blue, almost a bright black, though even that hardly did them justice.

The closest Toby could come up with was this: the old man's eyes were the color of the night sky flirting with the edge of a star.

On every book, their author's name was printed in towering letters above his beaming face. JEROME JEREMIAH WRIGHT—AMERICA'S PROPHET.

And Alyssa's grandfather.

"Jerome told you I was stopping by?" Toby asked Miss Lottie. He looked around the dusty Cracker Barrel. "Does he . . . shop here often?"

"He didn't tell me *here*. He told me on the show—on *The Prophecy Hour*! Do you have any idea all the years I've called and called just to touch the hem of that man's garment? And last week, guess who finally got to talk to him, right at the end of the broadcast?" Old Miss Lottie thrust a finger at her own chest. "Me."

"Congratulations?"

Lottie waved this away. "He didn't want to say a word about me. All he wanted to talk about was *you*."

After the car accident, sweaty Uncle Ezra had grudgingly accepted custody of his niece and nephew. In Ezra's house, there had been more cats than there had been rules, but of those few rules, the most important had been Ezra's edict that the entire family gather every Sunday morning for church service. Join him on the couch, that is: between his emphysema and "these damned oil prices" (had the man ever expected them to go down?), Ezra refused to drive the forty-five minutes to the nearest Baptist church. Instead, week in and week out, he'd tuned into a glitzy, exuberant, overwhelming televangelism program known as *The Prophecy Hour*.

The star of the show was none other than Jerome Jeremiah Wright, America's prophet.

Even as a child, Toby had found everything about *The Prophecy Hour* faintly deceptive, beginning with its title. A typical broadcast was, in fact, over four hours long, and each hour was stuffed to the brim with worship sing-alongs, talk show–style interviews with famous figures in the Christian world, short Bible readings and meditations, all of it punctuated by dramatic appearances from Jerome himself. With a swell of live music, Jerome strode grandly to a pulpit the height of a fence post to deliver a punchy sermon on "the roles of men and women in God's kingdom," or "purity of the body and spirit," and "our financial obligation to the Almighty" (a favorite topic) before taking live on-air calls from people around the world. "Speak, friend," Jerome began every call. "The Lord is listening."

It sounded like old Miss Lottie from the Cracker Barrel had lately been one of those callers. And apparently the Lord had had plenty to tell her.

Leaning against her counter, old Lottie spoke to Toby in a rapid, clipped whisper, shooting frantic looks over his shoulder as if terrified they would be interrupted. "The man with the fishhook scar will visit by the end of this week. This very week. That's what Jerome said to me. And here you are, just as he foretold."

Toby blinked, unnerved in spite of himself. After he gave up modeling, he'd worked for years as an aide in a nursing home. He knew all the signs of dementia: the bewildered eyes, the twitching hands, the sneaking inability to carry a conversation.

He wished he saw those signs here. He didn't.

"I'm . . . not sure what to say, ma'am."

"You're not supposed to say anything, you're supposed to *listen*." A toilet flushed in the back of the store. In a rush, Lottie jerked up three fingers. "Jerome made me swear—*swear*—that I would give you three warnings. Are you listening? 'Give that man three warnings from the Lord.' First: 'Warn that man with the fishhook scar that he is heading into a brood of vipers.' Do you hear me? You are heading into a brood of vipers. Second: 'Urge that man not to fall into the judgment the Lord his God has prepared for that brood.' Third, and this—*this*—is the most important of all: 'Warn that man that his son—'"

"Ready?"

A voice behind Toby made them both jump. It was Alyssa, emerging at last from the restroom. Her blond hair was piled high on her head in a way he'd never seen on her before. She'd daubed on some lip gloss and contoured her cheeks.

Toby was surprised. All this "comportment" looked false on Alyssa, desperately Texan. His wife hadn't even worn makeup to her own wedding last week.

Until this afternoon, the only cosmetics Toby had ever seen his wife indulge in were the gentle false lashes that somehow made her remarkable eyes even more astonishing. Six months ago in LA, Toby's world had stuttered in its orbit when she'd first turned those blue-black eyes his way.

"Miss Wright," Miss Lottie said, her voice sounding surprisingly calm and chipper for someone who'd just conveyed a message from God Almighty. "*Missus* Wright, I should say. I was just catching up with your new husband."

Luca emerged from the other bathroom, adjusting the shoulders of his shirt like he couldn't quite get comfortable in the nicest polo money could buy. He'd pushed his long hair behind his ears. "Is this enough comfortment?"

"Comportment." Alyssa smiled. She raised the key fob to her Mercedes in Toby's direction. "We should get moving. They're waiting for us."

"Is that right?" Old Lottie pushed away Alyssa's credit card. There was an unmistakable tremor in her fingers, at the edge of her smile. For some reason, her eyes never left little Luca's face. "Where are y'all headed?"

Before Toby could speak, Alyssa said, "Just a little birthday get-together. We wouldn't even bother celebrating if it weren't for this handsome man."

Alyssa dawdled near the aisles, clearly waiting for Toby to move for the door. (Was he being paranoid, or did it seem as if she didn't want to risk him and Miss Lottie spending any more time alone?)

Like a man in a dream, Toby smiled. "That's right. I'm off to meet my in-laws."

"I FOUND SOMETHING PRETTY in the bathroom." On their way back across the parking lot, Luca dug his free hand into his pocket and emerged with a scrap of brilliant blue wrapping paper that was patterned all over with sailboats and clouds.

"Very impressive," Toby said absentmindedly, his mind still standing at Miss Lottie's counter, wondering how many men with scars that resembled fishhooks were roaming around this quiet corner of Texas. What were the odds one of those men would step into this particular Cracker Barrel at the end of this particular week?

This—this—is the most important of all: "Warn that man that his son—"

Toby's mind snapped back into place. "Where *exactly* in the bathroom did you find that paper, Luca?"

His son sucked in his top lip, like he was afraid the truth might escape of its own volition. Toby knew that look.

"Did you find it in the trash can, Luca?"

"No! It was *under* the trash can."

Oh, Jesus. Ever since Luca had learned about recycled art last year at the private school in Echo Park where Toby had worked as a teacher's assistant, Toby hadn't been able to stop the boy from rifling through all the garbage he could find.

"Are you a raccoon, Luca?"

"Raccoons eat trash, Tobias. I *transform* it."

Alyssa beeped the Mercedes. "Please don't transform anything at Ramorah, sweetheart," Alyssa said. "My aunt Sarah Nella would have a cow if she found you rooting through the garbage."

"She can eat a whole cow?"

"She'd probably eat you if you're not careful. Believe me—you don't want to get on Sarah Nella's bad side."

A moment later, the Mercedes darted from the parking lot fast enough to give Toby whiplash. Raising her voice over the roaring engine, Alyssa said, "Speaking of which, I should probably warn you guys about a few things."

The little town of Hebron whipped past them—subdivisions, a strip mall, a few startled pickup trucks—until soon there was nothing to see but empty brass scrubland through Alyssa's window and the enormous green lake inching past Toby's. They were heading east.

"There's no cell service at the estate, so you'll need to use the Wi-Fi. I texted you the password the other day—did you save it?"

"Of course."

"And do you still have the list I sent you?"

Toby swiped open his phone and found his cell service already dwindling. He scrolled up through all the messages he'd shared with Alyssa last week, marveling at the speed with which their life had changed, the unnerving ease of it. Last Monday, he and his wife had taken a trip to city hall for a marriage license, a toothless bag lady serving as their witness. The very next day, Alyssa had quit her job at the private Silver Lake clinic where she'd worked as a pediatrician ("Why would they need two weeks? Those kids are too rich to die") and hired a crew of movers to pack up her house in Echo Park and ship everything, from the Mercedes in the garage to the last fork in the kitchen, to "a little place" she already owned in downtown Austin. Was there a reason she wanted to move so suddenly? "Does there have to be?" she'd said, in a tone that hadn't brooked much conversation. "It's not like we have anything keeping us here."

No, nothing but Toby's friends and work and a decade's worth of memories. Next to Alyssa's assets, he supposed that didn't add up to much.

On his phone, he found a file his wife had sent him. It bore the humble title *The Wrights Who Matter.*

Never taking her eyes off the road, Alyssa said, "So, from the top. Jerome was married to my grandmother, Abigail, for almost forty years. Grandma Abigail's been dead for twenty, but sometimes we still talk about her like she'll walk through the door at any minute. And we're not always looking forward to it."

"That bad?"

"Grandma Abigail liked things a certain way."

Toby grinned. "And you don't?"

"I like things *my* way." His wife grinned back. "You'll notice there's a difference."

"Noticed. Jerome has a sister at the house, too, right?"

"Corah, yes. Much easier to handle. Just smile and look pretty and say how brilliant Jerome is, she'll love you forever. Corah's getting a little fuzzy, but she's still strong as a horse. After Jerome had his fall last year, she became the best nurse you could ask for. Or bodyguard, depending how you look at it."

Toby wondered what he should make of this. "Then Jerome and Abigail had two children."

"Aunt Sarah Nella and my mom. Sarah Nella runs the house and grounds and a good chunk of the business."

"Sarah Nella is the woman you're afraid will eat Luca if he's not careful?"

"Sarah Nella . . . Aunt Sarah Nella is quite a bit older than Mom, and about eighty percent more terrifying. Sarah Nella's had two strokes. I'm pretty sure she took them as a challenge."

"And she never married?"

A funny look crossed Alyssa's face. "No. Aunt Sarah Nella never married."

Toby waited to see if his wife would add anything, but not for long. He and Alyssa may have only met in March, but he already knew that nothing, not even torture, could compel her to say a word more than she wanted to.

Toby and his wife had that in common, come to think of it.

Alyssa went on. "And, of course, you've already met Jerome's other daughter. Ruth. My mother."

Had Toby ever. Ruth Wright, Alyssa's mother, bore almost no resemblance to Toby's new wife. Whereas Alyssa was tall and sharp and imposingly slim ("Los Angeles made flesh," an old friend of Toby's had called her, not entirely kindly), Alyssa's mother was short and curvy and eager, her hair billowing from a massive blowout, her lips as plump and glossy as a Valentine heart.

Six weeks ago, Ruth had flown out to California—joined by Alyssa's father and brother—to meet Toby, the man who'd somehow stolen her daughter's heart. Alyssa's father, Hugo, was a towering bear of a man with wide shoulders and ham-hock thighs. Hugo was a former Marine, as evidenced by the Semper Fi signet ring and buzz cut and the old traces of strength that were slowly, inexorably, vanishing beneath a layer of fat. "So great to meet you, Tobes," Hugo had said at the airport. He was the first and only human in existence who'd ever called Toby *Tobes.* "What's popping?"

My back, Toby thought. Alyssa's parents had both hugged him so tight you'd think they were trying to squeeze out a sample of his marrow.

Alyssa's brother, Richard, had his father's height and easy smile, but where Hugo was softening into bulk, Richard seemed built of a solid slab of muscle. He, too, had done a stint in the Marines, something anyone with eyes would guess from his ramrod spine and rat-a-tat handshake. His teeth were straight and polished, his skin faultless, and in his loafers and tailored button-down shirt (the sleeves rolled up to reveal massive forearms and a tasteful tattoo of a cross) he looked like a man who'd just finished modeling for his seminary's alumni calendar.

"How's it going, killer?" Richard said to Luca. Recoiling, the boy had practically folded himself into the seams of Toby's jeans.

"Shy, isn't he?" Richard had said dourly to Toby, like he was commiserating over a cancer diagnosis.

The family's warmth hadn't lasted long. Over the course of three long days in restaurants and hotel pools, Alyssa's parents had grown cagey and quiet, their laughter forced, their eyes sweeping over Toby and Luca with such naked appraisal he'd almost been surprised they didn't ask for his blood type or his tax returns.

Richard had been the worst. Every time Toby turned around, he seemed to catch Alyssa's brother studying him with a perplexed unease, almost like he vaguely recognized Toby from a blurry night at the bar and was afraid he might have pissed on his shoes.

Which was strange: Toby had never met any of these people before in his life.

Whatever the Wrights had been looking for, Toby had been certain they hadn't found it. Before they left for the airport, Alyssa's mother Ruth had demoted Toby from a hug to a handshake. "Good luck with everything," she said in a tone that made clear she never expected to see him again.

Toby had been crushed, but almost unsurprised. This, he'd thought, was the end of the fairy-tale romance between a penniless single dad and a pediatrician heiress. There were a million more eligible men for Alyssa in sunny Los Angeles, men who knew how to dress a horse and play lacrosse and cover up an abortion.

Imagine his shock, the night after her folks left, when Alyssa had propped herself on her elbow after a particularly wild roll in bed and said casually, "Do you want to get married?"

1:4

Now, a week after the wedding and a million light-years from his old life, Toby sat in his wife's luxury car, swaddled in leather seats and adaptive climate controls, and wondered, not for the first time, if he hadn't made the greatest mistake of his life. *A brood of vipers. Do you hear me? You are heading into a brood of—*

"Your hands are shaking," Alyssa said.

"I'm about to see your family again."

"There's a bottle of Ativan in my bag. That'll calm you down in a hurry."

Toby's foot shied away from where it rested near Alyssa's purse. Pills had never mixed well with his family. Or rather, they'd mixed *too* well. The last thing he needed this weekend was to risk an addiction.

"I'll survive," he murmured.

Luca noticed none of this. He was in the back seat, playing with something Toby couldn't see in the mirror, blissfully oblivious. Alyssa, on the other hand, had turned her eyes from the road to study Toby with a frown. "What is it? Really?"

Typical doctor. "Not everything needs a diagnosis, Alyssa."

"You change when you get like this. It's like I see a gate shutting behind your eyes."

That wasn't a bad way to put it. A therapist would call it compartmentalization. Toby called it discipline. A long, long time ago, his sister had taught him the skill of sealing away memories that were too painful—too dangerous—to remember. (*Slam. Click.*) *Build a palace in your mind, the nicest place you can imagine,* Willow had said. *See the color of the walls, the texture of the floors. What color is the ceiling? Now imagine a door inside the palace. What material is it made of? What about the knobs and hinges? Look at the keyhole. Remember it well.*

Now open the door and see the empty room inside. See the walls and the ceiling. Check it for cracks. Make sure there's no escape . . .

Take a terrible memory, something you can't bear to remember again, and toss it in the room. Quick, before it can escape, **slam** *the door shut and turn the key. Hear it* click. *Make sure there's none of the memory still puddled in the hallway—they do that sometimes. Check the seals. Make sure none of it can slip through the cracks.*

And then leave it there. Sealed away. Build another hallway with more doors so you can never find it again. Forget it. Leave that memory sealed up so tight that even God himself couldn't find it if he looked inside your head.

Most people used such mental palaces to retain certain memories, perhaps even recover memories they'd lost, but the trick Willow had taught Toby—the power to seal them away—might have been the greatest gift she ever gave him (besides the obvious, of course). The palace in the basement of Toby's mind was made of marble, its doors hewn from glossy black granite. The palace was so old by now it had grown to encompass dozens of hallways, hundreds of doors, most of which contained memories of his sister. Memories of what she'd been through. Memories of what she'd put *him* through, after years of failure and addiction. It wasn't much of a palace these days. More a subterranean labyrinth.

Or a tomb.

Now, in the car, Toby shrugged all this away. He gave Alyssa his most brooding look, the kind the cameras adored. "Don't you like an enigmatic man?"

"My mom said you seem deep." Alyssa shrugged a bony shoulder. "Better than what my brother thought."

"Which was?"

"Richard says you're dangerous. But I think he's just afraid of anyone he can't impress."

Looking at the list on his phone, he said, "Richard's married to a woman named Kassandra, right?"

"That's a very smooth pivot. But yes. There isn't really much to say about Kassandra. She's pretty and charming and keeps her head down. Don't repeat that, Luca."

the corner of the white wall, she hooked a right, crossing the creek a narrower bridge, and headed through a dense copse of trees.

"What am I forgetting?" Alyssa said. "We keep some golf carts in the bles if you ever need to head out over the grounds. We call them *putters*, hough I can't imagine why you'd ever need one. Things around here should be pretty quiet until Sunday. Visitors aren't permitted if there isn't a broadcast on, of course. My mother also gave most of the staff the weekend off, so it'll just be Marie and Julian around the house. God knows why. It's not like we don't have a birthday party to throw tomorrow."

As they cleared the trees, Toby again caught sight of the white stone wall that bordered the estate. The wall stood at least twelve feet high, its upper edge dotted with the most elegant silver spikes a burglar could ever fear to meet. The sight of those spikes sent another sliver of ice rolling down the back of his neck.

Give that man three warnings from the Lord.

Surely old Miss Lottie at the Cracker Barrel had been pulling his chain: Why would the wealthiest televangelist in America say such terrible things about his own family on live TV?

And then Toby gave himself a little shake, like a man realizing he'd been dreaming within a dream. What was he saying? Did he seriously think Jerome Jeremiah Wright had known Toby would be stopping in that particular store on his way to meet the new in-laws? That Jerome even knew who Miss Lottie was? That God himself took any interest in Toby's tiny life?

It had been a long, long time since Toby had believed in the God that Jerome shilled for on TV. Uncle Ezra had seen to that.

"That woman at the Cracker Barrel is a little cracked, huh?"

"Grandpa Jerome has had that effect on people lately."

Toby wondered just how much of the conversation his wife had caught back there. As they crossed another bridge over another creek, a strange tension ran through Alyssa, a tightness in her mouth and in her grip on the wheel that seemed as wrong on his cool, competent wife as her lipstick and piled-up hair.

The boy looked up, bewildered, from whate·
the back seat. "Repeat what?"

"Exactly."

"But you're forgetting some people, aren't you?
"What about this Marie and Julian, 'the hired help
sister?"

Alyssa tapped a manicured nail on the ridge of the whe
need to worry about Marie and Julian—they just work at the h
be surprised how fast they turn invisible. I think they like it that
for Ginger . . . if I told you she was an only child for years and year
darling of the family, until suddenly my brother and I showed up to ru
it for her, would that tell you everything you needed to know?"

"Wasn't that thirty years ago?"

"And she still hasn't forgiven us for it, no. I envy you sometimes. There
must be so much less drama when you're on your own."

That sent some doors rattling in Toby's mind, echoing up and down
the halls of the marble labyrinth. Sometimes Alyssa's practicality could
go about a mile too far.

Slam. Click.

They'd finally left the lake behind and had begun to descend a tall hill.
Soon, Toby spotted another sprawling expanse of green in the distance,
though after a moment he realized he wasn't looking at more water but
at a great swathe of manicured grass, dotted here and there with white
buildings that gleamed like teeth in the hard sun. Glancing back, Toby
saw nothing of Lake Hebron behind them but a massive concrete dam.

VISITORS TO RAMORAH, TURN HERE (SUNDAYS ONLY) read a
tall sign mounted to a cross at a fork in the road. Alyssa whisked past it
and, moments later, drove past another, smaller sign.

ROADS FLOOD IN STRONG RAIN.

Through Toby's window he saw a wide green creek that ran along a
white stone wall. A bridge crossed the creek, leading to a black iron gate.
Through the gate's bars, he saw glimpses of a church, a satellite dish, a
parking lot. Alyssa kept driving.

The white wall turned a corner. They followed it and the estate's southern creek for what felt like ages before finally arriving at their final bridge. Like the first bridge they'd seen, the one that passed over the north creek, this one also ended at a black iron gate.

Alyssa clicked a button on the Mercedes's touch screen. The gate slid open without a sound. Up ahead, a new world loomed.

"Pass me my bag, would you?" she said, and shook two white anxiety tablets into her palm. She raised the pills like you would a shot glass. "We who are about to die salute you," she said, and swallowed the tablets dry.

A moment later, the gate whispered as it closed behind them. No going back now.

THE ESTATE HAD HARDLY changed since the last time Toby had seen an episode of *The Prophecy Hour*. Gone was the hard, brassy scrubland of central Texas, the sparse, sun-blasted gravel of the highway. Instead, here at Ramorah, a white stone drive cut through a perfect lawn of emerald grass spread out in all directions. Alyssa steered the Mercedes up a steep green hill, into a blinding flare of sunlight, and with every yard Toby felt himself slipping further and further away from any sort of life he recognized.

"Are we going to a Disney castle?" Luca murmured, clearly awed by the sight.

If only.

At the top of the hill, a cloud settled in front of the sun, and the great expanse of Ramorah unrolled beneath them. To the east, Toby saw what looked like an airstrip and a small aircraft hangar resting near the woods they'd driven through earlier. To the west was a steep rise that ended at the white concrete dam of Lake Hebron. To the north was a massive church with an enormous satellite dish on its roof.

And dead ahead, brooding in a soft pit in the earth, was the largest house Toby had ever seen. It was bone white, as if it was covered entirely in plaster, and with its rows of neat windows and elegant, restrained finishings it almost resembled the country home of some suitable bachelor in a Jane Austen novel. But only an American (and a newly rich American at that) could have ever desired a home as large as this. Two massive wings spread out to the east and west. A black iron cross stood on its roof, tall as the Tower of Babel.

Alyssa carried the Mercedes down the drive, down the hill, and parked, at last, on a great fan of white gravel that spread in front of the house. Not ten feet away, a stone porch sheltered a pair of oak double doors that, to Luca's credit, wouldn't have looked out of place in a castle.

The house's windows glinted in the sun. Toby stared at his arm.

Tell that man with the fishhook scar—

With a little hum of satisfaction, Luca dropped something over Toby's shoulder that settled, soft as a feather, on his thigh. It was a blue origami rosebud, patterned all over with sailboats. "See?" he said. "I make trash into *art*."

Alyssa shot the flower a swift, alarmed look before tossing it in her bag. With a tone Toby had never heard in her voice before, she said, "We'll work on that."

"Work on what?" Toby said, but there wasn't time for more. Alyssa hadn't even killed the engine before those tall double doors opened and a stream of Wrights flooded down the porch, led by none other than Alyssa's parents and her brother. Toby forced a smile as he climbed out. *We who are about to die salute you.*

To Toby's surprise, Ruth bundled him into a hug the moment she got him within arm's reach. Hugo thumped him on the back. Richard gave him a firm Marine handshake and said, "So great to see you again, man."

Richard says you're dangerous.

Gone was the blatant disappointment that had coated their eyes when they'd left Los Angeles six weeks ago. Today, Alyssa's family beamed at Toby and Luca like they were welcoming royalty. "It's great to see you safe," Ruth said. "I've ridden in a car with my daughter before." Oh, how she laughed.

Except Toby noticed the way Richard, as he gave his sister a hug, glanced from Luca to Toby with that same uneasy frown Toby had seen on the man in LA. A little behind him, Hugo was watching Richard. Hugo caught Toby looking. He flipped his smile back on.

As if to make up for this brief hitch of unease, Richard's wife swooped on Luca with a little *Eek!*, gliding through the air like a manicured bird. Toby remembered that her name was Kassandra, and in her floral sundress and white flats she did indeed seem pretty and charming, just as Alyssa had described her in the car. Kassandra was precisely the type of woman Toby would have expected a handsome man like Richard to marry: radiantly blond, filigreed with lashes and golden jewelry, nails burnished to a hard shine. *Perfect breeding*, Toby's uncle would have said, until Kassandra opened her mouth.

All the money in the world couldn't conceal an accent from the depths of the Texas countryside.

"Lord, it's good to finally meet you, Luca," Kassandra said. She pronounced it *Lard*. "You got no idea what it's like living in this big old house with nothing but *grown-ups*."

Luca, normally so shy, extended a soft hand with a giggle. "The pleasure is mine."

"Toby, hi, goodness you're handsome." Toby almost blushed when Kassandra turned her head his way. "I was so disappointed I couldn't make it out to LA with the others last month—we were so busy redecorating your suite I couldn't get two minutes away. Have you met Richard's sister Ginger? I know she's been dying to meet you."

Toby would never guess. Ginger didn't look like the sort of woman who would die to meet anybody, not even Christ himself. Ginger might have been only a decade older than Alyssa and Richard, but she carried herself like she belonged to a different generation entirely. Her face and figure were plain and unremarkable—Toby recalled what Alyssa had said about the way this older sister had never forgiven her younger siblings for overshadowing her—and so Ginger had apparently chosen to be striking if she couldn't be pretty.

Unlike all the blondes around her, Ginger's hair was a brilliant orange, styled up in a Betty Grable pompadour Toby had only ever seen on drag queens. She wore a man's white shirt, black slacks, ruthless patent leather pumps. When she produced a cigarette, Toby was surprised it wasn't fastened to an obsidian holder.

Was the orange hair dyed, he wondered, or was it the legacy of some distant relation of Hugo's? Did she always dress like a faded film star, or just when she was meeting a man from Los Angeles?

"I was up to my elbows in work while the others were on the beach with you," Ginger said, with a smile so sharp it could peel an apple. "But I feel as if I've met you already."

"What do you do for work?" Toby said, though a large chunk of his mind was busy trying to unpack this last sentence.

"You don't need to worry about that," she said smoothly, and shook Toby's hand for a second too long. She stared at his scar for a moment, and then a moment more.

And then, like nothing had happened, she looked him dead in the eye.

She said, "It's so good to finally meet you."

GINGER TOOK COMMAND A moment later, ushering the family out of the heat. "We'll have lunch in the sun lounge," she called over everyone's heads. "And after that—"

Following the family across the stone porch, Toby discovered a grand foyer where voices and footsteps rang on bright marble floors, echoed off white plaster walls, vanished up twin staircases that curved away to the east and west. There were ferns, urns, an enormous leather-bound Bible standing open on a tall gilt stand. Above the Bible, an image of something—it looked like a box being tossed on heaving waves—was carved into a chunk of white stone set into the wall.

Two more Wrights awaited them inside: a young man and a younger woman in crisp black uniforms stood at attention at the foot of the eastern stairs. The woman appeared to be in her mid-twenties, far too young to look as tired as she did, with a curved chin, a little nose, a wilting crown of black curls sunk around her face.

The man could only be her brother. He had her same curly hair—his was piled atop his head and buzzed on the sides—and features that were sharp everywhere his sister's were soft: diamond jaw, an elegant ridge of a brow, an arch grin like a cat watching a bird settle into his yard. Even to Toby's eye (an eye jaded by years of work in the Smoldering Factory), the man was astonishingly handsome.

This, Toby thought, must be Marie and Julian, the hired help from the end of Alyssa's list. Not that anyone bothered to introduce them.

With a polite nod, Julian presented a silver tray to Alyssa and Toby. "Mister Jerome sends his regards."

Two pieces of folded paper waited on the tray, one bearing Alyssa's name and the other bearing Toby's. Unfolding her note, Alyssa read aloud, "'My apologies, but I will be unable to see you until dinner. Welcome home, J.'"

Something curious crossed his wife's face as she read the note, a subtle hesitation, and then she folded the note and dropped it in her bag. Toby waited a moment. He was certain there was something on that paper she hadn't read.

Almost as an afterthought, he glanced over his own note with a polite smile, shrugged, said, "I'm sorry we won't be meeting him any sooner."

"Count your blessings," Ginger murmured.

"Your key, ma'am?" Julian asked, and like she was completing some arcane trade—two pieces of paper for one Mercedes—Alyssa placed her car's fob on the silver tray. "I'll get it parked in the stables for you, ma'am," Julian said.

Alyssa gave him a vague smile that might have been a thank-you.

"I'll get our bags first," Toby said, but Marie, the other member of the *hired help*, hiked up an eyebrow.

"That's what *I* do," she said, and followed her brother outside without another word. Toby caught a snicker from Ginger.

The family were already moving down a long main hall toward the back of the house. Toby watched with a pang as Luca giggled at something Kassandra, Richard's perfect wife, whispered to him in the din. The boy joined the procession without a single look back.

If Toby hadn't desperately needed to use the restroom, he would never have let the boy out of his sight.

He looked over his shoulder to ask Alyssa for directions, but his wife was embroiled in a conversation with Richard that looked far too serious to interrupt. Instead it was Ruth, Toby's new mother-in-law, who said, "Do you need anything, dear?"

"A bathroom, if that's all right."

"Of course it's all right." Ruth smiled. "It's your house now, you know."

What a thought.

She pointed out a door beneath the eastern stairs and left him to his business. As he stepped into the restroom, Toby caught sight of Marie and Julian crossing the front drive and climbing into Alyssa's car. He chided himself for not shaking their hands. Maybe it was normal for wealthy families to watch their staff park the cars and collect their luggage and vanish. Maybe it was even normal to treat them like they were hardly there at all.

But surely it was strange to employ members of your own family.

Because make no mistake: Marie and Julian might have had darker skin than the rest of the family, but they both possessed a pair of those remarkable blue-black eyes. Toby shook his head. The *hired help* tucked away at the end of Alyssa's list were Wrights themselves.

In the bathroom, Toby almost had a heart attack when the toilet slowed and gurgled and threatened to back up its contents all over the floor. At the last possible moment, the pipes cleared, the waters abated, and Toby shook his head, surprised. You'd think a mansion that could afford a marble vanity and a live orchid and a dainty granite trash can could afford to keep its plumbing in better shape.

He was so anxious he could have puked in the sink, but in the end he only straightened the orchid on the vanity, studied himself in the mirror, breathed.

That old lady at the Cracker Barrel had shaken him worse than he thought.

Leaving the bathroom and setting off down the long main hall, he was startled to discover just how silent a house this large could be. How oppressively *empty*. Alyssa had mentioned something about her mother giving most of the staff the weekend off, but even if there had been a full fleet of servants bustling around on their duties, there must still be long stretches of the day when a person could find themselves walking through the heart of Ramorah and feel the enormous weight of the house pressing in from all directions. As he followed the Wrights, Toby's sole companion was the nervous thud of his own heart.

Gilded sconces ran down either wall, each spaced wide enough apart to leave a narrow gulf of shadow between the pools of their soft light. Toby had just stepped into one of those gulfs, deep in thought, when all at once his survival instincts sprang into overdrive, like those of a man smelling smoke in his sleep.

Toby was certain—briefly, suddenly certain—that he wasn't alone.

But when he glanced over his shoulder, he saw nothing but the same empty hall. Saw no one but his own reflection, watching himself from a mirror on the western wall. A soft draft of air, quick and cool as mercury, passed over his cheek. In the mirror, he saw the draft ruffle his hair.

For a moment, Toby imagined he heard the faintest of sounds in that chilly air, something almost like a rushed whisper he couldn't quite make out: *ooreyetentaymetubayes*. And then it was gone.

Toby pressed a palm to his shoulder. Was that a patch of damp he felt on the fabric, or had he simply forgotten to dry his hands?

FOR A BROOD OF vipers, they passed lunch pleasantly enough.

The sun lounge lived up to its name. The room's long north wall was constructed almost entirely of glass. Its remaining three walls were covered in white plaster, and they trapped the brilliant glare of the afternoon so that the light seemed to tremble with a honeyed weight in the air. Toby found the family waiting for him at a ring of sofas and easy chairs, and in the center of the ring was a wide low table covered with so many plates and bowls and glasses he could hardly see a scrap of wood underneath.

Waiting for him also was another member of the Wright brood: Alyssa's aunt, Sarah Nella. The woman stood a foot taller than her sister, Ruth, and looked considerably older (how many strokes had Alyssa said the woman had already suffered? Two?), but Sarah Nella seemed healthy and brisk and perfectly in control of anything life might throw at her, even her pale blond hair frozen around her face in a perfect shellacked bob. *Don't get on Sarah Nella's bad side*, Alyssa had warned Luca, and yet this aunt, who was allegedly 80 percent more terrifying than Toby's new mother-in-law, spoke with a voice that was gentle, welcoming, and smooth. "We've completely redone the Ezekiel Suite for you, Mister Tucker," Sarah Nella said by way of greeting. "I hope it satisfies."

Toby raised an eyebrow. It struck him as strange, somehow, that Sarah Nella would call him by his unmarried name. Like so much about their marriage, Alyssa had casually informed Toby that he would become a Wright; she, Alyssa, would never be a Tucker. ("My dad did the same thing. You'll get used to it.")

There was more about Sarah Nella he found strange. The soft Texas twang in her voice felt almost out of place: Alyssa's aunt made him think of those tall, severe British actresses, the ones who appeared in period pieces and police dramas and quietly dominated every room they were in. As Sarah Nella seated herself on an easy chair, a ring of keys jingled on her hip, almost to ensure no one could ever forget she was there.

Alyssa's mother, Ruth, patted the place beside her. Toby sat, and Ruth unpeeled a damp film of Saran Wrap from the mouth of a tureen that rested on the room's round table. Ladling out a generous serving of lentil soup, Ruth said, "You *do* eat, don't you? I worry about you skinny Californians."

Toby and Alyssa shared a smile, but he couldn't bring himself to take more than a few sips. His hands might have stopped shaking, but that anxiety he'd felt on the road here had only gotten worse. The toilet under the stairs hadn't helped, nor that strange chilly draft in the hall, the rush of air that had sounded almost like a whisper in his ear.

Maybe he should have risked one of Alyssa's pills. Just one.

Kassandra begged Toby to recount the story of how he and Alyssa had met, and he did his best to oblige, though there wasn't a great deal to tell. Toby had been working as a teacher's aide at a private elementary school in Echo Park. One afternoon this past spring, as he ferried children into their parents' waiting cars, a sleek black Mercedes had pulled up at the school's door. The window rolled down to reveal an elegant, soft-voiced blonde with brilliant blue-black eyes. "I'm Alyssa Wright," she'd said. "You've been expecting me."

"Doesn't that sound portentous," Ruth said with a chuckle.

Alyssa let out a rare, uninhibited laugh. "I was picking up a friend's kid! I just wanted to make sure they had my name on the list."

"And what do you know? You found one." Ginger glanced at Luca. As she swapped her cigarette for a vape, a razor of a smile passed over Toby's handsome face as she added, "Maybe two."

Toby gave the woman his most oblivious look. Ginger, he noticed, had hardly touched her lunch either, but he supposed that wasn't a surprise. Wasps weren't known for their large stomachs.

Richard watched all of this with a gleam of capped teeth. He said to Toby, "And then you swept my sister off her feet."

"It was more the reverse."

"I couldn't leave the poor man alone." Alyssa laughed again. (Toby tried not to wince at the word *poor*.)

Kassandra beamed. "It was that way with me and Richard. But Lord, six months—I thought *we* rushed things."

"I wouldn't have minded a ceremony," Sarah Nella said.

Richard's eyes never left Toby's. "I wasn't surprised. We all saw it in LA—you were exactly what Alyssa was looking for."

Ruth smiled. "Sometimes you get lucky."

On the far end of their couch, Hugo balanced a small plate on a massive knee. He speared a Brussels sprout in silence.

Just as his note had promised, Jerome was nowhere to be seen. Neither, Toby noticed, were a couple other names from Alyssa's list. "Aren't we missing someone?" he said to Ginger. "You have a son here, right?"

"Matthias? He's like a feral cat. He turns up when he feels like it. We've tried to make him scrub up and smile for things before, and trust me—it's best to let him roam loose."

"Do you have any real cats?" Luca said.

"God, no," Ginger said. "Do you have any idea how allergic we are?"

Kassandra made a great show of sneezing all over her salad—"Ah-*CHOO!*"—that left Luca helpless with giggles. The boy had a high, pealing laugh, joyous as birdsong.

Toby smiled, only to hesitate when he noticed the way the sound made Alyssa's brother wince. Ruth refilled Toby's glass with sparkling water. Something about his brother-in-law's discomfort made Toby wish it was booze.

With a little flourish, Sarah Nella draped a napkin over a covered silver dish at the center of the table and whisked away its lid, revealing the most perfectly frosted cupcake Toby had ever seen. RIP MY 20S read a little golden gravestone standing up in the icing.

"A gift from the house," Sarah Nella said, and again Toby was surprised by how warm and gentle Alyssa's severe-looking aunt was turning out to be.

"Not as good as the cake tomorrow, of course," Ruth said. "A taster, if you will."

With a pointed glance at Toby that he couldn't begin to understand, Ginger added, "We were worried you wouldn't be able to celebrate this year, Alyssa."

Ah, yes. The big 3-0. Where some women might dread the date, Alyssa had been talking about all the ways she might celebrate it almost from the moment she met Toby. Venice had been on the table for a time, or perhaps Madrid "to save on the hotel," but in the end, with little warning, she'd settled on a trip home to see her family instead. "You'll have to meet them at some point, Mister Newlywed," she'd said last week in Los Angeles, rather like Toby was a new junior partner being dragged along to meet his company's board. "We might as well bundle all our obligations out of the way before Gstaad."

Gstaad, of course, was the resort town in the Swiss Alps that Alyssa had declared, more or less on her own, would be the site of their honeymoon. Toby couldn't ski and hated the cold, but he couldn't see a reason to argue with her, nor the means to do so: How could he hold an opinion on a place he couldn't even spell?

Here in Ramorah's sun lounge, Alyssa licked the gravestone free of icing before she flicked it at her sister. She took a single bite of her cupcake, *hmm*ed in pleasure, and passed the rest to Luca. "I have the cameras to worry about, don't I?"

"Are we taking pictures?" Luca never missed an opportunity for a selfie.

"Don't talk with your mouth full, bud," Toby said.

Hugo shot Toby a baffled frown, like there was something obvious staring Toby in the face that he couldn't see. A little chill, like that sliver of ice he'd felt at the Cracker Barrel, rolled yet again down the back of Toby's neck.

Why was Alyssa's big, cheery father suddenly so muted?

A high digital chime rose from Sarah Nella's wrist. She tapped the screen of her smartwatch and stood with a long yawn, the keys on her hip letting out a sleepy tinkle. "Siri says it's time for a nap."

The family stirred, gathering phones and downing the dregs of their sparkling waters and groaning as one when Sarah Nella added, "Jerome has informed us he wishes to have dinner in the formal dining room tonight. Yes, I know how you feel. Toby, y'all's suite is next to Richard and Kassandra's at the far end of the second floor. Alyssa will show you the way."

"Is that the east wing or the west?"

Ginger blinked at Toby. "East, of course. Didn't Alyssa tell you?"

"There wasn't time," Alyssa said.

With a pained little pause, Sarah Nella said, "No one's allowed in the west wing without Jerome's express permission."

"Like *Beauty and the Beast*," Luca exclaimed. "We *are* in a castle."

Sarah Nella shook her head. "It's simply a maze over there. If you got lost, we might not find you for days."

"Might be for the best," Hugo grumbled, but when Toby looked at his father-in-law in surprise, the man covered his mouth and coughed.

As the family filed into the hall, Toby noticed Luca staring into a distant corner of the room, wearing the frown he reserved for injured classmates and sad memes of dogs. "You all right, bud? Luca?"

"Why is everyone ignoring him?"

"Ignoring who?"

Luca pointed. "The man over there. The one in the nice suit."

Toby turned, bewildered, to an empty corner. A cloud passed over the sun. "What are you talking about? There's no one there."

"Never mind," Luca said, curling in his lip and turning away. "I think he's shy."

THE EZEKIEL SUITE WAS airy and ample, larger than most of the apartments Toby had ever lived in, its air still tight with the smell of fresh paint. It held two bedrooms (each with their own marble bathroom), a kitchenette, even a little balcony looking out on the estate's rolling eastern hills, the distant airstrip, the dense stand of woods. "Pity the Gulfstream's in Houston for repairs," Alyssa said. "We could have just chartered a flight here."

When he didn't respond, his wife glanced over her shoulder. "You've gone dark on me again."

Had he? Toby's mind was a perfect blank, though he knew from long experience that it always felt this way when another room was being constructed for the marble labyrinth, another cell going up to contain a new crop of fears and uneasy memories that didn't serve him. Into this new room, Toby tossed the way Luca's laughter had made Richard so uneasy, the way his wife had recoiled from the origami rose their son had folded in the car. Alyssa used to take Luca to drag queen story hour at the library in LA, once taught the boy how to contour his cheeks. She'd long assured Toby that the fire and brimstone on Jerome's show was just branding for the cameras. ("Don't worry—my family's too rich to be bigoted." Whatever that meant.)

Richard says you're dangerous.

Warn that man with the fishhook scar—

Now that they were here, Toby couldn't shake the feeling there was a lot about her family that Alyssa hadn't told him. Something he hadn't planned on. He thought of big, cheery Hugo, Alyssa's father, watching Toby with the pained frown of a man who'd just discovered an animal in a trap.

Best to lock all this away. *Slam. Click.*

"Are you thinking about Marie and Julian?" Alyssa said.

Toby blinked at her. "What?"

"They're my cousins, if you're curious."

Toby recalled the *hired help* that had waited for them in the house's foyer. "I noticed they had y'all's eyes."

"*Very* distant cousins."

Thinking of the pair's darker skin, Toby said, "I wonder if Thomas Jefferson said the same thing about Sally Hemings's kids."

"Oh, they're not working for us because they're part-Black. This family's too rich—"

"—to be bigoted. I still don't know what that means."

"Give it time."

They settled into the suite's sitting room, watching the way the sun played over the thick beige carpet. Alyssa sipped a coffee she brewed in the kitchenette and texted someone at a rapid clip. Luca was on the floor, coloring a book of mandalas. His colored pencils were new, imported from France on a whim of Alyssa's. *Everything* about the boy seemed new and imported: his polo, his shoes, his life. Six months ago, Toby had been collapsing under grief and capitalism, so broke he'd been debating whether it was worse for Luca if their little family were to lose their car or their apartment. And look at them now.

Six months. The day before the wedding, one of Toby's friends had looked him dead in the eye and said, "Do you love her, or do you love what she can do for you?"

("Can't it be both?")

Toby didn't realize he'd dozed off on the sitting room's couch until the sound of a distant door *creak-k-king* open made him stir. He stretched, rubbed his eyes, blinked—and froze. It wasn't Alyssa he saw seated across from him. The pale, waterlogged face of Willow, his sister, stared at Toby with clouded eyes. She'd freed herself from the prison he'd constructed in the marble labyrinth of his mind. She'd come back to haunt him.

His sister's flesh had turned a terrible white in her time away. Her wet hair stuck to her skin. A long ribbon of water bubbled up her throat and out her open lips and struck the carpet of the Ezekiel Suite with a steady *drip*.

Drip.

Drip.

Willow made a gurgling sound from deep in her throat. It sounded like a question.

What the fuck have you gotten yourself into?

Toby awoke from the dream with a gasp. Alyssa hardly glanced up from her phone. "You all right?"

He pushed his hands to his face. Sleep had always been the enemy of the memory palace: it was hard to keep his mind under control when his subconscious had taken the reins. Toby now imagined himself walking up and down the long marble halls of the labyrinth, turning one key after another, just as he did every morning lately. *Click. Click. Click.*

Luca, too, had fallen asleep, on the carpet, though his rest seemed far less troubled. The boy had taken the death of Toby's sister better than Toby himself. Toby sometimes wondered if such a thing was healthy.

A clock above Luca's head had somehow moved forward by almost an hour.

Toby picked up a glass of water Alyssa had left for him on the table. The glass felt more valuable than Toby himself, both light and sturdy, its lip as fine as a moth's wing. "How much did this cost?"

"You don't want to know."

"I feel like a Philistine around here. A barbarian," he added, when Alyssa gave him one of those blank looks. It was remarkable how little she knew her Bible.

"Dad said he used to feel the same way. Don't think about it."

"That's easier said than shunned."

"What?"

Toby felt like he'd swallowed a thorn, but of course that was just grief. *Easier said than shunned.* It had been one of Willow's favorite sayings.

Slam. Click.

"How does it feel being home?" Toby said, desperate for a change of subject. Alyssa had never sounded especially keen on her folks back when the two of them lived in LA. *My family's a whole production,* she used to say.

Now, however, his wife seemed more ambivalent. She glanced at her phone, at the freshly painted suite, at Luca drowsing on the floor. "Would that be so bad? If it was home?"

"If it was what?"

Luca's head snapped up. "What was that?"

"What was what?" Toby said, but then the sound came again, a distant high creaking like a door threatening to snap off its hinges, and for a moment he feared he was still dreaming.

But then they all recognized the sound for what it was: somewhere upstairs, a woman was screaming.

Alyssa took off running without a word.

"Solo protocol," Toby said to Luca, hurrying after her. It was an old code between them for *lock the doors and don't let anyone in.* The boy responded with a grave competence that always depressed Toby. Luca had had to grow up far too fast.

Toby followed his wife down the long hall that ran through the heart of the east wing, up a flight of stairs to the house's third floor, another scream rolling through the air to greet them on the way. They rounded a corner into the main wing, where they discovered the family gathered around an old woman in a tracksuit and sneakers who was screaming and shaking and sobbing.

This could only be Corah, Jerome's older sister. She had to be nearly ninety, but she carried an air of tight-wound strength that belonged to someone half her age. A cloud of gray hair seemed to flicker around her head, electric with fear. She was short, so short she'd rested her face on Ruth's generous chest, but still Toby wouldn't have wanted to meet her in a dark alley. When she wailed again, Toby brought his hands to his ears at the terror in her voice.

"He's *back*!" Corah screamed. "I was just coming to lay down for a few minutes and I found it, I found it on my door. He's back. Oh Lord Jesus, he's *BACK*!"

Richard and Ginger were here, as were Sarah Nella and Hugo, and then down the hall another new face appeared: a teenaged boy in a grubby shirt and jeans. He had a constellation of acne on his brow and a layer of gray-brown grime on his hands and a blank expression as he studied the scene. He looked at Toby, looked past him at the source of Corah's fear, and then vanished back around the corner without a word.

That must be Matthias. Ginger's son, the feral cat.

No one else seemed to notice the boy's arrival or his departure. Ginger herself tried to pat Corah's back—consolation was clearly a struggle for her—but her mother waved her off.

Which was when old Corah caught sight of Toby. All at once, the blue seemed to fade from her eyes, leaving behind nothing but a hard, hard black. "What is *he* doing here?" the old woman hissed to Ruth. "This is family business."

Toby hardly heard this. He was too fascinated, too appalled, by the sight behind her.

A bedroom door (Corah's presumably) had been covered with great slashes of red paint, the hue more vivid than blood. A wobbly cross had been painted near the top of the door, above the bold, bleeding word

REPENT

Below this, someone had left a message in rushed, violent letters.

GOD KNOWS WHAT YOU DID YOU OLD CUNT

AND SO DO I

1:9

AT DUSK, TOBY AND Luca emerged from their suite for dinner, dressed in matching shirts and ties, and discovered a changed house. The walls seemed closer, the carpet stiffer, like Ramorah's flesh and hairs had tensed for another shock. Toby and his son descended creaking stairs into the abandoned foyer and found sunset bleeding over the marble floors. Unease lingered in the air, faint and unmistakable.

"I have to pee." Luca seemed afraid to talk louder than a whisper. Toby pointed him to the little bathroom under the stairs and soon wished, foolishly, that he didn't have to be alone in Ramorah, even for a moment.

GOD KNOWS WHAT YOU DID YOU OLD CUNT.

No one had been in any hurry to explain how the hell such a message could appear on Corah's door (nor, for that matter, did anyone seem in a hurry to ask just what it was Corah might have done). The moment Alyssa saw it, she'd grabbed Toby's hand and pulled him away, guiding him as far as the stairs before she said, "I have to go help deal with that."

Toby had stared at her. "Does this sort of thing happen a lot around here?"

"That's a fantastic question," she said, and departed without another word. It was the last he'd seen of her all day.

Now, a few hours later, not long after Luca went into the bathroom under the eastern stairs, Ginger stepped out of the foyer's elevator and caught Toby flipping through the Bible perched on the golden stand near the eastern wall. "I can't remember the last time anyone read that thing."

Toby flinched. He turned a page. "I was almost afraid to touch it."

Ginger wore a black dress and tall black heels. Other than her scarlet hair, a brilliant silver bracelet was her only note of color. Her gaze seemed to possess a particularly lethal edge this evening, like she was not merely appraising this new member of the family but pricing him by the pound.

"I hear you like art."

"I do?" Toby said.

"What do you think of our grandmother's carvings?"

Ginger tipped her black vape at the bas-relief sculpted into the wall above the Bible. It was the long box on water that Toby had glanced at earlier, but now he saw that it was, of course, Noah's Ark being buffeted by the flood. Ginger was right, in a sense: Toby didn't particularly care about art, but after growing up with his sister—"our resident Picasso," their uncle had called Willow, clearly uneasy having so much raw talent under one roof—Toby knew how to recognize the good shit when he saw it.

(Though how Ginger knew this was a much more worrisome question.)

Either way, Toby saw the good shit now. The waves on the foyer's wall had been carved with a startling urgency, their crests towering over the little ark with such menace that the artist had accomplished the remarkable feat of making the viewer fear for the vessel's safety.

Toby said, "It's impressive. There are more of these carvings?"

"Four total, yes," Ginger said. "Some stranger than others. Did you get that scar in the accident that killed your parents?"

Toby froze. Ginger's eyes were fixed on the fishhook on his arm, just as they'd been earlier this afternoon. He said, "How did you know about that?"

"About your scar?"

"About the accident."

"Maybe Alyssa told me."

Toby was starting to see why his wife had been so unexcited to talk about her sister in the car ride from Hebron. He thought of the way Ginger had evaded his question when he'd asked her, earlier, what she did for work. *You don't need to worry about that.*

Toby was starting to suspect he might.

"Alyssa wouldn't have known about the accident," Toby said. "I told her my parents died when I was a kid. She never asked to know more."

"Isn't that funny, in a bride?"

"That she wouldn't want to make me uncomfortable?"

"That doesn't normally stop my sister."

The toilet under the stairs flushed. The bathroom was so well insulated it sounded like the distant lapping of a wave.

"You saw something upstairs this afternoon you shouldn't have, Mister Tucker. A few mean words painted on Corah's door," Ginger said. "You'd be smart to forget about all that."

"That's a tall order. I didn't think a good Christian family went in for that kind of language."

"Are you good at cards? Blackjack? Poker?"

"I usually just bluff."

Ginger smiled. "I don't."

There was a creak on the stairs, and a moment later he saw Alyssa for the first time in hours. She was dressed in a black evening dress and very high heels, her hair hanging loose over her shoulders like golden fleece. Her aunt Sarah Nella followed her down the stairs, the woman's eyes simmering with some private victory. "Be seeing more and more of you, I suspect," Sarah Nella said to Toby by way of greeting.

God only knew what she meant. Alyssa certainly wasn't going to enlighten him. His wife gave Toby the simplest of frowns and started down the long main hall.

Luca opened the restroom door, tucking something into his pocket on the way out. Without being told, he took Toby's hand like they were crossing another parking lot. He squeezed. *What's wrong?*

Toby squeezed back. *I don't know.*

Ginger watched all of this, her eyes bright with what might have been envy. "We never usually eat in the formal dining room, you know. Jerome must be awfully excited to meet you."

Unlike the sun lounge, Ramorah's dining room was the most oppressively gloomy place Toby had ever been served a meal. It was a long hardwood cavern, its meager light the product of a few apathetic wall sconces and a silver candelabra on the ceiling. The room had been out of service for so long the hissing candles sounded like they were burning more dust than air.

Most of the room was filled with a great oak table that was so large the family had abandoned a full half of it to darkness. Toby and Luca sat between Richard's wife, Kassandra, on one side and Hugo on the other. Almost to Toby's surprise, he saw Matthias the feral cat seated beside his mother Ginger down the table, the boy looking twitchy and sullen in a clean shirt, all the grime Toby had seen on his palms a few hours ago now scrubbed away.

Jerome and his elderly sister (*God knows what you did you old cunt*) were still nowhere to be seen.

As Julian and Marie, the "hired help," served salads off a pair of silver trolleys, Ruth rattled through the plans for Alyssa's birthday party tomorrow. "I gave Chef the weekend off, but she's set us up with more food than we could ever need. The cake, of course, we had brought in special from Austin, and that ice cream Alyssa loves just arrived from New York today—"

Alyssa sat across the table from Toby, listening to this in a benign silence. Her brother Richard leaned over to murmur something in her ear. She turned red and struggled to hide a giggle.

Neither made any effort to include Toby in this little joke of theirs.

Aunt Sarah Nella glanced at her smartwatch. Ginger looked at the empty seat at the head of the table. "Does Jerome want us to start without him?"

Ruth looked almost shamefaced, a sprig of salad poking from her lips. "Were you waiting?"

And then something curious happened. Across the table, as Alyssa was distracted by her mother, Julian the hired help rested a hand on Richard's shoulder as he leaned over to refill the man's sparkling water. Richard sat very stiff, something charged and startled flitting behind his eyes.

He didn't flinch from the man's touch. Nor did Julian pull his hand away.

From the edge of his eye, Toby saw Richard's wife notice this. Almost before Kassandra could register what was going on, Julian had moved down the table, refilling Ruth's glass with a smile.

"Of course, we'll have breakfast on the lawn," Ruth said, oblivious.

"No. No you will not."

A voice boomed from the darkness at the end of the table. With a whisper of rubber wheels, ancient Corah appeared from the gloom, pushing an old man in a wheelchair who seemed to fill half the room the moment he arrived. Toby suddenly realized he was holding his breath.

Few people can look imperious seated in wheelchairs. Perhaps Jerome Jeremiah Wright was the only one. He wore dark blue jeans and the most comfortable-looking black sweater Toby had ever seen. Around his finger was a bright gold signet ring. With the help of a brilliant onyx cane, he rose to his full height and towered over Corah, over the table, over all of them.

"Tobias." Jerome had a voice like a bell over water: austere, supple, inescapable. "Come, let me shake your hand."

Toby doubted he could have said no to Jerome's voice even if he'd wanted to. He pulled himself from his seat, went to where Jerome had stopped at the head of the table, extended his hand like a man in a trance. With a pang of agony, Toby saw his fingers shaking.

Jerome seemed not to notice. Instead, like Ginger, the old man's brilliant blue-black eyes (how could they be even *more* striking in person than they were on TV?) lingered for an eternity on Toby's scar. Even in candlelight, the shape of that pale fishhook was unmistakable.

Jerome looked up. His eyes swept over his family. For a moment, all of Toby's skepticism fell away and he wondered if Jerome was thinking about the command he'd given old Miss Lottie last week on *The Prophecy Hour*. Had the old man realized, at the sight of that scar, that the brood of vipers he'd warned of was the family seated in front of him?

Or had he known it all along?

Give that man three warnings from the Lord.

Finally, Jerome shook Toby's hand. He smiled. "It's so good to finally meet you, Tobias."

Jerome sat again in his wheelchair. Marie placed a salad in front of him. Julian filled his glass. Toby returned to his own seat as fast as his legs would carry him.

Waving all his food away, the patriarch stared at Ruth and said, "There won't be any breakfast on the lawn tomorrow."

"We were rather hoping we could, Daddy," Ruth said.

"It's not my decision. There's a storm coming tonight. A big one."

Richard gave his grandfather the patient, muted smile that men use when they don't want to be seen sneering at their elders. "There's not a spot of green on the radar, sir."

"The Seven Sisters were brilliant last night. It's a warning. Take it to the bank."

Across the table from Toby, Alyssa speared a chunk of romaine as if this exchange had never occurred. "You outdid yourself on the salad tonight, Richard."

"Chopped it myself."

Luca, heretofore occupied by something he was fiddling with beneath the table, piped up in his seat next to Toby. "The Seven Sisters. Those are called the Pleeah, Pleeud—"

"Pleiades. Yes. Very impressive." Jerome did, indeed, seem impressed: for the first time since he'd arrived, the old man grinned. "A seven-starred constellation in the autumn sky. 'Can you bind the chains of the Pleiades, or loosen the belt of Orion?' I always wondered how Job knew it was one of the few constellations physically bound into configuration with the strength of its stars' own gravity."

"You once preached a sermon on that. You said it was proof of the Word's divine inspiration," Sarah Nella said, then sipped her water.

Young Matthias sat beside her, staring at Jerome with a curious mingling of fear and eager anticipation on his face, the way you might study a match and a box of fireworks.

Jerome noticed none of this. His attention was focused on Luca. "But the gravity of the Pleiades misses the bigger question entirely—why have those seven stars been burning so uncommon bright these last few evenings? What are the Sisters trying to warn us about?"

"Daddy's always been so interested in astronomy," Ruth said to no one in particular.

"He has?" Ginger said.

"Are you an Aquarius, little Luca?" Jerome said.

Luca stared blankly at his father. Toby shook his head, surprised. It had been many, many years since he'd watched a full episode of *The Prophecy Hour*, and even longer since he'd stepped into a church, but he seemed to recall the zodiac—along with any other form of fortune-telling—as being soundly off-limits to any God-fearing, born-again Christian. Toby's uncle had practically considered the horoscopes in the local paper witchcraft.

"Luca's a Leo, I think. We didn't really keep up with that stuff at our house. Even in Los Angeles." Toby tried to force a laugh.

Jerome's smile was a pale, thin thing. "'That stuff' is some of the oldest science ever undertaken. Though perhaps that's just the Scorpio in me speaking."

"Have you considered incorporating star charts into the show, sir?" Richard said. "I'm sure the folks at home would love to hear why the Lord placed Pisces in the equinox this spring."

"That doesn't make any sense, son."

"Well that's a shame. I bet we could have really scared the pants off them with that."

A crippling silence spread down the table.

After a moment, Jerome scoffed. "What do you people care? The ratings this year have never been higher."

Ruth gave Toby a diplomatic smile. "I think we're all a little high-strung after last week's broadcast. It was a tough one."

Toby realized that last week's broadcast must have been when old Miss Lottie had been given a message from the Lord. *A brood of vipers, do you hear me? You are heading into—*

"Tough?" Richard attacked a tomato. "How many callers did you have pissing themselves by the end of the show last Sunday, sir? Three? Four? I didn't realize fear and anguish are part of our brand now. Should we add the occult just to keep things interesting?"

" 'The heavens declare the Glory of the Lord,' " Jerome said. "He guides the Mazzaroth in their seasons, boy. It's right there in Scripture."

"Guides the *what*?"

"The Hebrew zodiac, for goodness' sake. What did they teach you in seminary, Black grievance?"

Marie winced as she cleared a plate.

"Respect your elders, son," Hugo said.

Richard opened his mouth to reply, only to be interrupted by a chitter of metal against porcelain. It was Corah, Jerome's elderly sister, her cloud of gray hair twitching and anxious the way it had been upstairs outside her bedroom door earlier this afternoon. She threw her fork into her empty bowl. "You just can't wait for him to die," she said to Richard. "At the rate you're going, it's the only way you'll make a dime, isn't it?"

Someone, somewhere, gasped. Another great silence threatened to swallow them, perhaps permanently this time, but they were rescued by a cheery Ruth. Toby suspected the woman could have carried small talk through a meteor strike.

"Have you given any thought about what you'll be doing with us, Toby?" his mother-in-law said.

"Doing?"

"For the family. Now that you *are* family."

With a strange spite, Corah added, "We don't believe in trust funds and welfare checks in this house, you know."

"We don't?" Ginger said.

Ruth smiled wider. "We all do something to help keep the ministry moving. Sarah Nella runs the business and the house, Hugo and I handle the church and congregation, Richard's expanding our streaming offerings and taking on more preaching duties, Ginger—well. We all *work* around here."

"Is that right?" Toby said.

"Of course. You must know all about the new Health and Wellness program Alyssa is rolling out for us. It's the only thing we've been able to talk about for weeks."

Toby almost choked on a crouton. "Her *what*?"

"We finally hammered out the details this afternoon," Alyssa said. She didn't sound especially happy about it. "I thought I might start working for a hospital in Austin, but the . . . situation . . . has changed."

"I was wondering where you'd been all afternoon," Toby said. He couldn't help adding, "I was worried you might have found more painted doors."

Kassandra shook her head at him mutely. It looked like a warning.

Ruth didn't falter. "Do you think you'll be joining your wife in her ministry? Or is there anything else you're interested in?"

Toby wondered if he looked as blindsided as he felt. "I think for now I'll focus on taking care of Luca. I spent so many years just trying to keep a roof over our heads, I never got the chance to be much of a father. I'll be . . . what's the phrase? A house husband."

Richard didn't bother to conceal a derisive snort. Ruth chuckled. "That's precious, Toby."

Elderly old Corah lifted her cloudy head again. All her rancor from earlier was gone, now replaced by a gauzy, warm courtesy. "I think that's a lovely idea."

"Thank you, ma'am."

"It'll be harder for you to break anything that way. Your type usually do."

A muscle tightened in Toby's jaw. "I suppose you're right, ma'am."

"Your daughter doesn't look a thing like you, you know." Corah smiled at Luca. "Does she take after her mother?"

"My son, actually."

"Your what?"

"Don't worry, Toby, it's really quite comfortable work," Ruth swooped in again. "The compensation is more than fair, and of course you'll have free lodging here at the house—Sarah Nella's made sure your suite was completely gut-renovated, as I'm sure you noticed. Do you have a favorite verse picked out for Sunday?"

"Pardon?"

"Everyone gives their favorite verse on their first Sunday broadcast. Just be sure to run it by me so I can be sure no one's claimed it yet." A qualm of discomfort muddied her smile. "And I suppose little Luca will need one too."

"I'm supposed to be in the broadcast on Sunday?" Toby said.

Ruth laughed again, sounding like she sincerely thought Toby was playing with her. "Why else do you think you're here? We'll need to get your boy his haircut first thing in the morning. It's a little *too* California for us, I'm afraid."

Toby felt his teeth grinding. "My son's not going on TV. I lived in LA. I know what that does to a kid."

Which, of course, was when Luca finally decided to reveal what he'd been fiddling with beneath the table all evening. "I don't mind. I can show everyone how I make my flowers."

Later, to Toby's relief, he remembered that his first thought had been pride: for a seven-year-old, Luca had a remarkable talent for art, especially origami. He'd folded a small, crisp rose blossom out of some plain white paper (God only knew whose trash can he'd dug it from), and it was sturdy enough to stand upright when the boy eased the flower, with infinite gentleness, to the table.

Maybe it was the flower. Maybe it was Luca's high, gentle voice, a voice that was nearly as soft as a girl's. Whatever the reason, a wave of embarrassment swept through the Wrights, each and every one of them recoiling from the boy like he'd just vomited blood. Toby looked across the table for some scrap of support from his wife—a smile, a kind word, anything—but the moment he did, Alyssa dropped her napkin.

He could have killed her, right then, at the table. *My family is too rich to be bigoted.*

Bullshit. Luca turned his head up and down the dinner table, looking for the praise that always came when he presented some new art project back home in Los Angeles, and now found nothing but fear and disgust and shame. A smile tugged and collapsed at the corners of his mouth. The beads in his hair chimed a low, lonely note.

And then Toby caught Hugo studying him with a face of absolute grief. Silently, he mouthed, *I am so sorry.*

For what?

Richard sneered, utterly unaware of his father's sadness. "Forget the haircut—we need a few weeks to toughen you up at Camp Cleave, eh, Lucia?"

Marie and Julian stepped into the room with trays of roast duck just in time to hear this. Julian's handsome face soured. Even at a distance, even in the weak light, Toby could see a vein pulsing in the man's jaw. Julian began to say, "Do you have any idea—"

"ENOUGH!"

Jerome slammed his fists to the table and dragged himself to his feet, his eyes narrow and burning black. Ruth's glass fell into her lap. Sarah Nella let out a shocked yelp.

"Is this really what it's come to?" the old man bellowed at his family, his voice crushing them all like a great hammer. "All my decades of work and sacrifice, the politics and the insipid theatrics week in and week out, just to watch my spoiled spawn eat my money and shit out laziness and contempt and *greed*? You think the Lord God doesn't know how hard your hearts have grown, you insidious little serpents? Do you think I don't see all he has in store for you, for us, for this house?"

Every mouth in the room fell open.

"That warning on the door today was *far* from the first. Time and time again this year you've been enjoined to repent, but have you listened?" Jerome struck another fist on the table. "Have you stopped, even for a moment, to ponder what the Lord has asked of you? No! You've just brooded and hissed, lurked and sneered. As God is my witness, this family is so black with sin you couldn't find it in the dark."

Corah pressed her hands to her ears. Kassandra choked on a piece of something that wouldn't come free. A shrill digital beep rose from

Sarah Nella's seat, climbing in pitch and intensity until she unstrapped her watch and shoved it into her pocket.

It was Ginger who found the courage to speak. "You're one to talk about sin, old man."

A grim smile tightened Jerome's face. He made his way to the east wall, every thump of his cane's rubber tip echoing like the toll of some dread clock. With one hard jerk, he wrenched a panel of velvet drapery to the floor. Corah let out a low moan of dismay.

The fallen curtain revealed another bas-relief carved into the stone between two windows. The carving was enormous, far larger than Noah's Ark in the front hall, but it was cast with the same skill, the same violent urgency, as those towering waves, that vulnerable little boat.

On the wall of the dining room, a man lay sprawled in the dirt, his hand raised over his head in desperation. A second man kneeled over him with a massive stone in one hand, ready to crush the first man's skull. The fear and the fury on their faces was so carefully wrought, so agonizing, Toby almost glanced away in pain.

A small inscription was carved above the image.

And it came to pass, when they were in the field, that Cain rose up against Abel his brother, and slew him.

Jerome turned to his family with fire in his eyes. "Oh, yes. I know a thing or two about sin."

AND THE WATER TURNED TO BLOOD LIKE
THAT OF A DEAD MAN

2:1

THERE WASN'T A SINGLE scrap of cloud in the sky when Jerome warned of a storm. The first few drops had come hours later, shortly after midnight, followed not long after by a great crash of thunder that shook every window of the house. Toby had still been awake, seated upright in bed in the Ezekiel Suite, and listened as the storm landed on them like a bomb.

After the disastrous dinner, Toby had spent a fruitless half hour arguing with his wife about the way his family had treated Luca—"If that wasn't bigotry, then what was it, Alyssa? Branding?"—and the new job with the family she'd never mentioned and the surprising fact that Toby, a man who hadn't held any faith in God for as long as he could remember, was now apparently expected to take up work at Two Creeks Ministries himself. "Do you seriously think I want anything to do with your grandfather's fucking carnival act?" he'd said.

Alyssa had almost looked wounded. "That carnival act is going to pay for your son's education."

"Is that really why you think I married you? To pay for my kid's college?"

"Of course not. You needed a new car, too."

That had shut Toby up. How was this the same woman who used to take him to Lakers games, Coachella, who bought poppers off the gays in clubs in West Hollywood and always expected Toby to pay as much as he could afford whenever they went anywhere together, even if it was just a few dollars? ("If you're digging for gold," she'd once joked, "you'll have to work for it.") How was this the same woman who'd taken Luca to an art museum one afternoon and brought him back with a head full of beaded braids? Where had *that* Alyssa gone?

Had she ever been here at all?

Toby had abandoned that argument with Alyssa, walked away before his blood pressure and anxiety could rattle his mind to pieces. After helping Luca get changed into his pajamas—and after answering a knock on the suite's door to find Julian, the *distant cousin* turned hired help, waiting with a silver trolley full of linens and a sly smile and an offer to change the family's bedsheets and turn down their covers—Toby had returned to his bedroom to find Alyssa fast asleep. He'd still been so angry he'd been tempted to shake her awake and keep fighting, but what would be the point? He didn't plan to stay in this house long, whatever the Wrights might have thought. Toby lay down as far away from his wife as he could and stared at the wall. He knew he'd never sleep that night.

Imagine his surprise when Alyssa sat up in bed a little before eleven and whispered his name.

He didn't move. He was still turned away from her, breathing as steadily as he could, and listened as his wife gathered up a few clothes and slipped from the bedroom without another word. He heard the suite's main door click open, click shut.

She was still gone when the storm Jerome had warned of broke over the house a little after midnight. Toby's anxiety had only grown worse in her absence. His hands had been shaking, his heart beating so hard he could hear it ringing in his ears. He could practically feel his head vibrating, like the walls of the memory palace were threatening to collapse under all this pressure. What had he been thinking, doing any of this? Bringing Luca here? Bringing *himself*?

Deep inside his mind, he heard the faint low *creak-k-k* of a door swinging open. A bad door. The worst door. He heard a slow shuffle of feet, a wet *drip*.

Drip.

Drip.

He saw Willow, face pale, soaked to the bone, shambling down the halls of the marble labyrinth, free again from where he'd sealed her away. With a lurch and a gurgle, she came to stand at the foot of his new bed, dripping water onto the floor of Ramorah as she asked him, *What the fuck have you gotten yourself into?*

Toby was losing control of his mind, right when he needed it the most.

He relented moments before his mind caved in entirely. He threw his legs over the side of the bed, stepped into the closet, and dug open Alyssa's purse. He found the amber vial of anxiety tablets tucked into a pocket in the lining. He shook two into his palm and swallowed them dry.

We who are about to die salute you.

The pills worked. The trembling in his mind stilled. The door—the bad door, the worst door—*slammed* shut, sealing his sister away again with a *click*. It was the last thing Toby heard before he slipped into a dreamless sleep.

The storm raged on.

———

Toby stirred at seven o'clock sharp and saw that the storm showed no sign of letting up. In the en suite bathroom, he heard the unmistakable retch of his wife vomiting with one of the migraines that had started to plague her lately. She'd had one just like it Thursday morning.

He made no effort to comfort her.

A text message from a number he didn't recognize waited on his phone.

> Due to inclement weather, breakfast has been
> moved inside to the sunroom—Ruth.

At the thought of eating with the Wrights again, Toby stepped into the closet and returned to Alyssa's purse. He found the vial of tablets exactly where he'd left it the night before. Toby hesitated. He glanced over his shoulder.

He slipped three pills from the bottle. Tugging on a pair of jeans, he tucked two of the tablets into his pocket.

The third tablet he chewed dry. His sister had once told him that helped the drugs kick in faster.

She was right.

A few moments later, his mind already going smooth from the pill,

Toby stepped into Luca's bedroom. He rested a hand, as gently as he knew how, on his son's small, hot shoulder.

The boy started awake, the beads in his hair clinking. "Oh," he said. "I thought it was him again."

"Him who?"

"You look funny."

"I'm fine. I wanted to make sure *you're* fine."

Luca seemed to know exactly what he meant. "You mean because of dinner?"

"The family was mean to you, bud. Cruel. It means—"

"I know what cruel means."

His son wiped sleep-crust from his eyes. For the entirety of the boy's life, Toby had done his absolute best to keep Luca from ever knowing the pain of being laughed at, sneered at, humiliated simply for being who he was. Luca was only seven. Couldn't he enjoy a few more years before the world's bullshit started to pile up at his door?

"I like your flower." Toby picked up the white rosebud on Luca's nightstand and marveled that this small thing could have set off such a wave of embarrassment among a family of grown adults. Maybe Toby had just been living in Los Angeles too long, but surely there were bigger things a family of wealthy Christians could be aghast at than an origami rose?

Luca paid the flower no attention. He whispered, "Why don't they like me?"

"It really doesn't matter, bud."

"But they're my family now."

"Not really." Toby returned the rose to its place and brushed a handful of metallic stars, shed from Luca's bright pink bedtime socks, off the side of the bed and onto the floor. "I should have never brought you to this house. Let's just get through breakfast, all right? Hopefully we can get out of here for a bit after that."

But Luca didn't move. "Mister Suit said no one's leaving anytime soon. He woke me up to tell me."

"Who?"

Luca nodded at something over Toby's shoulder.

Toby turned, following his son's gaze, and found nothing but a dim corner, a rainy window, empty air. For a single second, he thought he saw a shadow there, a trembling black form whose source he couldn't place, but when he blinked, it was gone.

A draft of air, quick and cool as mercury, drifted over his cheek, just as it had in the hall downstairs yesterday afternoon. This time it was Luca who brought a finger to Toby's damp shoulder.

"Sorry. I think his hands are always wet."

TOBY CAJOLED LUCA OUT of bed in a hurry, refusing to talk any more about this: the boy had never had an imaginary friend in his life and he wasn't about to start now. On their way into the hall, they passed Julian pushing a silver trolley toward their door. "Laundry day," he said in explanation, his voice small and timid. "I'll . . . I'll get your things for you."

A marked change had come over Julian. Yesterday, Alyssa's *distant cousin* had seemed so suave and collected: the sly grin, the smooth steps, the air of bored competence. Now he watched Toby with a strange, anxious light in his eye, as if he was looking for some sort of clue, a confirmation, like a man who'd begun a secret handshake and expected Toby to return it.

Whatever Julian wanted from him, Toby's mind was too glassy with Ativan to either know or remember. "Thanks for that" was all he said, and guided Luca to the stairs.

The sun lounge was empty when he and Luca arrived. Now that he didn't have a family to entertain, Toby noticed an engraving in the stucco wall that he'd missed at lunch yesterday. It was another bas-relief, though his knowledge of the Bible was too anemic to recognize the scene: a robed man raised a hand to the sky while a herd of pigs hurried off a cliff into the ocean, a horrible cloud of eyes and teeth seething over their heads like a storm of gore.

Toby hated this house.

A glass door stood near the lounge's wall of windows, through which Toby and Luca discovered a cathedral of a room that stood three stories high. Most of its ceiling was constructed of glass, as was the entirety of the towering northern wall that looked out on the estate.

Round café tables—all bedecked with balloons and tinsel—were arranged around a great ocean of floor, while curving stairs led up to a wide balcony on the house's second floor that appeared to be loaded with sofas and recliners and palms in great alabaster pots. The diffuse light of the storm burnished it all with a dull glow, like a gloss of tarnished silver.

"You won't be so impressed when you see how much it costs to cool this place in the summer," Sarah Nella called to Toby from a table near the stairs. She stood with his mother-in-law, Ruth, looking tall and precise and fresh-pressed and utterly in control, just as she had yesterday afternoon. The sisters watched as Marie (the other half of the hired help) fussed with a great lavender bow. With a single glance at Toby, Marie tethered the bow to the table's centerpiece and hurried away across the wide floor.

Next to her sister, Ruth looked exhausted: no amount of makeup and hair spray could save the dark circles beneath her eyes, her crumbling blowout. With a great yawn, she said, "Once we realized the storm wasn't letting up, we decided to get creative about how exactly to host a garden party."

"Clever," Toby said.

"It was mostly Sarah Nella's idea, of course," Ruth said, turning to regard the soaked lawn outside, but her sister seemed not to hear her. The moment Ruth's attention was elsewhere, Sarah Nella turned to Toby with a nervous frown. She glanced between Toby and Luca, a finger running back and forth along the edge of her hair. Her bob was so sharp, Toby was almost worried she might cut herself.

That unease looked out of place on Sarah Nella, *wrong*. Toby had the fleeting, irrational fear someone else might have taken up residence inside her skin.

Ruth turned back from the window, catching the expression on Sarah Nella's face. "Are you all right? Is it your heart?"

Before Sarah Nella could answer her, Richard and Kassandra stepped, wordlessly, down the room's stairs, looking at no one, least of all each other. *They've had a fight*, Toby thought. Luca perked up at Toby's side, giving Kassandra a little wave, but the woman's eyes passed over him the way they did the rest of the furniture.

Luca wilted. Toby rested a hand on his head.

A pair of tall double doors on the main floor opened and Matthias the feral cat followed Ginger inside, saying as he did, "Who's Timothy Sage?"

He was studying his mother's phone too closely to notice the way the name made both Sarah Nella and Ruth go stiff and silent. Ginger was clad in heels and a long skirt and a massive black fur stole that covered most of her torso, but somehow none of her flair seemed to stick to her this morning. She was too spooked by whatever was on her phone. She shrugged her son away with a sharp elbow and pulled the screen to her chest. "I need the internet to come back up. Now."

"It only just died a moment ago," Ruth said. "It's probably the—"

"What is it? What's wrong?" Hugo blundered through the door behind Toby like he, too, had mistaken the sun lounge for the sunroom.

"Nothing." Sarah Nella tried to smile. "Nothing but a ghost."

"Marie! Coffee!" Richard shouted toward the kitchen. Kassandra patted her mother-in-law's arm. "You don't look so good, Ruth," Toby heard her murmur.

"Any sign of Alyssa, Tobes?" Hugo said, holding in a hard yawn.

"I think she's fending off another migraine."

Ginger looked up. "Since when does Alyssa get migraines?"

Coming closer, Hugo glanced from Luca to Toby with obvious concern. In a low voice, he said, "I hope you're hanging in there," and carried on across the room to hug his wife.

"I guess we're only missing Jerome and Corah," Toby said, though he was so curious what he should make of Hugo's worry he hardly heard the words leaving his mouth.

"Oh, we never see Daddy downstairs until almost noon." Ruth rubbed her eyes. "God only knows why. He used to be such a morning bird."

Ginger looked ready to throw her phone through one of the room's towering windows. "Does anyone have internet? Cell service? I need my email. *Now.*"

"Mister Tucker?" whispered a voice at Toby's side. "Mister Tucker, please, could I speak with you a moment? In private?"

It was Sarah Nella. Alyssa's aunt had practically materialized next to him, that anxious finger running again along the edge of her hair. She fastened her eyes on Toby's like she hoped to drag him away in some kind of thrall. "Please, Mister Tucker. It's urgent."

"Ah!" Ruth said. "Here she is."

It was Alyssa. She appeared at the head of the stairs, and as she floated down to kiss Toby softly on the cheek, he hardly recognized his wife. She wore a pair of plain blue jeans and a crisp white top with her usual effortless grace (did nothing look bad on her?), but he noticed a surprising new tranquility in her eyes, a calm light that might have been contrition, or at least an acknowledgment of how unpleasantly she'd behaved last night after dinner. When she mouthed silently, *Sorry,* Toby almost felt guilty for his own anger.

Almost.

Marie returned from the kitchen, tottering under a white tower of cake. Alyssa gasped in delight as the maid lit thirty candles, one by one. His wife kept glancing at Toby with her brilliant eyes like she needed some confirmation from him that the cake really was as beautiful as she thought. Sarah Nella was standing at Ruth's side again, her face a perfect blank, her eyes a mile from Toby's. Whatever she'd wanted to talk about, it would clearly have to wait.

Hugo let out a long hum, obviously ready to get a round of "Happy Birthday" out of the way. "Ready, everyone?"

And then the sunroom's grand double doors slammed open and tiny, powerful Corah tumbled inside, clad in nothing but a bathrobe and slippers, her gray cloud of hair almost billowing off her head. "Jerome?" she shouted. "Jerome? JEROME!"

Alyssa froze, a candle burning inches from her lips. Corah turned from face to stunned face, the knuckles of one hand rubbing away at the hem of her robe as she said, "He's not in his room. We're late for the party and he's not in his room and it's *not my fault.*"

A blur of something at the edge of his vision made Toby turn. It was a drop of rain, plunging from a leak in the skylight above. He glanced down just in time to watch the drop strike Alyssa's white cake with a muted *thump.*

Toby blinked. A spot of red had bloomed in the icing, like a rose petal drifting to the top of a glass of milk.

Another drop of rain struck the cake, a third.

Each brought a fresh bloom of crimson.

All eyes rose to the massive skylight above. There, at its southern edge, Toby spotted a small pale thing that rested on the glass like a beached fish. Water was pooled around the white thing. Red water.

A gleam of gold caught the dull light. A signet ring.

The small pale thing was a hand.

"Oh my dear Jesus," Ruth said. "It's Daddy."

ALL AT ONCE THEY were moving. With a crash of plates and cups, Ruth ripped the cloth off a table and flung it over the cake and Hugo stumbled away from the blood in horror and Corah pointed at the skylight and said, "I told you. *I told you he was back!*"

Sarah Nella's voice cut through the din with all her father's booming authority, her anxiety from a moment before long gone. "Tobias, Richard, I need you. This way."

Toby's feet were following her almost before his mind could catch up. He hesitated a moment, looking back at Luca, and found Marie the maid standing with a protective hand above his son's head. "Go on," she said. "*Go.*"

It would have to do: no one else was paying the boy any mind. Alyssa stared dumbly at the red rain spilling from the sky. Kassandra watched her husband hurry out the door, a stunned question on her face.

Toby caught up with Richard and Sarah Nella in the foyer. Richard had the door to the elevator propped open with his foot, an anxious vein pulsing in his hard jaw. "Are you coming or not?"

The elevator was spacious, its walls covered with a rich damask paper. A tufted bench waited to one side, and it was here that Sarah Nella sat, her brow sweating, her smartwatch emitting the same rapid shrill beep that had risen in response to Jerome's tirade last night. She fumbled at the screen to mute it. "Sorry," she said. "My blood pressure."

Richard stabbed the button for the third floor. The elevator rose with a great groan. They climbed the house in silence, Sarah Nella never once meeting Toby's eye. When the elevator's doors opened again, she climbed to her feet with a great effort, only to freeze again when she saw what awaited them on the landing.

The wall opposite the elevator had been attacked with more of the brutal red paint they'd seen on Corah's door yesterday. Someone had left another message.

THE LORD WILL HAVE HIS JUSTICE YOU FUCKS

AND I WILL HAVE MINE

"We'll deal with this later," Sarah Nella said, doing her best to sound commanding even with a hand pressed to her chest. She led them to the left, down a dim hall, and an icy chill swept through Toby as he stepped over the threshold, followed by a brief, perfect silence.

And then he was in motion again, plunging into the heart of the forbidden west wing.

Toby's sharp memory had always served him well with directions—give him five minutes with a map and he could navigate just about anywhere—but even he struggled to understand the maze that confronted them in the west wing. The walls were papered in a dizzying damask pattern, broken by nothing but a string of identical wooden doors. Every inch of floor was covered with the same endless beige carpet. There were no decorations anywhere, no landmarks, no obvious pattern to its turns and blind corners. Sarah Nella had been right yesterday: a person could wander this wing for hours and never find their way out.

She, at least, seemed to know where she was going. After what felt like an eternity of lefts and rights and lefts, she finally rounded one corner, veered sharply down another, and arrived at a hall that looked different from the others.

Jerome's wheelchair sat, empty, a few yards away. Near the wheelchair stood a large metal umbrella stand that carried nothing but a spare black cane. Past the umbrella stand, a narrow flight of concrete stairs rose to a wide metal door. At the top of the stairs, Sarah Nella gave the door a shove. It didn't budge.

"This is why I need you boys," she said. "Jerome is the only person with a key to this door."

Richard gave Toby's narrow shoulders a dubious frown. He needn't have feared. Toby had broken down his share of doors.

(And sealed shut plenty more. *Slam. Click.*)

"On three," Richard said, bracing himself at the edge of the door and motioning for Toby to stand beside him. "One."

"Two."

"Three."

The door buckled on its lock but held firm. It began to budge the second time they struck it.

The third time, the lock snapped. Richard and Toby stumbled out into the rain.

Ramorah's roof was enormous, a great expanse of black tar paper that seemed to stretch away forever. Close to the door were two tall black trash cans (the kind a family in the suburbs might wheel to the curb every Sunday night), both cans filled to the brim with some strange gray sludge Toby didn't have time to examine.

Further on, at the place where the west wing met the main body of the house, a bank of air-conditioning compressors rumbled and spat in the rain. The domed skylights above the sunroom stretched like boils toward the northern edge of the house. Past the skylights, that black iron cross Toby had seen when they first arrived towered thirty feet into the air.

As they neared the skylights, Toby saw a strange jumble of objects scattered across the tar paper on the nearer edge of the glass: a lawn chair, an Igloo cooler, a telescope that looked far too expensive to be resting on its side like it had been knocked over in some struggle. Near the telescope was a fallen black cane.

The beeps from Sarah Nella's watch grew frantic. She breathed in short, tight gasps.

"Are you all right?" Toby asked.

In reply, she nodded at the body sprawled at the skylights' edge.

The old man lay on his back, his arms flung wide. He wore dark jeans, leather loafers, a white cashmere sweater. Almost all of that white had been subsumed by a viscous brown stain.

A great gash yawned open in the sweater's chest. Like a lover or a nosy aunt, the wool had curled itself, almost delicately, into the deep folds of the wound beneath.

Jerome's face was frozen in a vision of terror. His black eyes brimmed with rain.

The Lord will have his justice, Toby thought.

And I will have mine.

Before Toby could see more, Sarah Nella's watch gave out a long, sustained wail and she fell to the roof with a *thud* beside him. "Oh, fuck," Richard said. "She's having another stroke."

2:4

AN HOUR LATER, SOAKED to the bone, Toby ran a towel over his hair and passed it to Marie with a small "thank you." She said nothing as she wheeled away her silver trolley.

Toby and Luca and much of the family were in the parlor, a snug room tucked away in a corner of the ground floor. It held a large television, a scrum of hulking leather chairs, dark windows. The sound of the endless rain ticked a steady *drip*

   drip

   drip down the chimney of a cold fireplace. Above the mantel, a glossy photograph of the Wright family brooded over them. The photograph was old enough to include a bony, silver-haired woman with a severe good cheer and a thin neck clotted with diamonds. She could only be Grandma Abigail, late wife to the dead patriarch seated beside her in the photograph.

Richard and his father, Hugo, stepped into the parlor just as Marie was about to make an exit. The woman struggled to hold in a sigh as she offered them two more towels.

"It's just like we were afraid," Hugo said. "Both the north and south creeks have flooded."

"Oh, Jesus," Ginger whispered.

Almost at the same moment, Ruth stepped through the room's other door, wiping her hands on her slacks, just in time to say, "What about the roads?"

"Gone," Richard said.

"Oh my Lord." Ruth seemed barely strong enough to speak.

Toby was right there with her. He felt like a sprinter coiled up at a starting line, ready to bolt at a moment's notice. But if the roads were out, where could he go?

Besides, he couldn't leave Luca with these people. The boy was seated on the floor with a bundle of colored pencils, pretending not to listen, but even a few feet away Toby could almost feel the boy speak to him, soundlessly, through the air.

I'm scared.

Me too.

Ginger tapped her phone, *tsked*, tapped it again. "The internet is *still* out."

"What does that have to do with anything?" Toby said. "You should be calling the police, not checking your email."

Ginger and Richard exchanged a muted frown. She pressed the television's power button and found nothing but static.

"We went completely digital a few years back. The satellite dish on the church roof is just for show. The cable and the Wi-Fi and the phones are all bundled together on the same wires. They promised us the networks around here were strong enough to never go down." Ginger glanced at the TV, tapping the tip of her vape against her teeth. For once, she looked sincerely uneasy.

"Meaning what?" Toby said. "There's no phone service either?"

"There's nothing, Toby," Ginger said.

"But we need the cops," Toby insisted. "A man is *dead*. Sarah Nella's in some kind of coma. Why aren't all of you freaking out about this?"

Richard rolled his eyes. "What do you want us to do? Rend our garments and weep?"

Ruth was way ahead of him. Toby's mother-in-law pressed a hand to her eyes, another to her mouth, and started to sob.

Ginger took a hard hit off the vape. With an unmistakable tremor in her voice, she murmured, "Christ. There's so much to do."

An hour ago, after Sarah Nella's watch had given out its last desperate beep and she'd fallen to the roof, Richard had sent Toby running to find Alyssa. "But she's just a pediatrician," Toby had said numbly. Richard had been too busy administering rough CPR on his aunt to answer him.

Pediatrician or not, Alyssa had been brisk and competent and strangely relieved when Toby brought her to the roof, as if grateful for the chance to do something. "I'm amazed you found your way through that labyrinth," she said. Richard had managed to carry an unconscious Sarah Nella inside onto the concrete stair landing—"I've hauled heavier," he said simply—and after listening to her aunt's wheezing chest and pressing a finger to her throat, Alyssa instructed Toby and Richard to carry the woman down the stairs, into Jerome's wheelchair. From there, Alyssa pushed Sarah Nella back to the main wing (she, too, Toby noticed, never lost her way in the west wing) before arriving, at last, at her aunt's suite.

Kassandra and Ruth had been waiting for them. "I was studying to be an RN when I met Richard," Kassandra said modestly when Alyssa wheeled Sarah Nella inside. Richard and Toby had eased the ailing woman onto her bed as gently as they could, nearly dropping her twice thanks to her wet skin, and Alyssa bustled around her before sending Kassandra into the bathroom for aspirin, crushing a few tablets into dust with the help of a heavy drinking glass, and dissolving the powder in water. "Prop her up and spoon-feed her," Alyssa said, passing the mixture to Kassandra. "Go slow—she probably won't survive a choke."

Toby wasn't sure if Sarah Nella could survive much of anything for very long. Her eyes were lidded, her lip drooping, her chest echoing with a pitiful high growl like a frightened dog. Even her bobbed hair had lost its form in the chaos, looking for all the world like a jagged helmet, shattered by a blow from the enemy.

Richard and Toby had left Kassandra by Sarah Nella's side and taken Alyssa back up to the roof. "I'm not a pathologist," she said more than once, but after Richard fetched an umbrella from somewhere and Toby held it over his wife's head, Alyssa examined Jerome's body with surprising acumen.

"You'd need an autopsy, of course, but judging by all the bleeding, it seems fair to say it was this stab to the chest that killed him: I saw a few wounds like it in my ER residency," Alyssa said. "It would have been a long flat blade—any decent kitchen knife would have done it. The rain's cooled the body too much to determine a decent time of death from his temperature, but his sweater is dry on the back. I think it's a decent guess to say he was already lying there, where we found him, when the rain started."

"Which was midnight," Richard said over the rain. "Or right around it. Could he have stabbed himself?"

"Theoretically, I guess. It would take some serious balls and a good grasp of anatomy to sever your own aorta."

"What about by accident?"

Alyssa gave her brother a narrow frown. "He *accidentally* severed his own aorta? By falling on his back?"

"So it's suicide. We all saw how unstable he was acting at dinner last night."

Alyssa had seemed ready to agree to this, but Toby cut her off. "Are you kidding? If he stabbed himself, what happened to the knife?"

They'd looked all around Jerome's corpse. None of them found any trace of a weapon.

Ruth had been waiting for them on the concrete stairs when they stepped back inside, her short frame so full of adrenaline Toby had worried his mother-in-law might dislocate a joint. "Y'all are just going to *leave* him out there?"

"The police will need to examine him," Alyssa said. "They'll need to go over the whole roof. It's a crime scene, Mom."

"Spare me—what sort of clues are they going to find after this rain?" Ruth snapped, and something in her voice made Toby ease away from her the way he would a barking dog. "I'm not going to allow my father to *rot* in the rain."

Toby positioned himself in front of the roof's door, almost without thinking. "You have to be kidding. If you move Jerome now, the police might never be able to figure out who did this."

Later, Toby wondered if his words had changed their minds, but perhaps not in the way he'd hoped. A silence spread over the landing, a small frown passing from face to face. With a little grunt, Richard motioned to Toby. "Let's get back out there and get him."

"No."

"It wasn't a question."

"You're serious? You're really going to sabotage the best chance the police have to make a decent investigation?"

"No," Ruth said. "We're going to show a great man the respect he deserves."

Richard made his way out the door—shoving Toby aside as easily as he would a stalk of corn—and returned, a few minutes later, with Jerome's corpse slung over his shoulder in a fireman's carry.

There was something about the way Richard handled his grandfather's body, his casual, unbothered grunts of effort as he hauled Jerome (bloody white sweater and all) down the concrete steps, that made Toby suspect Richard had seen violent action during his time in the corps. It wasn't a pleasant sight.

"Put him in his room," Ruth said, opening a door near the foot of the stairs, and Richard emerged a few minutes later, wiping his hands on a towel.

"Now to see about the roads."

———

Which brought them back here, now, to the parlor on the ground floor. Ruth was still shaking with sobs. Hugo rubbed her back. In a small voice he said, "It never stays flooded around here for long. The roads should clear in a couple hours once the rain stops."

"Can't we try to contact someone at the dam, get them to shut off the flow of one of the creeks?" Toby said, though he already felt he was grasping at straws.

Ginger looked stunned at the suggestion. "The county handles all the dam's business remotely—no one actually works on-site in this kind of weather. And even if we could reach them, they'd never shut off the creeks. Not unless they want to flood Hebron. What do you think the dam is for?"

Marie poked her head through the door. "I heated up some lunch," she said to no one in particular.

Jerome's sister, Corah, had spent the last twenty minutes seated alone in the parlor's corner, studying the photograph above the mantel, patting at her massive cloud of silver hair. At this, however, the elderly woman finally stirred. "Chef told me yesterday she was leaving us au gratin for lunch. Jerome loves au gratin."

A pained silence passed around the family as they waited to see if she would correct herself. She didn't.

"Corah makes an excellent point." Ruth rose, rubbing her cheeks and clasping her hands together like she was hoping to crush the tears from her memory. A lifetime on live television had clearly taught the woman how to switch on her bonhomie when she needed it. "Everyone has to eat," Ruth said. "That's an order."

Toby stayed where he sat. "Are you serious? There could be a murderer loose in this house and you're thinking about *lunch*?"

"It was a suicide, Toby. The knife will turn up somewhere," Richard said, heading for the door. "And if it *was* murder, well . . . it's not much of a mystery, is it?"

The rest of the family froze in their places.

Toby tried to speak, faltered, tried again. "What—what's that supposed to mean?"

"Jerome was perfectly safe in this house for years. Isn't it strange how that changed the night someone new arrived?"

Every eye in the room turned to Toby.

Richard shrugged, smiled. "What was it Grandpa always said? 'A coincidence is just God's way of tipping his hand.'"

"Is Mister Jerome really dead?"

Toby wasn't sure how long he and Luca had sat in the parlor since the rest of the family departed for lunch. The anxiety pills he'd tucked into his pocket earlier this morning had crumbled to dust, thanks to the rain soaking his jeans, but he found a few shards of a tablet and swallowed them with a wad of spit. They were too small even to chew.

They helped, a little. The medicine calmed him down enough for Toby to construct a new room in the marble labyrinth, fill it with new memories and new anxieties and suppositions that didn't serve him. He shut the door. He turned the key. *Slam. Click.* For a blissful moment, when Luca spoke, Toby didn't know where he was at all.

"Is Mister Jerome *really* dead?" Luca said again.

"Yes, bud," Toby finally said. "He's really dead."

Luca chewed the end of his pencil. Toby had never seen the boy so on edge. "No one but Miss Ruth seems very sad. Not like us when Mommy died."

Toby forced down a mouthful of bile, slammed his shoulder against a very dangerous door—the bad door, the worst door—before it even thought about *creak-k-king* open. Luca had a point: Ruth had been the only member of the Wright family to shed a tear for Jerome all morning.

Warn that man with the fishhook scar that he is heading into a brood of vipers.

Urge that man not to fall into the judgment the Lord his God has prepared for that brood.

Warn that man that his son—

That his son—

That his son—

The door opened and Marie the maid appeared bearing an empty silver tray, no doubt ready to clear away the family's cups, only to flinch in surprise when she found Toby still here. "You aren't hungry?" she said.

"Are you?"

Luca rose, gathering up a pair of dirty cups and easing them, with that infinite care of his, onto the empty silver tray. "I helped Miss Marie clean up the sunny room this morning," he explained. "She needs all the help they can get around here. She says the Wrights wouldn't know a broom from a kick in the head."

Marie started flinging dishes onto the tray with an unmistakable blush. In spite of everything, Toby almost found himself smiling. "I just hope he didn't get in the way."

"This little hustler? I wish I had his work ethic."

Luca buffed the glossy table with a rag. Toby saw the anxious elbow grease the boy was putting into it. He also noticed, almost in passing, that Julian the butler hadn't inherited all the good looks in Marie's branch of the family. Alyssa's *distant cousin* was rather lovely herself, her small features all resting in pleasant, poised harmony; she had an upward curl to her nose that a magazine or a beauty blog would adore. She spoke to Luca not with the breezy, confidential tone Kassandra had deployed yesterday (and abandoned just as abruptly this morning), but with the caution and careful pleasure of a woman unused to children and surprised to find herself enjoying one's company. Toby knew exactly how she felt. "Careful you don't buff off the polish, hustler."

And then fear came back over them all, even Luca, in a sudden cold wave. Lowering her voice, Marie said, "You should get to lunch, you know. My dad used to say the worst thing you can do is give this family time to scheme."

Toby sat back, considering this. Did it signify anything, he wondered, that Marie didn't appear to count herself as a member of the Wright family?

"Your father's not here, is he? He's not . . ." Toby struggled for the right word. "One of them?"

"He's dead. All Jules and I inherited from Sarah Nella are our eyes."

"Sarah Nella? Alyssa's aunt?"

"She's our grandmother, don't you know?"

Toby considered this, too. "I heard she was never married."

"She wasn't."

"Which makes y'all illegitimate."

"Dad was the really illegitimate one. And he was even darker than us."

That certainly put a spin on things. Ever since his arrival, Toby had been perplexed at the way Alyssa held such an aversion to her aunt when Sarah Nella, in person, had been nothing but polite and soft-spoken and very nearly kind.

Now, however, Toby found his appraisal shifting. What kind of woman would employ her own grandchildren as servants, illegitimate or otherwise?

And while he was on the subject of Sarah Nella, what the hell had she been so desperate to discuss with him this morning, moments before all hell had broken loose?

Mister Tucker, please, could I speak with you a moment? In private?

Marie had other things on her mind. Lowering her voice, shooting a careful look over her shoulder to be certain the door was still closed, she added, "I heard what Richard was saying at the end there. About a co-incidence being nothing but God tipping his hand. That's bullshit. Why would *you* want to kill the old man?"

"That is a fantastic question."

"Don't be so casual about this," Marie said. "I'm telling you—they scheme, these people."

"If I wasn't flippant, I'd probably be screaming."

Marie rose to go, adjusting the weight of her tray, hesitating at the door. She turned back.

"Sir—Toby—I hope this ain't too forward, but there's something someone needs to say. This whole family, what they do with the TV show and the money and all that—Christ ain't in any of it. You know that, don't you? I don't think the Lord's in a one of them."

"Jerome certainly didn't think so, judging by his performance at dinner last night."

"There's more sins in this house than murder, Mister Toby. You *really* need to go to that lunch."

"I'm touched, really, but I couldn't eat if I—"

"Who cares if you eat? You need to keep an eye on them in there. I just remembered what day it was."

"Saturday?"

"Alyssa's *birthday*. In all this madness I completely spaced."

"I don't think anyone's interested in celebrating my wife's birthday party today, Marie. Not even my wife."

"The law's certainly interested in it. The bank will be too."

A great rumble of thunder shook the house. The rain, far from abating, seemed to just be getting started.

"What bank?" Toby said.

A wry grin twisted Marie's mouth, an expression both stunned and deeply unsurprised. "Did nobody explain how the money works in this family, sir?"

"They certainly spend a lot of it."

"Oh, you poor soul. Your wife has done you dirty."

2:6

TOBY FOUND THEM IN the house's cavernous kitchen, a room on the main floor so large it contained not just three floating islands and a pair of cooking ranges, but a windowed nook with a rough-hewn oak table long enough to seat a dozen chairs. The family was in the midst of a rapid conversation there at the table, one they cut off with a sharp *shh* the moment he arrived. The sound of a single word—"circumstantial"—echoed over the skillets and stovetops and faded, at last, into the clatter of rain.

Marie followed him inside, pulling out chairs for Toby and Luca opposite Alyssa and Richard. "Thank you," Toby said, as the girl unfolded a napkin in his lap with an unmistakable tremor in her fingers.

Toby had questions about Marie and her strange eagerness to help him, but he also didn't see a reason she would lie to him. She had just finished explaining some exceedingly interesting details about his new wife's financial future. Toby gave Alyssa a hard smile. He might have been terrified—even the marble labyrinth had its limits—but for now he felt a welcome new emotion come over him.

Rage.

"Not quite the birthday you expected, is it, dear?"

Alyssa stared at him, a bead of water draining, unnoticed, from her damp hair and over her cheek.

A long silence followed. Matthias, Ginger's son, was nowhere to be seen. Nor, Toby noticed, was Kassandra.

"Is your wife still keeping an eye on Sarah Nella?" Toby said to Richard.

A funny expression passed over his brother-in-law's face, just as it had on the front drive yesterday and six weeks ago in LA. Yet again, Richard looked curious and uneasy, studying Toby with a faint air of recognition that seemed impossible to explain. Rather than answer Toby's question, Richard asked one of his own. "Did you ever spend any time with us at Camp Cleave?"

"Where?"

"The wilderness camp we sponsor outside Waco. Climbing walls, mountain bikes, leadership skills—ring any bells?"

"No," Toby said honestly. "My uncle was too poor to send me to something like that for fun."

Richard turned back to his sparkling water without another word.

Marie appeared from behind a pantry door bearing a great bowl of salad and her most deferential smile to Richard. "Not as good as the one you chopped for us last night, sir, but I did my best."

From the end of the table, Ruth fumbled for something to say. "Have... have you thought any more about what I asked last night at dinner, Toby? About what role you'd like to play in the ministry?"

"Do you still have a ministry?" Toby said.

"Of course. People don't tune in just to see Jerome," Ruth said.

"They don't?" Ginger said.

"Who knows how things will look when the roads clear and the phone lines come back up," Ruth plowed on. He saw tears leaking down over her fake cheer. He couldn't bear to look at her for long. "We might even announce Daddy's death on the broadcast tomorrow. Cardiac arrest. It's... not exactly a lie."

Toby had thought he was finished being surprised. "Are you serious? Won't the police want a say in that?"

"Who says we need to get the police involved at all? Why let all that fuss into the house?" Ginger took a long pull off her vape. Toby caught the way her hand was shaking. "This is a family matter. There's no reason we can't bury Jerome ourselves and move on."

Toby stared at his sister-in-law, certain she was joking, but Ginger looked as earnest as the rest of them. All around the table, Toby found Wrights glancing at their plates, their watches, the sky, no one but Ruth looking especially bothered by the fact that someone had apparently stabbed an old man to death on their roof. Toby wouldn't have expected anyone to be particularly bereft at Jerome's loss, but where was their sense of self-preservation?

Why did no one look scared they might be next?

As if to underline his unease, Alyssa said, "Who's to say we'll ever learn how the old man died? Most murders are never solved, you know."

"It could still be suicide," Richard cut in.

Ginger added, "And in a case like this, where all the clues would just be hearsay—"

"Circumstantial evidence," Richard said.

"Would anyone ever really be satisfied with the outcome of an official investigation anyway?"

"Provided we all find a version of events that we're happy with, we may never see a reason to look much further into the matter," Richard concluded.

Toby's mouth fell open. "Is that why you ruined the crime scene by dragging Jerome's body inside? So you could all decide on a version of events you could be happy with? Brush all of this under the rug?"

"What if it was a homeless person?" Marie spoke up, startling everyone: the girl was clearly never expected to open her mouth. "A vagrant, someone who broke in to steal something?"

Ginger narrowed her eyes. "Hardly. I checked—according to the security system in the office, all the doors and windows on the ground floor were locked by nine o'clock yesterday evening. They stayed that way until we started to get ready for the party this morning. We would have all gotten an alert on our phones last night if someone had broken in. Remember, the internet was still up until a few hours ago."

"What about cameras?" Toby said. "You must have a million of those posted around here."

"We do, of course. And we have private security that comes in to keep tabs on the visitors at the church on Sundays. But ever since Jerome had his fall last year, we've cut back on security throughout the week—it wasn't like he could go very far in that wheelchair of his. There's only one camera inside the house itself. It's posted in the hall outside the staff's quarters." Ginger settled her fork softly into her bowl. In spite of the calm in her voice, he heard the way the fork's tines *ting-ting-tinged* on the porcelain: her fingers were shaking. "The camera has a wired connection into the house's main server, so we can view its feed even with the Wi-Fi down. Which I did, the second I learned what had happened."

There was silence around the table. Even Luca watched her, rapt.

"Marie and Julian were both in their rooms by ten thirty last night," Ginger said. "They didn't emerge until five this morning."

"And according to my lovely wife, Jerome was already dead by the time the rain started at midnight," Toby said.

"He was lying on his back when the rain started," Alyssa began. "I never said—"

Toby cut her off. "So the hired help are the only two people here with alibis. That just leaves the rest of you."

"Let's not jump to any conclusions," Richard said.

"You mean like the conclusion you're acting suspiciously calm about this? Jesus, you'd think we were talking about the rain."

Hugo picked at his salad. In a low murmur (he clearly wasn't expected to speak often, either), he said, "Why was Jerome on the roof in the first place?"

Toby thought of the fallen telescope they'd discovered near Jerome's corpse, the lawn chair, the Igloo cooler. He said nothing.

"And what about the door to the roof?" Alyssa seemed to weigh every word in her mouth. She turned to Richard. "Was that door unlocked when you guys got up there with Sarah Nella?"

Richard gave a little grunt of a *no.* "We had to break the door down. Sarah Nella said Jerome had the only key. Which he did. It fell out of his pocket when I picked him up to carry him inside."

"And did you put it back?" Toby said.

"Of course I did. What were *you* doing around midnight, Toby?"

Toby's cool smile returned. Richard would have to do a lot more than that to scare him. "I was in my room. Trying to sleep. Wondering where my wife had snuck off to in the middle of the night."

One of those great silences spread over the table. Richard stared at his sister. Ginger stared at Toby.

"Where I *what*?" Alyssa finally said.

"You heard me. You got out of bed around eleven o'clock, dear, remember? I waited up for ages. You must have come back after I finally fell asleep, but that was well after midnight."

"I don't see how that's any of your business." The ice in Alyssa's voice could have frozen the rain.

"It's not my business to wonder where my wife is sneaking off to in the middle of the night?"

"What do you care? You haven't touched me since we got married."

Ruth and Hugo both turned pale. Even Ginger stared.

Corah, sitting by herself at the end of her table, exploded into laughter, rubbing her nose and spraying potatoes au gratin across her bowl.

Toby wasn't dissuaded. In that moment, all he could think about was the little secret that Marie had shared with him in the parlor a few minutes earlier, the bald-faced fraud his wife had tried to carry out right under his nose.

"It's funny you mention that, dear. *My business.* Like, wouldn't it theoretically be *my business* to know the terms of my wife's trust fund before I signed our prenup?"

There was another long silence.

"Oh, Alyssa," Ruth began. "Don't tell me—"

"No, Ruth, she didn't. For six months your daughter told me she'd never met a better man, that she loved me more than life itself, that her entire family would adore me and my son. She never bothered to mention how she needed Luca and I to access her fucking trust fund."

A muscle twitched in Alyssa's jaw.

"All of you had the same deal, didn't you? To get your share of the money, you have to bring fresh blood into the ministry. You need a spouse and a child by your thirtieth birthday." He shook his head at Alyssa. "There must be a lot of money in that trust, babe. You put on a hell of a show for it."

Ruth and Hugo both dropped their faces into their hands at the exact same moment. Ginger sighed and sighed like she'd sprung a leak.

Richard tightened his grip on his fork until the knuckles paled. "Oh, Toby. That was a mistake."

Before Toby could take this in, a blast of eerie string music tumbled through the quiet air, punctuated by the warble of a moody electric guitar. The music was bent and echoey, clearly playing at a loud volume from somewhere deep in the house, and while the sound was familiar, it took the arrival of a smooth, booming voice for Toby to recognize it.

"You're on *The Prophecy Hour*," said the spectral voice of Jerome Jeremiah Wright. "Speak, friend—the Lord is listening."

2:7

"IT'S COMING FROM A TV somewhere," Hugo said, but Alyssa was on her feet before the words had even left his mouth.

She took off for the hall. Toby hesitated just long enough to exchange a glance with Marie. For the second time that day, she rested a protective hand on Luca's head. "I'll be right back, bud," Toby murmured. Luca folded his cloth napkin without a word, struggling to form a rose.

Another familiar voice greeted Toby as he followed Alyssa into the hall. "I've been tithing and calling you for years and years, Reverend. It's such an honor to finally speak with you."

The sound of the voice sent Alyssa jogging toward the foyer, and a moment later Toby realized why. The voice belonged to old Miss Lottie, the round old woman at the Cracker Barrel. They were listening to last week's broadcast.

Judging by the way Alyssa was hustling, she knew what was coming next.

"It's an honor to speak with you, ma'am," Jerome's recorded voice said. "What do you need to lay before the Lord today?"

Alyssa reached the foyer ahead of Toby. She cocked her head, listening to the voice's echo, before she turned to the right and shouldered open a heavy door.

They were heading, once more, into the west wing.

"That's just it, Reverend. I always used to have so many questions about what the Lord had planned for my future, but I'm old now. I ain't got much more future left to worry about." Lottie's nervous laugh sent a murmur through Toby's heart. "But last night I had a dream that I was sitting here, now, calling you on the air, Reverend, and I—"

"'Lo, you shall know those times by their signs. You will see strange visions and you will dream strange dreams.'"

The ground floor of the west wing was just as much a maze as the third. It bore the same hypnotic damask wallpaper, the same beige carpet, the same endless rows of identical wooden doors. What were all these rooms *for*? Toby wondered distantly. Why did one house need so much *space*?

Whatever the answer, the TV was playing from somewhere deep in the wing's heart.

Jerome continued. "I knew you would be calling me today, ma'am. The Lord revealed it to me in the dark of night—oh, Hosannah, yes. The Lord God showed me that the woman who called at this quiet hour, the woman who would be my final guest on this glorious Sunday, she would be not a sheep in need of guidance but a *tool*, ma'am—do you hear me?—a tool of the Lord's service, oh praise his name. Are you willing to be that tool, madam? Are you ready to hear what the Lord God will ask of you?"

Miss Lottie seemed cowed by the urgency in Jerome's voice. "I—I suppose so."

"Listen to me now, ma'am, because time is short and the Lord demands much. Ma'am, I prophesy unto you that at the end of this week—*this very week*—you will encounter a man with a curious scar upon his flesh—a scar shaped like a fishing hook, you will know it without a doubt—do you hear me? A man with a fishhook scar. And when you meet that man with the fishhook scar, you must give that man three warnings from the Lord. Are you listening, ma'am? Three."

The sound of the broadcast was growing closer. Alyssa thrust her head into one room, another, a third, searching for its source.

"Ma'am, warn that man with the fishhook scar that he is heading into a brood of vipers. Do you hear me? A brood of vipers. Second, urge that man not to fall into the judgment the Lord his God has prepared for that brood. And third—ma'am, are you there? This is the most important warning of all."

"I'm here, Reverend."

Alyssa shoved open a door and the sounds of the broadcast grew almost deafening. Toby followed her into the room at a jog, stuffing his phone into his pocket, only to collide with his wife as she stood, frozen and trembling, before the ghastly sight inside.

Jerome was speaking from an ancient cathode-ray television that stood on a chipped pressed-wood dresser. Two twin beds sat before the dresser, both covered by the thin, dismal duvets of cheap lodging. Tartan curtains covered one wall. A crumpled pack of Marlboros rested on a greasy nightstand.

Crazy as it was, the entire room—right down to the thin carpet scarred with cigarette butts—was a perfect replica of an old budget motel.

A DVD player was hooked up to the ancient television. The screen of the TV was coated in a layer of bloody red paint. It pulsed crimson in the gloom, like some forgotten organ of the house.

Someone had painted another message above the TV.

BEHOLD

GOD'S JUDGMENT ON THIS FAMILY HAS BEGUN

AND I WILL HAVE MINE

Toby arrived just in time to hear Jerome deliver the final warning from last week's broadcast, the one Alyssa had interrupted yesterday at the Cracker Barrel.

"Ma'am," Jerome said. "Warn that man with the fishhook scar that his son, his *only* son, is in even greater danger than he could possibly imagine."

At Jerome's last word, the television's deafening volume climbed to a screech that made Toby and Alyssa cover their ears. Just as Toby thought he might lose his mind if the sound didn't abate, the screen shattered. Silence filled the room, tinged with a faint trace of smoke.

Toby didn't have time to be surprised by any of this.

Warn that man with the fishhook scar that his son, his only *son, is in even greater danger than he could possibly imagine.*

Luca. He had to get back to Luca.

Toby turned back to the hall, ready to take off running again, but

Alyssa beat him to it. She snaked around him, slammed the door shut, rose to her full commanding height. She stared him dead in the eye. He tried to slip past her. She planted a hand on his chest and shoved him back.

"No, Toby. We need to talk."

"**You humiliated me in** front of my family," she said.

Toby's mind was moving so quickly it took him ages to remember what she was even talking about. "You mean about your trust fund?" He thrust a finger at the smoking television. "Alyssa, fuck me, you think I care about money after hearing *that*? I want my son. Now."

"Calm down. Jerome made a lot of prophecies. It was sort of the business model."

"No, Alyssa. Not like that he didn't."

"How would you know?"

"Because my uncle made me watch your stupid show every Sunday for years," Toby said. "Your grandfather was a fucking grifter, Alyssa. I never once heard him make a prophecy with a *tenth* of the detail he gave that woman. How did he know we would stop at that Cracker Barrel yesterday? How did he know about my *scar*?"

Alyssa looked from the television to Toby to the furious warning painted on the wall. "You used to watch the show? You never told me that."

"Why would I? You never seemed to care about the family business until this weekend."

"Funny thing to stay quiet about, though."

"You're one to talk."

Alyssa turned the switch of a tasseled lamp, bathing the strange motel room in a noxious honeysuckle light. She took a breath, clearly trying to calm down. "Last week's show got a little weird, all right? They've done that a lot lately. It doesn't matter. What possible danger do you think Luca could be in? Is my family going to eat him?"

"Your grandfather called you a brood of vipers on live TV. A week later, the man's dead. Do you think I want my son anywhere near you people?"

"Jerome would have said something to you in person last night if that warning was actually serious. He saw your scar himself when he shook your hand yesterday. I saw him staring. You just said it yourself—the prophecies are all a scam. What kind of prophet doesn't see his own murder coming?"

Toby didn't answer her. He moved toward the door again, ready to push her aside if he needed to. "We're leaving. Luca and I can figure out the roads on our own."

Alyssa shoved him back into the room again, harder now.

"Jesus, would you think about this for five fucking seconds? You're acting like I'm your enemy because of what? The way I'm about to start collecting sixty grand a month from the trust fund? Sixty thousand dollars. A *month*. Half that money is yours, dummy. You just need to smile and keep your mouth shut and let all of this blow over."

"Smile and keep my mouth shut about an old man's murder?"

"Or suicide."

"Right. A suicide that didn't leave a knife behind."

"Details, details." Alyssa did something with her mouth that might have been a grin. "You really don't want to back me into a corner here, Toby."

"I raised a boy on my own with less money than you burn in a weekend. You can't scare me."

"I'm up to my eyes in debt, Toby. I'd say we both have a stake in this."

Toby laughed. "Debt? Your family has a house the size of Versailles and you're in *debt*?"

"It's not like they just hand out the money for no reason. When I was in school, the only things my parents paid for were my tuition and my housing and my food—"

"Is that all?"

"You're a fucking idiot if you didn't think something was off about all this." Alyssa's eyes darkened. "Did you really imagine a pediatrician's salary could afford a house in LA and a penthouse in Austin and a loft in Brooklyn and a bungalow in the south of fucking France?"

"I forgot about the place in Nice."

"It's not my fault you don't know how to read due diligence paper-work. It was all there in the prenup, Toby: I was mortgaged up to my goddamn eyes until 12:01 this morning."

"The terms of your trust weren't there. I'd have remembered that."

"Do you have any idea how hard it is to live responsibly when you know you'll be richer than God the day you turn thirty?"

"No, Alyssa, I don't."

"I don't recommend it. Especially when you spend your twenties dat-ing rich assholes who can jump on a jet and leave you."

"I'm glad to be of service."

Toby couldn't quite name the emotion in his wife's eyes: exaspera-tion, fury, fear? "This is a mutually beneficial arrangement, Toby. Your son can go to any school in the world now. We can pay for his intern-ships, his nonprofit work, we can give that kid a résumé that would make a billionaire cry. He has a future. *You* have a future."

"Right. Sure. As long as I stay with you." Toby laughed. "I read *that* part of the prenup just fine. 'Both spouses shall remain in harmonious cohabitation or risk voiding this agreement.' If I move out, it's over."

"You really do have a hell of a memory. Wait—where do you think you're going?"

"I just told you—I'm leaving, Alyssa. *We're* leaving. I don't fucking care if it voids the prenup. You want to talk about humiliation? I'm not leaving Luca anywhere near you people."

"So my brother wants to give him a haircut. Is that the end of the world?"

"That's not it and you know it's not. You heard what Richard said about toughening Luca up at some fucking camp in the woods. You saw the way Corah stared at my son like he'd crawled out of the creek. Your family is never going to accept my son for who he is. And good fucking riddance."

Toby put a hand on his wife's shoulder to ease her out of his way.

Alyssa hit him, hard, across the mouth.

"Listen to me, Toby. Listen very fucking well. The money from our trust fund isn't sourced out of passive income. Most of it's money that the ministry hustles out of the church donations. It's fraud and tax evasion and all the rest, but we've been doing it so long there's no going back. Do you see where I'm going with this?"

He touched a finger to his mouth. It found a thin ribbon of blood.

"All of our money, the real money, it comes from the donations people make to the ministry. We pull in a couple million in tithes every month. Do you hear me? A couple million dollars of tax-free money, all made out to Two Creeks Ministries and run through a half dozen shell companies in the Bahamas and then dropped into a big pot that the trust pulls from. But without the show, that money will dry up fast. If *The Prophecy Hour* goes under, we *all* go under."

"You hit me."

"Details, details. The good news is that Richard's been preparing to take over the show—we've all been preparing for it. We thought Jerome would hand over the reins at the next Christmas broadcast. Ratings were slipping before the old man started to get kooky earlier this year. We needed a refresh, something to draw in younger Evangelicals. Richard's run some focus groups. He knows what they like." Alyssa paused for breath. "A male lead, a female costar, and a young son."

Toby stepped away from her, slow and careful, as a realization dawned on him. The thud of his heart seemed to reach a new decibel level in his ears. "This is what you were talking about last night. The reason you decided to join the ministry. The 'situation' that had changed."

"Among other things, yes. Sarah Nella and Richard made the problem abundantly clear to me yesterday afternoon. Kassandra is about as charismatic on TV as a clothesline, and if someone else is going to join him on air, it sure as hell won't be Ginger. And until his wife can conceive a baby, Richard and I are going to need a kid of our own."

Toby sat at the edge of one of the motel's twin beds. He felt all the blood draining from his skull.

Alyssa didn't stop. "I didn't realize Richard would need me this soon, but hey, the Lord provides. I like you, Toby, all right? I really do. You're chill and you're funny and you're nice to look at and I would *really* like this marriage to work. Why the hell not? But if it doesn't work, there's something you should know."

He waited. Alyssa shook her head.

"This is not a forgiving family. They practically executed Sarah Nella when she came back from a mission trip to Korea with a Black baby forty years ago. My parents didn't talk to me for ages after my second DUI. Who knows what they'd do to you?"

Toby wanted to throw up. "That almost sounds like a threat, Alyssa."

"Maybe it is, Toby. Maybe Richard's onto something. We pay the salary of every cop in this county. You know what story the police will believe when they finally get here? *If* they ever get here? It could very easily be the story of how my new husband killed my grandfather in a fit of rage last night."

Toby stared at her.

Alyssa carried on in the same even voice. "After you were indicted for murder, we'd of course have no choice but to dissolve the marriage, which would lead to the question of who retained custody of Luca, and I can't imagine that would be a difficult choice for a judge. Should your son go to the heiress of a fortune who can guarantee the boy a life of comfort and privilege? Or to the father rotting in jail for the rest of his life?"

Alyssa narrowed her eyes. She didn't blink.

Toby was stunned, he was scared shitless, but he stared right back. "Or maybe I'll figure out who really killed Jerome before the cops even get here."

"I'd be careful poking around this house, Toby. We need your kid. We don't necessarily need you."

IF AN OBSERVER WERE to stumble into this strange motel room after Alyssa departed, they would see Toby seated on the edge of the bed, studying the red warning painted on the wall. Looks would be deceiving, however.

In truth, only Toby's body was there. He himself was somewhere deep below Ramorah, deep below his own mind, hurrying up and down the marble labyrinth of his memory palace. Toby was underground, sorting out fresh horrors from old ones.

What the fuck have you gotten yourself into?

Think, Toby. Think.

He needed to see his son—it was a physical pain, that need, like an ache at the root of his heart—but Toby knew that rushing headlong into the rest of this afternoon wouldn't do either him or Luca any good. This conversation with Alyssa had taught Toby a valuable lesson: he couldn't afford many missteps in this house.

His heart was a spring, coiling tighter than it had ever been designed to withstand.

Think, Toby. THINK.

Toby could recall almost every line of the prenuptial agreement he'd signed two weeks ago, and with every line the danger of his situation became more and more obvious. If Toby were to file for divorce without cause, Alyssa could bury him in penalties that would crush him with debt for the rest of his life. The same would result should Toby stay separated from his wife for more than three months "without the express written consent of both spouses and for matters pertaining solely to business."

That would never happen. Now that Alyssa had explained the family business and their vision of the show to him, Toby realized that he—and more specifically, his son—were too valuable for the Wrights to ever let out of sight.

And it was here that Toby's nerve started to fail. He could endure a great deal of abuse, but he couldn't imagine the same pain being thrown at his son. Early in his relationship with Alyssa, Toby had tuned into an episode of *The Prophecy Hour* to see if it was still as strange as he recalled from his childhood and found Jerome preaching a sermon about God's *rightful division of the sexes.* "The perversions of this country are holding us back from all true bounty," Jerome had decreed. "Men laying with men, women with women, a boy declaring to the Lord, 'No, Father, you made a mistake, I'm really a girl.' There shall be no peace in this country until such a practice is acknowledged by its true name—a perversion sent by Satan himself."

My family's too rich to be bigoted.

Who would ever be stupid enough to think that was just branding?

Now the Wrights wanted to include his son in that same show. Luca, a boy with long braided hair and pink shirts and delicate talents—a gentle, wild soul—who would never fit into the family business without some serious modification. *Pity we can't toughen you up for a few weeks at Camp Cleave*, Richard had said.

Toby knew too well what that sort of "toughening up" could do to a child. He had a horrible vision of Luca in ten years' time, standing under the brilliant glare of the church's stage lights, dead-eyed and smiling in an Ivy League haircut and starched button-down, a loveless girl on his arm and a hard, broken thing, like the cracked shards of an acorn, slowly turning to dust in the hollow of his chest where his heart should be.

Toby may have married a liar, but at the end of the day *he* was the fool who'd brought Luca into a brood of vipers. And for what? Nothing—*nothing*—was worth the danger in which he'd now placed his son.

If the family really was thinking about accusing Toby of Jerome's murder, there was only one obvious way out of this. He hadn't been bluffing with Alyssa, there at the end.

Toby took a few long breaths in the halls of the memory palace and made a plan. He peeked behind certain doors, skirted past others, considered every angle as carefully as his frayed nerves could allow. When he was confident he'd covered every angle, he made his way up and down the length of the labyrinth, his feet squeaking softly on the marble, and sealed away the pain and undiluted horror that this conversation with Alyssa had put inside him. He locked every door. He heard the key ring through the perfect, subterranean silence.

Click.

Click.

Click.

Toby rose from the motel bed. His mind was a perfect blank.

It was time to get busy. He'd never solved a murder before, but he couldn't imagine it would be any harder than anything else he'd already been through.

The hall outside the motel room was empty. The west wing silent. And yet Toby had only taken three steps and rounded a corner before he realized he wasn't alone.

Behind him, Ginger said simply, "Shall I show you the way back?"

"**MOM THOUGHT OF YOU** last week, the second Jerome started preaching about a man with a fishhook scar. She remembered it from when y'all met in LA."

Alyssa's sister led Toby confidently through the maze of the west wing, her vape hardly leaving her lips, red hair bobbing on her shoulders.

"Mom must have mentioned the scar to Jerome. God only knows why the old man wanted to scare old Miss Lottie at the Cracker Barrel half to death. It is funny though. None of us—especially not Alyssa—could recognize that woman's voice when she called in last week."

"So Alyssa and I stopped into that store purely by coincidence?" Desperate as he was to get back to Luca, Toby realized that something here felt important. "Exactly when Jerome said we would?"

"That Cracker Barrel is one of the only stores in town. And Jerome knew you were arriving at the end of the week, of course. Is it really so strange?"

Toby thought of Miss Lottie's dusty store, the stack of Jerome's books on the counter, the sign hanging behind her: KEYS CUT HERE.

Ginger guided Toby around one corner and another, past endless doors, never moving faster than a leisurely stroll.

Warn that man that his son is in even greater danger—

"Can we pick up the pace here?" Toby said.

"There's no rush. Your son is safe with Marie. She and her brother are probably the closest thing y'all have to friends in this house."

"And why is that?"

"Because they know what it's like to get fucked over by my family."

That wasn't exactly comforting.

"So what about you?" Toby said. "Are you a friend too?"

That seemed to confirm something for Ginger. She froze in her tracks, poked her head through a door, and ushered Toby to look inside.

The door led to a massive room, divorced from any intelligible sense of scale, furnished like a church sanctuary from the eighties. It held a raised lectern and a glossy maple wood cross, polished wooden pews with Berber seats.

"This is an *actual* sanctuary," Ginger said. "Every piece was broken down and shipped here on a flatbed truck. When Jerome and Grandma Abigail built this house, he gave her free rein over the other two wings. In exchange, he was allowed to do whatever he wanted over here. He called the west wing his 'memory palace.' Took him years to finish."

Toby went very cold. "He called it his what?"

"His memory palace. It's actually a very old idea. It dates back to the Romans, I think, but I'm not sure they built theirs out of *actual* palaces. Every rich man needs a quirk, you know."

Deep in Toby's mind, the halls of his marble labyrinth shuddered like they'd taken a blow to their foundation. The idea of a memory palace wasn't so rare, no—Hannibal Lecter had one too, though Toby supposed that still didn't put him in the best of company—but the thought that Toby might share anything with a man as bigoted and angry and cruel as Jerome Jeremiah Wright made him physically ill. He heaved the thought behind a door. *Click.*

"You still with me?" Ginger said. "You've gone quiet."

"No one killed Jerome for his memory palace, Ginger."

"What makes you so sure?"

Toby supposed she had a point. "Why are you showing me this?"

"We're getting there. Jerome was obsessed with his past. Do you know the name Tom Titer?"

"Vaguely."

"*He* used to be one of the richest preachers around, until he got sued into the poorhouse by all the kids he'd fathered on the side. Jerome was still on the traveling preacher circuit in the early eighties when he passed through this church sanctuary—it belonged to Albion Baptist at the time, up outside Frisco—and the pastor at Albion was so impressed with Jerome's skill at prophecy, he called his old seminary buddy, Mister Tom Titer. Tom had just started a television network modeled after Pat Robertson's CBN and he needed a main attraction to compete with *The 700 Club*. So Tom asked Jerome if he'd like to take his prophecies to the airwaves."

"And a star was born."

They left the sanctuary. "Jerome was a hit almost the minute he went on the air. He and Grandma Abigail settled in Houston awhile, founded a sister church to Tom's, spent their first few years broadcasting from there—my brother Richard would say they were 'growing the brand'— and when Titer's legal troubles got started, Jerome bought the network off him for a song. The money really started to flow in after that. Did you know this whole estate used to be Lake Hebron? The WPA dammed the lake in the Depression and parceled off the land to a few lucky farmers like Jerome's dad. Jerome and my grandmother Abigail used to be neighbors. Dirt poor. Literally. They always swore that when they hit it big, they'd come back and buy all the old farmland and settle a family here."

"Shouldn't we have taken a left back there?"

In response, Ginger opened another door and ushered Toby inside. This new room was decked out like a comfortable businessman's office from the late Reagan years. She came to stand behind a chunky wooden desk, framed on either side by artificial windows that looked out on a printed image of the sun setting in a downtown sky. JEROME JEREMIAH WRIGHT, CEO read a black nameplate on the desk.

The sole anachronistic detail of the room was the silver MacBook Pro on the desk. It rested beside enough loose papers and Post-it Notes to start a good fire.

Ginger said, "I was always Jerome's favorite, not that it's stopping my wonderful siblings from trying to take over the business without me. The old man let me use this room as my office. Please, take a seat."

"I want my son. I'll find my own way back."

Ginger sat, planted her elbows on the desk, tented her fingers. "Your full name was Tobias Martin Tucker. You did, indeed, get that scar on your arm in the car accident that killed your parents when you were six. They were both drunk. So drunk, in fact, the police wondered if they'd planned to kill your whole family when they ran into an oncoming truck. It didn't work. You and your brother survived."

Toby froze, midstep. "My sister, actually. Are you trying to impress me?"

Ginger shrugged, conceding a point. "Our investigators can't get all the details right. We can't, for example, figure out the name of your son's mother. I know that the minute your uncle died—his name was Ezra, I think? The only person who'd agreed to take care of you?—you and your sister moved to Los Angeles. She was in and out of mental hospitals and rehab centers and halfway houses almost from the second y'all got there. You supported her as best you could, but there's no fixing a drug addict, is there? She died of an overdose a little after this past New Year's. Did I miss anything?"

Toby sat.

"Why didn't you tell Alyssa how your sister only just passed away ten months ago? Alyssa was under the vague impression the girl died as a kid, years ago. I haven't enlightened her, don't worry, but please—enlighten *me*."

"My sister wasn't well. She never was. That kind of thing runs in families."

Ginger smiled. "And you were worried that if Alyssa learned the truth, she wouldn't want to marry you? For fear you'd bring mental illness into the family? How very Victorian."

Toby said nothing. There was more to that story than Ginger knew, but he didn't feel like enlightening her any further.

"You were so curious yesterday to know what I do for the family," the woman continued. "I'm chief counsel. I make sure the ministry's business is conducted legally and safely."

Toby thought of what Alyssa had said about the family's trust funds. "Is it always so legal?"

Ginger laid down the vape and withdrew a box of Marlboro Reds from the drawer of the desk. "Here."

"I don't smoke."

"Give it a shot. You're going to want it."

Toby wasn't sure about that: he hadn't smoked a cigarette since his modeling days. After two pulls he found he still despised it. "Who enjoys these things?"

"No one. But I need a vice until the internet can come back up. Though it might be too late by then."

Toby thought of the way Ginger had been so desperate to access her email this morning. Her son had mentioned a name right around the same time, something that had distressed more than a few of the Wrights. What had that name been? Thomas? Terrance?

It was lost to Toby now, tossed behind a door in the marble labyrinth along with so much else that happened this morning. He said to Ginger, "Too late for what?"

"Let's just say that Jerome might have known he had trouble coming. Trouble he couldn't wave away."

"You mean he had a reason to kill himself?"

"Perhaps."

"Then where—"

"Where's the knife? I know. I know. But if he was murdered, that begs another massive question: Who had another key to the roof? Who even knew he'd be out there in the first place?" Ginger smiled. "Not that *logic* is slowing anyone else down. There are plenty of awful ideas going around right now. Ideas about you, for instance."

"I know. Which is why I was on my way to find the actual killer when you interrupted me."

"Oh, that's adorable." Ginger tapped her filter with a crimson nail. "I like you, Toby. I really do. That's why we're sitting here this afternoon. A lot of stuff crosses this desk. There's not much that happens in this family that I don't know about. But there is one thing that's been nagging at me. Did your family ever give money to our church?"

"That's a strange question."

"Every few years, there's something in the paper about a family who gave their last dime to Jerome because he made some prophecy on the show they were certain was meant for them. 'Give all that you have so the Lord can give back tenfold.' Jerome loved that line. It was a shame when people took him seriously, of course, but hardly actionable."

Toby stubbed out his cigarette in a dry coffee cup. He said, truthfully,

"Nothing excessive. My uncle sent y'all a check every week, but never enough to get in trouble."

"Well, that settles it."

"Settles what?"

"Revenge. It was the only reason I could think you might have for wanting to murder the old man."

"Glad to know someone thinks I'm innocent."

"I didn't say that." She lit another cigarette with the butt of the first. "First lesson of law school, Toby—never commit to a position."

"You're wasting my time, Ginger."

"No, Toby. I'm trying to help you."

"You could help me by talking to Alyssa. My wife wants to turn my son into some sort of prop for your TV show. It sounds like they're willing to frame me for murder if that's what it takes to have him."

"Clause Seventeen of the prenuptial agreement: 'An indictment for a crime by either party will result—'"

"'—in immediate termination of this agreement and all penalties shall be enacted as outlined below,'" Toby finished for her. "Yes, I remember. Why can't they just use *your* kid for their shitty show?"

A dark look crossed Ginger's face. "They wouldn't risk that. Matthias . . . Matthias doesn't do well under pressure."

"And you think Luca would?"

"I don't know what the wonder kids think, Toby. But my brother and sister will get support from our parents in the end. The show must go on." Ginger watched a trail of smoke curl past her finger. "Has anyone told you about the way my daughter made the mistake of dying on a Sunday? Do you think a single one of my beloved brood were at the hospital with me when she passed?"

Toby sat a moment in silence. "You . . . had a daughter?"

"Yes. Had. Past tense. That's the salient detail here."

"I'm so sorry." Toby stared, the bitterness in Ginger's voice so strong he almost tasted it on his own tongue. "I know what that feels like. To lose—"

She held up a hand. "Stop. Please. A sister isn't the same as a child. I don't go a single day without wondering how I could be with her again. Isn't that pathetic? Spare me the fucking sympathy. We're a ruthless crowd, is my point. Not much prone to sentiment. Maybe that's why none of us are grieving Jerome and wringing our hands the way you wanted us to do at lunch."

Toby was hardly listening. A door slick with blood had started trembling deep in the heart of the marble labyrinth. It was the bad door, the worst door, and as the conversation turned away, Toby shouldered the door shut and *clicked* the key.

"Fine, Ginger, you want me to be ruthless? If I don't want Luca to get dragged onto *The Prophecy Hour*, then I need a smoking gun before the rain stops and the cops turn up. Is that what you're planning to offer me here?"

"I can offer you something better."

He waited.

"I can offer you a shield, Toby. Insulation in case the shit really hits the fan. Or maybe some leverage to get out of here in one piece."

"Pardon me?"

"Blackmail, you idiot." Ginger took a long, long drag of smoke. "I'm trying to help you blackmail my family."

SEEK HIS FACE ALWAYS

3:1

AN HOUR LATER, AFTER an incredibly strange conversation with Ginger, Toby found Luca in a cramped suite in a distant corner of the first floor's east wing, folding an enormous pile of laundry with Marie. The moment he spotted Toby, the boy leapt down from his chair and wrapped his arms around his father's waist with a squeal. "I *found* you!"

Toby never had time for movies or TV, even in LA. He got bored reading history and never trusted fiction (why would anyone enjoy feeling like God himself, peering into the heads of unsuspecting people?). He had few hobbies, in other words, but once, in a rare fit of ambition, Toby had dug out some of his sister's paintbrushes and a fresh canvas and tried to capture the seismic, eye-watering joy—like a bayonet of happiness straight through the throat—that seized him whenever his son, with no warning, reached out to share a little touch of love with him.

The painting had turned out to be an abstract scene, a wash of robin's-egg blue punctuated by cloudy silver shapes, all tinted by streaks of bright yellow and soft, soft lavender. Toby had tinkered for ages with the balance of cerulean and lemon and mauve, but in the end he never had his sister's elusive gift for shading. When he felt the painting was as near to finished as he could make it, he'd rolled a bar of white across the middle and written, in darkest black, *a happiness like this should be illegal.*

His sister, spoiling for a fight after an aborted round of rehab, had given the canvas a single snide glance. "The only happiness I've ever found *is* illegal."

That was the first time Toby had really considered it. Considered how much better things would be without Willow.

Slam. Click. He needed more pills.

In Ramorah's servants' quarters, Toby hoisted his son into the air and squeezed him until the boy started to wheeze with laughs. Toby felt Luca's heartbeat echo in every empty space of his body. "I'm never letting you out of my sight again," he whispered in the boy's ear.

Marie, meanwhile, was studying the scar on Toby's arm with a fresh appreciation. Alyssa's *distant cousin* must have heard the deafening recording of last week's prophecy echoing through the house an hour ago. How could she not? "I hope you don't mind me taking your boy. It seemed like you and your wife needed some . . . alone time."

"I just hope he hasn't been in the way again."

"I've never had so much fun folding socks in my life."

The servants' quarters were small, less than half the size of the Ezekiel Suite directly above them, and everything inside was mismatched and dingy and sallow with age. Rainwater seeped through the sitting room's sole window. Clothes and books and cookie dust were scattered across a cracked leather couch.

"Sorry," Marie said, motioning at the mess. "You'd think my brother would know how to keep a cleaner house."

"My sister always said, 'Why put away today what you'll drop tomorrow?'"

"They sound perfect for each other."

Toby hesitated, the thought touching him to the heart. "Maybe so. Maybe so."

"If your sister was a boy, of course." Marie laughed. "Thank God Julian finally stopped pretending otherwise."

"I'm sure the family is thrilled about that."

Marie gave him a dark look. "You don't know the half of it."

Toby joined Luca at the coffee table, matching socks. He tried to find it relaxing. Marie's words had sent something shimmering at the edge of his memory, like a ripple thrown by a stone that had sunk too quick to see. He'd watched Julian do something strange yesterday—something dangerous, knowing this family—but he couldn't recall it now for the life of him.

Just like he couldn't remember the name Matthias had read off Ginger's phone this morning.

That was the danger of Toby's version of a memory palace: sometimes it sealed away more than he wanted to lose.

"Where *is* Julian?" he finally asked Marie. "I haven't seen him since he came to pick up our laundry this morning."

"That's a fantastic question."

Luca had a question of his own. "Where's the bathroom?"

A moment later, when Toby was alone with Marie, he said, "You don't know where your brother is?"

Strangely, Marie ignored this. Shaking wrinkles off a blouse, she said, "What I don't understand is how anyone got hold of a knife in the first place. Sarah Nella locks up all the silver and utensils in the evening after we're done washing dishes. It's something the old British houses used to do, apparently. The way Miss Sarah Nella explained it to me, old Grandma Abigail—Jerome's dead wife, you know—demanded it be done that way, and so it's *stayed* that way."

"Like changing the bed linens every night."

"And doing laundry every Saturday, even if we're supposed to throw a birthday party at the same damn time."

"So where's Julian been all day?"

"He got all the laundry going."

The girl was evading the question. "So shouldn't he be helping you to *fold* it?"

"He's off on a break somewhere."

"You guys get breaks?"

"Not technically. But sometimes Julian goes AWOL." Marie gave a despairing look at the mound of clothing still to do. "Nothing to be afraid of."

"When did you last see him?"

"You sound like a detective."

"I'm trying to sound concerned."

"Really, Mister Toby, it's not some big ordeal, I'm just annoyed."

But her eyes flicked over his shoulder at the door, even as she said it. There was no hiding the worry there, at least not from Toby. The sight sent a fresh wave of anxiety rolling through his gut.

He knew that fear too well from his own life to ever mistake it in someone else.

"Jules will turn up again," Marie said, perhaps to herself. "He always does."

On his way out of the staff's quarters, Luca trailing by the hand, Toby stared at the small black camera mounted at the end of the servants' hall, directly above the hall's only exit. That camera was the reason Marie and Julian were the only people in the house with airtight alibis for last night. An hour ago in her curious office, Toby had asked Ginger to show him the footage from this camera. To his surprise, she had.

Marie and Julian had made their way down this same hall at 10:34 last night, a solid ninety minutes before Jerome's death. They'd stepped into their suite and stayed there until 5:02 this morning, when they'd both emerged and made the same route in reverse.

"And none of the doors or windows on the ground floor were opened last night?" Toby said.

"Precisely. Including the windows in the servants' suite."

"Meaning there's no way Marie and Julian could have left their rooms."

"No. And to be frank, I couldn't imagine why they'd want to murder Jerome in the first place. If anyone, I think Aunt Sarah Nella was always a little afraid of them."

"She was afraid of her own grandchildren?"

Ginger took a hit of a fresh cigarette. She gave an almost imperceptible nod of her head. "She made the staff sign away any hope of an inheritance before they came to work here, probably so they wouldn't have a reason to kill her. I suspect she still slept with one eye open. Wouldn't you?"

Toby led Luca by the hand to the main wing. "Are we going home yet?" the boy murmured.

"As soon as we can," Toby said, though if he wasn't careful, *this* would be Luca's home sooner than later.

Heading upstairs, they made a quick stop in the Ezekiel Suite. The crumbled bits of Ativan he'd found earlier in his pocket were already starting to wear off. Doors were shaking in Toby's mind. Anxiety was crushing him with a terrible pressure, like his memory palace had gone adrift and sunk to the bottom of the sea. If Toby couldn't keep his mind under control, it would all be over. For both of them.

Toby needed help.

Luca followed his father all the way into the master bedroom's large closet, where Toby opened Alyssa's purse and reached for the bottle of pills.

But then he hesitated. The bottle was exactly where he'd left it this morning, in a pocket in the purse's lining, only now it had company. A piece of white paper was folded up in the pocket with it now, a paper that hadn't been there earlier. "Keep an eye out for me," he said to Luca, and while the boy peeked his head out of the closet door, Toby unfolded this new arrival.

The paper in Alyssa's purse was some kind of printed confirmation from a bank. WIRE TRANSFER INITIATED, read the words across the top, beneath which something called ATW Holdings (headquartered in Nassau, apparently) had transferred $125,000 to the personal bank account of his beloved, Alyssa Wright, three weeks ago. The "agent initiating" the transfer was listed as Ginger Wright.

Toby didn't know much about the world of high finance, but he remembered the way Alyssa had mentioned the family hustling tax-free church money through shell companies in the Bahamas to feed their trust funds. This, however, seemed even stranger. The money coming into Alyssa's hands didn't appear to originate from a trust fund but instead from one of those holding companies. Ginger hadn't mentioned anything like this during his conversation with her in the strange office downstairs an hour ago.

Why had Alyssa been paid so much money from one of the family's shell companies, weeks before she was entitled to her trust?

Toby's phone was getting warm in his pocket; it had been working a lot this last hour. With a snap of the camera, he snagged a photo of this curious wire transfer before he stuffed the paper back into the purse's pocket and returned the purse to the shelf.

NO ROAD HOME

"You ready?" Luca whispered.

Toby shook an Ativan from its bottle. He hesitated, the bottle hovering over the mouth of the purse, before he made up his mind and stuffed the bottle into the pocket of his jeans. He noticed the way Luca stiffened at the clatter of the pills. The boy, like Toby, had seen too much of Willow's addiction to ever be comfortable around pharmaceuticals.

It's for your own good, Toby wanted to tell his son, but not even he could fool himself that much.

THE LORD WILL HAVE HIS JUSTICE YOU FUCKS

AND I WILL HAVE MINE

RAMORAH'S ELEVATOR OPENED ONTO the silent third floor around the time the Ativan kicked in and the doors of Toby's memory palace settled safely into their frames. The deep-water pressure of anxiety rolled away. Luca glanced, curious and unbothered, at the red warning splashed across the wall of the landing. The boy had grown up in some rough corners of LA. He barely gave the graffiti a glance.

Instead, Luca pressed his hand tighter into Toby's, a small tremor in his fingers. As Toby tried to step from the elevator, his son didn't move.

"You okay, bud?"

"Can you make me a promise. A *big* promise?"

"Of course."

"Promise you won't leave me alone here again. Okay?"

Toby went cold. "What's wrong? Did Marie do something to hurt you?"

"I'm not scared of Marie."

"Then who are you scared of?"

Luca looked from Toby's face to the little bulge of the pill bottle in his pocket. His silence said enough.

Toby's first instinct was a hot, shameful urge to strike the boy.

Instead he took a deep, deep breath. He wrapped Luca in his arms. "Don't worry, bud. I'll never let you go."

———

Downstairs in her office, Ginger had sketched Toby a crude map of the west wing's third floor, though she needn't have bothered. The route back to Jerome's dead-end hallway hadn't changed since Sarah Nella had guided him there this morning. Toby never forgot his way around.

It was strange, the way the west wing had no landmarks. In the other wings you might find a cross hanging here or there, some framed photograph of handsome Jerome and bejeweled Grandma Abigail smiling from the set of *The Prophecy Hour*, but up here there were only miles of damask walls and beige carpet and door after identical door. Toby poked his head through one such door at random. He discovered a spare old-style country schoolroom, its small desks so stiff and sharp it was a marvel any child could have graduated from them in one piece.

After so many years wandering a mental palace, it was more than a little unnerving to find himself deep in the bowels of a real one. But after a few minutes, Toby noticed a crucial difference between his marble labyrinth and Jerome's maze in the west wing: whereas every door in Toby's palace was locked up tight (especially now, thanks to the miracle of Ativan), all the doors in Jerome's physical palace were unlocked, as if they were eager to let a visitor inside. Toby felt almost like God himself, peering unbidden into Jerome's mind.

It was Luca who noticed the only true waypoints of the west wing. "We passed that wet splotch already. It's the one that looks like California."

Toby followed his son's eye, checked Ginger's map, shook his head. "I think that's another one. It looks more like Idaho to me, bud."

The rain was certainly making its mark on Ramorah. As Toby and his son finally arrived at the dead-end hall at the far edge of the house, he'd counted seven great black stains where the damp was creeping through.

Let it come, Toby thought. If it was raining, the roads were still flooded. If the roads were still flooded, then the cops couldn't come. It meant he had time. At least according to Ginger.

Blackmail, you idiot. I'm trying to help you blackmail my family.

In the end, his conversation with Alyssa's strange sister an hour ago had boiled down to a simple offer. "Jerome kept a journal," Ginger had said. "I want it."

"A journal?"

"Have they abandoned handwriting on the West Coast? A black leather journal bound with A5 paper." Ginger shaped a small frame with her hands in the air. "I caught Jerome writing in it every now and then."

"Why don't you go get it yourself?"

"You think I have time? I'm too busy getting our ducks in a row, succession paperwork, all the rest of it. You, on the other hand, have nothing but time, at least while it's still raining and the roads stay flooded. If I were you, I'd start looking in Jerome's study. I'll draw you a map."

Toby had waited while her pen scratched and scratched at a blank sheet of Two Creeks Ministries letterhead. She'd pushed it across the desk with the practiced, casual air of a loan shark.

He didn't pick it up. "Your siblings sound more than happy enough to tell the cops I killed Jerome. I'm supposed to believe *you* want to help me?"

"Maybe I like you, Toby. Maybe you deserve better than the bullshit my sister's dragged you into."

"But I still don't see what about this journal could be so valuable you'd blackmail your family for it."

"You don't seem like the sort of man to look a gift horse in the mouth."

"And you don't seem like the sort of woman to make an offer casually." He leaned back in his chair, doing his best to appear calm even though every muscle in his body had been twitching to get back to Luca. "You're asking me to find a journal so you can help me fix one crime with another. I'm not a lawyer, but that doesn't seem like the smartest deal."

"You won't *actually* be blackmailing the family. You'll just be making sure they know that *you* know something they would do anything to keep under wraps. Maybe it would get you a chance to renegotiate your prenup. I'm sure, as chief legal counsel, we could come to some very generous concessions."

"It sounds like your show might be doomed without Luca. What gossip could be more valuable than the family business?"

"If I were you, Toby, I'd look for the journal first and ask questions later. Who knows how long this rain will last? And even if you found a smoking gun in this house, do you really think it would do you much good?"

"If the local cops try to cover this up, then I'll call the state police. The feds. The Texas fucking Rangers."

"Or you can calm down and listen to a quick story. It'll help you. I promise."

"I've wasted enough time here."

He'd braced his hands on the office chair's arms, ready to rise.

"Wait."

The edge in her voice made him pause.

"I'm sure you've noticed, by now, that Ramorah has a resident graffiti artist," Ginger said.

Toby thought back to the wild streaks of red in the motel room down the hall. *God's judgment on this family has begun.* "It's hard to miss."

"It's been haunting us all year, almost literally. When Sarah Nella woke up the morning after the annual New Year's special, she found the first lovely note painted on her bathroom mirror." Ginger read off the screen of her MacBook. "'Repent, cocksuckers, for he has seen all you do in darkness.' Someone must have snuck into her room while she was asleep. We found eight other messages over the next few months, one for every member of the family except Jerome, and an extra one each for Corah and Sarah Nella. We've found them painted in closets, on doors, above beds, on the windshields of cars. I got mine here, on this very desk. I sanded it off myself."

"What did it say?"

"It followed the same pattern as the others. A little Old Testament rage, a sprinkle of dirty locker-room talk, a cross or a few extra 'Repents!' just to get the point across. None of the messages are ever precise enough to actually spell out *what* sins we're supposed to be repenting for, which led us to believe the vandal doesn't actually know anything dangerous."

"Or they don't want you to deduce who they are based on what they know."

"Clever boy. We had more staff living here at the time, five people just devoted to keeping the house running and the grounds maintained. We quizzed them all endlessly about the painted messages, watched footage from every exterior camera we had, but we could never place any one person near one of the sites of the vandalism around the time it must have been done. It was starting to drive us all a little crazy. A few of the staff started to insist the house was haunted. A few of us were starting to think it too."

A stray thought from early that morning flitted through Toby's mind like a glint of ice—*I think his hands are always wet*—and he slipped it under a door in the labyrinth, along with all his other irrational fears. "Ghosts can't hold paintbrushes."

"You say that like someone who's met one."

"Were you all living here when this vandalism started? All the family, I mean."

"Of course. We all came home after Jerome had his fall last October, a good two months before the paint started to appear."

"Everyone except Alyssa, you mean."

"No, she wasn't living here at the time, but Alyssa still plays a part in this little drama, don't worry. A few months went by and we'd all started to worry the vandalism would go on forever, until Richard found a message painted on the wall of his closet. He went into a rage." For the first time since Toby had known her, Ginger sounded genuinely uneasy. "You don't want to see my brother angry. He's already dangerous enough as it is."

"Dangerous?" It seemed funny that Ginger would use that word. According to Alyssa, it was the same word Richard (for God knew what reason) had used to describe Toby.

Ginger studied the screen of her MacBook, not meeting Toby's eye. "A woman named Guadalupe had managed our staff for years. The day after someone defaced Richard's closet, my brother went door to door, searching the staff's rooms, and found a red brush and an empty can of paint under Guadalupe's bed."

"That's convenient."

"A couple of us said the same thing, Mom especially. But what could she do? In the end, Alyssa sealed the deal. She was home visiting for Sarah Nella's birthday the weekend Richard found that message in his closet. Right when it looked like maybe Ruth could convince our aunt that Guadalupe was innocent, Alyssa came out with a marvelous story about the way she'd seen our housekeeper skulking around Richard's hall the night before."

"The convenience continues."

"They've always been like that, my golden siblings." A naked distaste puckered Ginger's lips, like her cigarette had soured in her mouth. "Whenever Richard needs Alyssa, she's there to serve, even if she doesn't stand to get a thing out of it. Your wife is a weak woman, at the end of the day. She just wants someone to pat her on the head."

"Or owe her a debt," Toby murmured, but he was busy thinking of the way Alyssa had snuck from their bedroom last night, a little less than an hour before the storm started. He said carefully, "So thanks to Alyssa, Guadalupe the housekeeper got the axe."

"Yes. She did. Off the record, I made sure Guadalupe was well-compensated. The woman had been with us since I was a kid."

"Did the graffiti stop after that?"

"That's the shitty part. Yes. The rest of the staff quit, naturally, either out of solidarity with Guadalupe or because they didn't want to be anywhere near Richard now that they'd seen what the man was capable of. I never for a minute thought our housekeeper was the vandal, but I assumed one of those other folks who quit must have been doing it. We went months without finding another message."

"Even after Marie and Julian started working here?"

"Indeed. That was in April, and we've had six months of calm since."

"Until I showed up."

"Yes, and Corah found a particularly nasty note on her door yesterday."
GOD KNOWS WHAT YOU DID YOU OLD CUNT.

"Who was Corah talking about yesterday when we found her in the hall?" Toby said. "She kept screaming that someone was 'back.'"

"Hell if I know. The staff who quit were all women. The only man we have on staff—other than Julian, of course—comes to do the grounds twice a week, but he's never lived here. You might have noticed that Corah gets confused. Sometimes today and sixty years ago seem to be going on at the same time for her."

Toby mulled this over for a moment, trying to figure out how any of it could do him any good. "Is that all?"

"You don't sound too impressed."

"What's impressive about it? Someone here has an axe to grind and paint to spare. You said Jerome never found a message for himself, right?"

"No, he didn't, but don't assume he was the one doing it. The man needed his wheelchair and cane after he recovered from his fall last year. It's hard to imagine him sneaking around with a brush and bucket without being noticed. What I'm still trying to figure out is whether the vandalism and his death are related. After all, the messages started appearing again not twelve hours before he died."

"You can't exactly take that to court."

"But you can't exactly ignore it, either. What was it Richard said about coincidences?"

"They're just God's way of tipping his hand."

Ginger gave Toby a long, hard stare before she rose from her chair. "Good luck finding that journal, Toby. I hope this story has proven instructive."

"Was it supposed to be some sort of riddle?"

"No, Toby—it's a warning. You could play detective and try to figure out what happened to the old man and waste all the time you want before the rain stops and the cops get here and all hell breaks loose. Or you can remember what happened to Guadalupe the housekeeper and get yourself some insulation."

Toby watched her stalk around the desk. Watched her smile and light up a fresh cigarette.

"You have no idea how much danger you're in, my friend. Like I said—I'd start in the study."

But Toby still had one more question. "Am I in danger from you, too?"

"You mean if you're not useful to me?" She perched her broad hip on the edge of the desk. "Do you really need me to answer that?"

TOBY WASN'T SURE WHAT to make of Ginger's offer—he wasn't sure he'd trust the woman as far as he could throw her—and he also doubted a journal could contain anything valuable enough that Ginger would actually help him blackmail the family in exchange for it. This felt more like an errand, something to keep him occupied and out of the way while she took care of the real business. Could that business have anything to do with the wire transfer Toby had found in Alyssa's purse a few minutes ago? It didn't seem impossible.

Toby went to the third floor of Ramorah in search of something else: there was still a bloody kitchen knife floating around the house, after all. A knife, and a handful of pressing questions.

He hesitated a moment in the dead-end hall at the far edge of the west wing, listening to the distant play of rain on glass, the sound of Luca's steady breath. Just when he felt certain they were alone, Toby took a step into the hall.

A door swung open and a pale face emerged, followed a moment later by a gangly body with big hands and feet.

It was Matthias, Ginger's son.

The moment he saw them, Matthias sprinted down the hall, looking frightened and found out, about the same way Toby himself felt. Before Toby could even think to ask the boy one of many obvious questions—Are you okay? What are you doing up here? Have you seen a murder weapon? A journal?—the boy had shot down the other side of the T-intersection and vanished back into the west wing.

"He looked sad about something," Luca said.

After a moment, Toby shrugged. "At least he was empty-handed."

The door to Jerome's study stood directly opposite the concrete stairs to the roof. To his surprise, the study was so bare he had it searched in a matter of minutes. Rows of walnut shelves were built into the walls, but all of them were empty, as were three tall wooden filing cabinets. A grand wooden desk rested between a bank of blinded windows. It didn't hold so much as a sticky note.

Toby twisted the wand of the window shades and found great sheets of gray rain outside, drowned grass, the distant black shape of the dam looming high above them to the west, vague and inescapable as an omen in a dream. Luca poked a hand into a heavy porcelain trash can under the desk. "Nothing," he said, and sounded almost heartbroken.

Toby might not have been a trained detective, but he also wasn't an idiot. It appeared obvious to him that the study had recently been cleared out. Faint lines of dust lingered on the shelves, outlining the places where books had stood not long ago. A stray pen cap rattled in the drawer of the desk. Empty picture frames were mounted to the wall; another stood atop the desk.

The only notes of personality left in the room were the plastic glue-on stars, a good two hundred of them, that were scattered across the breadth of the wide ceiling. As an experiment, Toby flipped off the study's light and saw the stars glow, faintly, in the rainy gloom.

Luca smiled. "They're just like the ones back home."

Indeed they were. Shortly after the start of the new year, after Toby's sister had vanished from their lives for the final time, Toby had dug into the small stack of cash Willow left behind upon her death (he didn't want to imagine what she'd done for that money) and bought Luca a few bags of these same fluorescent stars. At night, they burned a chemical green.

Odd. Those stars were an understandable design choice for a home with a seven-year-old boy, but it was hard to imagine old Jerome, bundled up in one of his nice sweaters, sitting at this desk and jotting in a handsome leather-bound journal while a tacky galaxy of plastic twinkled overhead.

Come to think of it, stars had been just about all the old man had wanted to talk about last night at dinner. *Why have those seven stars been burning so uncommon bright these last few evenings? What are the Sisters trying to warn us about?* In the old man's office, Toby toyed absentmindedly with a door that had once swung shut to conceal a stack of shelves. The door, he noticed, had a keyhole.

What kind of books would a minister need to keep locked away?

He searched the room again as carefully as he knew how, even pulling up the cushion of the desk's chair and tugging loose the drawers to check the space behind them, but in the end it was Luca who said, "What's that?" Following his son's eye, Toby spotted a glint of white in the dark behind the desk.

The desk was heavy, but with a little grunt of effort, Toby was able to pull it far enough away from the wall for Luca to reach in and grab a sheet of plain white paper. The page was smaller than the usual eight-by-whatever dimensions of standard copy paper, and its left edge was jagged and torn, like it had been ripped out of a small book.

Or a journal.

Yesterday's date was written in the page's top corner, along with the time, *11:42 p.m.* At the center of the page were three brief lines written in a crabbed, skittish hand:

Wet roses bloom on white sugar
From the muted mouth, he speaks
The wailing boy slips beneath green waves

"What does it mean?" Luca said.

Toby folded the page. All his anxiety was back at once, leaving his hand shaking so bad, it took him three tries to find his pocket. "I have no idea, bud."

———

Before he left the study, Toby snapped a half dozen photographs of the room with his phone, something he would have done on the roof this morning if he'd known the family was going to do their best to ruin the crime scene. He hadn't been bluffing to Alyssa or Ginger. If the Wrights really were willing to blame him for this crime to get his son, Toby would do some detective work of his own.

The missing knife seemed like the most crucial clue in this whole mess—where had it ended up? Could someone still have it?—but if Toby couldn't find that, then he could at least start collecting evidence the family couldn't cover up. It was why he'd snapped a photograph of the wire transfer in Alyssa's purse (and why his phone was burning so hot). Maybe he could gather enough insulation without Ginger's help. He sure wasn't going to find a journal in this study.

On his way out the door, Toby had the sense to tug off a shoe and use his sock to wipe down all the hard surfaces he had touched inside. Was he being paranoid, or was it possible Ginger might have sent him up here on a fool's errand just in the hopes he'd leave behind a few prints?

Luca watched him, curious and silent. Without being told, the boy poked his head into the hall and whispered, "All clear."

Toby's heart sank. Somewhere along the way, he'd made his son into an accomplice.

Back in the hall, Toby eased shut the door of the study and considered his options. He looked at his phone. There was still no signal.

The time was just past three.

Almost on a whim, Toby plucked up the umbrella Alyssa had left in the old-fashioned metal stand at the foot of the concrete stairs and climbed to the roof.

"Where are we going now?" Luca said.

"Just helping the cops do their jobs."

Thanks to the way Richard and Toby had broken its latch this morning, the door to the roof stood closed but wasn't locked. He hesitated. "Do you want to stay in here, bud? You hate getting wet."

Luca pursed his lip, shot a scared look down the stairs, extended his hand for Toby's. "You promised not to leave me."

Toby sighed. "Then stay close. It's slippy out here."

Not much had changed on the roof since this morning. The puddles were growing larger. The black tar paper had gotten slicker. Once, twice, Toby felt the roof buckle under his feet like it was threatening to cave in beneath him and changed course as quick as he could.

He glanced with unease at the gray sky. Houses in Texas weren't built to withstand storms that lasted for more than an hour.

When he arrived at the skylights at the northern edge of the main wing, he found the same curious jumble of objects he'd rushed past this morning: a reclining lawn chair, a fallen telescope, a sturdy little Igloo cooler. Inside the cooler he found a bundle of ballpoint pens fastened together with a rubber band, bottles of Ozarka water, a large bag of trail mix.

Beneath this, Toby discovered a thick laminated book entitled *The Starspotter Field Guide* ("The number one resource for identifying and tracking constellations for amateurs and experts"). He squatted down, passing the umbrella to Luca, and cracked the book open. According to a printed invoice tucked between two pages, the guide had been ordered online this past January.

The invoice served as a bookmark for a constellation with a familiar name. *"The Pleiades (or Seven Sisters) are a brilliant bundle of seven stars that were long ago ensnared in each other's gravitational pull."* In the margin nearby, Toby found a scribbled note: *Krittka/Azazel/Samhain—announcement of disaster.* The note had been written in the same cramped hand with which Jerome had scrawled the strange three lines Luca had spotted behind the desk in Jerome's study.

The Pleiades constellation, as photographed in the guidebook, was a brilliant cluster of seven electric-blue stars adrift in an ocean of white dots. When Toby began to turn the page, curious if Jerome had left any other notes inside, a glint of black ink made him stop.

Tilting the page in the weak light, Toby found that black lines had been drawn in ballpoint pen to connect other stars around the Pleiades. The lines formed a lattice of strange shapes across the page, like unlabeled constellations. The lines persisted across every photographed sky in the guidebook, forming patterns that seemed too carefully drawn to be random, yet so endless and all-encompassing they seemed to carry a faint air of madness. Toby found himself turning page after page, clueless as to what he was seeing, yet strangely hypnotized by it all the same.

And then, with no warning, the constellations ended and Toby found himself staring at a sheet of paper at the back of the book where Jerome had scratched out two cramped little lines.

We are nothing but motes of dust trapped in the orbit of a dead star.

Beneath this, he'd added,

God help us.

A bead of rainwater slithered behind Toby's ear and along his jaw, cool and sensuous as the caress of a corpse.

TOBY WIPED HIS PRINTS from the guidebook and put it back where he'd found it, snapped a few pictures of the crime scene with his phone (for all the good they'd do: the rain had already washed away almost every drop of blood he'd seen here earlier, and Richard had tramped through God knew what else), and headed back across the long stretch of tar paper above the west wing.

Before he stepped inside, Toby stopped to examine the pair of trash cans he'd noticed standing near the door to the stairs this morning. They were tall and sturdy and filled nearly to the brim with a thick gray-brown sludge he recognized, after a moment, as ash. Judging by the scraps of paper poking here and there from the mess, he suspected the cans had once been full of books and other documents, though it was anyone's guess what they might once have said. Stray words seemed to wink at him, their ink bleeding in the rain: —*by this process we*—, —*if true th*—, —*secrets of the Tibetan*—.

He snapped the umbrella shut and poked it through the ashen sludge in the trash cans. He hit nothing solid. Nothing like, say, a leather-bound journal.

Or, more important, a knife.

Inside, Toby shook rain from his hair and took Luca by the hand and stopped, at the foot of the stairs, to shine his phone's flashlight inside the old-fashioned umbrella stand.

"What are you looking for?" Luca murmured.

Toby didn't answer him. The umbrella stand was the perfect place to conceal a knife, but he found neither a weapon nor any blood inside. There was nothing in the umbrella stand but a spare black cane.

There were only two doors left in this hall for him to explore. With a sinking heart, Toby opened the first and said, "If you're coming inside with me, just stare at the wall."

Jerome Jeremiah Wright lay on a grand maple bed, exactly where Richard had rested him this morning. The old man was covered head to toe by a sheet. In some dim corner of the room, a leak in the ceiling was wearing down the carpet with a soft *drip*.

Drip.

Drip.

The air was frigid. The faint smell of iron was impossible to miss.

Iron, and spoiling meat.

His sock over his hand, his heart in his throat, Toby searched Jerome's closet and nightstand and dresser for anything of interest. He found nothing but clothes and shoes and an obscene quantity of bejeweled cuff links. Toby left all this where it lay.

He found no journal, not even any books. A stack of papers on the nightstand were clasped to a clipboard and covered all over in red pen— they looked like part of a manuscript for some new book entitled *A Prophecy of Profit*, which seemed blunt even for the Wright family—and after a quick glance through the pages, Toby saw they weren't of any use to him. Judging by the instructions in the margins, Ruth was responsible for typing up Jerome's edits, if not writing the book herself entirely. *R: Less New Age here, more Reagan.* Toby didn't envy her job.

The room's first surprise rested in the drawer of the nightstand. It was a large black King James Bible bound in crumbling fake leather, its pages yellow with age, the gilt on their edges turning to dust against Toby's sock.

The Bible's front page had been inscribed with a simple message:

This Bible is Presented to
Cleave Wright
On this, the 7th of April, 1943.
(Happy Birthday)

Toby puzzled on this, his mind going over Alyssa's list of *The Wrights Who Matter*. It had made no mention of a Cleave Wright, nor had anyone in the family mentioned the name all weekend. Was there anything strange in this? Might Cleave have simply been a nickname for Jerome in his younger years? Hell, maybe "Jerome Jeremiah" was simply a stage name he'd been using all this time, since 1943 was probably around the time Jerome had been born.

But no, that was wrong, wasn't it? Last night at dinner, Jerome had called himself a Scorpio, and while Toby was more or less clueless about astrology, he knew that the birthday of a Scorpio fell sometime near the end of the year, not on April 7.

So who was Cleave?

Oh, yes. I know a thing or two about sin.

A cool draft ruffled the pages of the Bible and stirred Toby's hair, quick and cool as mercury. He shivered. Standing here next to a cold corpse wasn't doing Toby's nerves—or his deductive faculties—any favors. He returned the Bible to the nightstand, started for the door, ready to tell Luca to keep his eyes down and follow him, before he stopped with a sinking feeling in his gut. There was something he still needed to check.

With a long sigh and a shaky hand, Toby lifted the sheet of the bed, only to recoil a moment later. Jerome was naked underneath, his marbled skin dry and smooth. The blood had been mopped from the wound to his chest, his hair had been combed, even his nails scrubbed. Someone had cleaned this corpse so well you could have propped it up for a public viewing.

And ruined any chance of discovering any forensic clues a killer might have left behind.

Toby found Jerome's wet clothes hung up to dry in the en suite bathroom. They stank of laundry soap.

But someone had forgotten to check the man's pockets. Threading a finger into one, Toby found the key that Richard had said fell out of Jerome's pocket when he carried the old man downstairs this morning. The key was small and silver and totally un-noteworthy, but a moment later Toby was glad he'd found it all the same.

Back in the hall, Luca followed Toby back up the concrete stairs and climbed to the roof a final time. Just to cover all his bases, Toby eased the key he'd found in Jerome's pocket into the lock on the roof's door. He tried it again, and once more just to be sure.

But the key's front teeth didn't even make it past the lock's first tumbler. Toby shone his phone's flashlight into the narrow hole, curious if maybe another key had snapped off inside, but the lock was empty. As far as he could tell, the bolt was the only part of the door that had been damaged when he and Richard had shouldered the door open this morning, not the lock itself. There was no reason that the key from Jerome's pocket—the key that presumably unlocked the roof, considering the fact that Jerome must have let himself outside somehow last night—wouldn't work.

And yet it did not.

Toby tried the key in the locks of both the bedroom door and the study. No luck. Luca followed him to the northern terminus of the dead-end hallway, a few yards past the stairs to the roof, and watched as Toby tried the knob of the door that waited there. It was locked. Toby tried the key he'd found in Jerome's pocket. No luck.

Toby felt a fresh cord of dread tightening around his heart. Something was wrong here. Why did Jerome have a key in his pocket that didn't unlock any of the doors in this hallway? More important, without a key to the roof, how had the old man gotten outside in the first place?

Whatever this key unlocked, it seemed like a bad idea to hold on to it. To be caught with it. He should return it to Jerome's pocket and solve this little mystery later.

But the moment Toby realized this, a voice echoed from down the hall, and Luca pressed himself to Toby's side in fear.

"I'm sorry, dear. Those stairs have been locked since Abigail left us."

It was Corah, Jerome's elderly sister, smiling so politely you'd think she found strange men, day in and day out, standing in forbidden wings of her house with socks over their hands and fear in their eyes.

"I'VE ALWAYS SAID JEROME'S late wife must have had the keys to the servants' stairs buried with her," Corah said, and let out a careful little laugh at her own joke. "But I suspect we've just lost them somewhere. Which is a pity, you know. It means we have to see the staff so much more often in the halls."

The old woman was certainly in better spirits than she had been earlier this afternoon, when Toby had left her in the kitchen staring numbly at a congealed bowl of potatoes au gratin. She was dressed in a pair of tan corduroys and a denim work shirt, her wild gray hair corralled with a scarf and dirt-spotted tennis shoes on her feet. A pair of gardening gloves poked from her pocket. She was a good two feet shorter than Toby and yet—absurd as it sounded—he wouldn't want to take the old woman in a fight. Even after decades of luxury, she still looked like the sort of sturdy farm girl who could tackle a horse to the ground.

"I'm sorry I'm not dressed for company, young man," she said, when Toby couldn't think of anything to say. "I just came to check on Jerome before I repotted the palms in the sunroom. I've been meaning to do it for ages."

Oh God, Toby thought. *She's forgotten he's dead.* He recalled what Ginger had said about her great-aunt: *Sometimes today and sixty years ago seem to be going on at the same time for her.*

Toby did his best not to glance at the door to Jerome's bedroom. He wasn't sure how he'd explain his presence up here if this delirious woman were to stumble over Jerome's corpse and bring the whole family running with her screams, just as she had yesterday afternoon when she'd discovered the red message on her bedroom door.

GOD KNOWS WHAT YOU DID YOU OLD CUNT

AND SO DO I

"That . . . that's all right," Toby said. "I think my son and I took a wrong turn somewhere. He needed the bathroom."

Corah shot a confused glance at Luca, just as she had at dinner the night before—Toby could clearly see the question on her face: *That's a boy?*—before her manners returned to her. "That's why we typically ask our guests to avoid this wing. It's so easy to get turned around over here."

Toby watched her another moment, waiting to see if Corah would betray any hint of recognition, but instead he only noticed the way her bright smile kept twitching into a frown, like some overlooked horror was nagging at the edge of her mind. He remembered that kind of smile well from his years distributing pills and mopping up urine in a private nursing home in Studio City.

He also knew how to work with it.

"We must have made quite a few wrong turns then. Story of my life." Toby chuckled and caught a faint blush rising in Corah's cheeks. There was nothing old women liked more than a handsome man who could laugh at himself.

"You poor thing."

"Didn't you see Jerome in the sunroom? We were talking to him down there not fifteen minutes ago."

A sudden frightened look, as much embarrassed as it was confused, came over Corah. "To tell you the truth, I don't remember if I've been down there yet this morning at all. Never get old, son."

"At the rate I'm going, I probably won't. But I bet you said the same thing at my age."

She had a hoot of a laugh. "Not me—that was Jerome. You wouldn't believe the scrapes I got that man out of."

Toby went still, careful. "Is that right?"

"Well, I'm sure I'm exaggerating." She grew reticent. "Who did you say you were again?"

"I'm Toby. Alyssa's new husband."

"You're a liar," she said, but her smile was more sly than accusing. "Alyssa's a smart girl. She knows her only job is to marry a handsome idiot."

"Is that right?"

"It's what we told both the daughters, you know. 'Get you a boy with a nice smile and an empty head.' They're not hard to find."

Toby gave her his nicest smile. As inconspicuously as he knew how, he tugged the sock from his hand, stuffing it (along with the key he'd found on Jerome's corpse) into his pocket.

Corah was too distracted trying to flirt with him to notice. "You're no fool, son. I can see it in your eyes."

"That's very kind of you."

"Sorry if I seem confused—we haven't had many visitors since Jerome had his fall last year." She lowered her voice. "You must be a friend of the family. You look just the type."

A friend of the family. "I suppose that's one way to describe me."

"Strange. Why aren't you out in the woods?"

"Where?"

With no warning, fear flooded her face, though God only knew why. *Oh, shit.* Toby knew from long experience the sort of meltdowns that came when someone this confused got too scared. Hoping to edge the conversation back to steady ground, he said, "Jerome asked me to come grab his journal for him. The little leather one, do you know it?"

"He sent you up here, to his study, unattended?"

"I've always got a chaperone." Toby smiled and patted Luca's head. Old women usually loved children.

It seemed to work, for a moment. "Well, if you haven't had any luck up here you could check his office at the church. It would just mean taking a ride in the rain."

"Why didn't I think of that? Thank you."

Toby started walking her way. Disgusting as it was to admit, most women her age, half-aware that their minds were failing them, desperately wanted a man—any man—to tell them what to do. "I'll head out to the church. Why don't you go work on those palms downstairs? Jerome will probably be happy to see you."

"Oh, I couldn't do that—I'd wake him, I'm sure. He always needs a

145

AD HOME

nap at this hour, ever since he started spending all night on the roof."

"The roof?"

"Of course. Time with his telescope. You know, you're the first person in this house to ask about him. None of the children give a flip about what Jerome got up to at night, I'll tell you that for free. Not even the staff knew what he did after they came to turn down his sheets every night. Jerome wasn't sleeping. Oh, no sir, he wasn't sleeping, much as I wish he would."

Toby stared at her. He said slowly, "Is that right?"

"I'm the only person in this family who's ever cared about that man. I support him. It's what a sister's meant to do. I might be afraid of what he's gotten up to out there on the roof, but it's not my job to ask questions, you understand? Not that I care for the company he's started to keep. Not one bit."

"That's so decent of you."

Toby took another step down the hall. Corah didn't move out of his way. A sudden flash of rage broke over her face. "The children are almost as bad as *him*."

"As Jerome?"

"*No!* The man who painted that *word* on my door yesterday! He's back, you know, even if none of them believe me. But I ran him off once, like Jesus with the demon Legion. I did it once and I know how to do it again."

This wasn't going well. Toby kept walking briskly in Corah's direction, giving her no choice but to turn and start heading up the narrow hallway with him. If he could just get her to the elevator, she'd forget all about this conversation by the time she reached the sunroom. It was cruel, how easy it was to manipulate a mind this muddled, but the last thing Toby needed was for someone to ask what he was doing up here with a key in his pocket, a few yards away from the scene of a murder.

For a moment, it worked. Corah made it all the way to the T-intersection on the hall's southern end, the grim tension in her shoulders easing, her breaths growing long. Toby was so concentrated on the old woman's mood he hardly noticed the damp, oily chill that had settled around them like an invisible fog.

It wasn't until Luca slipped a shaky hand into Toby's own that he felt an awful, primitive dread, a creeping sense that the three of them weren't alone.

A frigid draft whipped through the intersection, blowing into their faces, and with a startled cry Corah spun around as if to follow someone who'd just sprinted past her. Her eyes settled on Luca's. They were black with rage.

"You!"

Luca shrank into Toby's side. Corah jabbed a finger at him.

"You can't stay away, can you? Filth like you can't stay away from a good man for long."

Toby pulled on his hardest voice, the one he used to use at the home when nothing else had worked and an explosion was imminent. "I think you're mistaking us for someone else, ma'am. We'll be going now."

"Oh, you bet you'll be going. I won't let scum like *that* stay here. Corruption, that's all you are." Her eyes never left Luca's. "The sin of the world on two damned legs."

"That's enough, ma'am."

"Oh, is it? I know the things *he* gets up to in dark corners. Like an animal. A filthy animal in heat."

Toby stepped to within an inch of Corah's face. He thought he might be about to hit her after all. "You will *not* speak to my son that way."

For a moment, a shimmer of violence floated over her features like a heat mirage, all that strength coiling up inside her. Not that he cared. Toby didn't like his odds if he had to take this old woman in a fight, but if she said one more word to Luca, he just fucking might.

It didn't come to that, yet. With a long breath, he made one final effort to placate her. "Why don't we all go downstairs?"

"Why don't you take that sissy little shit to a barber?" Corah spun on her heel, stalked down the hall, spat over her shoulder: "Nobody wants trash like that here. This is a Christian family."

EVERY PARENT, HOWEVER RICH, lives in the shadow of the debt their children accrue under their care. It is the psychic debt, the debt of damage—the trauma and fear and insecurity and loss—that tallies up, day by day, in their children's minds, the debt that will take their children the rest of their lives to pay off.

Toby sometimes wondered where the line of no return was, the point at which his son's psyche would fall into permanent arrears. A mind in that much debt seldom ran in the black again. It needed liquor or pills or needles to keep the wolf from the door. Or maybe a gun.

As Corah stalked away from them, muttering under her breath like a bag lady, Toby saw the stunned expression in his son's eyes and practically heard a faint *screech* from somewhere inside the boy's mind: another tally on the board.

Toby dropped to his knees, took Luca by the shoulders, turned him around to look at him and only him. "She's a confused old woman, bud. She's a dinosaur. We don't have to buy any of the bullshit she's selling."

Luca looked down at the string of glass beads in his hair. He said nothing.

"There's nothing wrong with you. Nothing. I don't care what anyone says, you're perfect, all right? I love you more than you will ever know."

"I want to go home."

Toby didn't have the heart to say the obvious. This family had seen to it that they didn't have a home anymore. Thanks to the rain—and so much else—there wasn't even a road to go back and find it.

The chill in the air lingered, like a cold breath on the back of Toby's neck, all the way to the main wing. When Toby pressed the call button for the elevator, the muffled echo of a woman's sob drifted down the hall in response. Toby was so agitated he almost thought he was imagining things for a moment, that some awful memory was echoing up from the marble labyrinth, but no. With a pained little frown, Luca said, "That sounds like Mommy."

Toby shuddered. He hated when his son seemed to read his mind.

———————————

It was Luca who set out to find the source of the sobs. He followed the sound down a short hall in the main wing, through a cracked door and across an austere sitting room, into a bedroom draped in red silk and black velvet. They found Sarah Nella there, still resting where Toby and Richard had placed her this morning, her slim body covered by a brilliant crimson duvet patterned with black tigers and cranes. Her eyes were half-open. A horrible gurgling scrape, like a wrench dragging across the grille of a car's radiator, leaked through lips that had collapsed onto one side of her mouth.

Toby recalled the way Sarah Nella had materialized at his elbow in the sunroom this morning, murmuring, *Mister Tucker, could I speak with you a moment? In private? Please, it's urgent.*

He held in a sigh. He'd seen enough stroke victims to doubt the woman would ever speak to anyone again at all.

Kassandra, Richard's radiant wife, was the one they'd heard crying. She sat in a velvet chair by Sarah Nella's side, still clad in this morning's sundress and wicker wedges, a hand over her eyes, a fist to her throat. Tears forced themselves over and between her fingers in a way that made Toby think, with a queasy flutter, of the dam that loomed over the edge of the property.

"Is everything all right?" he said.

Kassandra recoiled, clawing tears out of her eyes. "Lord, you scared me. I didn't hear you come in."

"The door was cracked."

"Oh. Of course. I forgot to lock it again." Kassandra grabbed a wad of tissues from Sarah Nella's bedside table and blotted her face. "Do you mind doing that? I really can't handle any more surprises this afternoon."

He crossed back through the sitting room, shut the suite's door, flipped a silver dead bolt. Back in the bedroom, he found Luca standing awkwardly near one wall, fingering a red silk robe that hung from an old-fashioned coat stand. Kassandra's tears had subsided enough for her to study the boy with a distant smile. "Sorry I haven't been much of a friend to you today, sweetheart. My husband didn't care for the way we carried on yesterday."

"Why would Richard care if you were kind to a child?" Toby rested a hand atop Luca's head. His son withdrew his hand from the robe and rubbed something between his fingers, squinting in the soft light.

Sarah Nella watched them through her slitted eyes, gurgling away. Or perhaps she wasn't watching them. Even after two years at the nursing home, understanding what was happening inside the head of a stroke victim—if, indeed, there was anything happening at all—was like parsing Kabbalah.

Kassandra said to Luca, "Why don't you go watch something in Miss Sarah Nella's living room? I think she has some DVDs."

"That's okay," Luca said, with a careful look at his father: *Promise you'll never leave me again.* "I'll just go look at the painting."

The bedroom was big enough that Luca could study the wood-block prints on a distant wall without being much of a distraction. The boy was so deft at disappearing into himself, Toby sometimes wondered if he might have a memory palace of his own or if it was simply the innate talent of an only child.

Kassandra swiped a trail of spittle from her charge's chin with a fold of tissue and shook her head. "You know, it's funny—before I lived here, I used to get Aunt Sarah Nella and old Miss Corah confused in my head."

Toby gave her an incredulous look. "Corah? Jerome's sister?"

"I know, I know. Sarah Nella's not *that* much older than Richard, but she's always so precise and sharp and in control. Sort of terrifying, if you get on the wrong side of her."

"I don't know. Sarah Nella seems all right. Unlike Corah."

"I think I got them confused because neither of them ever married. They both seemed more devoted to Jerome than anyone else."

Though that didn't stop Sarah Nella from having a baby on a mission trip to Korea, Toby thought. He turned his attention to the woman's bedside table, where a massive ring of keys and a row of pill bottles were arrayed before a thick stack of books. He might not have cared for reading, but someone here certainly did. "*Cardiovascular Pathology: An Overview.* Just a little light browsing?"

Kassandra did something with her mouth that might have been a smile. "I brought some of my old nursing textbooks with me when we moved in. I still want to finish my nursing degree, even if Richard might kill me for it."

"And what have they told you? Will Sarah Nella recover?"

"There really ain't much to know about her condition without getting some brain scans. All we can do is keep her fed and hydrated. Alyssa's basically given up on her. Typical doctor."

"I see."

"Skinny woman like Sarah Nella, you wouldn't think she'd have all the cardiac problems she does. It's why she always wore that smartwatch—it beeped whenever her heart rate was climbing too high. She must have had some real scares in the past for her doctor to put her on these meds and dosages." Kassandra pushed around the pill bottles. "Three different hypertension pills, stuff for heart failure, blood thinners, anxiety meds, some of the heavy-duty sleeping aids. I wonder if all her doctors were on the same page. Some of these drugs have some pretty wild interactions."

Toby raised an eyebrow: now this was interesting. "What kind of interactions?"

"Well, I never finished my degree, so maybe I'm jumping at nothing, but . . . this one here, propranolol, it decreases blood pressure by slowing down the heart, but when you combine such a high dose of it with Xanax and Ambien at the strengths she's got here—wait, let me find it." Kassandra flipped open a book. "'There are reports of altered mood, vivid dreams, memory loss, night terrors, increased susceptibility to suggestion, and other marked psychological events.' It's a little amazing the woman was so productive during the days. I'd have thought she'd be a zombie with all this mess in her system."

As if in reply, Sarah Nella's head flopped to one side. Her hooded eye seemed to study Toby. With what looked like a terrible effort, her lips parted by an inch. "Gugh," she said.

Toby pulled his attention away from that hooded eye. He had something better to ask Kassandra. "What did you mean a second ago, that Richard didn't care for how you and Luca got along yesterday?"

"My lovely husband said I spent the afternoon 'encouraging' your son."

"Encouraging him to do what? Laugh?"

"More or less. Richard thinks the boy hasn't had enough of a 'masculine influence' in his life. He doesn't want me talking to him." Kassandra's pretty lashes twitched. "We had a horrible fight about the way he behaved at dinner last night. I know I can't apologize for another person, but I can apologize for myself. I should have never married that man."

Toby sank into a thick velvet chair, a hand pressed to his eyes. "You know that before we married, Alyssa told me this family secretly voted for Obama? That none of them gave a fuck about the conservative bullshit they sold on TV?"

"Then your wife is a liar." Kassandra adjusted the sleeve of her dress. "But would it really be any better if she'd been telling the truth? Is a family of lying liberals any better than a bunch of honest bigots?"

She had a point. "What did Richard tell you when you two were dating?"

"That I'd be richer than a Jew. His exact words. Which I know we ain't supposed to say, but I was young. I'd never owned a car that weren't coming apart underneath me. He treated me nice and bought me things and seemed like he was going places. He said he'd pay for me to finish nursing school, though I'm starting to think I should have written a deadline for that into our prenup."

"I doubt he's in any hurry to give you a means to support yourself."

"Precisely. Why should I have a degree when the church will provide for everything? I think they prey on desperate, pretty people, this family. Hugo had one foot in the poorhouse when he met Ruth. And you and Luca . . ." Kassandra shrugged a slim shoulder. "I guess I'm just lucky Richard didn't get my eggs tested first."

"Alyssa mentioned something about that. She said you two haven't been able to conceive a child."

"We have not. Hence why Richard's just a working man on the family payroll. Don't let Ruth fool you—the Wrights didn't get rich by paying their staff a living wage. At least not the way Richard likes to live."

"But he won't divorce you? Find someone else who can get him a kid?"

"We probably signed the same agreement you did. Unless one of us gets caught cheating or breaking the law, there would be a massive penalty in my favor."

Toby chewed his lip. He made a cautious calculation. He said, almost offhand, "I'm glad Alyssa made the same mistake with me."

Kassandra shot him a sly look from where she'd turned to dab sweat from Sarah Nella's forehead. "Don't tell me—you can't have them either?"

Toby showed her the scar on his arm. "I got this in an accident when I was a kid. I nearly got cut in half by a piece of metal, not that Alyssa ever bothered to ask. Thankfully everything still works fine. Or at least, almost everything."

"You're shooting blanks?"

"I shouldn't have mentioned it. I think she'd kill me for not telling her before the wedding."

Kassandra tilted her head back and laughed hard enough to make Sarah Nella shudder. "Oh, Toby, I needed that. Thank you. Your secret is safe with me."

Good, Toby thought. Now that he'd taken her into his confidence, he hoped she would take him into hers.

Before he had the chance, however, Kassandra shot a look down the room at Luca. "But if you can't conceive, how did you . . . ?"

That set off some very dangerous rumbling in Toby's mind. "He's mine," he said decisively. "Legally and otherwise. Can I ask you something?"

"You can ask. They keep me in the dark about most everything around here."

"If Richard is stuck working for the family and doesn't have any hope to get his trust, would that leave an inheritance from Jerome the only way he could expect to make any sort of big money around here?"

Kassandra eased herself away from Toby, a small, unmistakable shift.

"Well, of course. With the old man gone, I'm sure all of them are going to get some cash."

"How much are we talking here?"

"I don't know, Toby. Imagine a big number and then add the Lord's bounty to it."

Sarah Nella shuddered again. She swiveled her good eye from one of them to the other. "Gugh."

"You thirsty, dear?" Kassandra said. "Here, I'll get some ice chips."

"Gugh! Gugh!"

"It's all right, it's all right. I'll be right back." To Toby, Kassandra said, "Keep an eye on her, will you? I left her by herself for two minutes at lunch and found her choking in the shower when I got back. I wouldn't have thought it possible if I hadn't seen it."

Kassandra rose from her seat and hurried from the bedroom. Toby did his best to smile as Sarah Nella *Gugh*-ed at him with a mounting urgency. Between his demented encounter with Corah a few minutes ago and now this sad chaperoning of a woman slowly slipping into brain death, he was surprised how much use he was getting out of his old job at Silver Oaks. It was like the universe was trying to tell him something.

The universe, or something with a far more dangerous agenda.

As Kassandra returned from the suite's kitchenette with a cupful of ice chips, Sarah Nella jerked back the duvet with one good hand and revealed a slim, naked body. Deep red scratches were gouged along her breasts and stomach. Small red scabs, like insect bites, clotted her arms. "*GUGH!*" she bellowed at Toby.

"That's enough now," Kassandra said, scooping the duvet back over the woman's chest and easing down her head. "Do you need the bathroom? Do you want a little juice?"

"*GUGH!*" Sarah Nella thrust a bony finger in the direction of her robe. It shook wildly in the air.

"Hush, sweetheart, your heart's not going to appreciate all this excitement. Come on. I said *come on*. Hold her for me, will you? Help her feel safe."

Toby remembered this, too, from Silver Oaks. As gently as he knew how, he wrapped his hand around Sarah Nella's outstretched finger and eased it to the duvet, soft but unyielding, smiling as best he could. Even with the pills still working in his system, he felt his anxiety mounting. He was burning time here. Who knew how much longer the rain would last?

Sarah Nella finally stopped struggling. With a jerk of her chin, a final long "Gugh-h-h," she rested her head back on her silk pillow and turned away from them with an air of utter resignation.

"She was trying to tell us something." Toby's eye studied the silk robe at which Sarah Nella had pointed so violently.

"Poor thing. I think those days are past her."

Sarah Nella's breathing deepened and slowed. She was falling asleep.

"I should go," he murmured, motioning for Luca. Kassandra followed them from the bedroom, leaving open the door to keep an eye on her charge.

"Kassandra," Toby murmured in the suite's sitting room, finally asking an obvious question that should have occurred to him ages ago (he really wasn't cut out for detective work). "Did you notice anything strange last night?"

"Strange?"

"Out of the ordinary. Hear anything unusual, see someone who shouldn't have been where they were supposed to be?"

"No. Nothing. And I'm a light sleeper. I woke up the minute the rain started."

Which would have been around midnight, Toby thought. Alyssa had still been gone from his bed at that hour. "What about your husband? Is he a light sleeper too?"

"Richard was in the Marines. He can sleep like the dead when he wants to."

"So he slept all through last night?"

"How would I know?"

"Pardon?"

Kassandra's eyes darkened. "I have no idea what my husband was doing last night. I told you—we had a fight last night after the way he behaved at dinner. I told his ass not to come to bed. I didn't see him again until this morning."

She watched Toby, clearly seeing on his face what he'd heard in her words. If Kassandra was telling the truth, then Richard, like Alyssa, had no alibi for the time Jerome died.

Kassandra turned back to the bedroom without another word. Toby readied himself to go, taking Luca by the hand, but the moment he unlocked the suite's front door, he realized he'd forgotten to ask the most important question of all.

What had made her weep so hard he and Luca had heard her all the way down the hall?

"Kassandra—" he called to the bedroom. She poked her head out, but there wasn't time for more. Kassandra's eyes widened in surprise as the suite's front door swung open in his hand and Alyssa stood in the doorway, looking much the way he suspected she did at work: grand and peeved and showily exhausted, like a saint at the limit of her indulgence.

The moment she spotted him, however, Alyssa's face brightened into a sudden, bewildering smile. "Toby! Just the man I was hoping to see."

KASSANDRA KNEW WHEN TO make herself scarce. She closed the door to Sarah Nella's bedroom, leaving Toby and Alyssa and Luca idling in the sitting room like a perfectly normal family having a perfectly normal conversation. Alyssa herself seemed weirdly eager to play along. She smiled. She touched her hair. She appeared absolutely unlike the cruel woman she'd been not two hours ago in the strange motel room downstairs. "I've been looking all over for you guys."

Toby held tight to Luca's hand, not that the boy seemed in any hurry to let go. "Did you want to be sure we hadn't thrown ourselves into the creek?"

"I figured today must be difficult for you." Alyssa clearly had her mother's ability to carry on cheerfully in any situation when she wanted to. "I can't imagine what it's like to have another death in the family the same year as your sister's."

Just as it had downstairs in Ginger's office, this mention of Willow's death set a bad door—the worst, most dangerous door—rattling against its lock in the heart of the marble labyrinth.

It was Luca who said, "Tobias cried a lot after that. Why aren't any of you guys crying?"

"Mom certainly is. She and Dad ran off to the church the moment they could. I think it's where they keep the sackcloth and ashes."

Toby said, "And here I thought you'd never read your Bible."

"I've got a lot of surprises." She said it with a soft, flirty twinkle in those astonishing eyes of hers.

The sight made Toby shiver. Who was this woman, this cipher, who could slide so seamlessly between so many selves?

Who exactly had he married?

"Thirsty?" She stepped into Sarah Nella's kitchenette, plucked up a glass, held it to the light as if she was examining it for cracks. It threw a host of reflections across her face, reflections that trembled on the skin with a vague agitation. He realized her fingers were shaking.

Alyssa hadn't come here to shoot the breeze. She was scared of something.

"Did Ginger give it to you?" his wife said casually, finally filling the glass with water from a bottle in the fridge.

"Give me what?"

"The receipt for the bank wire. I know you saw it. It was in the same pocket in my purse where you stole my pills."

Toby froze. He said, truthfully, "I didn't put anything in your purse."

"Well, *someone* did. I'd never be stupid enough to leave anything that serious lying around."

"What's so bad about a money transfer?"

"Plenty," Alyssa said, as if to herself, before she clammed up, shifted gears. "You're still trying to get to the bottom of all this, aren't you? Do you think that if you guess the murderer, you can walk away and leave all of us behind?"

"Frankly, I'd just like to prove I didn't have the means or the motive to stab the old man."

"And what have you found?"

"You can't seriously expect me to answer that."

"Am I your enemy? Already?"

Rage burned behind Toby's cheeks. His phone burned in his pocket. "An hour ago you threatened to frame me for murder, Alyssa. Now you're obviously afraid of something a hell of a lot worse than a wire transfer in your purse."

"Which I burned, for the record."

Good thing I snapped a picture of it, Toby thought.

Alyssa took a single sip of water and dumped it in the sink. "Let this go, Toby. Let it all go. We won't cut Luca's hair, all right? We won't even have him onstage all day. You two can smile from the pews once a week and live in luxury in the meantime, and we can all get on with our lives. But I swear to God, Toby, if you keep rocking the boat, someone is going to push you overboard."

She laid a hand on Luca's shoulder. The boy flinched away like it stung.

Taking a step away from the woman and dragging his son with him, Toby realized, in a sudden flood of clarity, that he hated her. A part of him, the part that had grown up watching her family's awful television show, might have hated Alyssa from the moment he met her.

"How about you just let us go?" Toby said. "Terminate the marriage, cut me a check, and we all walk away before I turn up anything really awful."

A frown crossed Alyssa's face. It looked almost sincere. "You know we can't afford to do that, Toby."

"Then there's no way we're both coming out of this weekend happy. You see that, don't you? I've already learned you're not the only person without an alibi last night. Who knows what else I'll find if you don't let us go?"

Alyssa's back stiffened. Her eyes went black. With a tight twist of the mouth, she said, "Maybe Richard was right."

"About what? That I murdered Jerome?"

"Worse. I think you really are dangerous."

HE LEFT ALYSSA IN Sarah Nella's suite, guiding Luca by the hand all the way to the elevator. "Is she right?" the boy whispered. "Are you dangerous?"

"Only if they try to touch you, bud."

They took a detour on the second floor, stepping into the east wing and following the long hall to their room. The wire transfer was, indeed, gone from Alyssa's purse. He checked his phone and found the photograph still in its memory (and the phone's battery still holding up, despite how hot it had gotten), but he noticed, too, that none of the pictures he'd taken all day had uploaded to the cloud. How could they? There'd been no internet or network access since first thing this morning.

Heading back for the elevator with a freshly chewed Ativan tablet stinging his gums, Toby stopped halfway down the hall and knocked at the suite adjacent to his own. Yesterday at lunch, Sarah Nella had said that his family would be staying next to Richard and Kassandra's rooms, though by the sound of it no one was home now. Toby knocked again. The thick pile of the carpet swallowed the sound almost before his ears could catch it.

Toby slipped his sock from his pocket, shot a look down the hall, and tried the knob of the door. It was locked. He tried the key he'd found in Jerome's pocket—the key that didn't appear to unlock anything upstairs—and found that it didn't work here, either. Richard and Kassandra's room was sealed up tight.

The elevator opened to reveal Marie braced on her knees on the floor of the foyer, polishing the brass stand of the grand gilded Bible that rested beneath the carving of Noah's Ark. She smiled at Toby. In spite of everything, he found himself smiling back.

A boom of thunder rattled the foyer's windows. Their smiles shook apart at the sound. "You haven't happened to see Jules around, have you?" Marie said.

Bless her heart. She was still trying not to be worried about her brother. "No. I'm heading outside—I'll keep an eye out for him."

"But what would he be doing out in the rain?"

"He'll turn up again. They always do."

"They? They who?"

The question brought up a blank space in Toby's mind, a perfect gap where he'd tossed something behind a door of the memory palace and sealed it away. Where had this Ativan been all his life? It kept the marble labyrinth under lock and key better than anything he'd ever known. "Forget I said anything. Can I ask you something . . . personal, Marie?"

"I don't see how I can stop you."

"I heard that you and Julian had to sign away your inheritance before Sarah Nella would employ you here."

"We did. We don't stand to make a dime from any of this, just in case you were looking for a motive."

Toby gave the inside of his cheek an anxious nibble. "And you must have keys to all the rooms here, right? To clean them?"

"Every room except Sarah Nella's. She said she liked to clean her own space. I think she was afraid Jules and I might have had designs on her person."

"So you would have a key to Richard's suite."

Marie hesitated. She folded her rag carefully in her hand. "You're thinking about *his* inheritance. I can see it all over your face."

Toby stepped close to Marie, close enough to smell sweat and hair oil and a permanent, lingering worry. "I'm thinking about the knife. Somehow it still hasn't turned up."

"It's a big house. It could be anywhere."

"But we could rule out one place pretty quick." Toby lowered his voice to a whisper. "I'm worried. If I don't let them have Luca, I think they might do something crazy."

"Like what? Frame you?"

"Didn't you hear what Richard did to the old housekeeper? The one he convinced himself had been leaving the red graffiti everywhere?"

"But what would you and me sneaking into his room accomplish? Besides getting me fired?"

"It could help us rule out a few possibilities. He doesn't have an alibi for last night, Marie. And he has a hell of a motive."

For a moment, it almost looked like he'd convinced her: with an eye down the long hall, Marie rose to her feet and took a step toward the elevator. But at the last moment, she hesitated, her better judgment catching up to her. She stepped back. She shook her head. "I think . . . I think it's best if we let the police do their job when they get here. It's not like we'd find Julian in there, would we?"

Toby struggled again to catch a memory from dinner—something that had passed between Richard and Marie's brother—but it was gone, sealed up in the labyrinth. "I hope we get the chance."

He left Marie on her knees, polishing the Bible's stand, buffing a patch of brass so bright it gilded all of them with the gleam of a coin.

3:9

Toby led Luca down the long main hall where yesterday, after using the bathroom under the stairs, Toby had first felt that strange draft of air, quick and cool as mercury, as he made his way to the sunroom. Now, at the end of the long hall, he pushed open a door in the western wall and stepped back into the cavernous kitchen. The nook where he'd found the family eating lunch earlier was empty. The spotless counters bore nothing but a few napkins and a frozen bowl of chili thawing beneath a layer of Saran Wrap.

Through the windows, Toby saw the grand church at the north end of the estate, its satellite dish and its cross competing for prominence on the roof.

And a few dozen yards away from the kitchen's back door were the stables where the family apparently kept the golf carts they used to navigate the estate. *Putters*, Alyssa had called them. *Though I can't imagine why you'd ever need one.*

Toby and Luca made a dash to the stables, the beads in the boy's hair chiming weirdly in the rain. From somewhere nearby, Toby heard the unmistakable wail of a power drill.

Glancing back at the house, he saw a pale face studying them from an upstairs window. It was Matthias, Ginger's elusive son, though he vanished so quickly Toby soon wondered if he'd ever been there at all.

Luca saw him too. "I used to think he looked sad. But now I think maybe he's just got the lonesomes."

When they stepped into the stables, Toby wondered how one family could have ever owned enough horses to fill a building this size. These days its corrals housed three Benz S-classes, two Teslas, an assortment of Swedish decadents, and a small black Bugatti that Jesus, surely, would have approved of.

One end of the stables had been converted into a tool shop and a home gym (did expensive exercise equipment always smell like fresh rubber, Toby wondered, or was it bought new whenever the smell started to fade?). It was here that he found Richard, Alyssa's handsome, muscular brother, clad in nothing but jeans and work boots, standing before a pair of sawhorses on which a plain pinewood box stretched the length of a tall man.

Richard's blond hair was highlighted with sawdust. The tasteful Celtic cross tattooed on his forearm gleamed with sweat. A pale whorl of a scar, like an artist's signature on a canvas, marred any hope his stomach might have once had for a six-pack. "Shrapnel," he said, when he saw Toby looking. "Only action I ever saw overseas."

Luca, Toby noticed, couldn't stop staring at the man's bare drum of a chest. Toby had to physically turn the boy by the shoulders and point him toward the cars.

"I came for a putter," Toby said.

"You came to the right place." Richard stepped aside, revealing a row of gleaming white golf carts plugged into a strip of power outlets near the stable's wide back door.

Up close, Richard smelled of sweat and a private musk, an odor not unlike the heat of a straining engine. He guided Toby to the putters with the studied casualness of a bad model, all pecs and swiveling shoulders. He squatted down at just the right angle for Toby to study the rippling muscles of his back as he coiled up a golf cart's power cord.

Smiling over his shoulder, Richard said, "Y'all going for a joyride?"

Toby suspected it was no mistake Richard chose the cart furthest away from Luca's little ears: the man wanted some privacy. Toby might as well take advantage of it. "I understand you need my wife."

This had a much stronger effect than Toby had anticipated: Richard couldn't have looked more surprised if Toby had rammed a cattle prod into his balls. The shock passed, almost as fast as it had come, but not before Toby caught a distant glimmer of that odd unease—somewhere between fear and guilty recognition—that had occasionally come over Richard whenever he caught sight of Toby. "I beg your pardon?"

"For the show. Alyssa says you need a fresh female costar to bring *The Prophecy Hour* to a younger audience." Toby shot a look down the stables. "And you need a son."

"Oh. That."

"What exactly do you want to put Luca on the show for, Richard? He's seven. Who likes to watch seven-year-olds talk about Jesus?"

"Aspirational millennials and diabetic Black women, according to the focus groups I commissioned. We'd like more of each every Sunday."

"But what would he be doing, really? Singing? Dancing? Sitting there like a doll?"

"I have a lot of ideas. We'll do a few screen tests."

They both glanced across the stables to where Luca was balancing on one leg, point-toe, like a ballerina. His long hair swept in front of his face as he strained at a pirouette.

Richard said, "We can work on that."

With a sinking heart, Toby recalled Alyssa saying those exact words in the car yesterday. "There's nothing to work on."

"Woke moms from Shaker Heights aren't really our demographic, Toby. Give me four weeks with the boy. I'll have him camera ready before they're finished with your suit."

"I will eat glass before that happens, Richard."

Richard fished a key from above the golf cart's visor. "Here. I'll even let down the rain-flaps for you."

Toby didn't move. "Where do *I* fit into this new media empire of yours?"

"You'll sit in the front row and smile and rake in cash. Maybe tomorrow you can help Ruth anoint me in the Spirit. It'll be the start of my prophetic calling."

"You're seriously planning a broadcast tomorrow? Is Jerome's body even cold?"

"God's timing is strange." Richard pulled a phone from his pocket. "Speaking of which—Siri, remind the makeup team to cover up the scar on Toby's arm."

Toby had never been a strong man: his lithe muscles were superficial and mostly genetic. From the moment he hit puberty, he'd looked great with his shirt off but had never built up any real power at the gym. He'd never had to. Back when he'd been supporting himself modeling, back when he might have had time to work out, he'd never bothered. Clothes were expected to drape off models, not burst at the seams the way they did on a man like Richard.

Toby studied the power coursing through the other man's shoulders. Between his time with a barbell and his combat training, Richard could probably kill Toby with very little effort. The thought settled in Toby's mind with all the weight and force of an anchor striking the seafloor.

Yet Toby clenched his fists all the same. Ativan or not, rage rose through him. "I'm not going to let you have my son, Richard. I'm not going to let you people break him into whatever shape your audience wants."

"I really don't see how you're going to stop us, Toby." Richard smiled. He returned to his tools. It was only then that Toby realized what he was building.

A coffin.

"We'll put a pin in this conversation," Richard continued. "Frankly, I'm more concerned with burying my grandfather right now."

"That's understandable. It'll be a hell of a lot harder to order an autopsy if the man's already in the ground by the time the cops get here."

Richard laughed. "You're awfully cynical for a man who married his meal ticket. Personally, I'm just happy to use some of the old carpentry skills I learned at Camp Cleave."

"You're walking in Christ's footsteps."

"As best I can. You know, I always wondered—when Jesus was up there on the cross, do you think he had time to admire the woodwork?"

The rain rang like gunfire on the stable's tin roof. It made Toby think of carnage, blood, bombs. He realized, at that moment, that Richard wasn't merely strong. There was something strange in his mind— something dangerously off-center—that sent the flesh crawling on Toby's arms.

But Toby persevered. "Did you . . . did you notice anything odd last night, say between the hours of eleven and two?"

"Are you a detective now, Toby?"

"Call me an interested party."

"Then you can ask Kassandra what we were doing between the hours of eleven and two. She'll tell you the same thing I will: we were sleeping."

"That's what's funny, though. I did ask her. She told me she kicked you out of your suite for the night because of the way you treated my son."

Richard froze, a hammer in his hand.

"And the crazy thing is, *my* wife was gone for almost exactly the same length of time—from eleven to two. Which means that, as far as I can tell, you and your new costar both have no alibi for the time Jerome died." Toby took a moment to let this sink in. "What was it you called a coincidence? God's way of tipping his hand?"

"Where are you going with this, Toby?"

Toby shrugged. "Nowhere in particular, I guess. But Kassandra did tell me something else funny: since she hasn't had a child yet, *you* still haven't gotten a dime of the trust fund. You're working for the family, just another grunt on the payroll, and you're hardly making a great living. But with Jerome dead, you finally stand to make some real cash. Your inheritance doesn't have any strings attached. Even before you take over the show, you're probably on track to make millions."

Richard stood rooted to the concrete floor, one eye twitching like Toby had just stuck another cattle prod in him.

Toby put a hand on his arm. He smiled. "Let us go, Richard. Otherwise this is just going to get uglier."

Whatever response Toby had expected, it wasn't what happened. In a quick, sudden rush, Richard drew even closer—Toby wondered if he was going in for a kiss—and reached a hand for the front of Toby's pants.

But he wasn't reaching for Toby's fly. He dug a hand into Toby's pocket and pulled loose his phone.

"What the hell are you doing?"

"You wouldn't be recording this, would you?" Richard slithered out of reach, tapped the phone, turned it around after a moment so Toby could see what *he'd* seen. A red banner blinked at the top of Toby's screen.

That red banner had blinked there for hours. It was the reason Toby's phone had grown so hot in his pocket all afternoon. Richard was right: Toby had been recording every word the family had said since he'd caught up to Alyssa in the strange motel room a few hours ago.

Now, Richard only smiled. "Why should we let you go anywhere, Toby? We don't just own the police around here. We fund every public event in Hebron County, we pay for the schools, we shell out every dime that little town needs to survive. Say you recorded one of us confessing to killing the old man—what good would it do? You still wouldn't make it across the county line."

Toby made a grab for his phone. Richard pulled away.

"We always get what we want in this family, Toby. *I* always get what I want."

"Give me my phone, Richard. I'm leaving."

"Of course. One second."

With a single swift motion, Richard dropped the phone to the work-table and slammed his hammer on its screen. He struck it again, again, again, until nothing remained but chipped glass and flaking metal. He scooped the pieces into one palm and offered it to Toby with a smile. "All yours."

Toby barely remembered grabbing a stunned Luca and practically throwing him into the putter, gunning the engine, darting through the stables' door the moment it rolled open. Richard still stood with the shattered phone outstretched in his palm and a placid smile on his face. "Nice try, Toby. Nice try."

It had probably been a good idea. At lunch in the kitchen this afternoon, when the family had started to question whether they even needed to call the police once the roads were clear, Toby had begun to wonder if the Wrights weren't considering some kind of cover-up. It was why he'd hit record on his phone as he pursued Alyssa into the west wing, slipping it into his pocket a moment before he collided with her in the strange replica of a motel room.

Boy, had he gotten some gold since then. He'd recorded the details of the family's inheritance. The fact that neither Richard nor Alyssa had an alibi for the time of Jerome's death. The way everyone seemed ready to railroad Toby if need be.

But after what Richard had done to the phone, it was gone. The audio, the pictures he'd taken—including the photograph of the mysterious wire transfer he'd found in Alyssa's purse—had all vanished in a few strokes of that hammer. With the internet still down, nothing had made it to the cloud.

In the putter, Toby and Luca rocketed south down the estate's gravel drive, driven more by horror than conscious thought. The putter bounded through puddles, spread wet gravel behind its wheels in great hissing fans.

The emerald wonderland of Ramorah was drowning all around him. Where there had once been manicured grass, Toby saw nothing but a black abyss. Night would fall soon. The world, once more, was growing formless and void.

And yet something terrible finally occurred to him as he neared the southern gate.

The rain pelting the putter's plastic flaps sounded softer than it had all day. Slower. Toby hoped (prayed, even) that his mind was playing tricks on him, but it was no good pretending: the storm was weakening. At times the rain almost seemed ready to stop entirely.

Toby was running out of time.

When he arrived at the southern edge of the estate, he found that the creek was still so swollen it had come almost to the gate. The black iron bars slid open with the approach of the putter and Toby sat, a long time, watching the water whip past.

This family had deceived him—deceived him about a lot—but in this, at least, they had been honest. It would be suicide to try and cross that creek and reach the road beyond.

Toby dug the mysterious key from his pocket, the key that unlocked neither the door to the roof nor the servants' stairs at the end of the narrow dead-end hall in the west wing nor Richard's suite. It was funny, in a way, that Toby had been so critical of the family ruining the crime scene when he himself had inadvertently stolen a piece of evidence from the dead man's pocket.

Time for some damage control. Wiping his prints from the key, he ducked out of the putter, toed a deep hole in the mud near a bush, and dropped the key inside. He bent down to add the paper he'd found fallen behind Jerome's desk only to hesitate, think, take it back.

He buried the key. Returning to the putter, Toby shook a drop of mud from the fold of the note and stared, again, at the three lines Jerome had written last night at 11:42, mere minutes before he died.

Wet roses bloom on white sugar
From the muted mouth, he speaks
The wailing boy slips beneath green waves

"I still don't get it," Luca said, leaning over his shoulder.
"I hope we never have to."

THE FORMER THINGS
HAVE COME TO PASS

TOBY WANTED TO BE sure there really was no way out of this place. He rocketed east across the estate, past lakes of black water and shuttered guesthouses and the padlocked hangar of the family's private airstrip. East of the airstrip, there was nothing but the dense stand of woods that he and Alyssa had driven through yesterday. Only when he reached the woods did Toby recall the tall fence that ran through those trees, the spikes along its spine. There was no escape in that direction.

Except as he turned the putter north, a glint of glass in the trees made him stop. He drove across the airstrip and down a weeded gravel trail and into the woods.

A small building, little more than a shack, waited in a clearing set well back from the tree line. It felt like something out of a fairy tale: grandmother's house, a witch's hut. With every soft bend in the path, every foot closer to the clearing, a chill mounted on Toby's neck, a shiver in his fingers, and by the time he and Luca arrived at the front door, his teeth were practically chattering. A bitter breeze cut through the putter's rain flaps. The plastic whispered like a plea, or a warning.

"We don't like it here," Luca murmured.

Toby didn't have the heart to ask who he meant by *we*. "Stay in the putter."

Up close, the shack was almost homey. Bright gray paint on the walls, white trim on the eaves and the windows. The illusion didn't last long. When Toby cupped his hands to the glass of one window, he saw iron bars mounted to the other side.

On the front door, where the keyhole to a dead bolt would be, Toby found instead the lock's latch.

It was open.

He discovered a horse stable inside the little house, though it was a far cry from the elegant building that housed the main house's fleet of luxury cars. This stable was grubby, its floors covered with gravel and straw. It must have been another chamber of Jerome's memory palace, Toby supposed, a fragment of the old man's past that had been painstakingly re-created, right down to what looked like a few bales of hay rotting in one corner. It was such a good replica, indeed, there were no electric lights inside. He wished to God Richard hadn't destroyed his phone. Even without cell service, Toby would have really appreciated a flashlight in here.

Which was when he felt it: that chilly certainty he wasn't alone. He strained his ears for a distant breath, a rustle of clothing, but all he heard was the patter of rain.

"Hello?" Toby said. "Is there anyone in here?"

Silence. After a long silence, Toby fired a shot in the dark. Someone had left the door to this room unlocked, after all, and there was only one person unaccounted for around Ramorah.

"Julian? Is that you?"

Nothing.

Toby didn't take another step deeper into the dark stable, especially not after he examined the lock on the door. Just as he'd thought, the door's dead bolt was reversed, with its keyhole facing this direction, into the stable. Already Toby regretted burying the key he'd discovered in Jerome's pocket. What would it mean if it had fit this lock?

Because this door didn't appear designed to keep intruders out.

It was almost as if it had been built to keep someone *in*.

Toby heard an echo of something Corah had asked him in the dead-end hall earlier today. *Why aren't you out in the woods?* As he hurried back through the rain, a sharp breeze sliced across his cheek, quick and cool as mercury.

It felt familiar, that breeze. It felt dangerous.

And in the breeze, Toby almost imagined he heard a rapid rush of sounds, like a stranger whispering to him as they hurried past him: *doantfergetyoorprentstubuayes.*

Toby told himself he was imagining things. He told himself he was letting his anxiety run rampant with his mind. But a moment before he put the putter in reverse, he stopped and shivered and dashed back to the shack. He pulled his sock from his pocket and wiped both the front and back of the door's strange lock. He knew it was absurd, but it was as if his brain, a few seconds late, had made sense of that whispered rush of sound.

doantfergetyoorprentstubuayes

It almost sounded like, *Don't forget your prints, Tobias.*

"Hey," Luca said when Toby made it back to the putter again. "What does 'unfinished business' mean?"

Toby's head snapped around to stare at him. "Where did you hear that?"

But already the boy had grown shy again. He kicked his heels against the putter's seat. He frowned. "Your hands are shaking, Tobias."

"Probably because I don't like this place either."

Toby flipped on the putter's headlights. When they flashed over the shack's barred windows, he imagined he saw the shadowy form of a man inside, staring back at him.

Another flash, and the shape was gone.

TOBY FELT A SPARK of hope as he approached the estate's northern fence. Here, well away from the large gate that accepted visitors to the church, he found a smaller gate that let out onto the creek. More important, there was a boathouse on the creek's shore. Through the building's window Toby saw paddleboards, canoes, a great sturdy rowboat. The water of the north creek was surging no less violently than its twin to the south, but if push came to shove, Toby figured there were worse ways to risk an escape from Ramorah than a desperate paddle downstream.

Except two chains and two sturdy padlocks sealed shut the boathouse's solid door. There was no way he could shoulder that thing open by himself. To make matters worse, the window was too small for even Luca to climb through.

So much for that theory.

Toby was running out of options. He still hadn't found the knife that had killed Jerome, he had no evidence he could use in his defense, he couldn't even find Julian, Marie's missing brother.

Toby saw only one angle he hadn't given much thought to: Ginger's offer of blackmail. The whole proposition reeked with sulfur, the sort of devilish bargain people usually wound up regretting, and Toby was even starting to doubt if Jerome's small, elusive journal even existed at all. But with no way of fleeing the estate and the storm calming down, Ginger's "insulation" just might be his last decent hope of surviving this mess.

Of *Luca* surviving it, which was really all that mattered at the end of the day.

With a long sigh, Toby climbed back in the putter and headed for the only other building on the estate he'd yet to explore. A silver sunset burnished the waterlogged sky behind the satellite atop Ramorah's church. He glanced at his watch. It was two minutes to six.

Up close, the church was almost as imposing as the main house itself. It was a great hexagon plated all over with black glass, a honeycomb glossed with dark sugar. A white putter, identical to the one Toby was driving, stood in the massive visitors' parking lot on the church's north side, just beneath a sign that read ALL ARE WELCOME HERE.

Inside the church, Toby discovered a dark lobby the size of a car dealership. The carpet was black. The walls were a muted gray, and they were lined with photographs that glowed, museum-style, with the help of little curved lights atop their frames.

All was silent.

Discreet doors stood along the long wall nearby, but all of them were locked. Toby and Luca crossed the immense lobby and tried a large set of doors on the opposite wall, searching for a way deeper into the building, and discovered an immense sanctuary that he recognized immediately from TV. Black walls seemed to slink away into infinity. A standing army of empty pews awaited their duty. A wide stage, complete with drums and music stands and three lecterns and a great chrome cross all waited dead ahead.

Two people also waited on the stage, a man and a woman bowed in prayer. It was Ruth and Hugo, Toby's mother- and father-in-law, and before Toby could slip back out the door, Hugo waved a hand: *wait*.

The man left Ruth on the stage and hurried through the pews, catching up with Toby at the door. "She's just finishing up her devotional. She was hoping to talk to you, actually. We both were."

"I really don't have time to talk, Hugo. Can you just point me to Jerome's office?"

"His office? Why would you want to go there?"

Because crazy old Corah said I might find his journal inside, Toby thought. "Does it really matter, Hugo?"

"No. I suppose not. But you'll need Ruth's key to get in. This way."

Toby didn't see another option. He followed Hugo up the aisle toward the stage, his hand tight around Luca's fingers, never for a minute letting the big man get between him and his son.

"Can I just say I'm sorry for the way my daughter has treated you?" Hugo said over his shoulder. "For bringing you into this mess because she can't pay her bills?"

"Why apologize? She must have learned it from somewhere."

For some reason—probably because it was easier to be angry than afraid—Toby kept wanting Hugo to fight him. Instead, the man only lowered his voice further and said, "I saw your little putter heading toward the woods a few minutes ago."

Toby said nothing.

"Did you . . . did you find anything out there?"

Only a shack with bars on its windows, Toby thought. "Why do you ask?"

But before Hugo could say more, Ruth raised her head and watched Toby from the stage, still and silent, clearly straining to catch every word.

Hugo gave him a pained smile, a silent sigh, and gestured for him to climb the stairs of the stage.

4:3

RUTH WAS SEATED ON an amplifier, her chin propped on a fist. In the footlights, Toby saw tears on her cheeks.

"I come in peace," she said.

The woman seemed to have wilted since lunch. Skin hung off her face, darkened under her eyes, drooped from her arms.

In spite of himself, Toby said, "Are you all right?"

"I can't sleep. I dream too much."

The last thing Toby wanted to hear about were Ruth's dreams. "I just want to take a look at Jerome's office. Ginger's sent me on an errand."

"Keeping you busy. You probably make her nervous." Ruth climbed to her feet. "I'll show you the way. It's the least I can do."

That was too easy, Toby thought.

He followed his mother-in-law down the steps of the stage, never letting go of Luca's hand, and approached a black door that was almost invisible in the back wall of the sanctuary.

Ruth said, "You must have a lot of questions."

"I'm just trying to get us out of here in one piece."

"You're right to be scared."

"Who said I'm scared?"

"Every nerve in your face is twitching. Believe me, Toby—if I know one thing, it's anxiety. Alyssa's given you some pills, hasn't she?"

"She didn't exactly give them to me."

"I just hope they're helping."

They headed down a soft gray hall and mounted a flight of steps to the church's second floor. Ruth said, "You heard last week's broadcast."

Toby thought of the booming recording that had echoed through the house at lunch. He held on tighter to Luca. "Yes. The warning for the man with the fishhook scar. I had to watch a lot of your show growing up, Ruth. I never heard Jerome make a prophecy like *that.*"

"Neither had I. Not until this year."

"What changed?"

"Oh, nothing much. Daddy just took a show that used to be all about joy and God's loving plan and turned it into the courts of Judah."

"The what?" Toby tried to pick up the pace, but Ruth refused to comply, either out of exhaustion or pettiness or a strange need to talk. She trudged up the stairs, one stolid step at a time.

"The royal courts of Judah were where Isaiah spent most of his time prophesying doom and destruction for all and sundry in the Old Testament. The first caller on last week's show hadn't gotten three words out before Daddy cut her off and said, 'I know exactly what's going on in that motel room off the highway, Linda. I know it and you know it and now your husband does too.' How would anyone respond to that?"

"Was Jerome telling the truth? Did he really know?"

"Poor Linda certainly made it sound like he did."

"But how? Did you guys screen callers? Did you dig up dirt about them Jerome could use on air?"

"*Never.*"

Toby was surprised at her vehemence. They arrived at the second floor and started down a hall painted in the bright, neutral tones of any professional office building. Shooting a glance at Ruth, Toby said, "I don't recall the show being *that* upbeat when I was a kid. Jerome sure had a lot to say about what people did in their bedrooms, even back then."

"Oh, he just threw that in every now and then to placate old Corah. His sister's a bit of a relic, you know."

"Does that justify it?"

"No. But Daddy had a lot of masters to please."

"So why did he change this year? Did Jerome make the show darker to get the ratings up or something? Nothing gets people tuning into TV like live drama."

"There are a lot of things I don't understand anymore, Toby."

They rounded one corner after another. Toby had the strangest feeling of déjà vu and realized he'd done something much the same with Sarah Nella, Ruth's sister, as he followed her through the west wing early this morning.

Like motes of dust trapped in the orbit of a—

"Have you seen any sign of Julian today?" Toby said.

"The servant?"

"You mean Sarah Nella's grandson?"

"He's missing?"

"Well, he's not working and Marie's not sure where he's gone. Does that qualify as missing?"

Ruth seemed thoroughly unbothered by this. "That was only a matter of time. Ginger warned Sarah Nella not to hire that man. Her spies had dug up plenty of unpleasant things about him."

"What's that supposed to mean?"

"Julian has a lot of problems, Toby. I think Sarah Nella started locking up the silver at night again so he wouldn't steal it."

This wasn't a comfort. "Why does nothing scare you people?"

"Maybe because the Lord's looking out for us."

"Or you already know who killed your father and you aren't afraid you'll be next."

Ruth refused to take this bait. "Alyssa says Daddy had a telescope up on the roof. Is that true?"

"He did. Along with a chair and a map of constellations. The old guy seemed fascinated with stars."

"Oh. I see."

Toby said, "Who was Cleave Wright?"

Ruth paused. "How do you know that name?"

By snooping through your father's bedroom. "I heard it around."

"That's surprising. Corah expressly forbids anyone in the house from mentioning him. For Jerome's sake, obviously—it nearly drove Daddy out of his mind when they lost their brother."

"Cleave was Jerome's brother?" With a chill, Toby thought of the terrible carving Jerome had unveiled at last night's dinner.

And it came to pass, when they were in the field, that Cain rose up against Abel his brother, and slew him.

"Yes. Cleave slipped into the north creek. He didn't stand a chance against the current, Mother told me. It had been raining for days. The creek was swollen over its banks." Ruth folded her hands. "Just like this weekend, come to think of it."

Oh, yes. I know a thing or two about sin.

"When . . . when was this?" Toby said.

"Over sixty years ago, now. Not that it matters. A man never really gets over the death of a sibling, does he?"

Slam. Click.

Slam. Click.

SLAM. CLICK.

"No." Even with the pills in his system, Toby could hardly speak. "I'm starting to think he doesn't."

They rounded a final corner and arrived at a short hall. He paused at a door marked MR. WRIGHT. Ruth produced a ring of keys from her pocket. A moment later, the door swung open.

Toby stood in the doorway, studying his mother-in-law in the church's bland light. "Why are you helping me like this, Ruth?"

"Because the Lord told me to do it in a dream." She said it without a drop of irony. She didn't blink. "Though maybe I shouldn't have listened. You're a lot smarter than you look, you know."

4:4

UNLIKE HIS BARE STUDY at the main house, Jerome's office at the church was a rat's nest. It held three desks and a conference table, all of them overflowing with books and papers, letters and printed emails, two dozen Bibles in as many translations. Yet despite the clutter, it seemed just as empty, at least for Toby's purposes. What was he supposed to do with a hand-edited sermon entitled "The Lord Doesn't Work for Free" or the early plans for the Christmas telethon? On the smallest desk, drowned in sermon notes, was a landline telephone. Toby picked up the receiver. The line was dead.

"There's no stars here," Luca said, raising his eyes to the bare ceiling.

There didn't appear to be a journal either. Armed with his trusty sock—*Don't forget your prints, Tobias*—Toby tossed the office and found nothing but sticky notes, rubber bands, paper clips, Two Creeks Ministries merchandise: key fobs, coffee mugs, coasters.

Toby heard the faint hum of a golf cart's motor. He looked out the office's long window just in time to see Hugo and Ruth bounding away across the muddy drive. As he watched them leave, Toby's hand tugged absently at the drawer of the room's largest desk. The drawer was locked.

He searched every corner of the room for a key. When he couldn't find one, he returned to the desk, armed with a hefty letter opener.

The lock on the drawer snapped easily enough, but inside he found nothing but a small, washed-out photograph. The picture was so old its edges curled toward Toby's fingers like the ghost of an embrace.

The photo depicted two men of about the same great height, each standing with an arm over the other's shoulder. A weathered car and a modest house stood behind them. A chicken coop and a horse stable were just visible at the edge of the frame. In the far distance, Toby would swear he could make out the long, dark line of the Hebron dam.

The man in the left of the photograph wore slacks, a thin sweatshirt, an unmistakable smile. The man beside him wore shiny black shoes, a black tie, a sharp black suit. But at the end of his long neck, Toby found not a head but a furious cloud of yellowed scribbles where someone had scraped away the man's face with a knife.

Jerome Hitting the Road, 1956 read a note in a woman's curving hand on the back of the photo. *My handsome boy.*

Jerome was clearly the man smiling on the left. But who was this with him?

And what had happened to his face?

"Mister Jerome gets a lot of mail," Luca said from the other side of the room, and Toby returned the photograph to the drawer.

The boy was studying a thick bundle of open envelopes held together by a rubber band. In his halting, deliberate way, he read aloud the sticky note fastened to the top. "'J, more of the same. They just keep coming. Is another fire in order?—G.' Is 'G' Miss Ginger?"

"Probably so, bud."

Toby flipped through a mountain of magazines as Luca opened one of the many letters. "What does ter . . . ter . . . terminal mean?"

"Give me that."

The letter in question had come a month ago, from Missoula, Montana. *Mister Wright, you perhaps do not remember me, however we spoke on your program* Prophecy Hours *three weeks ago and you gave me news which I did not care to hear or believe, but you were correct. My grandson's blood disease was indeed terminal, terrible as that is to write, and sir please, I beg you, why has the Lord done this to us? Where is the great reward HE promised? I regret ever calling into your program now. I fear that to deserve this pain I have committed sins so old I've forgotten them and how can I ever ask forgiveness for them now?*

In spite of the time and failing rain, Toby found himself flipping through one letter after another, much as he had on the roof, trapped in the gravity of the star guide's strange hand-drawn constellations. By the time he bundled the letters back together with their rubber band, that awful chill that had haunted him all weekend was eating through the back of his neck.

It felt like someone was trying to tell him something.

"Let's get out of here."

But when they closed the door of the office behind them, Luca dug in his heels. "Wait. We promised Miss Marie we'd look for her brother."

Toby was tempted to ignore this, but a moment later he called up and down the hall, "Julian! Julian, are you in here? It's just us. We want to talk."

Which was true. Julian the missing servant was beginning to feel like some kind of wild card in this whole situation. The fact that he had vanished the same morning his great-grandfather was murdered on the roof of the house felt like the worst sort of coincidence. Julian and his sister had been here since April, more than long enough for Julian to have overheard something he shouldn't have heard, seen something he shouldn't have seen.

Or, perhaps worse, to say something he shouldn't have said.

Poor Marie. She was so desperate to conceal her fear whenever she talked about her brother; almost against his will, Toby recalled the many, many times his own sister had fallen off the wagon and disappeared into the night, sometimes for months at a time. Marie, at least, hadn't yet given up the strain of loving a troubled sibling.

He wondered if she'd already started thinking as Toby had, near the end, about how much easier life could be without such a burden.

Slam. Click.

Toby looked at his watch, saw that it was too soon to chew another Ativan, did it anyway.

He wished he had the time to search every room of this church, but it would be getting dark soon and he didn't care for the idea of crossing the estate by moonlight. After a few fruitless minutes spent wandering the church and calling Julian's name, Toby headed back for the lobby. "Sorry, bud," he said to Luca. "There isn't time to look for everything."

Luca accepted this with a small frown. He followed Toby mutely out into the thin rain, only to stop a moment later. "Where's the putter?"

He was right: their little golf cart was gone. Toby looked down both sides of the building, wondering if all this Ativan was locking away so many memories, he was making up new ones just to fill in the blank space. Had he parked somewhere else? Had he walked here?

But then he felt the putter's key in his pocket and knew he'd left it parked right here, steps from the door.

"Oh. There it goes." Luca huddled away from the rain under the church's narrow overhang. Following his finger, Toby saw a distant flash of white peeking over a hill and then vanishing on its way back to the house.

IT WAS LITTLE MORE than a mile between the church and the main house, yet it took Toby and Luca nearly an hour to cross it on foot. The soaked ground was too treacherous to walk with any speed, and twice a clap of thunder boomed over their heads with such violence, Toby wrapped himself around his son and dropped to his knees, certain a bolt of lightning was searching for something soft to strike.

But these were only the dregs of a dying storm. It was enough to soak them to the bone, but by the time Toby and his son reached the back door of Ramorah, the rain had grown so weak it vanished for steps at a time.

Toby ducked into the estate's nice stables before heading inside. Six putters were parked in six slots near Richard's exercise equipment. Three of them dripped with rainwater. Toby wondered if all of their ignitions started with the same key, or if a spare existed for the putter Toby had taken on his little tour of the estate this afternoon. He supposed it didn't really matter. One of these carts was wet because Ruth and Hugo had taken it out into the rain, another because Toby had borrowed it earlier.

The third was wet because some unknown party—a party consisting of two people, presumably—had driven to the church so one of them could nab Toby's cart while he was busy searching the church.

For the first stretch of his walk back, Toby had assumed that this had been someone's idea of a prank, an effort to punish him for playing detective, maybe some casual intimidation. And at first Toby couldn't think of two more likely culprits for the theft of his putter than the two new hosts of *The Prophecy Hour.* Not that it had worked, of course. If Alyssa and Richard thought a little thunder and mud would make Toby roll over and give up his son for their show, they'd clearly never seen what years of poverty did to a man's backbone.

But the longer Toby had walked, the more other pairs of Wrights began to filter through his mind: Wrights who might benefit from an hour without him around, Wrights who needed the time to get a few ducks in a row without the risk of being interrupted by an interloper. Had something happened in his absence? Had some new plan been set in motion?

Whatever the motive behind it, this walk had given Toby one thing he'd needed since he'd left the model motel room this afternoon: another chance to think.

As he neared the main house, he saw a face staring at them through a kitchen window, a face he'd seen so seldom, Toby almost thought it belonged to a ghost. And then he realized who it was: Matthias, Ginger's elusive son.

The sight of the boy connected two wires in Toby's brain with an almost audible spark. He realized he had an *excellent* reason to talk to Matthias.

If he could stop him. Matthias hurried from the window as they drew near, and Toby had to practically carry Luca inside to catch up with him. He stepped through the house's back door when Matthias was steps away from the door to the hall.

"Wait a second." Toby nodded to the pieces of a sandwich Matthias had laid out on the counter beneath the window. "Aren't you hungry?"

———————————

"When I saw you coming out of the rain I thought maybe Mom was right after all."

"Right about what?"

Matthias edged his way back to the counter. "You kind of look like a ghost right now, to be honest with you."

"Is that why you were trying to get away? You think the house is haunted?"

"No. It's 'cause Richard would kill me if he caught us talking. He's been going around all afternoon telling everyone not to say a word to you."

Matthias was tall and slim, bordering on scrawny, suspended at that awkward age at the cusp of puberty—twelve? Thirteen?—where his past and future selves seemed at war on his face. He had a child's lips and a man's hard brow, a streak of acne and a peach-fuzz mustache. He wore torn jeans, shoes that were coming open at the toe, and a baggy shirt that inexplicably read I HATE PONIES. If Toby had passed him on the streets of LA, he would have worried the kid was homeless.

"Why's Richard afraid of you talking to me?" Toby said. "It's not like you know anything, right?"

"Richard's nuts. Haven't you noticed that by now?"

"I'm starting to get the picture."

Toby said all of this as he gathered up dish towels and dried Luca as best he could. Now he wiped his own face so Matthias couldn't see the edge in his eyes. "How long have you been living here?"

"Since right after Grandpa Jerome had his *fall*." Matthias laid a curious stress on the word. "Mom said it was time for us to come home and take care of him."

"But she didn't bring your father?"

"He's . . . not in the picture."

"He's not dead, is he?"

"No."

"No siblings?"

Matthias blanched. "Never ask Mom that question."

With a lurch of guilt, Toby remembered the bitterness with which Ginger had said, *My daughter made the mistake of dying on a Sunday.* For once his keen memory had failed him.

"Shit. Sorry. Really."

Toby grabbed a banana from a copper fruit bowl on one of the kitchen's many islands and passed it to an exhausted Luca, who dragged himself to the table in the kitchen's nook and gazed out at the rain. A moment later and the boy's head fell to his hands. He was out like a light.

"Did you and your mom get along with Jerome?" Toby asked Matthias, doing his best to appear mellow, at ease, not thoroughly terrified at the way the rain was sinking to nothing but a soft murmur. How long would it be before the creek was low enough to cross?

"*I* got along with him. Jerome was the only person around here who didn't treat me like I was different because of my diagnosis. Like I might break if you breathed on me or something."

Toby snapped out of his thoughts. "What diagnosis?"

"Jerome was chill. We can leave it at that." Matthias shrugged a bony shoulder. "He gave me money sometimes, you know, for doing stuff around the house for him."

And here it was: the reason Toby had been so keen to talk to the boy when he'd caught sight of him in the window. "Stuff like burning everything in his study?"

Matthias had turned to the two slices of bread that lay on a sheet of Sarah Wrap on the counter, a jar of mayo, a spatula. At the sound of Toby's question, he froze. "How did you know about that?"

"You were covered in dirt yesterday when we all came running to see why Corah was screaming outside her room. That dirt was light gray. Almost like ash. Look—it's still under your nails."

"So?"

"There are two trash cans on the roof full of ash. Jerome's study's been completely cleaned out. It's not a difficult chain to follow."

Matthias shot a glance over his shoulder, looking past Toby to the kitchen's closed door. With a shrug that was too casual to be casual, he said, "Jerome asked me to keep it quiet. There was some stuff in that office he said he'd been meaning to clear out."

"Like what?"

"Why do you care?"

"I'm doing your mom a favor. She's looking for a journal Jerome was keeping."

"Be careful doing favors for Mom," Matthias said. "She usually gets a better deal than you. It's part of her job, you know."

"So did you burn the journal or not?"

"No."

Toby tried a different tack. "Did Jerome give you his key?" Toby asked Matthias. "The one to the roof?"

"Just for a second. I unlocked that door and propped it open with a few books and gave the key back. You can get back inside without the key, you know. You just can't go out."

"So you only had the key for a second? You didn't give it to anyone else?"

"Who would I give it to? There was no one in that hall but me and Jerome." Matthias hesitated. "And Julian, I guess, but he was leaving when I got there."

"Julian? The hired help?"

"Who else? He was carrying a silver tray and a couple notes on his way out of the study as I was heading in."

"What time was that?"

"Around noon yesterday. I think right around the time y'all were getting here."

Those must have been the same notes from Jerome with which Julian had greeted Alyssa and Toby yesterday. *My apologies, but I will be unable to see you until dinner.* "How did he seem?"

"Julian? Funny you mention it—he looked like crap, actually."

"Crap?" Toby arched an eyebrow. "He looked okay enough when I saw him in the foyer."

"He must have stopped crying by then, I guess."

A tremor coursed through Toby's head. He saw a dim shape, like a gap in his mind: something he'd overlooked, misunderstood, forgotten altogether. "What could Jerome and Julian have been talking about that would make Julian cry?"

Matthias shrugged, turned back to the sandwich laid out on the Saran Wrap. "Jerome wasn't nice to *everyone.*"

Toby switched gears, one eye on the door to the hall.

"So you and your mother moved here after the old man had his fall. When was that again?"

"Last fall. Funny, huh?"

"You mean October, November?"

"Those are typically considered the autumn months."

"So why'd you start painting that shit around the house? Were you bored? Angry about having to come live here?"

Matthias froze. "Say what?"

"Someone painted a fresh message in the west wing while the rest of us were at lunch today. They turned on last week's episode of the show as loud as they could to make sure we all found it. Kassandra was watching over Sarah Nella at the time. Sarah Nella's a vegetable. I'm starting to think Julian might not have even been in the house at all. That just leaves one person unaccounted for." Toby edged closer to Matthias. "You were also on the third floor, unmonitored, around the time someone painted a message on Corah's door yesterday afternoon. That's a hell of a coincidence, Matthias. So why'd you do it?"

Matthias laughed with a surprise so overwhelming, Toby knew in an instant that he'd completely missed the mark. "You were, like, so close to asking a smart question, bro."

"Then enlighten me. What should I have asked?"

"I don't see why Richard's afraid of you. You're a dumbass."

For a bright hot moment, Toby wanted nothing more than to slap the grin off the kid's pimply face.

"I'm exhausted, all right? I'm running out of time and trying to figure out what the hell is happening in this goddamn house and I would appreciate it if you would throw me a fucking bone about something you clearly want to talk about. All right, *bro*?"

It worked: Why did boys Matthias's age so enjoy being cussed at? The kid snickered. "You should ask literally anything about Jerome's *fall*." Again, Matthias stretched a pair of air quotes around the word. "You keep asking *when* it happened. Not *where* it happened."

Toby gritted his teeth. "All right. So *where* did it happen?"

"Most old people trip over their own feet, right? Or else they fall down some stairs?"

"I worked in a nursing home. I'm familiar with the process."

"Right. So. There's this little building out in the woods, yeah?"

Matthias lowered his voice. "Jerome apparently went there sometimes when he wanted some . . . some alone time."

A shiver passed down the back of Toby's arms. He thought of the strange, inverted lock on the door of the little shack in the woods. The shadowy form he'd imagined he saw in its window. "Is that where Jerome fell? The little shack in the woods?"

Matthias ran his knife through the sandwich. "Yeah. It's where they found him, at least. He'd been out there for a couple days by himself."

"He what?"

"How could Jerome have gotten home? He was broken all to shit—broken legs, broken hip, broken skull. The old guy had to have all kinds of surgery, couldn't walk for months."

"That's a hell of a fall to take in a building without any stairs."

Matthias took a bite of turkey. "You said it. Not me."

"What are you two lovebirds cooing about?"

Richard's voice echoed over the counters and the floors. Matthias went stiff; Luca, suddenly very awake, almost bounded down from the kitchen table like he'd heard a gunshot. Toby only turned, his heart beating so hard he felt its pulse in his fingertips as Alyssa's massive brother stalked toward him.

"I'm just jerking y'all's chain. I know there's none of *that* around here." Richard shot a wink at Luca. The boy stared at him, bewildered.

Pulling a fat ring of keys from his pocket ("Someone needed to keep them while Sarah Nella's out of pocket," Richard said), Alyssa's brother unlocked a wide drawer in a kitchen island and revealed a good two dozen knives arranged, blade-down, in a flat wooden block. Several slots in the block were empty, Toby noticed. It would be easy for no one to notice a knife was gone as they locked up the silver after a long day.

As if reading his mind, Richard made a show of lifting out one knife after the other. "Do you know where that nice wide one went, Matthias, the one I use to chop the salads every night?"

"I . . . I got no idea."

"Your nose is bleeding," Toby said to the boy, startled.

Matthias looked down at the sandwich in his hand. Three spots of red had bloomed on the white bread. When he wiped his nose with the heel of his hand, it came back shiny with blood. "Shit. I missed my pill."

Toby handed him one of the rags he'd used to dry his hair. He recalled what the boy had said a moment ago: *Jerome was the only person around here who didn't treat me like I was different because of my diagnosis.* "What pill? You okay?"

"No one here is okay," Richard said, casually drawing out one of the largest knives in the drawer with a *thunk*. "My poor nephew here had a tumor the size of a quail's egg cut out of his brain last summer, didn't you, Matty?"

Toby stared at Matthias. The boy had stuffed most of the rag up his nose.

"Of course, we were all so worried about Matty we hardly noticed the way his little sister picked up some bug when she visited him in the hospital. She was dead almost before anyone knew she was sick. Wild, isn't it? You think when God gives you one sick kid, at least that's insurance for the other one. But the Lord has a funny sense of humor, you know. Must be a terrible guilt for little Matty to carry around at his age. He's almost like a sacrifice the Almighty rejected."

Matthias started to shake. The rag in his nose was a brilliant red. Toby thought of the icy way Ginger had held up a hand in her office and said, *A sister isn't the same as a child. I don't go a single day without wondering how I could be with her again.*

Richard pressed on. "You must have been really grilling him before I got here, Toby. Stress gives my poor nephew horrible nosebleeds—it's why he's never going to appear on TV."

"He was doing fine until you got here."

Something had changed in Richard since Toby had seen him in the stables a few hours ago. His eyes were bright, his mouth twitching into a perpetual smile, his voice so pronounced and booming he might have been onstage. That dangerous imbalance Toby had detected in him earlier, the way the man's mind was clearly not entirely square, had only grown worse.

"Sometimes when Ginger forgets her Wellbutrin, she says it was God's judgment on this family, what happened to her little Elizabeth," he said. "But she's one to talk, you know, when you think about all the things she and Sarah Nella have buried for Jerome."

Matthias hurried from the room with a groan of pain.

"If you can't find your morphine, look for Julian," Richard called after him. "Five bucks says he's fallen off the wagon with it."

When Matthias was gone, Richard took a bite of the boy's sandwich. "Can't stand that fucking kid. I told him not to talk to you."

Toby's stomach turned: the man had just eaten the boy's blood. "What the hell is wrong with you?"

"Me? Nothing's wrong with me." Richard laid a hand on Toby's shoulder. He let it linger there. "Nothing's wrong with *me*, Toby. Not anymore."

Yesterday, a few hours after the family had discovered the red warning painted over Corah's door—*GOD KNOWS WHAT YOU DID YOU OLD CUNT*—Toby had led his son down the creaking stairs, pointed him to the bathroom in the foyer, flipped through the grand Bible on its golden stand, and felt the way the air of the house had shifted, tightened, so that every sound seemed to chime in a higher key.

The same was even truer today. As Toby led Luca down the main hall, a terrible tension hummed in the air, like a wire eager to snap. A flash of something—divine inspiration, parental intuition—sent sweat beading in Toby's hair, turned his stomach to slush. The end of the rain, Richard's strange behavior, that was all just the start.

Something had changed in the house while he was gone. Something *bad* was coming.

Luca seemed desperate to break the silence. "Did you know all this ground around here used to be a lake?"

"I think so, yeah." Toby's mind was flitting in too many other directions—opening too many doors, closing too many others—to remember if someone had told him this already or not.

"Remember the *biiig* lake we saw when we were driving in? That used to be *here*."

"That's crazy, bud."

"A long time ago they built the big dam to keep the water up there, and built the town around the dam, and then they turned all this old lake land into farms. Mister Jerome's family were poor, poor farmers. Then when he got on TV, he came back and bought all the land and built this big house."

They found the foyer empty. Toby called the elevator. "That's funny. Most rich people build houses next to the lake, not downhill from it."

"It's because of the lights in the town. Mister Suit said Jerome wanted the night sky to look just how he remembered it when they were kids."

The elevator arrived. Toby didn't move. "I still don't know who you're talking about, bud. I haven't seen anyone wearing a suit all week-end."

Except for the man in the photograph locked in Jerome's desk, he realized.

The man with his face scratched away by a knife.

Luca stared at Toby, bewildered. "But Mister Suit's been around all day. He was at the little house in the woods, remember?"

Toby recalled a flash of something—a tall, dark shape—glinting in the windows of the replica stable as he'd turned on his putter's headlights. He pushed the thought away.

"There was a shadow in the little house, bud. It was probably from a tree."

"But remember how you were so cold then? Mister Suit is cold. And wet. But it's not his fault."

"I was cold and wet because it was raining, bud."

"But he was upstairs in the hall with Miss Corah this afternoon, too, remember? It got real cold, and then she got all angry."

Toby stepped into the elevator. "Let's get changed into some dry clothes, bud. You're probably cold right now."

"I'm not cold." Luca waited as Toby pressed the button for the second floor, listened to the elevator creak as it started its ascent. Only when it stopped again did the boy murmur to himself, "But I guess I'm about to be."

They headed out of the elevator, hooked a right, rounded the corner to the long hall that ran the length of the east wing. Toby was moving so quickly he almost didn't notice the draft of air—quick and cool as mercury—that caressed the back of his ear.

He reached the hall. He stopped.

At the far end of the hall, very near the door to the Ezekiel Suite, a wall sconce was on the fritz. Its light flashed and died, flashed and died, the distant filament releasing an eerie hiss like radio static from some neighboring dimension. Darkness spread across the end of the hall. Dissipated in the flickering light. Returned.

When the light flickered to life a second time, a tall man was standing at the distant edge of its glow. He wore a sharp black suit and iridescent black shoes, his hair the color of engine oil. He had a hand raised in greeting. In the sputtering light of the dying sconce, the man's face was lost to shadow, but somehow Toby could still make out the wide, wide smile on his thin lips.

Something flashed in the darkness above those lips. They might have been eyes, blue-black, the shade of the night sky flirting with the edge of a star.

The sconce flickered again—off, on—and the man was gone.

"He said he wanted to meet you, Daddy."

Toby was so cold he could barely breathe. "I . . . I didn't see anyone ther—"

Before he could finish the word, every light in the hall went dark. A blast of frigid air blew over them, pounding at Toby's face like he'd opened an air lock into the void of space.

When the air finally stilled—how long did it take? A second? A minute? An hour?—it left droplets of icy water beaded across Toby's cheeks. And in the silence that followed, he heard a jumbled rush of noise, like a gleeful whisper hurrying past his ear.

Jeesusayeshahdowtertoebeyes

The lights flickered back to life. Luca wiped water from his brow and started down the hall. Toby stood, rooted to the spot, chilled to the bone. He felt a horrible urge to weep.

Luca reached the door of the Ezekiel Suite. Over and over in Toby's mind, he heard that rushed whisper, the sounds spoken just a little too quickly to understand.

jeesusayeshahdowtertoebeyes

jeesusayeshahdowtertoebeyes

jeesusayeshahdowtertoebeyes

The moment Toby reached their door, it clicked.

Jesus hates a doubter, Tobias.

He stopped. Turned. Looked back down the hall.

Was he crazy, or was that a glimpse of a suit he saw vanishing around the corner, the flash of an iridescent black shoe?

"You know Matthias isn't the person painting all the mean things around the house," Luca said casually, pushing open the door of their suite. "Otherwise why did Miss Sarah Nella have dry paint all over her red robe?"

THE EZEKIEL SUITE WAS empty. Toby cranked up the heat of the shower in Luca's little bathroom, grabbed the boy fresh clothes and dry socks, and helped him unpeel his soaked shorts. When he was down to his underwear, Luca gave Toby a long, level look that seemed to age him by a decade. "I can handle it from here," he said.

"You want to be alone?"

"Just when I'm naked."

Toby left without a word. When had his baby boy learned modesty? Was this family rubbing off on him already?

Every time Toby thought he was getting a handle on the situation here, some new detail emerged to throw it all into chaos again: a defaced photograph, the strange details of Jerome's fall, the spots of dry red paint Luca told him he'd discovered on the hem of Sarah Nella's robe. Toby remembered the way the woman, earlier this afternoon, had jerked back her duvet with her twitching hand, all but daring him to look at her bare chest: at the bruises she'd gotten in her fall on the roof, at the spots of red Toby had at first mistaken for scabbed blood.

I left her by herself for ywo minutes at lunch and found her choking in the shower when I got back, Kassandra had said.

There was more, something Toby couldn't see but knew was there, like the shape of a memory someone had sealed away. That awful certainty from downstairs, the creeping dread that something very bad was on its way, still hummed between the hairs of Toby's arms.

Jesus hates a doubter, Tobias.

Toby decided it was time for a new game plan. If the storm really was dying, then he would be ready to bolt the moment it was safe to cross the creek. Richard had warned Toby he wouldn't make it across the county line, but Toby would take his chances. He just needed three things: a warm bath to purge this lingering chill, a change of clothes, and the keys to Alyssa's Mercedes.

As Toby stepped into his bedroom, his eye caught on a square of paper resting by the lamp on Alyssa's bedside table. He thought for a moment it might be that wire transfer, undestroyed after all, but no: it was the folded note from Jerome that bore Alyssa's name, the one Julian had served on a silver tray yesterday afternoon when Toby and his family had first arrived at Ramorah.

Out of curiosity, Toby unfolded the note and found that it contained almost the exact message Alyssa had read aloud in the foyer: *My apologies, but I will be unable to see you until dinner. Welcome home, J.*

Under this, however, Jerome had added two curious words that hadn't appeared in the note the old man had written to Toby. Was it strange that Alyssa hadn't bothered to read them aloud yesterday in front of her family?

The two words were: *Good luck.*

Five minutes later, Toby was standing in the shower when he felt Alyssa herself slip into their bedroom, his wife's presence a weight he felt more than a sound he heard. Indeed, he thought for a moment that his mind was playing tricks on him again until he heard a faint, metallic *clink* from somewhere past the bathroom door. He let the water run, curious to see how long it would take Alyssa to announce herself.

A full minute later, she said, "Toby, can I talk to you?"

"Why would you ever want to do that?" he shouted over the shower.

"I wanted to apologize." She hesitated. "Really. I just don't know how."

"What could you possibly have to apologize for? Making me walk home in the rain?"

He killed the water, reached for a towel, stepped out of the shower just as Alyssa opened the bathroom door. She wore black pants and a tight jogging sweater, her face darkened with an anxious frown. She didn't look like his wife, and after a moment Toby realized why.

For the first time since he'd known her, Alyssa almost looked honest, and it had made her a stranger.

"I should have told you about the trust fund," she said. "Really. I should have told you earlier about how we need Luca in our show. If it wasn't for me, you and your son would have never been stuck here this weekend. I've treated you like dog shit, Toby, and I want it to stop before it . . . before it can get any worse."

Great white sails of steam drifted between them. The shower released a last gurgle of water, like it was choking on rainwater in its pipes.

"I'm sorry," Alyssa said. "I'm sorry for ever pretending I loved you."

Toby heard a door slam down the hall, only to realize it had come from his own mind. He heard the *click* of a lock. He shook his head at his wife, smiled, shrugged. "If it makes you feel better, I don't remember why I married you in the first place."

Alyssa grinned. She was slipping out of her honesty, her vulnerability, and back into one of her many guises. She propped herself against the frame of the door, turned up her chin like she was posing for a photograph. "Then can you please just let all this go? Let's treat the marriage like the business arrangement it is. Get with the program, let Luca be a star, relax. It's all here, Toby. Everything you wanted out of the marriage—everything Luca needs—we've got it."

"You made this offer once already today. You know my position."

"Please, Toby. This might be the last chance you get."

"Or what?"

Alyssa's gentle, caressing tone never changed. It sounded like the hiss of a snake. "Or we'll ruin you, Toby. I'm serious. No more threats. No more games. We will crush you and we will take everything you love and we will leave you bleeding in a ditch. Do you understand?"

Toby let out a long, long breath. "I'd like to see you try."

She sighed. She looked down. She looked, for a moment, genuinely pained at this answer.

And then she said, "Suit yourself," and turned on her heel.

When he was alone again, Toby glanced around the bedroom, curious what Alyssa might have been doing in here in that solid minute before she announced herself. He thought of what Ginger had told him, about the way the family's erstwhile housekeeper had been fired. *Whenever Richard needs Alyssa, she's ready to serve.*

But everything appeared just as Toby had left it: wet shirt and pants puddled near the bed, the junk from his pockets drying on the nightstand, shoes by the door leaking water across the rug. He grabbed the bottle of pills and stepped into the walk-in closet and found his clothes hanging just where Marie had hung them yesterday, drawers still full of tidy socks and underwear, luggage still stowed away on the closet's distant top shelf. He dressed to the faint sounds of thunder rolling out over the plains. A bead of water leaked from the closet's ceiling and curled around his throat.

As he tugged loose a pair of dark pants from the closet's shelf, something brown and heavy came with them, something that hadn't been there this morning. It landed between his feet with a soft *thunk*.

It was a pillowcase. Once it had been white, but blood had darkened most of the fabric to a hideous red-brown. The pillowcase's mouth had spilled open in its fall, revealing a long silver blade inside.

You have no idea how much danger you're in, my friend.

We need your son. We don't necessarily need you.

No more threats. No more games.

There was a knife in the pillowcase, its edge gummed with blood.

Toby thought his heart would rupture in his chest. In a panic, he bundled up the crusty pillowcase, rose on his tiptoes, and flung it over the back of his suitcase into the furthest corner of the closet.

Oh God, he thought. For the first time in years, he realized he was praying, though he was so afraid he found he couldn't form a single coherent thought. *Oh God, oh please, oh God.*

Toby shook like he was in the grip of a fever. With every tremor, he felt a vital piece of his mind rattling. Cracking. The marble labyrinth might crumble under this much pressure, its doors unlocking all in a rush. One door in particular, the door at the heart of the labyrinth—the bad door, the worst door—contained memories that Toby wasn't sure he could remember and still remain sane.

Pain waited behind that door. Pain and sorrow and fear like no one could imagine.

Only three tablets remained in Alyssa's Ativan bottle. Toby chewed them all at once, hard enough to bite off a piece of his tongue. He looked at the shelf where the bloody knife waited. How had it gotten there?

As if he had to ask.

Toby wanted his son. Now. Toby wanted his son and he wanted to *run*.

He wouldn't get the chance.

Toby somehow dressed himself, patted down his hair, stumbled from the closet. He didn't take two steps before he heard a man clear his throat in the sitting room. There was a rustle of fabric, like someone shifting in their seat. A woman sighed.

Toby had known, from the moment he'd returned from the church, that something terrible was brewing for him in this house.

And here it was.

"Toby," Richard called from the other side of the door. "We're ready for you."

AND SO THEY WERE. Stepping into the suite's sitting room, Toby found nearly every Wright in the house, even a startled Matthias and a morose Marie, assembled like they were about to undergo a wake. Only Sarah Nella was unaccounted for.

And Julian, of course. Always Julian.

Richard waited near the coffee table, erect and polished as a flagpole. He gestured toward the room's one empty chair. "Please, Toby. Take a seat."

Luca stood near Marie, looking sad and scared and confused. Corah sat on the sofa with Ruth and Hugo, all three of them bewildered and clearly unsettled, though perhaps for different reasons. Kassandra was propped against the kitchen's counter, Ginger perched in a small chair near the window, Matthias slouched against the wall.

Toby didn't notice Alyssa standing behind him, near the bedroom door, until she pushed him toward the empty chair. She said, "You'll want to sit down for this."

"What's going on?" Toby held out a hand for Luca, but Richard gave a hard jerk of his head. With an apologetic frown, Marie trudged toward Luca's bedroom, guiding the boy by the hand.

Luca turned back to watch Toby. He stared until the bedroom door closed in his face.

In his mind's eye, Toby saw the bloody knife resting not ten feet away in the back of his closet. Why weren't the pills helping?

We who are about to die salute you.

"What do you think you're doing, Richard?" Toby said, and heard a furious edge in his voice that almost surprised him.

Richard heard it too. That flash of something like recognition—the curious, confused expression that had crossed Richard's face time and time again since he'd met Toby—crossed the man's eyes now, only to be replaced a moment later by the deranged gleam Toby had seen in the kitchen a few minutes earlier.

But before Richard could speak, old Corah shifted anxiously on the couch. "Abigail," she murmured to Ruth. "Abigail, listen, it's time we put our differences aside. I know you like him but it's not right. I've seen him around the house all day, and you know as well I do that he shouldn't be here, he *shouldn't.*"

Ruth shushed the woman. She turned to Toby with such a sad, defeated exhaustion it almost made him sick.

"Don't worry, Mom," Richard said. "This shouldn't take long."

The man began to stalk the length of the suite's sitting room, his hands behind his back, his chin erect, looking for all the world like he was preparing to deliver a sermon. "I understand you've been poking around the house today, Toby."

"It's my house too. I'm family, aren't I?"

"Maybe. But Corah says she found you and your son skulking around outside Jerome's room, a place everyone in this house—everyone but her—is explicitly forbidden to go. Why was that?"

"Corah should be in a memory unit at a nursing home, Richard. You all know it."

"Why are y'all letting the friends of the family into the house now?" Corah murmured to Ruth. "Abigail, it must bother you."

Richard continued, undaunted. "Not only that, Toby, you've been asking us all the classic questions. What time did we get to bed last night, did we hear anything unusual, who stood to benefit the most from Jerome's death? I even caught you recording our little conversation in the stables, something everyone here has been *thrilled* to learn. It's almost like you were trying to do the police's job for them."

"And yet you're the one gathering all of us in the sitting room like Hercule fucking Poirot," Toby said. "What's the point of this, Richard? Let me have my son."

"The *point* is that you've spent all darn day working to make me look like a murderer. You've gone to great pains to understand our financial situations, the precarious position of the ministry, the need for new leadership to drag the brand into the twenty-first century. You've established I don't have an alibi for last night, and who knows *what* you found at the church."

"He didn't find anything at the church, Richard," Ruth spoke up, her voice both quiet and steeled. "I searched every inch of that office before Toby got there. You're letting him scare you for nothing."

Toby wasn't sure whether to thank Ruth for this or not. He didn't dwell on it. He was too busy thinking of what rested in his bedroom closet.

He stared Richard in the eye. "Don't forget that my wife doesn't have an alibi either. You know? Your new cohost. The two of you could have worked together. Killing Jerome would be your only way to get any money out of this operation, especially since the old man didn't retire after you beat him half to death in that little cabin in the woods last October."

A ripple of unease spread across the family. Alyssa said, "That's ridiculous. Richard and Kassandra were still living in Aspen when Jerome had his . . . fall."

Richard grinned. "Good try as always, Toby. But it won't—"

Ruth cut in smoothly. "Ratings were up for the first time in years, Richard. Jerome didn't have to die."

"Ratings were up because *The Prophecy Hour* had turned into a geek show!" Richard rounded on a heel to shout at his mother. "That couldn't last. It needed a new model, something sustainable."

"Sustainable. Yes. Is that why you and your siblings have been robbing the coffers blind? To *sustain* us?"

Everyone, even Corah, stared, stunned, as small, plump Ruth rose from the couch to stride across the room with all her late father's pride and fury. She thrust a finger in Richard's face. She said, "You think we didn't know? For months, Sarah Nella and I watched hundreds of thousands of dollars vanishing out of the companies in the Bahamas. She only confronted the three of you on Friday afternoon because she was tired of waiting for you to confess. Toby, if you were curious, that's why your wife decided to join the family business. If my children didn't earn back every penny they'd stolen from us, we were prepared to turn them over to the authorities."

Silence blanketed the room. Ginger looked at nothing but the glowing tip of her vape. Richard looked like he might strike his mother. Alyssa seemed ready to scream. She met Toby's eye, and he knew she was thinking about the same thing he was: the wire transfer he'd found in her purse.

No wonder she'd been so afraid of that thing. Toby would bet his life that transfer was proof that she and her siblings had been defrauding the family.

"Father was right," Ruth said. "This family is so black with sin you couldn't find it in the dark."

Toby decided to strike while they were off-balance. "So why make things worse, Richard? I've been looking around the estate all day and there's no blood anywhere, no forensics because you guys ruined the crime scene, no camera footage of the crime. It's all circumstantial evidence. You couldn't pin anything on me. I couldn't pin anything on you. We should all just walk away from this. You and Alyssa take over the show and bring it into the new millennium. Luca and I leave, and no one ever has to know about the money you've been stealing. We all just forget about Jerome. Maybe it really was suicide after all."

"Suicide. Right." Richard stared at Toby. "But whenever you mention suicide, Toby, I come back to the very obvious question you yourself asked this morning. If Jerome killed himself up on that roof, what happened to the knife?"

Richard met his eye. Toby went still. He felt something tremble deep within his mind.

"The locals in Hebron look up to us, you know," Richard went on. "What would they say if they knew we'd brushed this whole mess under the rug and played the police off with some story? If we let someone in this house get away with a murder?"

Hugo shifted in his chair. "Son, this is getting ludicrous. Whoever did this—"

"So you know what I think we should do, Toby?" Richard raised his voice smoothly over his father. "I say we knock another item off the police's to-do list. We search every room in the house. Tonight."

Richard's smile grew lethal, that gleam in his eye brighter and brighter—and in an instant Toby realized that they both knew where this was going.

They both knew what waited in that closet, and how it had gotten there.

Richard said, "What do we have to hide? We're all family, after all. Marie! Come back in here!"

She emerged from Luca's room, the boy slumped against her side like a frightened puppet.

"We're going to make a sweep of the house this evening. Starting with Toby's room."

4:9

RICHARD CLAPPED HIS HANDS like a camp counselor with some unruly charges. "Marie, here—I brought some gloves from the kitchen." From the back of his jeans, he produced a pair of dishwashing gloves and watched as she fitted them on. "I want you to look everywhere—inside clothes, bags, get creative. Come on, we don't have all night."

The family dragged themselves to their feet and watched from the door as Marie slowly poked through the suite's bedroom. Only Richard had any pep to him. He bobbed on his feet, his jaw anxiously working a piece of invisible gum, eyes flashing every time he turned his head.

Marie made a discovery that was as much a surprise to Toby as it was to everyone else. Fishing a finger into the pocket of Toby's sodden jeans, she produced a simple silver key. It looked so similar to the key he'd found in Jerome's pocket this afternoon that Toby wondered, just like he had when his putter was missing from the church, if he'd locked away too many memories, if he'd never buried that key near the southern creek at all.

But when she brought the key to the door for the family to examine, he saw that it was different. A small white label was affixed to the key's head, bearing the helpful word *roof* in tiny letters.

"Well, isn't that peculiar," Richard said.

Toby didn't move. Alyssa stood behind him, Luca somewhere behind her. Even at this distance, Toby could feel his son trembling.

The pills *still* weren't working.

"Keep looking," Richard said to Marie.

She stepped into Toby's closet. They listened as zippers opened, clothes clinked on their hangers, bags were pushed around. She seemed to stay in there an eternity.

But then Marie returned empty-handed. She shrugged.

"That was awfully fast," Richard said.

"What do you want me to say? There's nothing there."

Richard gritted his teeth. "Give me those."

Practically dragging the gloves off Marie's hands, he stepped into the closet. The girl came to stand with the rest of her family, staring after him.

Not a moment later, something brown and heavy sailed from the closet's open door and landed on the bedroom floor. A bloody blade poked from the pillowcase's mouth.

"Well then," Richard said, stepping out after it. "What do we have here?"

Toby kept his mouth shut. He shuffled backward a careful inch, toward Luca.

Alyssa clamped a hand on his arm.

"Well, this is awfully convenient, isn't it, Son?" Ruth said to Richard, that quiet steely tone taking on a keener edge. "You found a knife exactly where you expected to find it. How do we even know that's Jerome's blood? It could have been used to section the duck last night."

"I didn't know they shipped us whole birds, Mother."

"There's a lot about this house you don't know. But you're still so damned certain you can run it all." Ruth took a step into the bedroom, so livid she almost vibrated out of her shoes. "You got an idea into your head, Richard, that's all this is. You did it to our housekeeper and now you're doing it to Toby. You're just afraid. All your life you've been afraid."

"Never speak to me again like that, Mother."

"Or what? You'll plant a knife in my room too?"

"It's impossible, Son," Hugo said. "Our bedroom's on the third floor, right by the elevator and the stairs, remember? The way your mother's been sleeping lately, I've been up all night, every night. I would have heard Toby come up to kill the old man. I would have heard *anybody.* But they didn't. The stairs were quiet all Friday night. The elevator too."

Ruth's fury didn't abate. "Do you understand what he's saying? No one from this floor could have killed Daddy. No one."

"Isn't there a servants' elevator in this hall?" Richard said sharply. "Couldn't Toby have taken that?"

"How would Toby know where to find a *service elevator* on his first day in the house? How would he get a knife? How would he know where to find Jerome in that maze over there in the west wing? Toby's like the rest of us—*he* had no good reason to murder the old man."

"Ain't that the knife you use to chop the salads every night, babe?" Kassandra said softly.

"Think of what you're *doing*, Richard," Ruth barreled on. "You're trying to frame an innocent man for murder. For what? So you can take over a church? Do you have any idea the forces you're playing with, the rage God holds for false prophets, for greedy shepherds, for liars?"

"If that was true, then God would have wiped this family out a long time ago," Richard said.

"You know the Lord's schedule now? You haven't seen what I've seen. You don't know the sort of dreams he's sent me, Son. The nightmares."

"I saw him do it!" Alyssa's voice was so loud, even she recoiled from it, like a dog frightened by her own bark. She blinked, fretted, seemed desperate for someone to let her out of the mess she'd created for herself this weekend.

No one spoke.

"I . . . I was starving last night. It was why I stepped out around eleven—so I could get a snack. It was late. I hardly ate a bite at dinner," Alyssa said carefully. "I saw him as I was coming back to the suite. Toby. He was stepping into the servants' elevator right across the hall."

"You were gone for hours, Alyssa," Toby began, but Richard cut him off.

"You'd swear you saw that?" the man said. "In court?"

Alyssa shot her brother a scared, careful look. "Yes."

"Well done, child," Ruth said. "The perfect sister. Always ready with a lie when he needs you most."

But before Alyssa could protest, Ginger started to scream.

"Oh God. Oh God, oh God, oh God!"

Ginger stood near the sitting room's windows, staring out at the black estate, trembling and murmuring to herself and shaking her head.

When the family turned to see what was wrong, she pointed to the sky. "Why is it like that? *Why is it like that?*"

The sky was black, not a star in sight, but it was lit by a brilliant red moon—crimson as judgment, crimson as blood—that had come to burn on the eastern horizon. The Wrights, as if possessed, all hurried to the sitting room's windows to stare. Even Toby, heathen as he was, couldn't shake the horror of the sight. He'd never seen anything like it. That red moon felt primitive, eerily on cue, like an ancient curse.

Or the sign of a prophecy come due.

They were still standing like that, massed near the windows, when every light in the room flickered, flickered—and died. The moon's red glow oozed over their skins like a violation. A terrible cold sprang up on every neck.

"The stars—shall withdraw—their shining."

A voice spoke from the room's dark door. It was a stranger's voice, a choked, strangled sound like that of a dead man struggling to breathe. A dread omen. A mad prophet.

"And the moon—shall turn—to blood—before—his judgment—arrives."

There was a heavy step from the hall. Another.

"The time—for repentance—is past."

Sarah Nella appeared in the moon's crimson light, her head cocked at a perverse angle, half her body limp as a corpse, a heavy can swinging in her good hand. She was naked from her hair to her toes and gleamed with red paint like a scion of that infernal moon, and from her drooling mouth she let out a voice that wasn't her own.

"Weep—for the day of the Lord—is nigh."

RUTH SCREAMED. KASSANDRA RECOILED and landed against a window hard enough for it to crack. Hugo started to pray.

Luca squeezed through hips and thighs and pressed himself to Toby's side. Toby scooped the boy up and held him tight and Luca whispered in Toby's ear, "That's not her. It's *him*."

With a *klunk*, the can in Sarah Nella's hand dropped to the floor and sent gobs of red paint lurching over its sides. Sarah Nella—or whatever was inside her—bent painfully at the waist and withdrew a gleaming red brush. *"Behold."*

She swung the brush in a wide arc, and before anyone could think to move, the family was doused in paint.

"Listen—for the God—of Israel—speaks."

"Sarah," Corah said. "Sarah, what in the world is wrong with you, child?"

"Sarah—is—gone." That drooping mouth made a ghastly smile. *"I speak—for the Lord."*

And then something even stranger happened. The droop to Sarah Nella's lip, the pitiful slump from the stroke that had rendered half her body useless, suddenly stiffened, twitched—and was smoothed away. Sarah Nella stood as tall and powerful as Jerome had once stood in his pulpit.

A new voice came from her mouth, a voice unlike any Toby had ever heard before: a deep, gothic baritone that seemed to resonate in the hollows of his chest. The voice made his heart quail. Maybe his soul.

"MY JUSTICE IS WIDER THAN THE EARTH," said the voice in Sarah Nella's mouth. "MORE POWERFUL THAN THE WATERS AND DEEPER THAN THE GRAVE. I HAVE BLESSED THIS BROOD OF VIPERS FOR DECADES HENCE. I HAVE GIVEN YOU WEALTH AND COMFORT, POWER AND ABUNDANCE, THE MEANS TO SHOW MY LOVE TO ALL THE PEOPLES OF THIS EARTH."

That paintbrush swept through the air again.

"AND AS WITH SAUL BEFORE YOU, I REGRET YOU TO MY VERY HEART."

Against all reason, Sarah Nella's ruined body took a smooth step forward, the paintbrush in one hand and the can in the other, and flicked Ginger with a spray of red. "I SEE THE VIOLENCE YOU HAVE WORKED SO HARD TO CONCEAL."

Paint swept over Kassandra. "I SEE THE SILENCE YOU HAVE KEPT."

Over Ruth and Hugo. "THE CORRUPTION YOU HAVE SPENT YOUR LIVES IGNORING."

Alyssa gasped as red flew over her. "YOU PATHETIC GIRL. DO YOU THINK I AM BLIND TO THE SECRET YOU CARRY? YOU THINK I CAN IGNORE WHAT YOU'VE ALLOWED TO GROW INSIDE YOU?"

Paint flew into Corah's wailing mouth. "WHERE WERE THESE SCREAMS WHEN MY LOVE WAS STILL WITH YOU? WHEN I COULD STILL FORGIVE EVEN THE GRAVEST OF YOUR SINS? THE TIME FOR MERCY HAS PASSED. MY HEART HAS BECOME AS STONE TO YOUR TEARS."

Richard stepped forward, his hand tightened into a fist, arm raised, ready to strike.

Sarah Nella swung on him, blanketing him in red. "AND YOU. YOU. YOU ARE MY GREATEST DISAPPOINTMENT. EVERYTHING HAS BEEN GIVEN TO YOU, EVERY BLESSING FOR WHICH A MAN COULD HOPE AND PRAY, AND YOU HAVE USED IT FOR HARM. MY FLOCK HAS BEEN CHEATED—YOU WANT TO EXTRACT THEIR BOUNTY TEN-FOLD. THEY HAVE BEEN WOUNDED—YOU WISH TO CRUSH THEM INTO THE GRAVE. YOU ARE A BROKEN, MEWLING CHILD WHO DRESSES HIMSELF IN THE ROBES OF A PRIEST. YOU WILL NEVER BE ANOINTED. YOU WILL NEVER PROSPER. YOU WILL DIE WAILING, AND THE FISH WILL HAVE NO USE FOR YOUR BONES."

Arcs of paint flew through the air as Sarah Nella heaved the can in the air. "MY JUDGMENT IS ON THIS HOUSE, ON THESE GROUNDS, ON THIS FAMILY."

Finally, Sarah Nella turned to where Toby stood, very near the open door, and said, "YOU FOOL—WHY DO YOU SEARCH FOR ANSWERS YOU ALREADY POSSESS? DO NOT WASTE THE OPPORTUNITY I HAVE GRANTED YOU. LET MY WORDS BE BRANDED IN YOUR MIND. I HAVE SPOKEN. BUT DO YOU HEAR? *DO YOU HEAR?*"

At that, Sarah Nella's body went slack, like a plug had been pulled from her back. She collapsed to her knees, lips slumped again, neck struggling to hold her head aloft.

Yet with a painful effort, she seemed to smile with another man's grin. That strangled voice spoke a final time.

"*Tobias—remember—what was written—on the roof. Like motes—of dust— trapped in the orbit—of a dead star—*" Sarah Nella shook her head. "*Things— have a habit—of repeating—in this family.*"

Richard struck her, hard, with a roar of pain and rage so profound, Toby feared he might keep hitting her until there was nothing left.

He didn't stick around to find out.

Toby knew an opportunity when he saw one. He was out the door. He was running. He was halfway down the long hall, Luca squeezed tight to his chest, before a cry of alarm went up behind him.

He didn't know where he was going, what he would do, how he planned to escape this estate without a car and with the creeks still flooded and all the Wrights pursuing him. Maybe he and Luca would take their chances with the water. Maybe they'd hide in the woods until the tide abated. Maybe he'd make a last stand in the kitchen with its drawer full of knives.

Toby knew this: whatever he'd just seen, whatever had just spoken through Sarah Nella, it had frightened him to the foundations of his mind. Maybe the foundations of his soul. Something terrible was coming for this family, and he didn't want his son anywhere nearby when it came.

What had Jerome warned on his final broadcast last week? *Do not fall into the judgment the Lord has prepared for them.*

Toby squeezed Luca tighter, and when he did, he felt a strange delay between the impulse and the action, like a buffer had come between his body and his mind.

The pills. The pills were finally kicking in, right when Toby needed every one of his wits. All at once, he realized that taking three tablets had been a mistake. A dire one. His legs felt sluggish, his mind flat and weirdly dilated. Luca whispered in his ear. "Be careful. He says it's—"

Wet. Toby cleared the carpet of the long hall, rounded the corner, and started across the hardwood floor of the landing, sprinting for the stairs. What he didn't notice until it was too late—what he might have noticed, had his mind been sharper—was the water that had seeped through the walls and pooled across the slick wood.

If Toby had been sober, he might have been able to step around the water. Jump around it. Keep his balance.

But thanks to the pills, he didn't. Toby's foot landed in the puddle of water at the top of the stairs and flew out from under him.

Time slowed. Clarity struck. His mind moved into that realm of split-second thinking, the moment when catastrophe was no longer an abstract concept.

He knew he was about to fall down those stairs. He knew that if he released Luca, the family would catch up to the boy before Toby could shake off whatever pain he was about to inflict on himself and grab the boy and keep going.

But if he held on to Luca, he might crush his son, or lose hold of him in the air, or awaken from a daze to find his son's neck bent backward around a banister.

Promise you'll never leave me alone again.

But Toby didn't have a choice.

With as much momentum as he could muster, Toby turned and flung the boy away from the stairs, aiming for the relative safety of the carpet.

An instant later, Toby was falling.

He landed, first, on his elbow. Electricity spread up his arm. Stars shot over his eyes. He let out a gasp of pain.

It was nothing compared to what came next. He bounced off his elbow and spun over and landed, knee-first, on the wooden landing with a sickening *pop*.

He started to scream. His head struck the wall.

The world spun before it went dark. Sounds grew muddy, sensations strange. Upstairs, through a muffled commotion, Toby heard his son say the one word he'd waited all his life to hear.

Luca shouted, "Daddy!"

And then silence.

THE DAY OF THE LORD IS AT HAND

5:1

SHE USED TO VANISH for months at a time.

All addicts relapse; few addicts relapsed with the panache of Toby's sister. Sometimes it was a bad day at one of her menial jobs that triggered it, sometimes it was a failed painting, sometimes she was gripped by a passing fancy that Toby could never, later, understand. Whatever the cause, he would come home to whatever little squat they were struggling to maintain on the fringes of Los Angeles and discover Willow gone, the fridge empty of any portable food, her dresser empty of whatever clothes she could fit in two small backpacks. The first few times, she left notes (*"Need some space. Love you."*), not that that stopped Toby from searching for her in every dive bar and sketchy motel he could find.

She always came back, her returns as unpredictable as her departures. The first time it happened, Toby came home from working a double shift at Silver Oaks to discover Willow in an armchair, wearing nothing but a pair of Toby's boxers, sifting through the pile of mail that had accumulated in her absence. She nodded to a sheaf of crisp hundred-dollar bills on the kitchen table. "For back rent," she said. "And no—you don't want to know what I did for that money."

Nor, for that matter, did he want to know how she'd gotten those scars on the crooks of her arms.

Eventually, the little farewell notes stopped, and Toby stopped searching for her too. Love may not die, but sympathy certainly can. At a certain point, he'd simply become too exhausted to care. Eight years ago, when the chance for her first real break had utterly collapsed—Willow had once been productive enough to convince a gallery to show her work, but not lucky enough to keep the gallery from going bankrupt a week before opening night—Toby hadn't even been surprised when she'd evaporated without a trace.

What he never could have predicted was how long she would be gone this time. Three months passed with no sign of his sister. Six. Nine. He

232

took on a second job to keep a roof over his head without Willow's help, then a third. All the work gave him a pain in the side of his neck that persisted until Alyssa, years later, started giving him free cortisone shots at her clinic.

And then one evening in the rainy depths of an LA winter, right around the time he'd started to think Willow might be gone for good this time, her key turned in the lock. He was almost surprised at how furious he was at the thought of having to face her again, to start over from scratch the whole process of living with her (because that's the thing about addicts: their lives are circles, not lines), and so he refused to look up from his phone, to acknowledge her, to smile.

But Willow didn't speak. The newborn boy she clutched to her chest let out a low, tired mewl and burbled in his sleep. "Sorry about the smell," Willow said. "He's needed a change since the Greyhound station."

That made Toby look up. His sister looked skinny, haggard, old.

But the baby in her arms looked more alive than anything Toby had ever seen. The baby was pure and perfect and overflowing with potential, and when he awoke to study Toby, his little green eyes were like maps of a new country no one had yet to ruin. The baby smiled.

"Oh my God," Toby said. "What have you done?"

"What does it look like? I had a kid." Willow passed him the hot little bundle. "His name's Luca. Unless you want to change it. I think we both know you're going to wind up raising him."

SUNDAY MORNING AT RAMORAH, Toby awoke alone in a room he didn't recognize. He heard a rumble of voices outside the door—it sounded like two men arguing—but he paid the sound no attention. Even before he opened his eyes, Toby knew his son was nowhere near him. He could feel the boy's absence like a hollow in his heart.

When he blinked, he saw Willow standing at the foot of his bed, water dripping from her mouth, shaking her head. *What the fuck have you gotten yourself into?*

A blink, and she was gone. Toby tried to *slam* the door on her memory. *Click* the lock closed. But without those pills, he didn't have much faith in it.

Those fucking pills.

Luca was gone, and it was Toby's fault. He should never have started taking those fucking pills. Who cared if his anxiety nearly overwhelmed him at the sight of the knife that had been planted in his closet? Who cared if there had been doors in his mind—specifically one very bad door—threatening to break open and spill out memories he was terrified to face?

Toby had made a grave miscalculation coming here. Being in this house—being in this entire fucking state—was simply too much for the safeguards he'd erected inside his head. Now that the pills were gone (good riddance), he knew that the doors of the marble labyrinth wouldn't stay locked for long. If this fleeting vision of his sister was any indication, it had already started.

God help him.

Toby thought of Luca, and the way he'd once sworn that he would never, ever, let his son be hurt the way Uncle Ezra (and so many others) had harmed his sister. Toby had sworn he would keep Luca safe. That he would let the boy become whoever he wanted to be.

Promise you'll never leave me alone again.

"Never make a promise," Toby's uncle used to say. "Take it to the bank, one day God'll call you to deliver."

Gladly. Toby swung his feet to the floor and wondered where he might find the closest weapon. He would kill every Wright on earth if it meant keeping his promise to his son. He'd burn this house to the ground.

And if Richard or Alyssa or anyone else had harmed a hair on the boy's beaded head, Toby would take it out of their flesh first.

But of course it couldn't be that easy. As Toby tried to stand, his left knee—the one that had landed with a gunshot's *POP* on the hardwood landing of the stairs last night—now buckled beneath him. With a gasp of agony, Toby collapsed back to the thin bed, draping a hand over the knee as carefully as he could and blinking back tears. Pain roamed across his body like a living thing. Bile climbed his throat.

Outside, the rumble of voices he'd heard a moment ago was fading into the distance. Toby recognized one of the voices as Hugo's. The other—cocky and chafing, even through a thick door—could only be Richard's.

By the time the two men were gone, the pain in Toby's knee had abated enough that he felt he could open his eyes again. He found that he was in some junk room, the sort of place that could hold a half dozen broken chairs, but not a single pillow. He'd spent the night on a hard bed wedged between a stack of boxes and a ceramic vase the size of a short man.

To his left, a narrow window looked out over the soggy remains of Ramorah's lawns, or what he could see of them in the darkness of the early morning.

Except it wasn't all that early. According to his watch, the time was already seven a.m. The sun should have long since begun to rise, and yet the world outside rested beneath a cloak of cloud so thick it had blotted out even the sun.

The stars—shall withdraw—their shining.

And then Toby finally noticed an ominous silence. In spite of the thick clouds, the rain had finally, totally stopped.

A cool draft slithered past his cheek. It brought a rushed jumble of sound.

Teyemtogettbisseetubeyes

Time to get busy, Tobias.

With a new urgency, Toby's eyes searched the junk around him for a cane, a walking stick, anything that would help him stand. He needed to get moving. Who knew how long it had been since the storm had finally abated. The roads might have already cleared by now.

Luca. He needed to find Luca and get the hell out of—

"Here. Use this."

The hinges on the room's door were so silent Toby hadn't heard Marie slip inside behind him. He might not have even recognized her out of her little black uniform. Today she wore a blue hoodie, frayed sweats, a pair of rugged Timberland hiking boots. An enormous backpack was slung over her shoulders. In her hand, she held out one of Jerome's shiny black canes.

Toby grabbed it without thanking her, struggled to stand, and made it three steps before the pain in his knee grew so bad he had to retreat to the bed again.

"Lord Jesus, slow down. I brought you some pills, too, if you'd sit still."

"My son." Toby forced the words through gritted teeth. "Where is he?"

Marie rooted around in her backpack. She didn't meet his eye.

"Here. These were in Jerome's room. They say they're for pain."

From the massive backpack she produced an amber vial of tablets, a water bottle, a bag of granola. The bottle contained nothing more exciting than ibuprofen. Toby took two, draining half the water before he realized how thirsty he was. The moment he could speak again, he said, "Is Luca in your room?"

Marie let a taut silence stretch. She tested the strength of a chair and dragged it to face Toby on the bed. With an anxious sigh, she dug a small leather-bound Bible from the backpack and placed it on his leg.

"I need to know, hand on the Gospel, if you did it or not."

"If I killed Jerome?"

"Yes."

Toby didn't blink. Resting his hand on the Bible's cracked leather, he said with total honesty, "No. I didn't kill him."

Marie nodded. She pulled the Bible away. She said, "You're in the shit, sir."

"Tell me about it. I didn't put that knife in my closet, in case you were curious."

"I wasn't. Same with the key in your pocket?"

"Richard and Alyssa's work. Obviously. To be honest with you, I really don't care. Where is Luca?"

"You should care. The internet's back up. Richard texted everyone a few minutes ago to say he called the police. And the congregation will start turning up around ten, road or no road. In a few hours this whole area is going to be crawling with people."

"Then I want my son. I want my son and I want to leave."

Marie ran a finger over the frayed edge of the Bible's cover. She nibbled her lip. "I hope it's that easy."

Toby moved as fast as he could, even before the pills could kick in. Marie followed at his side as he dragged himself along by the cane, filling him in with as much as she knew. He'd apparently spent the night in a room just down the hall from the staff's quarters, with Richard himself sitting watch in a chair outside his door. Last night, after all the chaos had subsided, Richard had forced Marie to hand over the key she'd discovered in Toby's room and had assured the family he would lock it and the bloody knife in a safe in his own room.

"You know what's annoying?" Marie said. "None of them bothered to see if that key really did unlock the door to the roof."

Toby picked up the pace, even though it sent his knee screaming. "I'm sure it did."

"How's that?"

"Richard was by himself with Sarah Nella and Jerome on the roof for a good twenty minutes after she had her stroke yesterday morning. He would have had plenty of time to swap the key to the roof that Jerome had in his pocket with a key from the ring Sarah Nella always had on her."

"How do you know Jerome had the key to the roof on him at all? All this time I figured the killer must have stolen it somehow."

"Or gotten it copied. The Cracker Barrel twenty minutes away cuts keys." Toby rounded a corner. "I found a plain key in Jerome's pocket yesterday afternoon. I have no idea what it opens, but it *wasn't* the key to the roof."

"If you're right about Richard swapping it with one of Sarah Nella's keys, then it probably just opened some utility closet somewhere. What'd you do with it?"

"I buried it near the southern creek. I figured it was probably best if I wasn't found carrying a key on my person."

Marie muffled a laugh. "They sure fixed that for you."

They certainly had. Toby thought of the way Alyssa had lingered in their bedroom for almost a solid minute last night while he was in the shower, moving so softly he'd felt her presence more than he'd heard it. No doubt that was when she'd slipped the key to the roof into the pocket of his waterlogged pants. No one else would have had the opportunity.

And while Alyssa was at it, she'd deposited the bloody knife in their closet.

Toby remembered the hounded, honest frown with which Alyssa had studied him in the bathroom. *I want to apologize. For all of it.*

Had Toby been a fool to rebuff her apology? Had she been hoping to divert the catastrophe that was coming? Had Toby put Luca in danger by refusing to risk yet another deception from his clever, beautiful wife?

She'd warned him, after all, that the family was ready to ruin him.

"It sounds like Richard's been setting you up to take the fall almost from the minute y'all found that body on the roof," Marie said.

"Why not? He had practice—he did the same thing to the family's housekeeper." Toby's foot landed funny. He swore through his teeth. "You haven't seen Julian yet, have you?"

"No."

"You're getting scared for him."

"Is it that obvious?"

"I used to get the exact same look on my face when my sister went missing. She used to go AWOL too." Toby looked Marie in the eye. "And probably for the same reasons as your brother."

Marie pushed this away with a visible effort. "Richard was watching your door down here until just a few minutes ago. Hugo came and dragged him away, but Lord only knows where to. Richard sure didn't sound happy about it."

"So where's Luca? Why didn't he just spend the night with you?"

"I wanted him to, but Richard wouldn't let me. He's supposed to be upstairs with Ruth and Hugo."

"What do you mean, supposed to?"

"Because your boy was fighting tooth and nail when Richard dragged him away from those stairs last night. Don't you think he would have come to find you by now?"

THEY RODE THE ELEVATOR to the third floor and stepped into the suite nearest the landing.

Inside, Toby found the first place in this entire house that actually resembled a home. Ruth and Hugo's sitting room held a large sofa littered with pillows, a sheaf of crackers, a sticky iPad in a tacky case. Photos of the family rested on a marble mantel. A pair of tall windows looked out on a day dark as any night.

The moment Toby stepped inside, he knew the suite was empty.

"They were supposed to watch him last night," Marie murmured. "I don't know—"

"Luca!" Toby shouted. "Luca, where are you?"

Through another door they found an unmade bed and a couch where a tangled blanket and cold pillow waited on the floor. A few sparkly plastic stars still clung to the blanket's fabric. Toby plucked one of the stars between his fingers, shocked but somehow unsurprised. He'd known this wouldn't be so easy. "Luca slept here at some point last night. These stars come off his favorite socks."

A door clicked open in the sitting room. They returned just in time to find Ruth stepping in from the hall, blinking at Toby like she'd seen a ghost. "Here you are. The man of the hour."

If Ruth had looked exhausted yesterday, today she looked ready to come apart. Her tall hair was collapsing around her face. Her plump lips had sunk so deep in her mouth Toby could see the shape of her skull.

He didn't give a shit. "Where is my son, Ruth?"

Of all things, the woman laughed.

"Alyssa told me you aren't a believer. Did last night change your mind?"

"What does that have to do with anything?"

Ruth had to practically drag herself to a tufted bench along one wall, settling at last with a heavy thump. She patted a place beside her. "Here. Sit."

Toby watched his mother-in-law cautiously. Yesterday at the church, he'd half wondered if Ruth's kindness, her willingness to answer his questions and lead him to Jerome's office and all her talk about Christian decency hadn't been some sort of performance. (Her daughter, after all, must have learned how to manipulate men from somewhere.) Ruth had even admitted, later, to searching Jerome's office before Toby arrived, just to ensure the old man hadn't left any incriminating evidence lying around.

But there'd been no mistaking the force with which she'd fought Richard on Toby's behalf last night, the righteous rage, the sadness in her eyes. Ruth might have been one of the few people in the house brave enough to possess any principles. Or at least a heart.

That didn't mean Toby had time to sit and chat with her. "I asked you a question. Where is my *son*?"

"You never had a mother, did you? I can see it in your eyes."

The question was so surprising, it literally sent Toby back on his heels. When he recovered, he almost struck Ruth, probably because she was right. He didn't remember his mother. He didn't remember anything before the car crash that killed her.

Instead, Toby remembered this: years ago, back when they still lived at Uncle Ezra's house, Toby had stepped into the kitchen on a dewy golden morning and discovered his sister dressed in a sundress and pumps, scrambling eggs for him. Turning away from Ruth Wright, from the pity in her eyes, Toby found not one of Ramorah's little kitchenettes waiting for him in the corner of her suite, but the greasy kitchen from his uncle's house, a perfect replica in every detail, right down to the yellow wallpaper, the window with the single broken blind, the smoke stain on the wall above the fridge. Toby and his sister used to swear the stain looked like the face of Jesus.

And there was his sister, turning to him with a skillet in hand, her long hair glowing like honey in the sun as she said—

"No. We never had a mother."

Toby turned to Ruth with a shudder. It was just as he'd feared. Cracks were forming in the marble labyrinth. Locks were coming loose.

Memories were starting to *leak*.

"I'm sorry," Ruth said. "In another world, I would have liked to be that mother for you. I really would."

"Marie says you and Hugo were supposed to watch Luca last night. Where—is—he?"

"Your guess is as good as mine. We put him to bed on that couch in our bedroom. When I woke up this morning he was gone. I just spent the last hour wandering the west wing shouting his name. Thank you for coming up here, by the way. You saved me the trouble of going to find you."

It was all Toby could do to keep his voice level. "But isn't Hugo a light sleeper? How could he not notice someone coming into your room to steal my son?"

"Steal?" Ruth blinked at him. "No, you don't understand. I locked this door last night. I even pulled the chain. All of that was open an hour ago. It had been unlocked from the inside. You see that chair there? It was standing right by the door when I woke up. I think your boy climbed up to pull back the latch."

"Luca left on his own?"

"I don't see any other explanation. If I had to guess, he went looking for you."

Marie seemed to materialize above Ruth in an instant. Her arms were crossed over her chest, a livid frown braced over her mouth. She looked for all the world like a dubious cop ready to crack a few heads. "Who's to say it wasn't Hugo who unlocked that door?"

The sound of Marie's voice made Toby lean back, startled. Did this quiet maid ever run out of surprises?

Ruth, however, seemed thoroughly unfazed. "That's impossible, dear. Last night the Lord granted my husband his first good night's sleep in weeks. I may have also slipped him some of Sarah Nella's sleeping pills. Quite a few of them. He was so exhausted after the ordeal she put us through, I was worried he might fall apart in my hands. We seem to run on pills in this house, if you haven't noticed. And they worked. Hugo slept like a stone until just a short time ago."

"So let's say Luca let himself out. Did you tell him before bed where Toby would be sleeping?" Marie said.

"No, of course not—I didn't want him leaving this room. Not that that stopped him."

"What about the security system?" Marie didn't let up. "Even if Luca didn't know where Toby was sleeping, he knew where *we* slept. Did anyone check the camera footage to see if he came down our hall last night? What about the locks on the doors and windows—did anyone come or go out of the house after we went to bed?"

"I thought of all that. Look." On her phone, Ruth opened an app with the icon of a padlock. "This is the security system. If anyone had done something like that last night, it would have created an alert on this page here. But there's none—see for yourself."

Toby took the phone from her hand. She wasn't lying: a long list of tabs stretched down the screen (<u>DOOR EXT 1 EAST, DOOR EXT 2 MAIN</u>) and beside each tab was a pleasant green checkmark. <u>ALL CLEAR</u>, the app said.

He took the liberty of opening the same record of Friday night and found the same <u>ALL CLEAR</u>.

"Nobody came or went from the house last night," Toby said. "Just like the night Jerome was murdered."

Ruth nodded. "And there was nobody in your hall last night but Richard. He's dead set on pinning you to the wall, Toby. There's nothing else I can do about that."

"You made things easy for him, though," Toby said. "You made Richard drag Jerome's body inside yesterday. You cleaned Jerome's corpse, too, didn't you? You wanted to ruin the crime scene and sabotage any hope of a decent investigation before it could start."

Up close, Toby saw a small, perfect circle of red paint, like a dab of clown's makeup, dried to Ruth's left cheek. She scratched at the paint with a nail. It didn't budge.

"I didn't . . . I didn't want Richard framing anyone. I figured if we ruined the crime scene, he wouldn't be able to blame *anyone* for the killing."

Toby lowered his voice. "Because you think he did it."

Ruth said nothing.

"Was it the money they stole?" Marie said. "Your kids, the three of them—you said they all had their hands in the till."

"I didn't know about that until a few days ago. Not . . . conclusively. I wasn't entirely honest with Richard last night—Sarah Nella had suspected wrongdoing for some time, but she didn't have proof until Friday."

Marie scoffed. "She must not have been looking very hard. Ginger leaves all her papers and log-in details laying around everywhere when I go to clean her office. Julian and I figured out she was embezzling cash months ago."

Ruth and Toby both stared at her.

"What?" Marie said. "We thought all of you were in on it."

"No. No, we were not. Sarah Nella and I spoke to my children on Friday. It's just like I said last night—if they didn't pay back every penny they'd stolen by the end of the year we would notify the authorities, even if it caused a scandal."

Toby said, "Would that have given them a motivation to kill Jerome? With the inheritance—"

"There is no inheritance. Zero. They stole it all."

That took Toby aback. Not Marie.

"But it could *still* give them a motivation to kill Jerome," she said. "If the old man was out of the picture, Richard and Alyssa could take over the show and pull in a way larger cut of the take. It would have made it a hell of a lot easier to pay back the debt they owed y'all."

"That's a stretch. Sarah Nella was on the verge of cutting them all out and bringing in outside talent."

A memory flashed through Toby's head. "Yesterday morning in the sunroom, right before we saw Jerome's body through the skylights, Sarah Nella tried to pull me aside. She looked scared of something, said she needed to talk in private. It sounded urgent, but she never got the chance to say what it was about. Do you have any idea?"

"Sarah Nella? Urgent? No. Except—" A little light dawned on Ruth's face. "My sister *did* say something, now that you mention it. But it didn't have anything to do with you. Yesterday, as we were getting the party together, she said something had occurred to her when she woke up."

Toby held his breath. "Did she say what it was?"

"No. Just that it was about an old friend she'd forgotten."

Marie wasn't done with their first line of questioning. "You still think Richard killed him, don't you? Even if the inheritance was gone and Jerome was his meal ticket, the second you found out the old man was dead, you started covering for your boy anyway."

"I did clean Daddy's body, yes."

"But why?"

"Like I said—I thought it couldn't hurt to . . . to keep our options open. I just hoped that if there wasn't enough evidence, it would all just go away, you know? That's how it usually works in this family. But I had nothing to do with the knife or the key they found in Toby's room last night. I had no idea that was coming. Truly."

Marie looked at her phone. "We should get moving. There's no telling where Luca's gotten to by now."

She was right. Jerome's pills were starting to kick in, reducing the agony in Toby's knee to a distant, pulsing ache. He couldn't run, but he could move again.

And yet he realized, after what he'd seen in his suite last night—what he'd heard come out of Sarah Nella's mouth—that one last, obvious question needed to be answered.

"Jerome was a traveling preacher for a long time, wasn't he?"

Ruth seemed surprised by this turn in the conversation. "Yes. For years. It's a terrible life."

"And what about his brother, Cleave? Did he stay home while Jerome was on the road?"

"Of course not. They toured together. Until Cleave drowned, that is—it happened when they'd come home from a long tour to recharge."

"So they were some kind of double act? Two prophetic brothers from Nowhere, Texas?"

"Hardly. From what I've heard, it was Cleave's show back then. Jerome just handled all the smaller details." Ruth turned to stare out a black window.

"Jerome handled the small details. But not the actual prophecy."

"Daddy was . . . a quick learner."

"Just not a prophet."

"He had his moments, truly. And the Lord did give Daddy the gift of reading people. Jerome knew what they wanted to hear. Isn't that a blessing, of a sort?"

Marie rolled her eyes. "I could have told you that for free."

"That Jerome was running a scam?" Toby said.

"Of course he was. What kind of prophet doesn't see his own murder coming?"

Toby had heard that question yesterday. He didn't linger on it. To Ruth he said, "Everything changed at the beginning of this year, didn't it? After he recovered from his fall and came back onto the show and turned it into the courts of Judah?"

"He wasn't the same man after his fall, no. I think it broke something in him, Toby. Or maybe it let something loose."

ON THEIR WAY OUT of the suite, Ruth asked if they'd seen any sign of Hugo. "He was still sleeping when I left to look for your boy an hour ago."

"He was just downstairs a minute ago, dragging Richard off somewhere," Marie said.

"To where?"

Marie only shrugged. Toby let the door fall closed behind them and called the elevator. He noticed as he crossed the hardwood landing outside the suite that Hugo had been telling the truth about something last night: the boards of the landing creaked loudly enough to wake a man from a light sleep, which was exactly what they would have done if anyone had used the stairs or elevator late on Friday night.

Downstairs, Toby and Marie made their way across the second floor in silence, Toby's mind churning faster than his feet could move. He stopped at the juncture to the east wing and leaned on his cane to catch his breath. He studied Marie, marveling again at the way this shy, quiet girl, so reserved and nervous the first two days he'd known her, seemed to have shrugged off an old skin in the night. She was taller now, tougher, altogether more capable.

Except her fingers still twitched around the straps of her backpack. Her teeth wouldn't stop chewing at the corner of her lip.

"Why are you helping me like this, Marie?"

"Because you need it. You *both* need it."

Toby didn't entirely buy this. Marie and her brother may have both had airtight alibis thanks to the camera in their hallway, but that didn't mean the girl didn't have another agenda at work here.

"Richard won't appreciate it," Toby said. "He seems like a vindictive man."

"Screw this family. Screw Richard. The roads should be clear any minute. Jules and I are getting the hell out of here." She bit a nail. "Soon as we find him, of course."

Something obvious finally occurred to Toby. "Not to be rude, but all the cars in the stables are luxury models. They seem a little out of y'all's price range. Is there any chance Julian might have left in your car on Saturday while we were all distracted by Jerome's body, but before the roads totally flooded? Is it possible he's been gone all this time?"

"Our old Dodge died just about the minute we got here. We don't have another ride. Neither of us have left this estate for months."

Toby nodded, considered this, came to a decision. "I think I can help with that."

"Once we have your son, of course."

"And your brother."

They started down the long hall to the Ezekiel Suite. "Jules was getting edgy these last few weeks," Marie said. "Scared. He wasn't sleeping, barely eating, kept saying something bad was coming to this family. On Friday I'd swear he'd been crying."

"Crying?"

"You heard me. Old Mister Jerome always wanted coffee and croissants brought up to his study around eleven thirty every morning. Julian's always the one who took it up to him. On Friday, maybe twenty minutes after he went up with the day's coffee, I found Jules standing in a little room off the main hall, wiping his nose and staring at the wall. He looked like he'd been bawling."

Toby considered this. "Matthias said the same thing—he saw Julian leaving Jerome's study when the kid was on his way in to burn the old man's things. He said your brother had tears in his eyes."

"To burn what?"

"I'll tell you later. Did Julian say why he was crying? Had Jerome said something to him when he brought that coffee?"

"You clearly didn't know Jules. He never says a word about what's bothering him. It's probably why therapy never worked." Marie let out a sigh. "My brother is good at pretending nothing's ever wrong. The second

I found him, he straightened himself up and blew his nose and stepped out into the foyer just in time to greet you and your wife and kid."

Toby chewed his cheek. Down the hall, he caught a flash of a woman in a sundress and cheap pumps as she rounded a corner, fine and flickery as a moth's wing, and vanished before his eyes. In the months after his sister's death, back before he finished work on a new wing of the marble labyrinth, Toby had seen his sister everywhere, just like this, stepping around corners and vanishing up stairs and slipping into cars at the edge of his vision. Without the help of Alyssa's anxiety pills, who knew what else Toby would see as the doors of his palace kept coming open?

"Whatever made Julian cry, it happened at the same time Jerome gave him those notes for you and Alyssa," Marie said.

Toby pulled himself back to the hall with a shudder. "I forgot all about those."

"You think they're connected? Those notes and Julian's tears?"

Toby thought long and hard before he answered her. He thought of the curious words Jerome had added to the bottom of Alyssa's note: *Good luck.*

What kind of prophet doesn't see his own murder coming?

"I have no idea," Toby said truthfully, and found himself walking faster.

———————

All the way down the long hall, Toby waited for the sconce near his door to go on the fritz again, for a tall man in a black suit to appear at the edge of its flickering light, but nothing happened: no cool draft, no rush of whispers. He thought of those strange icy sensations on the back of his neck, the breezes that brushed his cheek as quick and cool as mercury and left a faint damp on his clothes.

Toby thought of Luca saying, *I think his hands are always wet.* Thought of Ruth saying, *He slipped into the north creek.*

When they reached his suite, Toby ignored the overturned furniture, the violent splashes of paint Sarah Nella had flung from the ceiling to the floor last night. He headed straight for Luca's bedroom and found it empty. No surprise.

As he gathered up a change of clothes for his son—wherever they went after this, the boy would need clean underwear—Toby noticed that Luca's pink sparkle socks, the ones festooned in dozens of tiny reflective stars, were indeed missing. He was right: the boy must have worn them to sleep last night in Ruth and Hugo's bedroom.

"You know what they'll do to your boy, don't you?" Marie said matter-of-factly, stuffing Luca's clothes into her backpack. "If they find him first and get you out of the picture?"

"If they don't have him already."

Toby sat on the edge of Luca's bed to give his knee a break. He toed at one of the pink sparkly stars that had shed from his son's socks Friday night. He felt a horrible powerlessness wash over him, a sense of absolute failure as a parent. Wherever Luca was, was he hungry, was he scared, did he need to pee? Who would help him now?

"At least Luca's too valuable to risk him coming to any harm," Marie said. "Nothing that would kill him, I mean. They'll still send him to that camp of theirs. Same as they sent my brother."

Toby nodded. Richard had mentioned the place plenty this weekend. "Camp Cleave. To 'toughen him up a little.' Julian went there?"

Marie chewed her cheek. "Fifteen years ago, when Jules was seventeen, our dad tried to get us a share of the family's money. Dad said it was only fair, seeing as we were Wrights just as much as the rest of them, even if Sarah Nella hadn't been married when Dad came along. Apparently, the family agreed to bring Jules into the ministry, on the condition he spend two weeks at Camp Cleave first."

"Why would they do that?"

"Isn't it obvious? The family already knew that Julian batted for the same team."

"They knew he was gay?"

"Lord knows how they figured it out. Maybe they were monitoring our internet. I wouldn't put it past them. Sarah Nella told our dad the same sort of thing Richard told you about Luca—that Julian needed a couple weeks at their wilderness camp to get a little hair on his chest before they could bring him into the operation. She made it sound very pure and Christlike. And Dad bought it. He never was very smart."

Briskly, Toby rose to gather knickknacks from Luca's nightstand. "What happened out there?"

"I've wondered that ever since. My brother left for the woods and two weeks later it was like a different man came back wearing his clothes. He was never the same again. I think that's when he first got hooked on pills, right there at the camp. And of course they never brought him into the ministry afterward, even though he stayed at the camp the full two weeks. I guess the folks at home wouldn't know what to do if a Blacker pair of Wrights ever turned up on the broadcast. Maybe the family decided the camp hadn't straightened Jules out enough, or maybe they hadn't thought we'd go through with the deal in the first place. Either way, Dad had been an idiot to ever trust Sarah Nella. And Julian's never been the same since." Marie stared Toby in the eye. "You can't let them do the same to your boy. Whatever it takes, you can't let him turn out like Jules."

"I have no intention to."

Toby's trembling fingers knocked an origami rose to the floor. Marie studied the flower as she bent down and passed it back to him. Toby tucked the rose in his pocket.

"I just need one more thing from this suite," he said.

Marie watched from the doorway as Toby ducked into the bedroom he'd shared with Alyssa and rooted through his wife's nightstand. It didn't take him long to find what he was looking for.

And then he realized they weren't alone. A guttural retch came from the other side of the bathroom door, a splash of water, a moan.

A woman was puking up her guts in there. It wasn't hard to guess who.

MARIE EVAPORATED BEFORE ALYSSA opened the bathroom door. Toby's wife probably wouldn't have noticed her anyway: Alyssa seemed too surprised to see Toby to pay attention to anything else. She leaned against the wall, a wet towel pressed to her forehead, and studied Toby a long time before a wave of nausea washed over her and she fell into one of the room's tufted chairs with another moan.

"I can't tell if I've had the same migraine for four days or if a new one just keeps coming over to party," Alyssa said by way of greeting.

"Where's Luca?"

"Upstairs. With Mom."

"No he isn't. She hasn't seen him since she went to bed last night. He left their room. He's somewhere in this house."

Alyssa laid back her head, closed her eyes. "Oh, Jesus. You think that's my fault too, don't you?"

"Luca's your meal ticket. Your way out of jail, too, now that your mom knows about all the money you and your siblings stole."

"Mom would never go to the police about that."

"That still leaves Sarah Nella. What if she recovers?"

"She won't. She died last night, under Kassandra's care."

A long, long silence stretched. Toby propped his shoulder against the wall. "Sarah Nella's dead?"

"Cardiac failure. Not a surprise. I have to go write out the death certificate."

"That's . . . Jesus. People are dropping like flies."

"It's been a stressful weekend."

"But things are looking better for you and your brother by the minute. With Sarah Nella gone, that's one less person who knows about the embezzlement."

"What are you saying? I stuck a pillow over Sarah Nella's face in the dark of night?"

"It certainly raises a good question," Toby said. "What *did* you do last night after I fell down the stairs?"

"You're still playing detective?"

"No. I'm being a father. I'm looking for my son."

"I had to tranquilize old Corah with a few Ambien from Sarah Nella's stash—Corah was falling to pieces after Sarah Nella's little performance in our sitting room. I was worried I might have overdone it, so I stayed by Corah's bed."

"Until when?"

"I don't know, Toby—two, three o'clock? Then I came back here to get some sleep."

"Did you take the stairs?" Toby's eyes narrowed. "Or the service elevator across the hall? The one you'd swear in court you saw me use on Friday night to go kill the old man."

Alyssa lowered the rag from her brow to study him. It revealed a long stroke of red paint clinging to her forehead. "You're awfully angry, Toby. You've been angry all weekend."

"Can you fucking blame me? Was it your idea to put the key to the roof in my pocket last night?"

"Nothing's ever my idea, Toby."

"What about going to the church yesterday to steal my putter?"

"That was Richard. It was *all* Richard. After you and Luca went to the church, Kassandra went out to the stables and started screaming at him."

"About what?"

"I have no idea. Truly—Richard never told me. He never tells me anything. But he changed after she left. He got . . . colder. Angrier." With what seemed a sincere fear, Alyssa said, "Scarier. He seemed kind of like you right now, come to think of it."

Toby remembered that wild gleam in Richard's eye he'd seen yesterday upon his return from the church, the violent energy that had thrummed through Richard once he'd gathered the family in this suite.

And yet still Alyssa had the gall to add, "Why are you so certain my brother killed Jerome?"

"You guys planted a knife in my closet, Alyssa. Where the hell would Richard have gotten one of those if he hadn't held on to it after the murder?"

"What if someone was trying to frame *him*? Just like someone was trying to stick *me*, planting the receipt for that wire transfer in my purse. Please, be honest with me now—did you do that?"

Toby laughed. He said truthfully, "No, Alyssa. I never put anything in your purse."

"Truly?"

"Alyssa, I haven't lied about a thing all weekend. Why would I risk it? I was recording half of my conversations yesterday."

"It would have been clever of you. That wire transfer was just what you would have needed to get me in trouble with the law."

"I thought it looked shady."

"Oh, you have no idea." Alyssa seemed almost to be gloating. "It was payment for blackmail. *Ginger's* the one who started embezzling the money in the first place. I think she's been doing it ever since her kid died last year, don't ask me why. Richard and I found out about it a couple months back. We made her pay for our silence. Only fair, right?"

Toby shook his head. Alyssa had a point: if the police had found that wire transfer in her purse and followed a few very obvious threads, they would have caught her tangled up in a very obvious white-collar crime.

And then, the moment she was indicted, Toby could have voided their prenup and taken a fat payout that could have probably supported him the rest of his life.

So much for that.

Toby pressed on. "Maybe the simplest answer is the correct one: Richard killed the old man, and you helped him cover it up because you thought you could take over the business and make all your troubles go away. Push out Sarah Nella, maybe even Ginger, start totally fresh."

Alyssa didn't answer him. Not quite. She watched Toby with a naked appraisal, or the scrutiny of someone for whom the scales had finally fallen from their eyes. She said, "Actually, Toby, I *don't* think you've been honest with me all weekend. I don't think you've been honest with me *ever.* You weren't just pretending to love me to get your kid an education. I think all this time, maybe from the minute we met, you've been angry. Angrier than you want me to know."

"What's that matter?"

"Maybe it was all those episodes of the show your uncle made you watch as a kid—people have hated us for less."

"Who says I hate you?"

"Oh, Toby. I think you've hated this family since before we ever met."

Toby found Marie in the suite's sitting room, studying a crinkled square of paper someone had left on the coffee table. It was the page that Luca had found fallen behind the desk of Jerome's study yesterday afternoon. The page on which Jerome had written a few last words shortly before his death.

The three lines were blurred with damp—the page had spent a very wet afternoon in Toby's pocket yesterday, after all—but they were still plenty legible.

> Wet roses bloom on white sugar
> From the muted mouth, he speaks
> The wailing boy slips beneath green waves

"You saw when he wrote this, right?" Marie said.

"A little before midnight on Friday. Yes."

"Weird how he'd know about your wife's cake."

"What do you mean?"

"The 'wet roses' in 'white sugar.' That almost sounds like the blood that dropped onto the cake's icing Saturday morning." Marie chewed a nail. "And Sarah Nella's mouth had definitely been muted by the stroke."

"I thought you didn't believe any of this prophecy stuff?"

They both stared at the page's last line.

"I don't. At least—I hope I don't."

A cool draft blew over their shoulders. In the draft, Toby heard an unmistakable rush of whispered sound.

ceapetmuhvingtuhbeyes

Keep it moving, Tobias.

"Did you just hear something?" Marie said.

Toby dug his fingers into his pocket and removed what he'd gone into the bedroom to retrieve in the first place: the key fob for Alyssa's S-class. "I got our ride figured out. I need your help finding someone."

MARIE LED TOBY STRAIGHT across the hall from the Ezekiel Suite and pushed open a panel of brocaded wall that didn't even look like a door. The wall swung inward, revealing a drab closet large enough to contain shelves of fresh linens, paint thinner, nails and hammers, bleach. (Quite a lot of paint thinner, in fact: Toby supposed the family must have stocked up on acetone when the red warnings had started appearing everywhere with the new year.) Parked in front of the shelves was one of the silver service trolleys Marie and her brother had spent all weekend pushing around.

In the back of the closet, tucked behind a rusted metal grate, was a small compartment just wide enough to carry two people.

"Ah, yes," Toby said. "The infamous service elevator."

It carried them upward without a sound.

Ramorah's library was tucked away in a quiet corner of the third floor's east wing. It was small, practically an afterthought, its walls fitted with built-in shelves that held few books. It reminded Toby, in a sad way, of the library at Silver Oaks, the nursing facility in Studio City where he'd once worked. Even the ancient Sidney Sheldon paperbacks were the same.

Kassandra, Richard's elegant wife, sat folded up on a drab recliner, clad in yet another of her bright floral sundresses, staring sightlessly at an Agatha Christie. A nerve pulsed, ceaselessly, along the line of her perfect jaw. Her head snapped up when they stepped inside.

"We won't stay long," Toby said, trying to calm her. "Unless you can tell us where to find Luca and Julian."

Out in the hall, they heard a crash of something, a muted curse. Kassandra curled away from the sound. "That was . . . that was Richard's voice."

"I'll go keep watch," Marie murmured, and slipped out the door.

They waited. Silence filled the third floor again.

Finally, Kassandra's lips started to move, though it was a long time before she could form a word. "Marie led you here, didn't she? She must have known I love this little library. She knows so much about us."

Toby said nothing.

"Do you like novels?"

"No," Toby said.

"Why not?"

Toby didn't have time for this. "Because they make me feel like God, poking around inside someone's head."

Kassandra gave him a dark grin. "You're definitely in the wrong family, then."

"What makes you say that?"

"If there's one thing rich people like to do, it's to feel like God."

When she drifted off, Toby dropped into the room's sole other chair. "I don't have a lot of time here. You don't have any idea where they are, do you? Julian or Luca?"

"No. I haven't seen your son since Ruth took him to her room last night. I assume he's not there anymore?"

Toby shook his head. "And Julian?"

He was surprised at the sourness in Kassandra's face when he said Julian's name. "He's got his own agenda somewhere, I'm sure. If you're lucky, he's looking out for your son."

"You don't sound too keen on him."

She toyed with the book in her lap, brushed a lash, said nothing.

Toby lowered his voice. "What about yesterday in the stables?"

"What about it?"

"Alyssa says you went out there to scream at your husband not long after Luca and I left for the church. Why?"

"What's it matter, Toby? You heard Sarah Nella as well as I did last night. It's over. We're fucked."

"*I'm* not fucked. My son isn't fucked. But he's gone and I think your husband might have something to do with it."

"What makes you say that?"

"Because Richard's had his finger in every pie this weekend. So please, tell me—why were you so angry at him yesterday?" When she still wouldn't answer, Toby said, "Did it have anything to do with the way Luca and I found you crying in Sarah Nella's suite?"

Still Kassandra evaded him. "Did you hear that Sarah Nella died under my watch last night?"

"Alyssa mentioned it."

A sudden bitterness came over Kassandra. "It's no surprise—Sarah Nella's performance in y'all's suite put a serious strain on her heart. She was wheezing and hitching something terrible from the minute they laid her back down. But maybe if Richard hadn't wanted to talk to me so damned much, I'd have been there to see the poor woman slipping under. I could have done something."

"I'm confused. Was this last night?"

Kassandra nodded. "Richard came and found me at Sarah Nella's bedside, said he needed to apologize. He said that all the stuff I told him after dinner, after the way he treated your son—he said I was right. He said he's a horrible man. He admitted to some . . . some terrible things."

"What kind of things?"

"Not murder, if that's what you're thinking. Affairs. As if I hadn't guessed." She tossed her head. "I just assumed all of them had been with women."

Toby titled his head. "Richard sleeps with men?"

"He sleeps with anything breathing, by the sound of it."

"That's . . . quite a confession."

"Explains why he hates your boy so bad, doesn't it? The worst bigots are the ones who want a piece for themselves, ain't they?"

Toby tried to get back to the matter at hand. "What time last night did he come to tell you this?"

"It was more like this morning. One o'clock, maybe one thirty. He talked my ear off for an hour, and by the time I finally got back to Sarah Nella's room, she'd passed."

"Got back?"

"Richard dragged me all the way to our suite for that lovely conversation. I don't know why we couldn't have talked in Sarah Nella's sitting room. I don't know why he even told me in the first place."

Toby leaned forward. "Maybe he went to your room because he was scared you'd cause a scene. Like when you went to scream at him in the stables."

"You're not going to let that go, are you?"

"Not as long as you keep avoiding it."

Kassandra rose to place her book carefully back on its shelf, to study the black sky through the room's one narrow window, to adjust her hair in the dark glass. She raised her arm to show Toby a spot of red paint on the back of her hand.

"Have you ever felt so guilty you don't think you'll ever get it off your skin?" Kassandra gave the paint a scratch. It didn't budge. "Have you ever wondered if even Jesus has a limit on how much he can forgive?"

Toby hesitated, fingers tight around the rubber head of the cane. A door trembled in the bowels of the labyrinth. He couldn't recall when or where or why, but he was certain that someone else had asked him that same question this weekend, almost verbatim. "I stopped asking Jesus for help a long time ago."

For a moment Toby feared he'd lost her. Kassandra laid a palm over the spot of paint on the back of her hand, closed her eyes.

But when she lifted those long lashes, she didn't look frightened any longer. She looked furious.

"I know Hugo keeps saying no one from the lower floors could have killed Jerome, but . . . that knife, that disgusting knife that turned up in your closet last night? I found it yesterday—found it in that same grubby pillowcase—hiding behind the suitcase in *Richard's* closet."

"Why were you going through your husband's closet?"

"Why else? I was afraid he killed Jerome."

Toby studied Kassandra. "Because of the inheritance?"

"That. And the fact he didn't have an alibi. Yesterday after the body turned up and everyone left me with Sarah Nella, I went downstairs to our room and started going through his closet and found the knife. It was like all my suspicions came true at once, and I didn't have a clue what to do about it."

Toby sat very still.

"You and Luca found me crying in Sarah Nella's suite not long after. When y'all left for the church, I made up my mind. I went out to the stables and confronted Richard. You'd think I had a death wish, the way I talked to that man. But he was cool and quiet and just said, 'Thank you for letting me know.'" Kassandra studied Toby. A hard breeze shook the library's black window. "I think it was a sin, you know. A sin for me to do something stupid when I knew better. A sin against the God who gave you a smarter mind. Because of course Richard found Alyssa and the pair of them went off to the church to steal your putter and got busy setting things up here at the house. They're nothing but vipers, all of them. I should have left that blade right where I found it. Then the *police* would have found it. They'd have searched the whole house for evidence the minute they got here and found that knife right where the dumb bastard had left it."

5:8

THE HALL WAS EMPTY when Toby emerged from the library, and he was overwhelmed by the sudden fear that Marie had abandoned him. He was surprised at the depth of his relief when she poked her head around the corner and motioned him over. He hadn't realized, until that moment, just how badly he wanted an ally in all this.

Even if he couldn't shake the feeling there was still something Marie wasn't telling him.

"I heard a commotion by the main stairs and went to check it out," she whispered. "It was Richard and Hugo. They were hauling something down the hall. Something big."

"Could you see what it was?"

"No. But they're heading to the west wing."

Considering this, Toby recalled the long pinewood coffin he'd seen Richard constructing in the stables yesterday afternoon. *When Jesus was up there on the cross, do you think he had time to admire the woodwork?* "Why are we whispering?"

"Because they might come back."

"Then let's get moving."

————————————

Toby filled Marie in on everything Kassandra had told him. When he got to the part about the knife Kassandra had found in Richard's closet, Marie let out a sigh. "I was worried about that."

"About what?"

"You asked me for my help yesterday afternoon, down in the foyer. You asked me to unlock the door of Richard's suite."

Toby and his cane thumped along. "Yes. I did."

"We would have found that knife. We would have found that knife in Richard's closet and none of this would have happened."

"I wouldn't be so sure about that."

"You think Kassandra's lying?"

"No. I'm just not sure it would have made a difference."

Marie chewed on this a moment. "But why was Kassandra going through her man's closet in the first place?"

"I asked her the same question. She was worried that Richard might have killed Jerome for all the obvious reasons."

"She's not dumb."

"Yes and no. After she made a scene with Richard in the stables, screaming at him about the knife, she just let the matter drop. Of course the knife wound up in my closet after that. It must have gotten all the wheels turning." Toby stopped to massage his knee. "But that's not all she had to say. At some point last night, after all the chaos in my suite, Richard confessed to Kassandra that he'd been unfaithful for years."

Marie arched an eyebrow. "Who with? Some woman over in Hebron?"

Toby's cane squelched on a wet patch of carpet. All around them, dark blotches of damp had spread across the damask wallpaper. A memory that Toby had been searching for since Friday night finally returned to him. "You and your brother moved here in April, right?"

"Yes." Marie's voice was unmistakably guarded.

"So Richard and Kassandra were already living here when you guys arrived."

"Of course. The whole family turned up after Jerome's fall last October. Like vultures, Julian said."

The memory he'd just reclaimed was a brief one: Friday night at dinner, Julian had rested a hand on Richard's shoulder as he refilled the man's glass.

Richard had tensed at Julian's touch.

He'd tensed, but he hadn't pulled away.

Toby thought of the intense look Richard had turned on him, Toby, every time Richard thought Toby's attention was elsewhere.

Maybe it wasn't fear or curiosity Toby saw there, but that terrible admixture of the two.

Maybe what Toby had seen in Richard's gaze all this time was desire.

"He was sleeping with someone in town," Toby said. "Sure."

The silence that leaked from Sarah Nella's suite was thicker than mere quiet. Even in the hall outside, Toby could smell urine and fresh paint and the same sickly-sweet scent of rotting meat that he'd noticed yesterday in Jerome's room. When he nudged open Sarah Nella's door, he discovered the final red warning that would ever bleed on the walls of Ramorah:

THE TIME FOR MERCY HAS PASSED

THE MARK OF HIS WRATH IS ON THIS HOUSE

AND I WILL REJOICE AS YOU SCREAM

"I saw that last night," Marie said. "I helped Hugo carry Sarah Nella down here after Richard socked her in your suite. The paint was still damp when we got here. I figured she must have painted it right before she left to start her little show."

Toby thought of what Luca had told him yesterday evening on their way upstairs from the kitchen. *You know Matthias isn't the person painting all the mean things around the house. Otherwise why would Miss Sarah Nella have dry paint all over her red robe?*

Two terrible questions occurred to Toby, almost at once:

What else had Luca figured out about this family?

And who else had known that he'd known it?

"A hell of a thing," Marie continued, staring at the red message on Sarah Nella's wall. "All this time, I'd half thought it must have been old Corah painting all that shit around here. I didn't think there could be *two* nut cases in one house."

Toby followed Marie into Sarah Nella's bedroom. It was empty but for the woman herself: Sarah Nella lay very still on her broad bed, her face covered with a red silk sheet. When Toby raised the sheet, he saw that, unlike Jerome, no one had bothered to bathe her. Sarah Nella was still naked and coated with crimson paint, her hair matted and her eyes closed and a sly grin frozen on her mouth.

Something about her expression made Toby flick the sheet back in a hurry. That grin was familiar.

Toby noticed the way Marie was toeing at a pile of throw pillows. "Are you all right?"

"Why wouldn't I be all right?"

Because this is your grandmother lying here, Toby wanted to say, but he knew he was barking up an empty tree. Instead he said, "I'm not sure Sarah Nella was crazy."

"You don't cover your house in Old Testament prophecies if you're playing with a full deck of cards."

"Probably not. But what if she wasn't the one painting them?"

"We saw her literally red-handed last night, Toby."

"Her body was there. But maybe not her mind."

Toby described what Kassandra had told him yesterday about the medications spread across Sarah Nella's bedside table, the way they could cause *altered mood, vivid dreams, memory loss, night terrors, increased susceptibility to suggestion, and other marked psychological events.*

"Increased susceptibility to suggestion." Even as he said it, Toby imagined a pair of shadowy lips whispering into Sarah Nella's ear as she lay down for an afternoon nap. He imagined the woman awakening in her shower an hour later, spattered with paint and with no memory of how it got there.

He recalled the way Luca had frantically whispered in his ear when Sarah Nella had arrived in their sitting room last night. *That's not her. It's him.*

Could Luca's "Mister Suit" really be the person responsible for the warnings painted around the house? Worse, could Mister Suit have something to do with the boy's disappearance? Or had Toby grown so desperate for an explanation he would grab any straw he could find?

Marie looked thoroughly unimpressed. "I highly doubt Sarah Nella had no idea she was behind all the vandalism. Look at this."

Marie flung back the skirt of Sarah Nella's bed, waving for Toby to look. Crouching down as far as his bad knee would allow him, he found rows and rows of silver cans lined up beneath the bed. Each bore a label marking them as SHADE 271: URGENT CRIMSON.

"Sarah Nella always kept the door to this suite locked—eventually I stopped asking if she wanted me to clean in here. You look at this and it's pretty obvious why. She must have ordered all this paint from God knows where, made sure it arrived when no one was looking, then hidden it away. Or are you saying she did all that in her sleep?"

"Not exactly. But it's also hard to picture Sarah Nella calling Corah a cunt."

"So who did? Some ghost took possession of her when she was drugged and asleep? Maybe an angel of justice sent from God himself?"

"Why can't it be both?" Toby murmured.

Marie only rolled her eyes.

"We may never know exactly what was going on there," Toby continued. "Maybe Sarah Nella wasn't herself when she painted the messages, or maybe she'd just had a gutful of this family and wanted to scare them. But the fact remains, Sarah Nella was one of the only people who could have gotten that episode of *The Prophecy Hour* playing in the west wing yesterday while the rest of us were at lunch. Unless it was Julian."

"He avoids that show like the plague, Mister Fishhook Scar. I bet you twenty bucks Julian had no idea about that prophecy on last week's show." Marie shook her head. "I still don't understand how Sarah Nella could have dragged a can of paint and a DVD player down two flights of stairs. The woman could barely breathe after her stroke yesterday morning."

"Maybe she had some help."

"From Kassandra?"

No—Sarah Nella must have gone downstairs when Kassandra, her erstwhile nurse, had left her side yesterday to go search Richard's closet. When Kassandra returned to this room, she'd found Sarah Nella nearly choking to death in the shower. No doubt Sarah Nella had been washing off the red paint she'd spread across the motel room on the first floor.

GOD'S JUDGMENT ON THIS FAMILY HAS BEGUN.

"Not Kassandra. You saw the way Sarah Nella was moving in my suite last night. For a minute there it was like she'd never had a stroke at all."

"Maybe it was adrenaline."

Listen—for the God—of Israel—speaks.

"Or maybe she had some other kind of help."

When Toby turned to go, he noticed the way the suite's main door, the one that led into the hall, was standing open now, even though he was certain he'd closed it on his way inside. He remembered what Kassandra had said yesterday afternoon about forgetting to lock that same door when he and Luca had discovered her weeping by Sarah Nella's bedside.

There must have been something wrong with the door's latch: if someone didn't lock it, the door opened of its own accord.

And then Toby's eye caught a glint of pink at his feet.

He eased down into a squat, ignoring the screams of pain from his knee. He held his breath, plucked up a little piece of metallic plastic from the bedroom's carpet, held it to the light.

It was a star. A pink sparkly star.

"Luca," Toby said. "Luca was here last night."

5:9

TOBY WANTED TO pace, but his leg was screaming for a break. He sat on the suite's couch, beneath Ramorah's final red warning, and thought out loud. "Did you notice that star in the carpet when you were bringing Sarah Nella to bed last night?"

"No. But I wasn't exactly looking for it."

"What time did you and Hugo bring her down here? Around ten?"

"Give or take. Around the same time Ruth was getting Luca ready for bed. Did Luca wear those socks on Friday night, too? Could he have come in here then?"

"He wouldn't have left our suite on Friday. He's never in his life slept more than twenty feet away from me. At least not of his own volition." Toby strummed his fingers on the couch's arm. "Besides, when we came to this room yesterday, Luca looked around like it was his first time seeing it. There's this curiosity in kids the first time they visit a place, you know? You learn to spot it."

Marie studied her phone. She tapped out a message. "All right, so let's say Ruth is telling the truth and Luca left her suite of his own accord last night—why would he come *here*?"

"Maybe he got distracted by something. Ruth and Hugo sleep right near the stairs. Maybe as Luca left their suite he saw someone coming up to this floor and followed them."

"Or maybe he just came to make sure Sarah Nella was all right. That little star may not mean much, Toby. According to Kassandra, Sarah Nella was by herself from almost one to two in the morning. Luca could have come in, found her sleeping, and left again."

Toby said nothing, only watched as Marie lifted her phone to her ear and lowered it with a furious little jerk. She tapped out another message. Desperation tightened the skin around her eyes.

"I *still* can't get hold of Julian," she said, more to herself than him. "His phone isn't even ringing anymore."

Toby spoke almost without thinking. "I remember that feeling. My sister used to put me through the same kind of hell."

Marie chewed a nail. Not quite meeting his eye, she said, "Did your sister ever get better?"

Toby felt a dangerous shudder ripple through his mind. Once again he saw his sister here in Ramorah in a sundress and pumps, this time standing in the corner of Sarah Nella's suite, staring into a cabinet with the benign smile he only ever saw on her when she was really, truly happy. That smile was so rare he always forgot what it looked like between one appearance and the next.

Only the sister Toby saw now wasn't the same sister he'd seen earlier in Ruth's suite. The Willow he'd seen there had been a much younger woman, the Willow who Toby remembered from his teens, back when they still lived in Texas. The Willow that Toby had seen in Ruth's suite was the Willow who still stood a chance.

The Willow that he saw here, now, in Sarah Nella's suite, was the Willow who Toby had discovered in his kitchen in LA at the start of this year, ten months ago, on the worst day of his life.

Willow had been missing for months. One of her disappearing acts, another long one, one that finally ended when Toby and Luca had come home from a trip to the grocery store and discovered her standing in their apartment's tiny kitchen. They'd found Willow wearing a new sundress and new pumps, scrambling eggs just like she had on that distant afternoon in Texas. They'd found Willow looking happier and healthier than Toby had seen her in ages.

As Toby set down the day's mail and Luca wrapped his mother in a hug, she smiled to Toby over the boy's head. *I did it*, she mouthed silently.

"Did what?"

"Rehab."

A blink, and Willow was gone, though Toby doubted she would stay away for long. Everything was coming back to him now. All the joy and horror of that golden afternoon—the worst day of his life—had begun to leak from beneath the door at the heart of the marble labyrinth. The bad door. The worst door.

"She's dead, isn't she?" Marie said in a low voice. "Your sister."

"Yes."

"An overdose?"

He nodded. Even now, ten months later, Toby could barely bring himself to admit it.

"Does it . . ." Marie trailed off, tried again. "Does this ever get any easier? Every time Jules disappears like this, I think—I think this is it. This is the time he doesn't come back. And then when he does turn up . . ."

"It's almost a disappointment."

"I've spent my whole life worried about that man. I sometimes wonder how I haven't killed him."

Toby looked away. The leaking door at the heart of the labyrinth—the bad door, the worst door—gave a violent shake against its lock.

Marie bit off a sliver of nail. "Did you ever figure out what started it for her?"

"What do you mean?"

"Every addict has some trauma they keep circling around. At least that's what Dad said. What was your sister's?"

"If you'd known my uncle Ezra, you wouldn't have to ask."

"Did he . . . touch her?"

Toby studied his hands. After a long moment he said, "What's Julian's trauma? That fucking camp they sent him to?"

"What else?"

Marie put her phone down on the table, so gently Toby wondered if she was afraid she might break it. "Do you think it could be connected, Luca and Julian both going missing? They're both . . . sensitive, right?"

"You mean light in the loafers? Queer? You think some homophobic psychopath is out to purge the house of evil?"

"It sounds crazy when you say it like that," Marie said. "I just keep wondering about that conversation Jules had with Jerome right before you and Alyssa showed up. Do you think . . . do you think there's a chance

Julian might be missing because he knew too much? That he might have said something to the old man that afternoon that he shouldn't have? Or the other way around: the old man told *him* something that someone else wanted to keep secret?"

"It's certainly possible. But how does it connect to Luca? The boy's only been here for two days, and he's spent almost all of it with either me or you. That's not time to learn something *we* don't know, is it?"

"Unless we *do* know it. Unless it's just staring us straight in the face."

Toby tapped his cane on the carpet in a steady *thump-thump-thump.* "I want to know why Luca left Ruth and Hugo's room in the middle of the night. Even if he'd wanted to find me, Luca's still young. He'd be afraid to wander around a huge house at night all on his own."

Marie, however, wasn't listening to him. She was mouthing something to herself, her mind suddenly miles away. *Straight in the face*, her lips said. *Staring us straight in—*

She sprang to her feet. "Let me see the stuff in your pockets."

Toby complied, puzzled. He withdrew the key fob to Alyssa's Mercedes, the crumpled page he'd found behind Jerome's desk yesterday (*The wailing boy slips beneath green waves*), and the blue rosebud Luca had folded out of the discarded wrapping paper he'd discovered at the Cracker Barrel in Hebron.

Marie waved it all away. "No, no. The other flower."

Even more puzzled, Toby withdrew the larger white rose Luca had produced at dinner on Friday night, the one that had made every Wright at the table blanch. The flower had been nearly crushed flat by his pocket. It toppled over the moment Toby set it on the table.

Marie pointed. "There. I saw it earlier when you dropped it on the floor. I thought I was imagining things."

Following her finger, Toby saw two tiny black marks peeking from the fold on the underside of one of the white rose's petals. Peering closer, he realized the black marks were letters: *Ma.*

"I caught your boy going through our trash yesterday," she said.

"He goes through *everyone's* trash," Toby said, his voice barely above a whisper.

Raccoons eat trash, Tobias. I transform it.

Marie unfolded the large white flower without a sound. Toby watched, stunned, as words began to appear from inside the folded petals.

The flower had once been a note.

Half a note, at least. With the paper unfolded, Toby and Marie saw a few handwritten lines scrawled in a hurry across the middle of the page, something that had (perhaps inadvertently) left a great deal of white space all around it.

"That's Jerome's handwriting," Toby said.

"Someone's ripped it in half."

The note had been torn roughly across the top and lengthwise down the middle, so that only the first few words of each line were legible. They were still enough to send the hairs rising on Toby's arms.

I know why
Meet me o
Midnig
Don't be la

"'Meet me,'" Marie murmured.

"'Midnight. Don't be late.'"

Below the main note, almost like an afterthought, Jerome had added,

Remember Matth

Toby and Marie stared at that last line for ages. Toby felt a stirring in his mind, a deep hollow space, something enormous he'd forgotten.

"What if we've been worrying about the wrong person all this time?" Marie seemed almost afraid to say it. "And what if Luca knew it too?"

"Are you thinking what I'm thinking?"

"Matthias. Jerome wrote this note to Matthias."

A SMALL DOOR WAITED at the northern end of the main wing's third floor, through which they found a secluded balcony barely large enough to hold a rattan armchair, a small table, and a single orchid, all of it overlooking the cavernous sunroom. From this height, Toby could see the cross on the house's roof through the skylights overhead, the distant twinkle of the north creek through the sunroom's glass wall.

Matthias, Ginger's strange son, sat in the armchair, reading a small black Bible. Like Kassandra before him, he jumped when they stepped through the door.

"I thought I was the only person who knew about this place."

"Please." Marie nodded at a sweating Coke resting on a little table at the boy's side. "Who do you think clears away your trash every night?"

Matthias rubbed his head. He didn't look well. "Sorry, I don't really—"

"What is this?" Toby didn't have time. He thrust Jerome's torn note under the boy's nose. They watched as Matthias scrutinized the few lines, the boy mouthing what few words he could make out.

> I know why
> Meet me o
> Midnig
> Don't be la

Finally Matthias looked between Toby and Marie with a confused frown. He repeated Toby's question back to him. "I don't know. What *is* this?"

"Where's the other half?" Marie pulled on her jaded cop routine again. "What did it say?"

"I've never seen this paper in my life."

"Then why is your name on it?" She pointed to the note's final line: *Remember Matth—*

"That's not my name."

"Is there a Matthew living here we don't know about?" she said.

A drop of blood struck the white paper. Another. Matthias rubbed his temples, rubbed his face, dug a tissue from his pocket and plugged his nose.

"My son is missing, Matthias. He's had this note since Friday. It has your name on it." Toby tightened his grip on the cane. "Do you see why I'm not believing you?"

"That's *your* problem. What the shit would I do with a kid?"

Marie tried a subtler tack. "You have to admit it looks strange. Why would an old man want to meet you somewhere in the middle of the night?"

With a little keening sound, Matthias said, "I told you, I never saw this before. Jerome wrote a lot of notes, all right? How do you even know he wrote this on Friday? What if it had been in the trash for a week by the time your kid picked it up? Mom says he likes to do that."

Toby opened his mouth. Hesitated. "You've got a point."

"You mean Jerome made a habit of meeting people on the roof at midnight?" Marie said. "And then one night they decided to murder him?"

Matthias pushed the note into Marie's hand. "I don't know, man, I just live here. Is there, like, actually a chance your brother took my pain pills? I haven't been able to find them since breakfast yesterday and I really need one. Like really."

The thought of yesterday's aborted party made Toby think of the way Matthias had followed his mother into the massive sunroom shortly before the chaos started, the boy reading aloud something from Ginger's phone. It had been a name: Thomas, maybe, or—

Marie clearly wasn't thinking about this. She said, "Let's make a deal, then. You tell us about this note, and we'll talk about pills."

"But I don't *know* anything. I swear to God, I've never seen this in my—"

"You didn't see this note when you burned Jerome's things?" Toby said. "He didn't give it to you Friday afternoon?"

"Jerome didn't give me anything on Friday but two hundred bucks. He paid me and asked if I could get everything burned by dinner. He said he wanted to start fresh on Saturday." Another wave of pain crossed Matthias's face. "I had to work my ass off to burn it all in time. Jerome's study was such a freaking mess, I wouldn't have noticed this note if it had already been on fire, you know?"

Marie opened her mouth to barrel on, but Toby raised a hand: *wait*. In a softer voice, he said, "What *was* in that study, Matthias? Why would Jerome want all of it burned?"

A shimmer of tears gleamed in Matthias's eyes—his pain seemed more than genuine. "It was all random. Really. Lots of Bible stuff, some medical books, a bunch of printed-out emails. And some . . . some weird shit."

"Weird shit?"

"I didn't even want to touch some of it."

"You mean it was dirty? Sexual?"

"No, no. I don't care what anyone says, Jerome never treated me like that."

"Whoa. Wait. Hold up," Marie interjected. "Don't care what *who* says?"

Instantly, a gate closed behind Matthias's eyes. "Never mind. Forget I said anything."

Marie shot a glance at Toby, as if to confirm that he'd just felt what she'd just felt: a massive hole had opened up at their feet, a terrible new possibility. She swallowed hard. "Did Jerome . . . did Jerome treat *other* people like that? In a dirty way? A sexual way?"

"I don't know what you're talking about."

"Then what are you talking about?" Toby said.

Matthias seemed too tired to resist them for long. "I just heard he hired hookers sometimes, all right? A man's got needs. That's it."

"Hookers." Marie said the word like it soured in her mouth. She and Toby both shook their heads, feeling too jaded by this family to be surprised. First Richard had confessed to his wife his numerous infidelities, and now here was Jerome indulging in the same sins of the flesh. *Things have a habit of repeating in this family.*

"So Jerome hired prostitutes?" Toby said.

Matthias was far too young to seem as bored by this conversation as he was. "He flew them in on his private jet and took them out to that cabin in the woods, all right? He'd been doing it for years. Except one of them beat the crap out of him last fall and messed him up bad."

"Jerome might have been old, but he wasn't frail and he wasn't small." Marie, again, was incredulous. "What kind of women was he hiring who could break half the bones in his legs?"

Matthias rubbed blood from his nose, dug out a fresh tissue. "I don't know if they were females."

Toby and Marie stood in silence a moment, staring at each other. Finally, she said, "Jerome hired *male* prostitutes?"

"Timothy Sage." The name had finally come back to Toby, the one he'd been struggling to recall. "You were looking at Ginger's phone on the way into the birthday party yesterday morning. When you asked her who Timothy Sage was, half the family got spooked."

"I'd heard the name around the house a few times, that's all. I always kind of guessed he was the guy who beat up Jerome. Then I saw an email on Mom's phone yesterday morning, it seemed to freak her out. It was sent from someone called Timothy Sage and the subject was, 'From a Friend of the Family.' That's what Mom and Sarah Nella used to call those people. 'Friends of the family.'"

Oh, yes: Toby had heard *that* phrase before. Yesterday in the hall outside Jerome's study, not long before she started heaping abuse on Luca, crazy old Corah had asked Toby why he wasn't "out in the woods." She'd said he looked just like "a friend of the family."

"But you're telling me Jerome was gay?" Marie said.

Matthias shrugged. "Who knows what he was? Maybe he just got an itch sometime, you know."

"He was the same as Richard, by the sound of it. Just like Kassandra said." Toby shrugged. "The worst bigots are the ones who want a piece for themselves."

"Listen, I don't know anything else, okay? It's not like me and Jerome ever talked about this shit." Matthias squirmed. "I really need my pills, please. Because of the tumor they took out. It's like my brain starts to go backwards when my headaches get this bad."

Toby listened to the desperation in the boy's voice, the confusion and fear. It sounded genuine. "So this note—"

"I don't know anything about your fucking note!"

Matthias's voice cracked. Toby glanced away: whatever was going on with this scrap of paper, the kid knew nothing about it.

And then Toby's gaze fell again on the black leather Bible in the boy's lap. It looked awfully small for a Bible, he thought now. Awfully slim, too. It looked less like a Bible and more like—

"The journal."

Matthias followed Toby's eye. "Of course. What did you think it was?"

"Your mom had me looking everywhere for that."

"Then she's an idiot. She shouldn't read it. I wish I hadn't."

"What's that supposed to mean?"

"I told you—Jerome had some weird books in his office. Stuff I didn't think a preacher was supposed to have."

"Such as?"

"You'll laugh."

"Trust me." Toby thought of the drafts of air that had haunted him all weekend, quick and cool as mercury. "I won't."

"Jerome had, like, books on dark shit in there. Black magic. Demons. Ghosts."

Toby thought of the doors over the bookcases in Jerome's office. Their locks. "You're right. That is strange reading material for a preacher. Did you ask him about it?"

"It wasn't my business. But I was glad he wanted me to burn it."

"So where did you find the journal?"

"On his desk. Yesterday. After everything calmed down about the body and all. I went up to the west wing one more time, you know? I poked my head into the study to make sure I hadn't forgotten to burn anything on Friday—he'd paid me to do it, you know, I wanted to do a good job. It seemed . . . respectful or whatever. I saw the journal just sitting right there, under a paper with some crazy stuff written on it."

"This paper?" Toby produced the water-stained page with its three cryptic lines.

> Wet roses bloom on white sugar
> From the muted mouth, he speaks
> The wailing boy slips beneath green waves

"Yeah. *That's* the only note from Jerome I ever saw, and I don't even think it was meant for me. It slipped behind the desk when I went to pick it up." Matthias raised the journal. "I took this instead. I thought maybe I could figure out why Jerome had all that weird shit in his office. And why he wanted me to burn it."

"Is that when Luca and I saw you running out of Jerome's study?"

Matthias nodded.

"Funny—you weren't holding the journal when you were in the hall. I looked."

"I'd stuck this in the back of my shorts. Later I hid it in my room. I kinda figured the police would have considered that stealing evidence, you know? And then when I finally talked to Mom yesterday, she never once asked me how I was feeling, how I was holding up with everything that had happened. All she asked me was if I'd seen his journal and did I know where it was, and I was so mad I told her I had no idea what she was talking about. Serves her right. Ever since my sister died, it's like Mom forgot she still has another kid left over."

Toby didn't know what to say to that.

It was Marie who asked, "Do you believe in any of that stuff? Black magic?"

With one last look at the journal, Matthias said, "I didn't use to."

BEFORE THEY LEFT, MARIE shrugged off her backpack and fished out the bottle of tablets she'd shared with Toby earlier this morning. She shook out a few for Toby to thrust into his pocket before passing the rest of the bottle to Matthias. "I don't know where Julian or your pills are. God's honest. But will these help?"

Matthias read the label. "Maybe. They're not the good stuff."

"That's probably why my brother didn't steal them."

Out in the hall, Toby found it impossible to read Jerome's journal on the move. The man's handwriting was as cramped and harried as ever, and after struggling for several steps to read a page one-handed while walking with the cane, Toby gave up and passed it to Marie. "Want to give me the SparkNotes?"

She wasn't so quick to take it. She gave the torn note they'd found concealed inside Luca's flower a final glance.

> *I know why*
> *Meet me o*
> *Midnig*
> *Don't be la*
> *Remember Matth*

"This still means something. What if it was *meant* for Matthias but someone else found it first?"

"Who would care? Everyone seems to let that kid do whatever he feels like around here. Even his mom called him a feral cat."

"But look here, the way it was torn across the top of the page too. It's almost like there was something else written here that someone wanted to get rid of."

"You're going to drive yourself crazy if you're not careful." Toby nudged the journal her way. "Seriously. Maybe the answer's in here."

She tucked the note into her pocket, accepted the journal with a little frown, but she didn't make it much further than Toby. After flipping pages for a time, seemingly at random, she snapped the book shut as they neared the main elevator and thrust it back into Toby's hand. "I see what Matthias meant."

"What do you mean?"

"I don't play around with heresy."

Perplexed, Toby sat on the elevator's bench and opened the journal again on the ride down. The first entry was dated the end of last October, around the time Jerome had taken his alleged "fall" (a fall that had, in fact, been a beating) out at the replica of a horse stable he'd built in the woods. Indeed, the journal began, *Writing with a broken hip is an agony few could comprehend.*

And yet Jerome *had* written, describing his pain in the wake of the beating, his private frustration at the way the family had swooped home to Ramorah to keep an eye on him—*Vultures, one and all. Vipers.*—before settling into a pensive, musing tone that felt at odds with the bitterness of the preceding page or the bombast of his televised self. In private, alone, Jerome had apparently been drowning in floods of nostalgia.

In the Renaissance, an Italian thinker named Nicolo Nicorelli theorized that all the memories of a man's life remain in his brain; the mind simply loses the route back to them, like "Theseus en la labyrinthos senza il filo." Nicorelli believed that with the careful reconstruction of one's memories in a mental palace, a man could either seal away the memories that no longer served him or reclaim lost moments of his life.

In an aside, Nicorelli theorized that if one were to go so far as to build actual physical replicas of scenes in one's past and play-act the events that took place there, one could either seal away or reclaim every aspect of a lost memory. That one could bring back "even the contours of a missing face."

How much expense have I devoted to that one aside? How much flesh?

I discovered Nicorelli right around the time The Prophecy Hour *began. I wonder if the Lord knew how many dioramas of my youth I would build with the money that program brought in. How much re-creation it would fund. A life-size replication of my entire life. A memory palace.*

All to reclaim a face I lost sixty years ago.

But I was a fool: Nicorelli's palace has done nothing to dredge up the past. I wanted simply to see my brother again, if only in my mind. I tried everything to have him back. I ran countless experiments on countless young men until the last of them I brought in for the purpose nearly killed me out there in that godforsaken shack. Did I ever enjoy it, the things I did out there in the woods? Was it ever like it was?

Regardless, it accomplished nothing. My palace has sealed Cleave further away than he's ever been.

When I lay in that shack with my body broken to pieces, wondering if I would die out there before anyone found me, I realized I'd been going about this the wrong way for all these years. There are . . . other ways to reclaim the dead. It's all right there in First Samuel.

The elevator arrived at the ground floor. Marie rose but Toby held up a hand to stop her, never lifting his eyes from the journal. Just as he had on the roof, when he found himself turning through page after page of mad constellations in Jerome's *Starspotter Field Guide* (*We are nothing but motes of dust trapped in the orbit of a dead star*), Toby found himself turning through page after page of the man's journal. He felt his mouth falling open. Hairs rose up and down his arms.

Matthias hadn't been lying: over the course of the last fall and winter, Jerome had assembled a collection of texts behind the locked doors of his study that would have horrified his audience. Not only that; the man's Skype call history was a veritable index of expert occultists from around the world. As the year had come to a close, as Jerome had regained the mobility in his legs, the man had gathered his tools. Made a few careful experiments. Done things on that roof that would have sent half his family running from this house if they had known.

Smoke. Candles. A little blood.

And then last December, shortly before the Christmas broadcast, Jerome wrote, *Tomorrow is the solstice. The thinnest night. Everyone agrees it's my best chance. God help me.*

Toby read the entry on the next page. He was shaking so hard, it was all he could do to keep the journal in his hands. "Oh, fuck."

"Don't tell me," Marie said. "Really."

No worries there. Toby wouldn't have repeated what he saw in that journal if you stuck a gun to his head.

God help me, Jerome wrote at the bottom of the journal's final page.

God help me, he's back.

A draft of air slithered through the ventless elevator, strong enough to riffle the pages of the journal. Toby would swear he heard a man laughing in the sound of the draft. He thought of Mister Suit, smiling and waving at the end of the long hallway yesterday evening.

He thought of what Ruth had told him at the church, that Cleave had always been the real prophet.

Of course. Of course. So much was finally beginning to make sense. A great blank space in Toby's mind, one of those hollows that had haunted him all weekend, was starting to fill in. He thought, of all things, of the question Kassandra had asked him in the library. *Have you ever wondered if even Jesus has a limit on how much he can forgive?*

Where had Toby heard that before?

But there wasn't time for more. Just as Toby felt a door opening in his mind, a scream came from outside the elevator, loud enough to scare the dead.

———————

Toby and Marie discovered Corah, Jerome's ancient sister, standing in the house's foyer, clad in a turquoise windbreaker, a nightdress, and a pair of muddy tennis shoes, her cloud of gray hair almost crackling with rage. They arrived just in time to watch the woman wrench the brass stand from beneath the foyer's grand gilded Bible and swing it, like a baseball bat, against the wall. The Bible fell to the floor. The golden stand slammed against the stone carving of Noah's Ark. The boat and half the waves rained to the floor in a clatter of dust.

Toby had been right to feel nervous around this woman. Even at her age she still had the strength of a horse.

Corah spun to stare at them, dark eyes aflame. "Why are you still here?" she said to Toby. "Why haven't you taken your money and gone?"

She held the brass stand in front of her. Toby and Marie edged a careful step away. "We were just coming to grab our things," Toby said, toggling into the voice he'd once used for the really tough nuts at Silver Oaks. "We forgot we'd left everything down here. I know it was stupid of us."

"Stupid? Stupid is commissioning an artist to carve your 'favorite scenes from the Bible' around your new house just to make *me* miserable. To humiliate *me*. Forty years I've lived in this house and stared at these awful carvings about drowning and murder and wanted to cry every time I saw them. Just like Abigail intended." Corah almost vomited the words, they so disgusted her. "She got ideas in her head, Jerome's wife. She never understood *love*."

The brass stand wobbled in the air, and for a moment Toby thought Corah's strength was failing her. He passed Jerome's journal to Marie so he could take a step forward, one hand on his cane, the other raised placatingly in the air. "We all loved him, Corah. It's terrible what's happened."

"You're a liar! If all of you loved him, he'd still be alive!" She struck the wall again. "'Blessed are the pure in heart, for they shall see God.' No one understood how hard it was to protect my Jerome. To keep my perfect boy safe and pure."

Pure enough to bring prostitutes to his strange little stable in the woods? Toby thought. *To re-enact some lost moment in his past?*

Corah seemed to collapse in on herself. The brass stand fell to the parquet floor with a bang. To Toby's surprise, the old woman stumbled across the foyer and collapsed against his shoulder. She sobbed.

"They think I'm crazy," she said. "But all I've done is make this family what it is."

From the edge of his vision, Toby saw Marie staring at Corah, willing the woman to say more. He looked away. He knew from experience that this wave of tears would pass, soon to be replaced by whatever card Corah's mind would draw next from its small, fraying deck of emotions. He considered asking her about the story Alyssa had told him about last night (*Did my wife really stay with you until two in the morning?*), but he knew he only had one shot to get something resembling an unguarded answer out of Corah. He only cared about one thing.

"I feel the same about my boy. I'd do anything to keep him safe." Toby patted the old woman's back; it was hot as an ember. "Have you seen him today, Corah? My Luca?"

The woman leaned back to look at him, bewildered. "A child?"

"Yes, Corah. The child I brought with me on Friday. He's only seven. He's too young to be on his own."

"I haven't seen a child in this house in years, young man. Who are you again?"

Toby's heart sank. He watched as Corah slithered away from him in a rush, and he tightened his grip on his cane. Her face was clouding over again. Her mind was readying its next trick.

Judging by the desperation in her voice, Marie saw it too. "Ma'am, what did you do for this family? What do you mean, you made them what they are?"

As if in reply, a bitter blast of air swept through the foyer, gusting toward the stairs, and before the breeze had settled, Corah's eyes were gleaming once again with rage. She rushed to the stairs with an astonishing speed. She climbed them two at a time. "He's taunted all year," Corah called down to Toby and Marie. "He's made everyone think I'm out of my mind. He's back, and everyone thinks I'm crazy for it."

"*Who?*" Marie called after her.

"He was just there a moment ago, you stupid girl!" Corah thrust a finger to the head of the stairs. Coming around the banister to follow her gaze, Toby saw only a great wall carving of Pharaoh's forces being swallowed by the Red Sea.

"I know how to fix this," Corah said. "I did it once and I'll do it again."

She whipped around the landing and vanished up the same slippery stairs. He noticed two flashes of red paint on Corah's hands: they coated her palms like fistfuls of blood.

"Should we follow her?" Marie turned back to look at Toby. "She knows something."

Toby watched the landing. Another rush of cold air made the sconce above Pharaoh's forces flicker and spark. When it passed, it left behind the faint echo of a rushed whisper.

atlastatlastatlast

At last, at last, at last.

"No," Toby said. "Leave her be."

5:12

THEY FOUND GINGER IN the parlor, tapping out an email with a cigarette burning between two fingers. On the room's enormous TV, Jerome strode across the grand stage of the estate's church, a finger raised at his audience above a banner that read THE LORD DEMANDS PURITY ABOVE ALL ELSE. It might have been a rerun, but the logo of every major credit card was still plastered to the corner of the screen, a toll-free number and website and a photo of Jerome's latest book: *I Have Received My Reward (and You Can Too!)*.

Ginger gave them a single glance. "Tobias. How are you this glorious Sunday?"

"I've been busy. I'm not sure what kind of insulation you can offer me that I haven't already figured out."

Ginger looked strange this morning. The brilliance of her ruby hair had dulled. Her shoulders were tight. A long ribbon of red paint had dried along the length of her arm, surrounded by deep red scratches where she'd clearly been clawing at it for hours. Even as Toby watched, she clamped her cigarette in her teeth to gouge two fingers along the skin.

Toby held up the black leather journal. "If you were going to tell me about the friends of the family that Jerome used to take to the little cabin in the woods, then I'll keep this—your son told me all about them."

Ginger's fingers stilled. Her eyes fixed on the journal. "We don't have friends in this family."

"That's probably why Jerome had to pay them," Marie said.

"Pay them?" Ginger scratched at the paint on her arm. "Sure."

"Why did Timothy Sage email you on Saturday?" Toby said. "Matthias suspected he was the man who beat up Jerome and left him to die in the woods. But if that's the case, why would he contact you?"

"Timothy wanted more money. Most of them do, eventually. He was threatening to go to the news. He said he'd already written to Jerome and the old man hadn't replied. I was worried Timothy would do something stupid before we could shut him up."

Marie said, "But why would this Timothy person beat Jerome up in the first place? I take it he wasn't hired to do that?"

"You want to hear the good news? You don't need to know." Ginger's eyes had yet to leave the journal. "Give me that, Toby. The police will be here any minute. You're going to want some cover."

"Are you going to tell me where to find my son?"

She blinked. "He's missing?"

"No one's seen him since last night," Toby said.

"And no one's seen Julian since yesterday morning," Marie added.

"I wouldn't be so sure of that."

Toby eased himself onto the couch beside Ginger, struggling to play it cool. "And why is that?"

"Someone must have seen those two, right? Why else would they be missing?"

"You're talking in riddles."

"I'm saying the obvious. You're just too distracted to notice." Ginger dug a Marlboro from a crumpled pack beside her. Lit up with the smoldering butt clamped in her teeth. "And I don't care. We made a deal, Toby. Give me that journal."

He held it away from her. "Are you sure you really want it? There's some stuff in here I wish I hadn't seen."

"What are you trying to do? Protect me?"

"Is that so bad? Jerome did something right before the end of the year. Right around the time the red graffiti started to appear in this house." Toby tapped the cover of the journal with a nail. "And after that, the show changed. The *prophecies* changed. But you already suspected all that, didn't you?"

"I don't know what you're talking about."

"Yesterday afternoon, Matthias said you thought the house was haunted. My son seemed to think the same thing. All weekend long, he kept talking about someone he called Mister Suit. At first I thought it was just an imaginary friend he came up with, but after what happened to Sarah Nella last night . . ." Toby trailed off.

"Are you listening to yourself?" Ginger said.

"I wouldn't have believed it if I hadn't seen the letters you left for Jerome in his office at the church. There were dozens of them in there, and they only went back three months. You've been getting them all year, haven't you? After Jerome recovered, he came back to the show and started making prophecies for the first time in his life. *Real* prophecies. And they started coming true."

"I don't think my grandfather could see the future."

"Not without help." Toby took a long breath, waving smoke from his face. "Jerome brought his brother back, Ginger. He brought back his brother Cleave. The man who'd always been the real prophet."

Ginger studied the journal. Marie studied the TV. Toby waited.

"Do you think the police are going to believe that story?" Ginger finally said.

Toby didn't buy the disdain in her voice.

"I don't get why you want to help him at all," Marie cut in: she was clearly getting restless. "You and your siblings are deep in the shit, thanks to the way you've been siphoning away the money. Shouldn't you be trying to get Toby out of the way so you can keep his kid and save the whole operation?"

"Who says I give a *fuck* about the operation?" Ginger pulled her eyes from the journal long enough to scowl at her. "I already have a plane chartered out of Houston. The second the roads clear, I'm headed to the Bahamas. I've been piling up money for years. I couldn't care two shits if Richard and Alyssa starve or strike gold with their new version of the show. I'll be fine. I will *always* be fine."

"They found out, though," Toby said. "Alyssa says she and Richard were blackmailing you to keep the embezzlement quiet."

"Sure. If that's what they want to think. My siblings were too stupid to realize all I did was make them accessories after the fact. If I go down, they *all* go down."

Something seemed to dawn on Marie. "Just how broke *is* this family?"

Ginger gave her a dark smile. "I'd say they have about three months left."

"You weren't just making yourself a nest egg, were you?" Marie said. "You were trying to ruin them."

When Ginger didn't deny it, a small piece clicked in Toby's head. He realized, at last, why Ginger had done everything she'd done. And why she wanted this journal so badly.

"It's because of your daughter, isn't it? The one who died on a Sunday. You stole all that money as revenge for the way nobody left the show to be with you when she passed."

A cruel grin spread over Ginger's mouth. "Maybe. Or maybe I'm just a bitter bitch who's gone off the deep end. First rule of law school, Toby: never commit to a position."

"Well, I'll commit to this: it's all in here. Everything you need to do to have her back."

Silence. Toby recalled what Ginger had told him in her strange office yesterday afternoon. *I don't go a single day without wondering how I could be with her again.*

Ginger stared at him, looking for the first time like she was afraid he might be wrong.

Or right.

"Are you serious?" she said, clearly struggling to remain composed. "Does it really . . . does it really say how Jerome did it? How he brought his brother back?"

"In gory detail. I'm not an expert, but if you're crazy enough to play with this kind of thing I don't see why it wouldn't work for you, too."

Toby held out the journal. Ginger wrapped her fingers around it.

He didn't let go. "Now show me this proof you're so certain will save me."

That cruel grin returned. Ginger opened her phone again, tapped a few keys, and a moment later Marie's phone pinged with a message.

Watching her screen, Toby saw that Ginger had sent a text containing a single photograph.

"Oh my Lord," Marie said. "Is that Alyssa? And . . ."

Of course, Toby thought. *Of course.*

He released the journal. Ginger all but snatched it away. He stared at the photograph on Marie's phone as an entire constellation of assumptions and clues reassembled itself in this new gravity. He said, "That certainly will complicate things around here, yes."

They sank into a final silence. Even Jerome froze on the screen of the TV, his image caught between one step to the next, casting them all in a perfect tableau.

The old man's image started to flicker and tear. His face dissolved into a pulp of glitching pixels.

Soon, all of it vanished into a sea of static.

A familiar sound came from the window.

Tap

Tap

Tap-tap-tap-tap-tap-tap.

The rain was back. Within moments, it was coming down as hard as ever.

"Would you look at that. The Lord just gave you a little more time." Ginger clawed at the paint on her arm. "Go get your kid while you still can, Toby. And pull the house down while you're at it."

And yet they weren't quite finished with Ginger. Toby rose to go, ready to ask Marie for a favor, when Marie herself withdrew the torn page from her pocket and said, "Luca had this note with your son's name on it. Do you have any idea what it might mean?"

Neither of them could have predicted the effect the torn scrap of paper would have on her. Ginger read the note first with boredom, then unease, and by the time she arrived at the last line, a look of horror came over her face so profound it made the skin crawl on Toby's arms. Her lips mouthed the words slowly, like she couldn't believe them: *Remember Matth—*

Ginger pushed a sudden spring of tears from her eyes. She champed her teeth on her cigarette the way a soldier would bite their belt as a medic took off their leg.

It took Ginger three tries to say, "Where . . . how . . . but he's so young."

"Young?" Toby said. "Who are you talking about? Luca?"

"No, not—but I thought the old man learned his lesson last year. I thought . . ."

Ginger thrust the note back into Marie's hand, pushing herself away along the couch like the paper had bitten her. "Get out."

"What's gotten into you?" Toby said.

But Ginger wasn't even looking at him. "Jerome didn't. Matthias would have told me if the old man had . . . had . . ."

"Had what?" Marie said.

Ginger blinked, as if seeing the two of them for the first time. "I said leave. Now."

"Ginger—"

"Now!"

And then, with a scream that echoed in Toby's bones—the scream of a parent who had failed both of her children utterly and permanently—Ginger's shell finally cracked. She folded herself around Jerome's journal and wept, harder and harder, like she was making up for lost time.

5:13

THEY FOUND THE MAN waiting for them in the kitchen, a glass of water in his hand and a thick track of sweat down the back of his shirt. He was watching the return of the storm as it pounded the dark estate. Toby said, "Thanks for answering our text. This won't take long."

Hugo pushed his great bulk away from the woodblock counter and toyed with the wad of Saran Wrap Matthias had left there yesterday afternoon. Like Ruth this morning, Hugo looked drained, half-there, and nervous as an enormous rabbit. A quick dash of red paint underlined one eye. His frown was so deep it seemed to have carved a handful of flesh from the bottom of his face.

Yet despite his exhaustion, he smiled. "Tobes. I'm so glad we can finally talk privately. It feels like the family's kept us apart all weekend."

Toby didn't know how long this new storm would last, if it would keep the roads flooded or just breeze on by. He didn't have time for small talk, especially not with a man who'd apparently let Luca vanish right under his nose. "I only came to ask if you heard anything last night, Hugo. Anything strange at all."

"This is about your son, isn't it? I noticed he was gone when I woke up. Both he and Ruth were out of the suite."

"And yet last night you were insisting you were such a light sleeper you would have heard anyone if they'd come up the stairs to kill Jerome. How could a kid disappear from your bedroom and you didn't hear a thing?"

"I was on some of Sarah Nella's sleeping pills last night. Ruth insisted." Hugo ran a thumb on the lip of his glass. "But it's nagged at me all day. I feel like I *did* hear something, but then it could have just been a piece of the dream. I was dreaming of—"

"Don't waste my fucking time." Toby thumped his cane. "Say you did hear something—what time would that have been?"

"I'm not sure. Truly. Not enough to swear in court." When Toby opened his mouth to say more, Hugo added, "But if I *did* hear something, it would have been around one in the morning. The Marines beat a clock into a man."

That was just what Toby had thought. From the moment he saw the photograph Ginger had sent Marie, one obvious answer after another had become clear to him. He didn't have any actual proof, but Hugo had just given him enough ammunition to cause some real trouble.

"Thank you. Have you seen my wife around recently?"

"As a matter of fact, I have. She was on the third floor a few minutes ago, heading into the west wing."

"That's what I thought. Thanks, Hugo."

Toby turned for the hall without a word, gesturing for Marie to follow him.

"Wait. Please."

There was a strange weight to Hugo's voice, a sadness and concern that dragged at something deep inside Toby. He turned back, surprised. He waited.

"I . . . I've done everything I could to get Richard off your back today, Tobes. Dragged him halfway around the estate and back." Hugo gave a great, humble shrug. "Father to father, tell me, please—did it help? Do you know where to find your son?"

"No. But I have a pretty good idea who to ask."

"I hope you do. I hope it works. I hope *something* finally works."

"What do you mean?"

"I tried my best to keep you from marrying into this family, Tobes. I'm the reason Ruth was so cold with you at the airport in Los Angeles six weeks back. I thought if I could convince her that you were a bad fit for us, she could persuade Alyssa to call it off. Stupid of me, I know. My daughter's never listened to anyone but herself."

"But why would you want to keep me out of the family?"

"Not *you*. It was your boy I was afraid for. I was afraid for Luca. The minute I met him, I knew these people would ruin your son. I didn't know about the show, Richard needing some child for the cameras, any of that. I just knew that if this family had half a chance, they'd poison your boy like a weed." Hugo stared at his big hands. "Richard was so like Luca at that age—and look what they've done to him."

Toby went still. "Richard was what?"

"Smart, sensitive, gentle. A good kid. A perfect kid. And they broke him. Simple as that. And they'll do it again to your boy. Sarah Nella—or whatever it was inside Sarah Nella last night—she was right. Things really do have a habit of repeating in this awful family." Hugo wiped a big paw over his eyes. "Anyway. I got Richard away from you this morning so you could go find your son and get the hell out of here."

Toby nodded. He didn't forgive this man for all that had happened this weekend—he didn't forgive any of them—but then Hugo wasn't asking for forgiveness, was he? "I'll get it done."

"Before you go, can you answer a question for me? For my own curiosity?"

"If you can ask it quick."

"I started to ask you at the church, but Ruth would have heard me. I saw your putter going toward the woods yesterday while Ruth and I headed out to do our devotional. Did you find anything strange in those woods, Toby? Anything . . . out of place?"

"I found a replica of an old horse stable stuck inside a house. It was eerie, to be honest with you."

"I see. Yes. I suppose that makes sense. Another room in the memory palace. The woods have been off-limits for me, you know."

Marie said, "Off-limits?"

When Hugo hesitated, Toby said flatly, "I've heard Jerome used to take prostitutes to that cabin. The 'friends of the family.'"

Hugo let out a sigh. It sounded like he'd been holding it for years. "Those weren't prostitutes, Toby."

TEN MINUTES LATER, THE elevator deposited Toby and Marie on the third floor for the final time. Sound had grown strange up here. It echoed with rain, hard wind, with the distant, insistent drizzle of what sounded like a hundred little leaks. The wall on the landing that had been defaced Friday night—

THE LORD WILL HAVE HIS JUSTICE YOU FUCKS

AND I WILL HAVE MINE

—was now so soaked it resembled that of a cave, brown and yellow and gleaming with a ceaseless trickle of wet.

"Jesus," Toby said. "It's getting worse up here in a hurry."

With a crash like a head-on collision in the sky, a peal of thunder burst over their heads, rattling the lightbulbs in their sconces. The storm was raging again, harder than it ever had before.

Toby hooked a left, hurrying west as fast as his knee would allow. Neither he nor Marie seemed quite able to discuss what Hugo had just told them in the kitchen.

Instead, Marie pressed her phone to her ear, again and again. "The service is cutting out. Not that Jules's phone is even ringing anymore."

"Do you think he did it?" Toby said. "That your brother killed Jerome?"

The girl looked ready to vomit just thinking about what they'd learned from Hugo. "I think you might be onto something."

A few minutes ago in the kitchen, Hugo had folded and unfolded his big hands, scratched at the paint dried beneath his eye, struggled to speak. "A long, long time ago, maybe a year or two after Grandma Abigail died, I was out for a walk and I heard a scream in the woods. Screaming and—and—crying. I thought my mind was playing tricks on me, but when I got closer and closer, the sound just got louder and louder. I followed the noise to that little house. I saw who was screaming. It was a young man. A teenager, dressed in . . . in a black suit. He was banging on the bars of the windows, begging for someone to let him out. By then I was close enough I could see the way the lock on the front door was built backwards." Hugo swallowed. "Like it hadn't been built to keep people out. Like it had been built to hold someone *in*."

Toby had felt a wave of nausea wash through him. He'd had the same thought when he'd seen the lock yesterday afternoon.

"That boy—that child—he'd been locked up in there. He saw me, Toby. He saw me through the window and started screaming for me to help him. To open the door. To take him back."

Marie looked ready to be sick. "Take him back? Back where?"

"To Camp Cleave. To that awful wilderness camp where my son wants to send Luca. That's where Jerome found them, those 'friends of the family.' Somehow he got them from the camp and stuck them into that little house, and then I suppose he sent them back eventually. God only knows what he did to them in the meantime. Judging by the way that boy was crying, it couldn't have been . . . Christlike."

Thunder shook a line of dangling saucepans. A horrible weight seemed to warp the air around them.

Hugo went on. "Sarah Nella must have seen me heading back from the woods that day. She grabbed me the minute I got back to the big house. She told me that the boys who visited that cabin were well-compensated, that we paid them some enormous sum of money to make sure they kept their mouths shut, even kept a list of their names in case they ever wanted more money. Ginger's taken over for her since then. I know because she never used to look so haunted." Hugo shuddered. "I'll never forget what Sarah Nella said. 'They all live in poverty, those men. Really, Jerome's done them a favor.'"

"What . . . what happened to him?" Toby said. "To the boy you saw in the cabin?"

"I left him there, of course. I'm a coward, Toby. At the end of the day, I'll never have the stones to do anything really good and brave. A few years later I didn't even stop Ruth from sending our son to that same exact camp after he got into some trouble. He's never been the same since."

"Hold up," Marie said. "Richard went to Camp Cleave?"

"Yes. Fifteen years ago, he spent a summer working as a counselor. Taught archery, rock climbing, rowing. Or so they said. Whatever was really going on out there, it finally destroyed my boy. He came back . . . broken. I ain't ever been able to put him right since."

Toby and Marie stared at each other. *Fifteen years ago*, she mouthed. He knew exactly what she was thinking:

Julian and Richard had been to Camp Cleave at the same time.

"Be careful if you run into my son upstairs, Tobes," Hugo said. "He's still a Marine. He brought a gun to this house, and he knows how to use it."

The big man drained his glass of water, squeezed Toby's shoulder with one massive hand and nodded to Marie, and heaved open the kitchen door. "Now if you'll excuse me, I'm going to go be with my wife."

They didn't say a word to stop him. Hugo stepped out into the storm.

Now on the third floor, Marie was talking a mile a minute. "Maybe we've been looking at this all wrong. Again. What if money never entered into the equation? Richard might be crazy, but if he knew what Jerome was capable of, maybe he killed the old man to put a stop to it. And Julian would have made the perfect accomplice. He had the opportunity to set everything up beforehand. He could have hidden the knife somewhere during dinner, well before Sarah Nella locked up the cutlery. Left it somewhere Richard would be able to grab it later and take it up to the roof to kill the old man. Richard could have taken a service elevator to make sure his dad didn't hear him on the landing and stabbed Jerome while Kassandra thought he was sleeping in the doghouse. Afterward, Richard put the knife in his closet to frame you with it later, or maybe just to scare you into letting him have Luca. Two birds with one stone, right? It was just dumb luck Kassandra found the knife first."

"And you're sure it's Richard?"

"There are just too many coincidences, Toby. Jules and Richard both changed after they went to that *same* camp in the *same* summer. Now we know what Jerome was up to out there with those 'friends of the family.' The old man might have—might have interfered with Richard or Jules. With both of them."

Toby thought of the hand Julian had laid on Richard's shoulder at dinner on Friday night, hours before Jerome had died. Thought of the way Richard had tensed but hadn't moved away. "But Richard and Julian have both spent the last six months living with him in this house. Why wait to get revenge until Friday?"

"I don't think they wanted revenge. I keep coming back to that torn-up note, the one addressed to Matthias. I think one of them might have intercepted the note before it got to Matthias. They realized Jerome was up to his old tricks—I'll bet you money that's the same exact thing Ginger thought when we showed the note to her. Richard and Jules would have known the old man had eyes on Matthias, so they decided to kill Jerome before the old man could hurt the boy the same way he'd hurt them."

Marie hesitated. Toby listened to the rain pounding the walls of the west wing. Somewhere behind him, he heard a long *creak*, a moan of wood and metal straining against a joist.

He couldn't be sure if the sound had come from Ramorah, or from deep inside his mind.

An epiphany struck Marie between one step and the next. "It would even explain why the note was torn in half. If Richard or Julian had found that note before it got to Matthias, they could have torn up the page and split it between them. One half got destroyed like it was supposed to, but the other . . ."

Toby saw where she was going. It made a horrible sort of sense. "Luca found the other half instead." He thought about what Ginger had texted them downstairs, the picture he'd traded for the little leather journal. With a shudder he said, "That might not have been the only thing Luca found."

"I just can't figure out the key to the roof. How did either Richard or Jules—"

She broke off. Up ahead, a foot hurried through a puddle of water.

Someone else was up here. Just as Toby had hoped.

The house seemed to be coming apart around them. Cracks spread through the walls, fracturing the mad velvet brocade with lines of glistening black. Windows wept. Soaked doors groaned as they swelled and swelled, ready to burst from their frames. It was as if, without its creator, Jerome's memory palace was coming undone, ready to cave in at any moment.

It felt almost identical to the damage Toby felt spreading in the base of his mind. Up and down the halls of the marble labyrinth, doors were coming open, walls were being breached, a whole wing collapsed inside him. Memories were coming to him that were so old he'd forgotten he'd forgotten them. The past shimmered everywhere at the edges of his vision.

And one memory—the afternoon when he and Luca had returned home from the grocery store earlier this year to discover his sister in a sundress and pumps, scrambling eggs for them just the way she had when Toby was a teenager—the memory pressed against him, always, with a dull weight. He smelled the warm butter through the damp air of Ramorah. He saw streaks of sunshine glinting off his sister's hair and shining on the soaked damask walls.

He heard the rustle of paper and plastic as he set down his groceries and the day's mail. He wrapped her in a hug. He told his sister, *You really had us worried this time.*

And there, behind Willow, Toby saw the bloody door—the bad door, the worst door—as it rattled against its failing lock.

Marie whispered, "I'm lost."

Toby came back, fully, to Ramorah. He got his bearings. The house might have been rotting, but at least the configuration of its halls hadn't changed. Toby could still recall the map he'd seen of this floor. "I'm not."

They stopped at a four-way intersection, ears straining through the drips and the wind, listening for any sound of the person they'd heard running earlier. Instead, it was Marie who spotted something at the end of one hall: a door was standing open.

Inside they found a wood-paneled room with bare pine floors and nails in the walls hung with a few shirts, an assortment of bags, three tired hats. Bunk beds filled the room, enough to sleep at least eight men in close quarters. Or sixteen, if they wanted to save a dollar.

"It's like an old-fashioned rooming house," Marie murmured. "They had places like these all through the backwoods until well into the sixties."

"I bet they did." It was exactly the sort of place two poor young preachers would sleep on the nights between their tent revivals.

The wood ceiling was spattered with hundreds of fine drops of red paint, like constellations of blood.

Around a corner was another open door, this one leading to a small country store, complete with soaked bags of seed and an ancient cash register. Further on, they found a room painted to look like the outdoors: moonlit farmland rolling out in all directions, real dirt turning to mud on the floor, a wooden hand pump jutting up in one corner. Gazing at the staggering night sky painted above, Toby realized why Jerome would have grown so interested in astronomy living in this isolated corner of Texas. It would have been impossible not to.

Another crash of thunder echoed overhead, followed by a sound that made Toby's stomach twist. The sound was a sort of low, metallic groan that seemed to last an eternity. He told himself he was just imagining the sound, that it was some noise he'd invented as another piece of the labyrinth collapsed, but without the pills, it was impossible to deceive himself.

Toby blinked. That ominous sound was coming from the west.

And then they heard, from much closer on the third floor, the unmistakable murmur of a woman's voice fading around the corner. "I *am* going back, but I'm telling you . . ."

It was Alyssa.

They found her in a small bedroom. Judging by the room's spare decorations, it had once belonged to a pair of young boys: two baseballs and two gloves rested on a rough-hewn pine dresser, two dress shirts hung on a thread of wire. A pair of initials had been carved into one wall.

JW

CW

The ceiling had been painted a deep, bright black, almost the exact shade of the Wrights' eyes, and fine dots of white stars had been painted over it. The dots were constellations, labeled with a child's careful hand.

Ursa Minor.

Big Dipper.

Pleiades.

The room had once held two narrow beds, but they'd since been pushed together into one. The beds' sheets were tangled and stained.

The unmistakable funk of old sex still muddled the air.

The beds stood at a strange angle to a large pine armoire across the room. Alyssa stood past them, peering into the armoire, a phone pressed to her ear. "But how the hell could a kid have pushed open—"

Toby took a step inside, letting his cane land on the wood floor with a heavy thud. His wife went still, silent, before she turned to him with a look of perfect, unalloyed fear.

"Alyssa." Toby's hand tightened around the cane. "It's over."

5:15

HE SAW, IN AN instant, that his wife really wasn't cut out for this sort of thing. In the hour since he'd last seen her, she'd grown pale and fidgety, her eyes unfocused, her hair—like her mother's—falling everywhere. A phone dangled in her hand. She looked ready to cry.

Past Alyssa, Toby saw that the floor of the empty armoire was dusted with sparkly stars.

"Luca caught you killing her, didn't he?" Toby said.

Alyssa only stared at him.

"Last night, you forgot that the door to Sarah Nella's room will open up on its own if you don't lock it. You were in a hurry. You weren't sure how long Richard could keep Kassandra occupied. Because it was Richard's idea to put Sarah Nella out of her misery, wasn't it? It's always Richard's idea."

Alyssa seemed almost relieved to whisper, "How did you know?"

"You didn't make it very hard. Your only alibi was Corah, a woman you admitted to drugging with sleeping pills after whatever the fuck happened in our sitting room. The timing is too convenient. You didn't realize it, but Luca had left his room around one o'clock, right around the same time Richard dragged Kassandra away from Sarah Nella's suite to talk her ear off about stuff she didn't want to hear. You went into Sarah Nella's room after it was empty, just like Richard told you. And Luca must have seen you, followed you inside—maybe he thought you would lead him to me." Toby took a step into this bare little room. "And instead my son saw you killing her."

In the hall behind him, Toby could feel Marie stiffen. Another groan of metal, louder than the first, rolled in from the west.

"You're her doctor, after all. You'd be the one writing her death certificate."

Alyssa watched him with an expression he'd never seen on her face before. It looked almost like respect.

"You know what, Alyssa? I—don't—care." Toby thumped the cane on the floor with each word. "Just give me my son."

"I would if I could, Toby. At this point I think I really would. But I don't know where he is. I was able to get him out of Sarah Nella's room before Kassandra came back, but he started crying, he wanted you, he was making so much noise I didn't know what to do. I had to carry him up here kicking and screaming. It's a wonder he didn't wake the whole fucking house."

"You put him in there." Toby stared at the armoire. "A seven-year-old boy. You put him in a closet barely wide enough for him to turn around."

Promise you won't leave me alone again.

"It was just going to be for a few hours! The rain was calming down, we figured the roads would be open by dawn. The cops would come to arrest you and the media circus would start, but as long as we had Luca we could keep the kid insulated from everything. But then Richard got some email from the county and told me to come get Luca, to keep him safe, but he—"

Before she could say more, another groan of metal came from the west, this one even louder, and Toby finally realized what it was.

Someone else did too.

"Alyssa!" A voice rose from the phone in Alyssa's hand. "Alyssa, you need to get over here, now!"

It was Richard.

Alyssa made to run. Toby spread his arm over the door. "I'm not letting you leave until you give me my son."

But panic had already set his wife moving. With a jerky lunge, she snatched up one of the old baseballs on the room's dresser and flung it, hard, at Toby's face.

He ducked.

Marie didn't see it coming. Toby heard a quick bright *snap* as the ball struck her face.

Toby's cane left him off-balance as Alyssa rushed his way. She shoved him over easily, elbowed past Marie, and took off down the hall.

For an endless, awful moment, Toby was falling. He feared he would land again on his bad knee. If he did, it would be the end for him. If that knee took any more damage, he wouldn't be able to walk, let alone chase his wife. If he landed on his knee, he would never get Luca back.

The floor was coming up fast. He felt the agony of the collision before it even occurred.

With a second to spare, he was able to twist his body far enough around to land on his ass instead. It sent a jolt of pain down his leg, almost knocked the cane from his hand, but after a few seconds he was on his feet again.

Marie, too, wasn't out of commission for long. A hideous bruise was spreading over her cheek, but she didn't look like she was in pain.

She looked furious.

Marie tightened the straps of her backpack, nodded to the west. "Is that what I think it is?"

"Yes. And Richard knows it too."

Good thing Toby knew exactly where Alyssa must be heading, maybe better than Alyssa herself. His wife clearly didn't know this floor very well; otherwise she would never have headed south down this hall.

For his part, Toby turned north. With any luck, he'd reach Alyssa's destination at the same time as she did.

"She sounded scared," Marie said. "Like she doesn't know where Luca is."

"Then I hope Richard does. For his sake."

Toby and Marie hurried left, right, straight, left, the wet *thump* of his cane on the carpet growing faster and faster, the pain in his knee worse and worse, as another low groan started from the west. This one gave no sign of stopping. It rumbled and rumbled through the air, like a thunderhead that couldn't find release.

They rounded a corner and found themselves in a branch of the T-intersection that waited at the edge of the west wing, just in time to watch Alyssa hurry up the dead-end hall that contained Jerome's study and bedroom and the locked door to the servants' stairs.

Marie took off after her at a sprint. Toby followed as fast as he could.

Alyssa ducked to the right, vanishing onto the landing of the concrete stairs that led to the roof. Toby hoped—prayed—that Luca was up those stairs.

Marie was right behind her.

But when Alyssa disappeared onto the landing of the stairs, Richard stepped into her place, planting his feet wide and raising his arms in front of him. In his hand was the largest pistol Toby had ever seen. Just as Hugo had warned them.

Richard's face was coated, from his hair to his jaw, in urgent crimson.

Marie skidded to a halt, barely a foot from the gun's muzzle. Toby stood maybe a yard behind her.

Richard cocked the gun. He looked taller than ever, his eyelid twitching, rage and fear and animal desperation burning off his skin. He looked just as he had last night, when Sarah Nella had turned on him with the most dire prophecy of the evening.

You will die wailing, and the fish will have no use for your bones.

Yet Richard seemed unsure of what to do now that he had Toby and Marie frozen in their places. He simply watched them as the metallic groaning from the west grew louder.

Louder.

Louder.

Over Richard's shoulder, down the dead-end hall, Toby saw his own sister, fresh from rehab and clad in her sundress and pumps, smiling at the letter that had come for her in the day's mail.

It was Marie who said, as gently as she could, "We're not trying to get you in trouble, Richard. We know you were trying to do the right thing. You and my brother, you knew you had to protect Matthias from the old man."

Richard couldn't have looked more confused if she'd started speaking backward. "We had to *what*?"

"The note. The note he'd written to your nephew."

"What the *fuck* are you talking about?"

Toby didn't have time for this. He jerked his head back to the present, nodded to the west, said, "You and I both know what that sound is. Give me my son before it's too late."

Richard only grimaced. His eyes flicked from Toby to Marie and back again, the muzzle of his gun twitching in the air. That dangerous light in his eye was growing brighter.

"There's no point keeping him, Richard," Toby said. "The show's over. I know everything."

"You don't know shit."

"I know Alyssa's pregnant."

Richard's eyelid twitched. "What?"

"Think about it—those migraines of hers only ever seem to make her sick in the mornings, right? And what did Sarah Nella say to her last night? Something about knowing the secret she's allowed to grow inside her? It's obvious, Richard. Did Alyssa really never tell you?"

Richard's hands tightened on the handgun. His eyes cut toward the landing. "Is it true?"

Alyssa eased herself out from where she was hiding. She stood behind her brother and tried to smile at her husband and said, "I was going to tell you, Toby, but I could never find the right time. I lifted a pregnancy test when we stopped at the Cracker Barrel. You're right. You're . . . you're going to be a father."

"No. No, I'm not." Toby took a step forward. He held up his arm so they could see the pale fishhook in his flesh. "Do you know what caused this scar? When my dad crashed our truck into that semi, a piece of the bumper cut him in half and sliced through his seat. I was sitting behind him. I guess I put up my hands for the bumper to cut me like this, but it still pinned me down bad. By the time the fire department cut me out, I hadn't had any blood below my waist for nearly an hour."

Richard seemed bewildered by this. Alyssa, however, only watched him with a mounting horror. She was a doctor, after all.

"The folks at the hospital were afraid I'd lose all function down there. Thank God they were wrong. In the end, there was only one long-term consequence." Toby's eyes fixed on Richard. "I'm sterile."

Richard's eye twitched again. "So what?"

"So it's not hard to guess who the baby's father is. Even if you make it through today, even if that noise from the west isn't as bad as it sounds, even if you do salvage the ministry and take over, if my son and I don't walk away from this family alive and unscathed, I've taken steps to make sure everyone *else* knows too."

Richard's jaw clenched. The gun bobbed in the air. Marie seemed to have stopped breathing.

"Knows . . . what?"

"Ginger sent us a picture, Richard. I used Marie's phone to send it to some friends back home while the internet was still up. If they don't hear from me in four hours, they're sending that picture to the news. It's a picture from your trip to LA six weeks ago. Six weeks. I'm not a doctor, but isn't that about how long it takes for morning sickness to set in?"

All the color had drained from Alyssa's face.

"One of Ginger's private investigators snapped it, you know. She'd told them to cover every angle of your trip to meet me. Which they certainly did." Toby shook his head. "Jesus Christ, Richard—how bad did you want to fuck your own sister you didn't think to close the hotel blinds?"

"You son of a bitch," Richard said.

Toby realized, a moment too late, that he'd miscalculated. Rather than breaking Richard's nerves, the words had tightened every muscle in his body. That wild light in his eye burned brighter, brighter—and died.

Richard swiveled the gun an inch, aimed it straight at Toby's head, and cocked the hammer. He bellowed again, "YOU SON OF A BITCH!"

Toby watched Richard's finger on the trigger. Watched it tighten.

And then this strange day somehow grew even stranger. At the precise moment the groaning metal from the west took on a new, dangerous *screech*, a section of the wall behind Richard and Alyssa swung inward and Marie's brother, the one and only Julian Wright, stepped into the hall.

Lazarus himself couldn't have looked much worse. Julian was soaked to the bone, his skin a ghastly washed-out shade of brown like a blanched acorn. He was so wired with adrenaline and God knew what else, his eyes seemed ready to burst from their sockets.

And like a mad prophet from the wastes, Julian had a warning for them. "Put down the gun, you idiot! The dam—"

He didn't need to say more. With a final, furious *SCREECH* of metal, followed by a booming cannonade of exploding concrete, the thunderhead to the west finally found release. The dam burst. Lake Hebron, swollen by rain, came rushing down the hill to reclaim its old home.

A fresh horror came over Toby.

Promise you won't leave me alone again.

"My son!" Toby shouted to Richard, to Julian, to anyone who would listen. "Where is my—"

The flood struck the house like the fist of God himself.

VI

ALPHA AND OMEGA

FIRST JULIAN

IN HIS DEFENSE, JULIAN had been clean all summer.

Like most of his accomplishments, this was less impressive than it sounded. Can you really be proud of your sobriety when you didn't have much choice in the matter? He hadn't had the literal *time* to ride the white horse, let alone risk his job. His duties around Ramorah had been endless: cooking, cleaning, fucking candlestick making. He'd washed the dishes every evening, changed the linens every night, washed the cars every Wednesday and washed the laundry every Saturday and covered every inch of this house with a vacuum cleaner at least four times over. Julian had worked harder this summer than he'd worked in his entire goddamn life.

In more ways than one.

Do you know how hard it is to dust a boy's bedroom, week in and week out, and oh so casually *not* slip a few white morphine tablets from the little amber vial that Matthias always kept on his desk? Really, when you thought about the endless mounting tension of the past six months— when you thought about what had happened Friday, when Julian had brought Jerome his usual twelve o'clock coffee—you almost had to be proud of Julian for *not* cracking until he did.

Because crack he certainly had. Saturday morning, minutes before the family discovered Jerome's body on the roof, Julian had made his rounds with his little silver trolley, gathering up laundry and dropping off a few items and doing everything that was expected of him. It was a miracle, for example, that Alyssa Wright hadn't noticed Julian sticking that bank transfer in her purse, seeing as she'd been throwing up in the bathroom not ten feet away. Julian was so invisible to these people, they didn't even realize when he was in their suite with them.

Compared to the bank transfer, it had been child's play to take a few steps down the hall and do what needed to be done in Richard and

Kassandra's closet. They'd already headed down for the birthday party by the time he arrived to collect their laundry.

When he was done with the morning's errands, Julian's hands had been shaking so bad he'd knocked a half dozen cans of paint thinner off a shelf with his big silver trolley. He rode the service elevator down to the first floor and stuffed all the family's laundry into the industrial washing machines in the east wing. He'd been on his way to the sunroom—was literally stepping into the kitchen to help Marie with the birthday cake— when everyone started screaming. "Oh my dear Jesus, it's Daddy."

They'd found Jerome early.

Nope. Nope, nope, nope, nope, nope, nope. As the rest of the family had started scrambling, Julian had dipped back into the hall, made a beeline to the same service elevator he'd used not fifteen minutes earlier, climbed back out onto the second floor like he was rewinding his life (if only). In what felt like the space of a single long breath, Julian was in and out of Matthias's bedroom with that amber vial finally tucked into his pocket and a pill slipping down his throat.

Morphine, morphine—what made you so mean?

Julian knew, even as he did it, that in stealing Matthias's pills, he was doing exactly what this family would *think* he'd done when word got out that he was AWOL. In the end, that was the worst part about an addiction: you really do behave as horribly as everyone expects you to. Marie sometimes still asked Julian "what his wound was," what had made him so sad, so angry, so desperate for a little chemical consolation. Julian always told her he had no idea what she was talking about.

He'd long since stopped feeling bad about lying to his sister.

The truth was this: Julian needed pills because fifteen years ago he'd learned too much about the world—about its capacity for pain, its inventory of monsters—on a long, endless afternoon on a crumbling rock wall in the woods just west of nowhere. That day, that summer, Julian had let down the one person he'd ever loved. Let them down in the most irredeemable way possible.

After an experience like the one Julian had endured at Camp Cleave, how was he supposed to handle a world so cruel without a little help? The Lord had made poppies, right? Surely the God of Israel expected us to use every resource his bounty had provided?

The Big Guy in the Sky had certainly made it hard enough to live here.

The boy back then, the one at Camp Cleave, the one Julian had let down: his name had been William. *Beautiful* didn't begin to describe their face. There were old souls in the world, funny souls, tender souls—Pisces, in other words—but even now, fifteen years later, Julian was certain there'd never been another soul like William's. The two of them, William and Julian, had arrived at Camp Cleave on the same day, been assigned to the same cabin, had kissed almost the moment the lights went out. By the end of the week, they were in love. They were both seventeen, the age at which such a thing is perfect and easy.

Their only problem had been Richard Wright, Julian's cousin: a tyrant with a large dick and a tiny heart who'd already spotted William for himself.

Richard Wright had been working at the camp as a counselor that summer, and even at seventeen Julian had understood him at a glance. The suburbs of Dallas where Julian grew up were infested with boys like Richard, angry Christians so desperate to prove their worth (which is to say, their masculinity), they're convinced they can intimidate their own hearts into compliance. Show-offs. Athletes. Brawny hunks with bumper stickers like I DEADLIFT FOR JESUS. That summer fifteen years ago, Richard had just reached the age where he was finally beginning to realize that the harder he fought his heart, the harder it fought back.

God help them all.

When Richard saw someone like William, someone with a woman's gentle throat and a man's deep voice and a body like silk wrapped around a stone, he'd been helpless. "Your cousin's bi, you know," William had said to Julian one evening, not long after the cousin in question had pulled William into the woods for a *private prayer session*. A few spots of dry white were still crusted to the corner of William's mouth. "Richard hates himself for it. I almost feel sorry for him."

"You're seventeen," Julian had said. "Isn't that rape?"

William shrugged the shoulders of his khaki camp uniform, tugged at them in the mirror like he couldn't make them fit. "It was kind of hot, honestly."

Julian had been so jealous of Richard, he'd thought it would suffocate him. Jealous and aghast and sad.

It was nothing compared to the horror that came the next day. Sunday. The day Jerome was scheduled to come preach at Camp Cleave.

"Richard told me your grandpa sometimes takes a special interest in a boy or two here," William said as they dressed for breakfast.

"My *great*-grandfather," Julian corrected. "Wait, what?"

———————————

Julian never learned how Richard discovered what he and William were up to in their cabin after lights-out. Maybe William told him, perhaps under some sort of duress during one of their *private prayer sessions*. Maybe Richard just had a nose for what he could never really possess (love, in other words).

However it happened, Richard sidled up next to Julian at the breakfast buffet that Sunday morning, a few hours before Jerome came to preach, and said, "Hey, cuz."

"Oh, look. You finally admitted we're related." Julian didn't meet Richard's eye as he shoveled eggs onto his plate. "Does that mean I can leave early?"

"Are you afraid of heights?"

"How did you know?" Julian winced the moment the words were out of his mouth. He hadn't been nearly so good at concealing himself back then.

"No reason," Richard said, and stalked off with a smile.

But of course there had been a reason. Not two hours later, Richard had pulled Julian out of an archery class and driven him in one of the camp's little golf carts to a limestone cliff at the far edge of the property, talking nonstop, full of horrible rumors he'd heard about Jerome and the unfortunate boys at the camp who the old man took a shine to.

"Apparently, Grandpa always asks the staff if there's anyone here who needs special attention from the Lord, you know. He takes them for a ride in his private jet, shows them the world—if you know what I mean." Richard snickered. "I've been wondering all day who I should recommend." Richard smiled. "And then I thought of your boyfriend."

"My . . . my what?"

"Let's make a deal, cuz."

Julian had already been too scared to speak. It makes your memory blurry, a fear like that. The next thing Julian remembered, he was halfway up that limestone cliff, wearing neither a harness nor a rope nor any decent shoes, his heart in his mouth and his bladder threatening to fail and, high above him, the pale, frightened face of William was looking down over the edge at him. Gentle William, who'd never done a thing wrong but exist.

"Hurry up, Sir Galahad," Richard said, laughing from the top of the cliff. "Your princess needs saving."

"Let him go!" Julian shouted, though he was so out of breath, his voice came out with a mewling sound like a cat's. "Leave him alone."

"I will. He's all yours. If you have the balls to get up here and take him."

"He's really high up," William had said in a low voice to Richard, no doubt hoping Julian wouldn't hear him (if only). "He shouldn't be so high up without any gear."

Richard grinned. "My family sent me here to make a man out of Julian. I sure hope he gets a move on. Grandpa will be here any minute now."

It wasn't that Julian hadn't *wanted* to climb that cliff and grab William by the hand and run into the woods together (and beat the shit out of Richard along the way). He just didn't know *how*. Every handhold Julian found in the soft rock seemed to crumble into chalk under his fingers. Every little ledge felt like it was evaporating under his feet. Somehow, through pure desperation, he'd climbed a few dozen feet and found a stable shelf and couldn't bring himself to rise another inch.

He made the mistake of looking down. Never look down.

He was still standing on the same shelf an hour later when the sound of a jet screamed through the air overhead. Richard had long since grown quiet at the top of the cliff, almost sullen, and when he looked over the edge to shake his head mutely at Julian, there was an unmistakable fear in his eyes. At the sight of that expression, Julian had hoped for a brief moment that Richard would say that of course he was joking, that he'd just wanted to torture Julian for having the audacity to love the object of his own desires, that they'd never speak of this again.

But no. Richard was the sort of man who followed through on his threats, even when he didn't want to. (A monster, in other words.) He left, taking William with him, and no one found Julian until that night, by which point he'd pissed himself and nearly collapsed from heatstroke.

They didn't see William again for three days. When the boy returned, there wasn't much left of him.

The night William returned, as they whispered in the dark of their cabin, Julian finally found the courage to ask, "What happened? Where did you go with Jerome?"

Twenty minutes later, when William wound down his story, Julian wished he hadn't asked. "Why would Jerome make you wear the black suit?" he whispered to William. "And why would he have a horse stable that looks like a house? At his own estate?"

"If I think about it anymore it would probably kill me," William said. "The old guy gave me some pills. Wanna share?"

Morphine, morphine—what made you so mean?

Fifteen years later, on Saturday morning at Ramorah, as Julian's awful family had scrambled to the roof to study Jerome's corpse, Julian himself had stepped out into the rain, the taste of Matthias's morphine still stinging his tongue. He knew they'd crossed a river, this family. He knew there was no swimming back.

Jerome had told Julian as much the day before, Friday at noon, right before the old man handed over those notes he wanted delivered to Alyssa and Toby. God help them all.

Julian didn't pack a bag as he left Ramorah. He didn't say goodbye to his sister. He didn't even take a putter, though that was probably the morphine's fault. Julian had walked out into the rain, walked the southern drive to the gate—

And discovered that the road was flooded. Then he saw that the phones were dead. Even drugged as he was, Julian realized what it would mean for the rest of the weekend if the police couldn't reach the property and he couldn't leave. Oh dear.

He popped two more morphine and wandered. What else was he supposed to do?

Julian knew that last year a "friend of the family" from Camp Cleave named Timothy Sage had beat the shit out of Jerome to flee the stable where he'd been held. The boy had escaped through a hole in the wall in the woods. Julian knew this mostly because he was an excellent eavesdropper, and the family had made him repair that same hole: there was no escape that way now. And so as the storm grew more violent, Julian instead found his feet carrying him to the one building he'd avoided ever since he'd arrived, the one corner of Ramorah he hadn't mapped out, examined, pondered over.

The old man took me to some weird building out in the woods, William had said, years and years ago. *A horse stable that looks like a house from the outside.*

Julian had found the stable without a problem. If you followed the path from the family's private airstrip there was no missing it. Inside the stable, Julian took two more pills—or was it four, six, eight, the whole fucking bottle?—and the last thing he remembered he was sitting down to rest his legs. Or maybe looking for a place to die. At least he'd had the bright idea to slip behind the rancid hay bales in the corner of the stable in case someone came looking for him. If Julian was on his way out, he didn't want any interruptions.

He should have died on Saturday, he really should have, but even after six months of sobriety, his tolerance was simply too high for things to be that easy.

Instead, Julian had slept for twenty-four hours straight.

At one point, Julian dreamed that Toby had stepped into the stables and called his name. He dreamed he saw Jerome guiding William into those stables and discovering a dozen other broken boys piled up, like unwashed laundry, in heaps and piles around the gravel floor.

He dreamed he saw a much younger Jerome step into the stables with a man his same age. Julian dreamed the other man said, *We need to stop. This isn't good for us.*

And Jerome had replied, *Of course we'll stop. After one more time.*

Julian dreamed that a damp hand had gripped him by the shoulder, that cold lips had whispered frantically in his ear: *gehtepgehtepgehtep.*

Get up, get up, get up.

And then he was awake.

Julian didn't know it was Sunday morning when he finally stirred. He didn't know that the knife had been planted in Toby's room or that Luca was missing or that the police had been called.

Julian didn't know that the dam was ready to fail.

His phone was dead and the sky was dark, so he assumed it was still Saturday night. He stretched his stiff back and took a piss in the woods and started back for the main house just as the rain began again. He needed food. He needed more pills. He knew how to get in and out of Ramorah without being seen. Maybe he could—

"Let me go! Let me go!"

Julian was nearly to the stables—the family's fancy stables, that is, the ones that corralled nothing but luxury cars—when Luca's little voice cut through the air. It was coming from very close by.

Julian had no interest in being a hero. If anyone else—literally *anyone* else—had been in danger, he would probably not have done what he'd done. But Julian's heart was with Luca. How could it not be?

The moment he heard the boy scream, Julian dropped into a crouch and hastened around the side of the stables, ducking out of sight a moment before the building's door rolled open and a white putter darted out into the rain.

Julian wiped water from his eyes. He stared after the putter, straining to see its occupants in the dark. A flash of lightning did him a favor. Luca sat in the golf cart's passenger seat, looking small and trembly and scared.

And next to him was Corah, the old woman who Julian had always thought was a shade crazier than a shithouse rat.

She certainly looked it now. Corah's gray hair was flying everywhere, her tatty bathrobe practically falling from her shoulders. Little Luca tried to climb from the putter's seat, and Corah clawed him back in without ever taking her eyes off the road. She flipped on the putter's headlights. She rocketed north.

What the hell was she doing? Where was Toby? Where was Corah taking his son? There was nothing in that direction but the north creek, which presumably was just as flooded as the south.

Flooded.

Luca shouted, his voice already vanishing into the storm. "Help!"

Oh fuck, Julian thought. *Oh fuck, oh fuck, oh fuck.*

With a hard shake like a dog trying to rouse himself, Julian lumbered into the stables, unplugged a putter, grabbed its key from the visor. Dropped it. Grabbed it again, gunned the engine, and backed the putter straight into an Audi with a deafening crash of glass and metal.

The morphine clearly had not worn off.

By the time Julian had guided the putter out of the stables, Corah's lights had almost vanished into the void.

FIRST LUCA

IT HAD TAKEN HIM a long time (long enough to make Tobias worried), but Luca finally knew his days: Monday, Tuesday, blah, blah, blah, Friday. Friday was when he'd first seen him, Mister Suit, looking tall and sad and lonely in the corner of the room where the rest of the family had all eaten lunch and pretended to be happy to meet Luca and his daddy. Mister Suit had watched them all, silent and so perfectly still. Luca had thought at first he might be some kind of dummy—what did they call the plastic people they hung clothes on at the dead malls? Manatees?—until the man glanced down to adjust the button of his nice suit's black sleeve.

When Luca had pointed to the man and asked his daddy, "Why is everyone ignoring him?" a look of stunned surprise had passed over Mister Suit's dark face and Luca had wondered, as he would soon wonder all weekend, if he'd *Stepped in It*, as Tobias used to say. For some reason, Luca Stepped in It a lot at this house.

When Luca's daddy looked confused in the sunny room—when it seemed for all the world like Tobias couldn't even *see* Mister Suit—Mister Suit tilted his head at Luca and brought a finger to his lips. *Shh.*

"Never mind," Luca had said to Tobias. "I think he's shy."

Luca saw Mister Suit again that evening, standing in the bathroom at the bottom of the stairs in the big front hall before dinner, waiting for him with a cautious sort of look, like he wasn't sure Luca could see him at all. When Luca started to excuse himself—did they not lock the door in this house???—Mister Suit had held up a hand (*wait*) and then pointed a long finger to the potted flower on the counter. Luca eased up the orchid's pot, looked at what was hidden underneath, looked back to say thank you, but Mister Suit was gone. Maybe they didn't say goodbye in this house either. Luca hated it here.

They didn't get a chance to talk until that night, right as the storm was starting, when Mister Suit had wrapped a cold hand around Luca's ankle in the dark and scared the libbing bajeebus out of him. Luca had opened his mouth to scream, but in the weak light of the vanishing stars he'd seen Mister Suit's face studying him (if that was the word for it) with a shadowy sort of concern.

Mister Suit's mouth didn't move, but somehow he managed to talk in fast little whispers.

kanooseemee

Can you see me?

"Yes," Luca whispered back. Outside, the storm had started.

anndoounnerstanmee

And you understand me?

"Doesn't everyone?"

When had the room gotten so cold?

Then don't be afraid. I'm a friend. I'll keep you safe.

Safe? Wasn't that what his daddy was for?

Maybe. Except last night, Saturday, after Tobias fell down the stairs, Mister Richard—how could someone who smelled so nice be so *mean*?—grabbed Luca by the waist and dragged him back to the room with all the paint splashed around it and smiled to Miss Alyssa and said, "You're ours now, little guy." Like Luca was a dog.

Luca was allergic to dogs. And assholes. ("You don't need to use every word I teach you, bud.")

Miss Ruth had stepped in. Luca liked Miss Ruth. She'd helped Luca change into his pajamas and his sparkle socks and taken him to a *very* comfy couch in her room and given Mister Hugo a pill and said, "You both get some rest now. Tomorrow is going to be a long day."

But how could Luca sleep when poor Miss Ruth spent all night moaning and mumbling and crying in her sleep? And then when Mister Hugo started up in the same way? They both sounded like they were being tortured in their dreams.

What was *really* wet-your-pants creepy was the way it sounded like they were both dreaming the same dream.

It was almost a relief when Mister Suit had slipped into the room and stood at Luca's side.

doouoowenttooseeuorfathr

Do you want to see your father?

Luca nodded, not making a sound.

Then follow me.

Mister Suit led him into the suite's main room, showed him how to climb on a chair and turn the latch, and then held up a hand—*wait*—even though Luca didn't hear anyone outside. After a moment, Mister Suit nodded.

itstime

Luca opened the door just in time to see Alyssa step into Miss Sarah Nella's suite down the hall.

Follow her, Mister Suit had said.

Luca's heart sank. He'd never liked Alyssa, and he didn't think his daddy did either. Luca didn't really understand money or education or any of that ("I have to plan for your future, bud"), and so he'd never understood why his daddy had married a lady who smirked at Tobias whenever his back was turned. Like she was getting ready to play a prank on him.

Luca had tried to tell his daddy about this. Tobias had brushed it aside. Luca let it go. After Luca's mommy died, Tobias had been so sad and sick and lonely ("Why did I ever give her that fucking letter?"), Luca had worried his daddy might never get better. It was why Luca had never let himself cry. Luca was afraid that if he started crying, then neither of them, he or Tobias, would ever be able to stop.

But when Tobias had met Alyssa, he'd started to get better. Tobias had locked up his sad memories in the weird basement he'd built in his brain and gotten married. Once, a few weeks ago, Luca had asked, "Do you remember the time we came home and Mommy was making us eggs?" and Tobias had stared at Luca with a perfect, blank frown. "When she what?"

It sometimes scared Luca, how much his daddy could make himself forget.

Last night in Ramorah, Luca did as Mister Suit instructed him. Alyssa didn't hear him come through the cracked door of Miss Sarah Nella's suite (like everyone else, she'd forgotten to lock it). She didn't notice Luca as she grabbed one of the heavy pillows off the floor and pressed it over Miss Sarah Nella's face and Miss Sarah Nella started thrashing around all crazy-like.

It wasn't until Miss Sarah Nella went still—went completely still, like Luca's mommy had done—that Alyssa finally glanced over her shoulder and saw Luca standing there, puzzled, wondering why a doctor who was supposed to fix people would do something like *that*.

Luca had thrashed around like crazy too, when Alyssa snatched him up and smacked a hand over his mouth and dragged him halfway across the house and threw him into a weird wooden closet in an even weirder bedroom and said, panting, "Just stay put for a while, all right? I'll come get you later."

Slam. Thunk. Luca waited until she was definitely gone before he tried to push open the door. There was something heavy on the other side, locking him in.

His father, it went without saying, was nowhere to be seen.

So when Luca felt Mister Suit slip out of the dark to come talk to him a few minutes later, Luca realized for the first time that maybe he'd been dumb not to be a little afraid of a man made of shadows who talked in whispers. It was thanks to Mister Suit he'd followed Alyssa in the first place. It was thanks to Mister Suit he was here at all, trapped like a bug in a rug.

And now there was no getting away from him.

SECOND LUCA

OORSKAIRED

You're scared.

"You said you were taking me to see my daddy." Luca edged away from Mister Suit's voice, but where was there to go? The wooden closet was the size of the bathroom on the airplane they'd taken from California.

Mister Suit seemed to consider this. *Yes. But I didn't say it would be tonight.*

Luca frowned. "You tricked me."

No. I'm helping you. But I need you to help me first.

"You should have asked."

Yes. I'm sorry. I'm out of practice.

"At what?"

Helping people.

Luca considered this. People said all the time that children have good *instincts* for people ("Yeah—most people in-*stink*," he'd said when he'd first heard this, and had laughed at his own joke for days), and frankly,

Luca had no idea if this was true. He found himself relaxing in the dark closet not so much because he trusted Mister Suit, or even because he liked him very much right then, but because if the man had wanted to hurt him he probably would have done it by now.

Right?

"*Should* I be afraid of you?"

No. Not you.

"Who are you anyway?"

I was a man. A man a lot like you.

Luca struggled to think what this could mean. "You liked sparkled socks?"

I probably would have worn them when I was young, yes. Mister Suit made a wheezy sound that Luca guessed was his version of a laugh. *People would have been just as bothered by it then as they are now. More so.*

"Who cares about pink socks?"

Idiots.

"Oh. Tobias says the same thing."

He loves you very much, Luca. You're lucky to have a father who loves you like that. The luckiest boy in the world.

"I know."

You don't. You never will.

"Were you lucky too?"

No. No, I wasn't.

Luca shivered. "So you're dead."

Yes.

"Have you seen my mommy?"

No. She's already moved on. Like I want to do.

"But you can't. Because you have unfinished business." Mister Suit had mentioned that already, when Luca's daddy had driven out to the little house in the woods yesterday. *No one* liked that little house in the woods.

Yes.

"If I help you finish your business, can you go see her? My mommy?"

I think so. Yes. Is there something you'd like to tell her?

Luca gave this a great deal of thought. "No. I just want her to have a friend. A friend who won't get her into trouble like the ones she had back home."

I'm out of practice at that, too. Being a friend. Mister Suit hesitated. *But I'll try.*

"Then I'll help you finish your business. Deal?"

He could feel Mister Suit smile. *Deal.*

Luca shook hands with the dark.

They talked a *lot*, almost all night, in fact, with little breaks when Mister Suit departed to *Get things in motion.* Luca had no real sense of time to begin with, and the bedroom outside the closet had no windows, which made it a surprise when Mister Suit seemed to gather himself (which must have been hard to do, when you weren't really anywhere at all) and said, *It's time.*

"Time to pee?"

Time to see your father.

Oh. That was *much* better. "Is he coming now?"

No. A woman will be coming soon. The craziest cunt who's ever walked this earth.

"That sounds scary."

It should. She's the reason Jerome warned your father to look out for you, even though Jerome didn't really understand why until right before he died. That woman is the danger the Pleiades have been warning of for days. The lethal sister. The one who set all of this in motion. Mister Suit hesitated. *She's more dangerous than you could possibly imagine, Luca.*

"I'd really rather see my daddy if that's okay."

Mister Suit didn't get a chance to reply. Miss Corah came bursting into the bedroom a few seconds later, panting and sweaty and loud—"You can't run from me anymore, Cleave! You can't hide!"—and Luca had done his best not to be afraid. He'd let Corah drag him from the closet and around a corner and down the hall where Mister Jerome had slept dead yesterday. Luca watched her wrench a ring of keys from her pocket and unlock the door at the end of the hall that she'd told his daddy, yesterday, didn't have a key anymore. She was crazy *and* a liar.

And she got him wet a minute later, dragging him out into the rain, mumbling to herself all the while. "No one knows this," she said. "But I'm still strong for eighty-six."

Luca didn't like to admit it, but she had a point. He started screaming as she dragged him into the stables, but who could hear him now that the storm had started up again?

Corah threw him into the putter and went rocketing into the dark.

The darkness around them was so thick, Luca wondered if they'd somehow sunk to the bottom of the lake. Miss Corah was hunched over the wheel of the putter, muttering to herself, looking for all the world like the sad women with shopping bags and no shoes who used to sleep outside their apartment building in LA.

She was too busy talking to herself to notice the way Mister Suit had started whispering in Luca's hear. *Repeat after me, Luca. I hope it works.*

Luca did as he was told.

"Cleave used to be so angry because of what you did, Miss Corah."

Corah shuddered. She stepped on the gas.

"He used to be angry, but now he's grateful you did what you did," Luca went on. "It's given him a long time to learn and think. A lot of quiet nights to study the stars."

"Oh, yes. Cleave always loved his stars. Like a pagan."

"'The heavens declare the glory of God.' The Lord put the stars in place for us to study them, Miss Corah. Jesus said it Himself—'there will be signs in the sun, moon and stars.' Daniel was put in charge of astro-lo-gers. The same school of astro-lo-gers who followed the stars to find the baby Jesus in the manger. Mister Suit says it's not pagan to study what God's trying to tell us. Why would he have gone to the trouble of arranging them up there otherwise?"

"Oh, yes. Cleave's been working on you, too. Just like I thought. Just like he worked on Jerome when they took their first long tour together. My brother Cleave was an illness, child. A corruption that dirtied everything it touched." Corah bounced them over a rock. "And now he's taken up residence in you, child. I've known it from the minute I saw you. Cleave's grown so terribly worse since you arrived."

"What are you talking about?"

"Possession, dear heart. Spiritual warfare."

Even Cleave paused at that. "You think he's . . . taking over me? Like he took over Miss Sarah Nella last night?"

"Oh, I think it's worse than that, child. Not that anyone listened to me all weekend." Corah cut a glance at Luca. "You look just like him in this light, you know."

What the heck was that supposed to mean?

They were coming near the north creek: Luca could hear its water up ahead in the dark, a distant roar like a river. Mister Suit started whispering with a fresh urgency. Luca was getting scared.

"Mister Suit says you didn't understand what you saw that day in the horse stables sixty years ago, Miss Corah. That day after he and Jerome got back from their first tour. Mister Suit says he can't blame you for being confused. You were young. Sheltered. Nai . . . naive."

"Shut up, child."

"Or maybe you were jealous. Maybe you wished it had been you."

"QUIET!"

"Mister Suit said he was trying to stop it. He knew it wasn't good for Jerome, none of it, it was confusing things in Jerome that didn't need to be confused. Mister Suit was trying to stop it in a way that wouldn't make things worse. He knew it could cause an ob . . . ob . . . obsession for Jerome if Mister Suit didn't end it right. But because you did what you did, that's exactly what happened. Jerome became obsessed with what he'd lost. Obsessed. What's that mean?"

Corah eased off the gas. She turned, very slowly, to stare at Luca. She said calmly, "There's nothing confusing about what I saw my brothers doing in our old stables. Cleave was mounting Jerome like a horse. I think they'd been doing it since they hit the road. Cleave was a disease, child. I had to do something about him before he ruined Jerome."

Lightning cracked, straight above their heads.

"Mister Suit says it hurts to drown, Miss Corah," Luca said in a tiny voice. "He says it hurts worse than anything you could ever imagine."

"I didn't drown him! I just wanted to talk to Cleave, privately, about what I'd seen that day in the horse stables. Has Cleave told you everything *he* said to *me* that afternoon by the creek? The *language* he used against me? You would have done the same thing, child. Any woman would." Corah gunned the putter's engine. Still in that horrible, calm voice she said, "I just gave Cleave a little push. Is it my fault he never learned how to swim?"

Luca went very cold. This woman might have been even more dangerous than Mister Suit had said.

"Abigail saw, though," Corah continued. "Our neighbor. She'd stayed home at the farm next door even though she'd told me she was going into town with Jerome that day. She saw two people leave for the creek and only one person come back. She never breathed a word about it, not even to me, but twenty years later she built this house and filled it with those awful carvings on the walls. All those pictures of drowning and death. Abigail commissioned those carvings to punish me, child. To punish me for doing something she would have never been brave enough to do in the first place."

THIRD LUCA

LUCA THOUGHT HE'D BEEN scared before in his life, but nothing had prepared him for the fear that hit when something finally loomed up in the putter's headlights: the north gate. The creek on the other side was so swollen with water it bucked and seethed over the creek's banks. The creek's water was a funny color. It looked green.

The wailing boy slips beneath green waves.

Oh, jeebus.

The gate slid open. Miss Corah led the car into its path. Stopped. Breathed.

A terrible silence passed between them.

Luca opened his mouth to speak, and the old woman grabbed his arm and dragged him out into the rain.

He told himself not to be afraid, but that was getting to be a challenge the closer she dragged him to the water's edge. Miss Corah really was strong for her age.

And Luca didn't know how to swim.

He started screaming.

Luca.

Mister Suit's whispers were almost completely swallowed by the storm.

Luca, listen.

Luca dug in his heels to slow Corah down. They only slipped on the mud, and he fell on his butt.

She kept right on dragging him.

Luca lis—you mu—, Mister Suit said, but his voice vanished in the breeze.

Miss Corah brought Luca to within a few yards of the water before she stopped with a little pant and wiped rain from her eyes. "I really don't want to do this, boy."

After all this screaming, Luca, too, had to catch his breath. "Then why are you?"

Behind him, the putter's wipers let out a desperate *cree-eak* as they struggled against the rain.

Cree-eak.

Cree-eak.

"Because—" Corah heaved him another pace. "Because I can't let another child like you take root in this family. Jerome was never the same after Cleave was through with him. They crossed a line when they were out on the road together. A line that no siblings should ever cross."

"What does any of that have to do with me? I don't have any brothers."

"Maybe not yet. But Sarah Nella is always right. Things have a habit of repeating in this family."

A big loud *GRO-O-O-OAN* came from the darkness to Luca's left. It sounded like it was coming from up the hill.

Corah turned her head in that direction. Rain had plastered her hair against her skull, so flat and thin you wouldn't think she even had hair at all. "Ah," she said to the metal noise. "Yes."

With a loud grunt, she dragged Luca right to the edge of the green water, so close he could feel drops of creek jump up from its banks and leach through his filthy sparkle socks.

Luca started babbling. "Mister Suit . . . Mister Suit told me things about you last night, Miss Corah. He said you'll never understand how bad you hurt this family."

"Please, be quiet, child."

"You hurt *everyone.* You started all of this. All the horrible things Mister Jerome did with all those friends of the family, it was just because he wanted to get back that afternoon in the stables with Cleave. Back when he was happy. He was never happy again after he lost Cleave, Miss Corah. All Jerome ever wanted was to see his brother's face one more time."

The words made the voice hitch in Luca's throat. He'd wanted to do the same thing with his mommy for ages and ages, ever since she left the house for the very last time.

Corah gave Luca's arm a jerk toward the water. He dug his heels into the mud and, to his absolute luck, finally struck against a rock that didn't budge. Corah wobbled. She wobbled but she didn't let him go. "Move. I said move!"

Luca just kept on babbling because he couldn't think of anything else to do. He'd never talked to an adult like this before. He wished he could enjoy it.

"Mister Suit says you poisoned this family when you killed him. You made a dead star and you sent everyone spinning around it. It's already starting again with Richard. Cleave says you can see it in his eyes. He says Richard's already getting bored with his sister. Maybe this time it'll be young girls he gets interested in, or it'll be boys, or all the people in the middle. But whatever he does, Cleave wants you to know that inno . . . innocent people are going to suffer all over again. Things *do* have a habit of repeating in this family. And it's all your fault."

Corah hit Luca, hard, across the mouth. He'd never been hit in his life. The shock of the blow turned his limbs into jelly. Corah gave a great roar, wrenched him off his feet, and flung him toward the creek.

Luca was up. He was airborne.

He was flying.

And then a hand reached out and grabbed his ankle in the dark.

Corah's eyes widened in surprise. She hadn't yet let go of Luca's wrist, and with her momentum interrupted, she stumbled toward the creek. The hand around Luca's ankle tightened. It pulled him free.

Corah fell. She landed on all fours, right on the water's edge. She turned back over her shoulder to see who had grabbed Luca and never noticed the *other* hand—the wet, cold hand—rising up from the green waves of the creek.

She didn't notice the hand from the creek until it had wrapped its fingers around her arm.

A hideous shape, worse than anything from Luca's deepest nightmares, rose from the green waves. The thing in the water had once looked like a man—a tall, thin man—but strips of skin and rotted black fabric dangled from his gaunt frame like ribbons. Water drained out of his mouth and ears and nose, just like Luca imagined it had done when they'd pulled his mother out of the bathtub where she'd drownded. Drowned. Like Mister Suit.

The shape's voice was suddenly speaking from everywhere. He wasn't whispering anymore.

"THE LORD WILL HAVE HIS JUSTICE!"

Mister Suit pulled Corah's arm so hard that Luca felt-heard-*saw* the bone come loose from the shoulder with a *crack*.

"AND I—"

Mister Suit crushed Corah's face into the waves. Into the rocks.

"WILL—"

He held her down. Blood and water bubbled around her wild hair.

"HAVE—"

He grabbed her hair, wrenched up Corah's face to stare her in the eyes.

"MINE!"

Caught in the glow of the putter's lamps, Mister Suit opened his bone-mouth in a roar of absolute dizzy joy. He fell backward into the creek, roaring all the while, and vanished downstream.

He dragged Corah, screaming, along with him.

There wasn't much to see after that: a few green waves, a single desperate hand, a flash of a muddy foot. The creek swept Corah away, and Mister Suit with her.

SECOND JULIAN

IT WAS UNNERVING, TO hold a child in his arms. Fifteen years ago at Camp Cleave, a counselor had once told Julian that his sinful attractions to men were born out of a satanic desire to corrupt innocence, especially the innocence of young boys. A diagnosis of demonic possession wasn't off the table. Julian had been stupid enough to laugh.

Now, in the dark wilds of Ramorah, he realized (because somehow, he always needed reminding) just how deeply those two weeks at Camp Cleave had cut into his soul. He released Luca the moment Corah vanished into the water, almost like he was afraid his touch might expose the boy to some incurable disease. "Are you . . . all right?"

Luca seemed strangely unfazed by the way Corah, to Julian's eyes, had just drowned herself in the creek. The boy studied his muddy feet. "My sparkles are gone."

"Sounds like a net win, honestly." Julian wiped rain from his face. He felt stone sober by now, at least he could say that much, and the coast appeared to be clear for the moment. Julian opened his mouth. There was something he'd thought he'd never get the chance to tell Luca: that the boy could be whoever he wanted to be, for however long he wanted to be, that no one had it in their power to take away a single iota of his worth or value or joy.

Julian wanted to tell this small, sturdy child that he was perfect just as he was, but life didn't give him the chance. The moment Julian opened his mouth, another great groan of metal rumbled down from the darkness to the west.

He'd heard a similar sound a moment ago, though he'd been so busy running to grab hold of Luca before the house's resident psychopath could heave the boy into the creek, he hadn't had time to register just what it meant.

Now he had no choice. "Oh, Jesus. It's the dam."

Julian's putter hauled ass across the dark fields. They bounced over gravel and standing water and stones, whizzing toward the house like a bat out of hell.

They were halfway to Ramorah when he spotted another pair of headlights coming his way, and moving just as fast. Julian hesitated, slowing enough to see who was in the other putter and what they wanted (while still having plenty of momentum to make a break for it), but there was no need to bother.

Hugo whizzed by them, heading northwest with a grim frown.

"Hey wait!" Julian shouted after him, but Hugo didn't slow. The man looked like he was on his way to the church, where Julian could just make out the distant shape of a small, plump woman waiting in an open doorway. Ruth. She was waving, though Julian had the strangest feeling she wasn't waving at her husband.

It was like she was waving to him, to Julian. Like she was waving goodbye.

The groaning from the dam climbed an octave. Julian turned away, tightened his knuckles on the wheel. If that dam was going to go—and frankly, the way it was sounding, that was more a *when* question than an *if* question—there was only one place on this estate that might be high enough to survive the coming flood.

"Hold on to something," Julian said to Luca, and floored the gas.

"That way!" Luca shouted as they neared the house. "She left a door open in the left wing."

"You mean west?"

"*Go!*"

Following Luca's finger, Julian spotted a door standing open in the wall of the west wing. The ground was so soaked the putter nearly skidded into the house when Julian slammed the brakes. "Let's move."

Julian didn't have a remarkable memory. It had taken him ages, but Julian had finally mapped the entirety of the west wing after moving into Ramorah with his sister last spring. That mental map now served him well. Without a moment's hesitation, he shot through a maze of empty halls, Luca hot on his heels, and shouldered open a section of brocaded wall that didn't even look like a door.

God was on Julian's side: the elevator in the west wing's service closet—a closet identical in every way to the one in the east wing, right down to the silver trolley and half dozen bottles of acetone—was waiting for them.

They were nearly to the third floor when Luca looked up at Julian and said, with a plain, simple kindness, "I think you're a good person, Julian."

The words sent a wad of sobs rising up Julian's throat. He forced them down. "I'm really not. But it's nice of you to lie."

A moment later, the elevator stopped at the third floor, just in time for them both to hear Richard shouting at someone in the hall outside. "You son of a bitch. YOU SON OF A BITCH!"

That didn't sound good.

"Stay here," Julian whispered to Luca. "I want to make sure everything's okay."

Julian really got a kick out of his own optimism sometimes. He stepped out of the service closet and into the dead-end hallway, where he discovered Alyssa and Richard and Toby and Marie and a very large gun, and yet somehow, *somehow*, they all had even bigger problems.

The groaning from the west climbed a last desperate octave. "Put down the gun, you idiot!" Julian shouted. "The dam's about to—"

Break. Which it did, quite stupendously.

The flood struck the house like the fist of God himself.

FIRST RICHARD

HE'D SURVIVED BOMBS BEFORE. Mortar shelling. Had felt a buddy next to him explode into a dozen pieces with the help of a Taliban RPG fired from a roadside cart in the middle of a perfect spring afternoon in Iraq. That buddy, the man who exploded, had had the nicest biceps Richard had ever seen. Strange, how an arm loses its appeal when it's no longer attached to a body.

The point is, sir, that Richard had felt the effects of heavy fire and it was nothing next to the force of a lake striking a three-story mansion.

At the moment of impact, right after his cousin Julian—of all fucking people—emerged from the service closet looking like a drowned rat, the entire world seemed to tilt on its axis. Standing where he was in the hall at the foot of the roof's concrete stairs, his gun trained on Toby's smug face, Richard stumbled sideways into the wall, discharging his firearm and worrying, for an agonizing moment, that he'd actually hurt someone.

His father Hugo had always said that Richard used to be softer. Kinder. And the man probably had a point: deep down, Richard didn't want anyone to suffer.

But if it was a choice between another person's suffering and his own—well.

The bullet grazed Toby's ear. Julian shouted, "Jesus, are you out of your mind?"

And then a moment later, a tiny figure bolted out of the service closet. It was Luca.

The boy dashed toward his father with a cry of "Daddy!" that made the hairs on Richard's arms stand on end. Richard grabbed Luca by his long hair as the child darted in front of him and tugged Luca toward the stairs.

The kid screamed. Toby, his face contorted with rage, tried to lunge toward Richard, but his cane landed at a strange angle on the canted floor and he fell to his knees with a roar of pain.

"You're hurting me—" Luca began, when a deafening *CRACK* of wood split the air.

Richard followed the sound, twisting at the hip just in time to see the end of the hall—hell, the entire western wall of the house—fall away.

One moment, Julian was standing there, right near the end of the hall, looking stunned and stupid and scared.

A moment later, he was gone.

"No!" Marie screamed. For all the good it did her. There was nothing at the end of the hall now but rain and sky and open air.

A horrible pain swept through Richard's chest. He refused to examine that pain. He gave Luca's hair a hard jerk. "Hurry. This way."

"Let me go!"

But Richard wouldn't do that, for the same reason he'd told Alyssa (the moment the rain returned and the county started sending him frantic emails about the dire state of the dam) to dig Luca out of whatever hiding place she'd stuck him in last night and bring him to the roof. Luca was too useful to lose, after all. Still—*still*—Richard was certain he could turn all of this around.

He would take over the show. He would steer the ministry into the future.

People would tune in to watch him preach. Millions of people. Millions of people would love him.

Richard would finally be loved.

Speaking of Alyssa, she was already well up the stairs by the time Richard started dragging Luca to the roof. Toby's words were still knocking around inside his head. Watching as his sister vanished onto the roof ahead of him, Richard wondered if it could really be possible that she was pregnant. That Richard would be a father.

The thought stirred a muddy puddle of emotions, none of which he had the wherewithal to process. He was not a man in touch with his emotions, Richard. Ever since his summer at Camp Cleave, Richard had fucked women, he'd fucked men, he'd fucked everyone in between. He'd fucked his own sister, it was true, off and on throughout the years, every time he needed to prove to himself that those *other* times with the fags and the trannies were aberrations, surprises, infectious itches to scratch and forget.

Richard fucked Alyssa whenever he needed to forget about that one boy at Camp Cleave, all those years ago. That perfect, smart, beautiful boy about whom Richard felt nothing. Nothing.

There was nothing wrong with Richard. No man who could get into his beautiful sister's pants could possibly bat for his own team, right?

Right?

Alyssa never complained, not even six weeks ago when Richard and their parents had come to LA. Nor had she complained this past Friday, when she and her new family had arrived at Ramorah and Kassandra had taken Luca by the hand down the hall and Toby had gone to the restroom and Richard had whispered into his sister's ear, *I want you. Tonight.*

Not even Richard, a man blind to the workings of his own heart, could miss the obvious. The last two times he'd felt the urge to be with Alyssa, it was when he'd been around Toby, a man who felt so familiar and beautiful and unnerving it set Richard's teeth on edge.

Toby and his strange, impossible son.

Now, here at Ramorah, Richard wrapped an arm around Luca's little chest and bundled the boy up the concrete stairs of the trembling house. They followed Alyssa to the roof. They arrived at the doorway just in time to see a patch of tar paper open up beneath Alyssa's feet.

A hole in the house swallowed his sister whole.

Richard shouted her name. She'd turned back to stare at him, looking stunned to have finally encountered a problem she couldn't spend or sweet-talk her way out of. One second Alyssa was here. The next she might as well have been a ghost.

Richard raced to the edge of the hole in the roof and saw nothing inside but a long drop through pipes and joists that seemed to stretch for miles before it ended in churning green water. A long red blanket he'd never seen before was stretched between the ends of two exposed pipes. A moment later, Richard realized it wasn't a blanket. It was the mother of his unborn child.

So much for that kid. Jesus. When little Luca turned to peer into the hole in the roof, Richard turned him away, kept him moving. No child needed to see that. Even one that could use some hair on his chest.

(It went without saying that Richard had yet to worry about his wife at all. She'd long since worn off both her luster and her usefulness.)

They hustled across the roof toward the main wing, Luca fighting and flailing with every step. It sounded like the house was coming apart beneath them. Not surprising. Ramorah was old, and Sarah Nella had always been stingy with repairs. But still. It's hard to stay frosty when your every move might send you plunging to your death. Richard had never cared for danger. A hole cracked open in the roof right beside him. If he hadn't been holding on to Luca, the boy would have been a goner.

Forward. That was Richard's motto, maybe his only guiding principle: always press forward.

They'd just reached the juncture of the west wing and the main house and hooked left around the boxy A/C compressors when Luca let out a scream. "Daddy!"

Hazarding a glance over his shoulder, Richard saw Toby and Marie headed his way. Of course. Toby had one arm braced on his cane, the other arm draped over Marie's shoulder. There was a resolve in Toby's eyes that sent alarm bells ringing in every corner of Richard's head. It was so familiar, that resolve. It had nagged Richard all weekend. Nagged him ever since he'd met Toby in LA.

Richard couldn't tell, for the life of him, if he found Toby beautiful or terrifying. It was like he'd met him before: in a past life, a past body. Or maybe he'd just always wanted to meet a man like Toby in the first place, disgusting as that was to admit even to himself.

That was all it was. It had to be.

Right?

Turning left, Richard started up the roof of the main wing, heading straight for the cross mounted above the north wall. Luca wasn't making it easy. The boy screamed. Flailed. Dug in his heels. In short, sir, he did such a goddamn fantastic job of slowing down the operation that by the time they neared the grand stretch of skylights above the sunroom, Toby and Marie had caught up to within twenty yards of them.

Close enough for them, too, to see what waited past the skylights, tethered by a length of rope to the base of the cross.

A steel rowboat.

Through the years, Richard's father had done his best to instill certain values in him. Humility. Respect. Faith. Not much had took, but that wasn't Hugo's fault: Richard had done his best to teach himself the same things and he'd never had much luck either. How could anyone be decent in a family like this? When the bedrock of their entire fortune was a glorified theft?

When their grandfather vanished, sometimes for days at a time, into a little shack in the woods that no one dared to speak about?

Another value that had never taken hold in Richard was any sort of respect for his mother's strange dreams. They used to come infrequently, like inland hurricanes, leaving behind nothing but an irritable, sleep-deprived father and a shaken mother liable to say things like, "I never appreciated how irrelevant time was to the Lord." Cool. Great. Glad to hear it.

But this morning, after Richard had spent the night seated outside Toby's door, Hugo had come trudging down the hall and said, "Get up. We're headed to the boathouse."

"The what?"

"Your mother had a dream."

"And bears shit in the woods."

"It wasn't just her. I saw it too. I had the same precise dream. I'd bet my life on it."

Richard rolled his eyes. "I guess we're all prophets in this family now."

Hugo had popped him across the mouth with the back of his hand. How long had it been since that had happened? "We need a putter and some rope. Come with me. Now."

Richard was thirty-two years old. He could deadlift twice his body-weight. Held the record at his old CrossFit studio in Aspen for most successive pull-ups. But when his father lifted himself up to his full height, he looked like a bull rearing on its back legs, and Richard was suddenly a soft, spooked child again, desperate for a hug.

He'd followed Hugo down the hall without a sound. Ridden to the boathouse near the north creek in silence. Lashed the steel rowboat to the roof of the putter and ridden back and hauled the boat up three flights of stairs, because of course it couldn't fit in the fucking elevator. They'd lugged it all the way through the west wing, getting lost twice, before they finally reached the concrete stairs and crossed half the length of the house and tied the boat here, to the base of the cross, and not to a more convenient and accessible place (like, say, the A/C compressors), all because his mother and father had had a dream that the boat needed to rest here and here alone.

And now look: the flood had come, and salvation was at hand. Maybe Richard should have paid more attention to his parents through the years. Maybe he would have missed them more now that they were surely gone.

The sunroom's skylights were so large they required a long central beam for support. The beam ran down the middle of the glass like a catwalk, connecting the solid tar paper of the main wing's roof to the sliver of concrete at the front edge of the house where the cross was mounted and the boat rested. The catwalk was maybe thirty feet long and barely wide enough to hold two men walking side by side.

When Richard reached the catwalk, he turned around. Toby and Marie weren't more than ten yards away. That was a lot of ground to cover with a bum knee, but Richard knew it wouldn't slow Toby down. The man had a kid on the line.

And that fire in Toby's eyes was burning brighter than ever.

Richard leveled the gun at Toby's face.

"Marie. You're family. Get in," Richard said.

"What about me?" Toby said. "Aren't I family?"

"The boat only seats three."

"So what's your plan?" Toby took a step forward. "Shoot me? Leave me here to drown?"

Toby took another step.

Another.

Richard swallowed a bubble of self-loathing. He pointed his M18 at Luca's temple. "You killed my grandfather, Toby. You're not going anywhere."

SECOND RICHARD

TIME FROZE FOR A moment. All sound ceased, like God had pulled the needle off the record. Toby stopped walking. His knuckles went white on the grip of his cane.

And then he laughed.

"Do you seriously think that, Richard? That I killed Jerome? How? How could I have gotten a knife from a locked drawer in the kitchen? How could I have gotten to the west wing without waking up Hugo on the landing? How would I have gotten out here onto the roof? How would I even know to look for Jerome up here in the first place? Fuck me, Richard, you tried to frame me for the murder and you still think *I did it*?"

"Someone's trying to frame me!" Richard bellowed. "Me and Alyssa both. Someone planted that paperwork in her purse to make sure the cops knew we were robbing the family, and then my wife found a knife in my closet to make them think I killed Jerome. I hadn't seen that knife since I used it to chop the salad for Friday's dinner. I never came within ten feet of the old man that night."

Except that wasn't exactly true. On Friday night, Richard had waited for Alyssa to creep from her room and meet him at the usual place they went to when they were home: the strange replica Jerome had made of his childhood bedroom in the west wing. That night, Friday, they hadn't lasted long. Richard had lain in Jerome's childhood bed and watched his naked sister slip into a deep sleep beside him. Jesus. What kind of animals had they become?

Richard had been very much awake. He'd been too anxious to sleep, soaked in thoughts and fears and pain. Richard was so divorced from his own heart—his desires, wishes, needs—that he sometimes felt like a man in a small boat adrift on an endless black sea. Dangerous tides governed that water, dragged him to places he never wanted to go. Tides that rose from a void too deep to ever dare explore.

Too terrifying even to name.

But as Alyssa started to snore in bed beside him on Friday night, Richard swung his legs to the floor and pulled on his jeans. He left the little bedroom. He headed west.

He found the old man in the dead-end hallway just as Jerome was stepping out of his study. Jerome had changed into a white sweater since dinner. For the first time in ages, Jerome looked surprised about something. The sight of Richard, specifically.

"What are you doing here?" Jerome said. "Do you know what time it is?"

Reflexively, Richard looked at his watch. It was six minutes to midnight. "I wanted to talk to you."

"Can't it wait?"

"No." But now that Richard was here, at the place those black tides of his heart had dragged him, he hesitated. "I need . . . I need guidance. Spiritual guidance."

"Now's not a good time."

"To help your grandson? To tell me what the Lord's done to my heart? I just fucked my sister, sir. Right here in your house. I've fucked men. Women. Trannies and lady boys and whatever the fuck you want to call the hookers in New Orleans. I've fucked people and I've hurt people and I don't know why. Sometimes I get so scared I think it'll kill me, sir. Do you hear me? Scared out of my mind. I think I want to be faithful to my wife, I think I want to be faithful to the church, but no matter how hard I try, I never am. Sir, please, just say it—what is wrong with me?"

Ramorah itself seemed to let out a murmur of surprise at this. The walls buckled. The floor seemed to tilt, ever so subtly, like even the house wanted to get away from this conversation.

Somewhere down the hall, a clock was ticking.

"You're asking *me*?" Jerome had fixed Richard with a smile that wasn't quite compassionate. "Do you remember the summer you worked at Camp Cleave?"

"Yes." But Richard would rather not.

"Do you remember the boy you told me could use some special attention? The one you said was struggling in his walk with the Lord?"

"Yes." Richard remembered everything about that boy: his long neck, his thick hair, his hard eyes. Richard remembered everything about the boy but his name. William Something. Poor Will.

"Did you know what would happen to that boy, thanks to you?" Jerome went on. "Didn't the other counselors mention that the boys who left with me on the Gulfstream never quite came back the same? Didn't you ever wonder what I did in that little house in the woods here?"

They had. He had. And still Richard had done it. He'd pointed William out to Jerome because he'd wanted to torture Julian, a distant half-breed cousin no one in the family wanted around.

Except that wasn't the full story, no sir. Richard had also sent William off with Jerome because William was the most beautiful person Richard had ever seen. Richard had noticed guys in high school, of course, but then he'd also noticed the girls, too. That was normal, right? That was just hormones.

But that boy at Camp Cleave, William: he'd done something to Richard. It had terrified him, the things that boy made him want. The things they did in the woods. The life Richard had almost dared to imagine with him.

William had terrified Richard and Richard had been scared and Richard had snuffed out the boy's spark. It was the only way to be safe.

Jerome glanced at his watch. "You're just like me, son. Practically identical. You want to be loved. Happy. Safe. You want the power to make your heart behave. The power to get back a moment that almost felt like Eden. But you'll never have it, boy. You were born in the wrong family. The wrong home. I've spent my whole life striving for the precise same things as you, and look at the damage I've done. Decades of horror, boy.

Decades." Jerome put a hand on Richard's shoulder. "I pray to God you never get the same opportunity."

Outside in the night, a late bird called to its flock, looking for a home. Somewhere in the distant wing, a floorboard creaked.

Jerome waved Richard toward the service closet down the hall. "Take the little elevator and get out of here. I have nothing for you. The Lord and I parted ways a long time ago."

Numb as a whipped dog, Richard had done exactly as he was told.

Richard had gone down to the first floor. He'd encountered no one else along the way. He'd slept fitfully in a guest room at the edge of the house because Kassandra had said she never wanted to sleep with him again after the way he'd behaved at dinner, and frankly, Richard couldn't blame her. He listened to the start of the rain.

Richard remembered the way Jerome had stood at the foot of the concrete stairs, staring at his watch, desperate for him to leave. Richard had looked at his own watch in the service elevator. On Friday evening, Richard had left Jerome alone at precisely one minute to midnight.

Now, on the roof on Sunday morning, the M18 still pressed to Luca's head, Richard shouted over the roar of the rising flood, "I never came within ten feet of the old man that night."

"And you think *I* did?" Toby shouted back.

To be honest, Richard didn't, really. Toby had never set foot in the kitchen before the knives were locked away on Friday night; he seemed unaware there were service elevators that could circumvent the creaky stairs, would have probably spent ages wandering the west wing his first time here and still never have found the roof.

And even if Toby had had help from someone—someone who could get him a knife, a map, a key to the roof—why would he kill Jerome? Apparently, Toby's family had never gone bankrupt thanks to the church, nor had Toby ever been to Camp Cleave, never suffered any abuse at Jerome's hand. Richard had wondered if maybe Toby had had a brother who'd experienced the same fate as poor beautiful William, but no: Toby just simply had a dead sister, according to Alyssa. Girls had always been safe from Jerome.

And besides, the old man had been Toby's meal ticket. The key to Luca's future. The start of a better life. Why would Toby want to hurt Jerome?

So for a time, Richard had been certain that Marie and Julian must have done it, maybe out of some convoluted revenge against their family. But Richard himself had checked the camera in their hall and found no sign anyone had tampered with it. He'd studied the security footage front to back. He'd watched the siblings step into their rooms at ten thirty on Friday night and not come back out until five in the morning.

But with the three most obvious suspects out of the way, where did it leave him? Nowhere useful. Here's what Richard knew: *someone* had planted a knife in his closet and that wire transfer in Alyssa's purse. And Toby might have been innocent, but he'd been snooping into things that weren't his business. He'd learned things he shouldn't know.

Richard wouldn't be sad to see Toby out of the picture, he really wouldn't. Someone had to take the fall for all this chaos, after all.

Richard took a careful step backward along the catwalk between the skylights, gun pressed to Luca's temple, picking his way through the jumble of junk Jerome had left there: lawn chair, Igloo cooler, fallen telescope. Richard didn't let go of Luca. Didn't let go of the gun.

Richard took another step. Another.

He thought he caught a blur of motion from the roof of the west wing. He glanced over, found nothing, looked back. Toby had come a step closer.

"You're not taking my son, Richard. And I'm not dying here."

"You—"

They felt a tremor in the house a moment before it happened. With a deafening *BOOM*, the east wing—the entire east wing—split away from Ramorah and fell into the water. Richard stared at the massive wave it sent up.

Lightning arched over their heads. A green sea surged in every direction.

The roof tilted at a queasy angle. Another tremor, a warning, shook the house.

Richard needed to get in that boat. Now.

But when he turned his attention from the vanished east wing, he found Toby standing right in front of him.

Toby swung his cane like a baseball bat.

The cane struck Richard in his shoulder. It sent a jolt of electricity down Richard's arm, enough to loosen his fingers. Richard dropped the gun. It skittered away over a skylight.

Enraged, Richard released Luca's hair and swung a fist into Toby's face.

Toby took the blow. Stumbled sideways. Fell.

But as he fell, Toby slammed his foot against Richard's ankle. Grabbed a handful of his shirt. A moment later, Richard was falling with him.

The two men landed—hard—on the eastern skylights.

The glass around them let out a startled *creak*. Somewhere very close by, a pane of the skylight exploded and crumbled from its frame. Richard and Toby both froze, petrified, certain the glass on which they rested was about to do the same.

It didn't. But through the skylight, not fifteen feet below, a flash of lightning revealed churning green waves. The water was rising fast. It was nearly here.

The lightning revealed something else, too: a glint of dark metal. The M18, resting on the glass not a foot away. Richard lunged for the gun, got his fingers around the barrel, brought it to Toby's temple. Toby didn't blink. Didn't weep. Didn't flinch.

He only stared at Richard, that same determined fire still burning in his eyes, and finally Richard knew where he'd seen that exact same expression before. Fifteen years ago. The tender agony of a summer in the woods.

Does he take after his mother?

Richard turned to stare at where Luca was watching them from the boat.

Oh, God. Oh, God.

Richard had been looking at this the wrong way all along.

It wasn't Toby he'd recognized.

It was Luca.

"Holy shit," Richard said. "How did you do it?"

Something hard and heavy struck Richard on the back of the head. Dazed, he felt a strong pair of arms wrap around his chest. A man's voice said in his ear, "Good job, cuz."

And then Richard was flying.

THIRD JULIAN

JULIAN HAD TRIED EVERY type of therapy in the book, taken all the antidepressants, tripped on mushrooms and acid and burned his life to the ground several times over and still, after what had happened at Camp Cleave, he was afraid of heights, he was afraid of climbing, he was so afraid of letting people down, he kept himself (and their expectations) as low to the ground as possible.

The best shrink Julian ever had was a stout lesbian named Trina who used to drag his scrawny ass to a climbing gym every week and billed it to Medicaid as therapy. God bless Trina. Julian had fallen off the wagon eventually, of course, but she and that gym had kept him sober way longer than methadone.

And it had taught Julian how to balance footholds and handholds. How to keep his core tight, his center of gravity tighter. How to react when you're standing at the end of a hallway that's suddenly gone crumbling into a lake.

You grab on to whatever you can and you start praying.

When the west end of Ramorah collapsed and Julian went plummeting with it, he didn't fall far. He caught himself on a frigid pipe somewhere on the second floor. He crashed sideways into a wall joist, a blow that would probably have incapacitated another man with pain. Not Julian. There was still enough morphine in Julian's system that he felt it as nothing more than a dull ache.

Julian found a foothold on a floorboard. He made the mistake of looking down, but only once, and saw Richard's wife, Kassandra, and Ginger's son, Matthias—the two most overlooked members of the family, come to think of it—bobbing in the water, quite dead, wrapped in each other's arms. Had they been friends this whole time, unbeknownst to anyone, or had the house's façade merely crushed them into this final intimacy?

A lurch of water, and they were gone.

Julian jerked his eyes away and refused to look down again. Never look down.

He climbed. Handhold. Foothold. Center of gravity. Pray.

It had taken Julian longer than he'd thought it would (*you* try climbing wet pipes and splinters in a pounding storm), and by the time he made it back to the dead-end hallway on the third floor, everyone was gone.

Julian climbed the concrete stairs three at a time.

He hesitated as he took in the scene on the roof. He didn't exactly have a game plan here, nor many options. Richard, with his gun and Luca, held most of the cards, though that clearly wasn't stopping Toby and Marie from following him as fast as they could. Julian suspected they'd need his help, though how he could get near Richard without scaring the man into doing something stupid was another question. The only cover on the roof was yards and yards away. And Richard had already started crossing the main wing.

Julian guessed he'd figure it out as he went, like everything else. While Richard's back was turned, Julian darted from the door and out onto the roof, moving at a low crouch, dodging holes in the tar paper with a little prayer, every few steps, that another wasn't about to open up to swallow him.

He was five yards from the juncture to the main wing when Richard finally noticed him. Time slowed down as the man began to turn in his direction.

Julian fell flat across the roof because there was nowhere else to go. He didn't breathe.

It worked: between the rain and the black tar paper and Julian's black hair and the black uniform he was still wearing from yesterday, Richard didn't see him. The man was clearly more distracted by Toby anyway.

"Someone's trying to frame me!" Richard was shouting. "Me and Alyssa both. Someone planted that paperwork in her purse to make sure the cops knew we were robbing the family, and then my wife found a knife in my closet to make them think I killed Jerome."

Oh, yes. Funny story about that paperwork. That knife.

Julian didn't risk moving again until the east wing collapsed and everyone's attention was turned away. He took the last stretch of the west wing at a sprint and skidded to a halt behind the tall A/C compressors at the juncture of the main wing. He peeked around the corner just as Toby swung his cane at Richard and Richard socked him in the jaw and the two went tumbling onto the skylights.

"Oh, fuck," Julian said. He was really getting tired of saving the day.

It was all a blur after that. Luca went sprinting down the catwalk to the boat at the foot of the cross. Marie stood paralyzed at the edge of the glass, clearly thinking the same thing as Julian: How could anyone hope to help Toby without endangering him and themselves to the creaking skylights? She jumped when Julian placed a hand on her shoulder. He pressed a finger to his lips. *Shh.*

There wasn't time for goodbye. Richard grabbed his gun. Leaned back. Pressed it to Toby's forehead. Julian grabbed the only weapon he could see: the shaft of Jerome's telescope, still resting on the tar paper near the skylights and Igloo cooler. Julian heaved the telescope over his head and dashed across the skylights.

He'd just reached Richard when the man finally, finally, put it together. Looking from Toby to Luca and back again, Richard said, "Holy shit. How did you do it?"

Jesus, Julian thought. Morphine was nice and all, but was there any high as satisfying as revenge?

Toby was putting up a hand for the gun. There was no need. Julian thwacked Richard with the telescope hard enough to daze the man. Before Julian could go in for another blow, the wet metal slipped from his grip. *Screw it.*

Julian wrapped his arms around Richard's chest and did the only thing that made any sense. He sprang forward, knocking Richard off Toby and rolling with him along the slanted glass. The skylights let out another dangerous moan.

"What are you doing?" Richard said, panic in his voice. "Let me go!"

But Julian wouldn't let Richard go. How could he, after what Jerome had said to Julian on Friday afternoon? When Julian had found the old man in his office, Jerome had been seated at his cluttered desk, scribbling something on two pieces of plain white paper. Julian had laid out the man's coffee and croissant without a word. After six awful months in this house, he still couldn't stand to be around Jerome a minute longer than necessary.

If all went as planned that night, this would be the last breakfast Julian ever served the man.

Julian looked at the clock. It was a little after noon. Toby and Alyssa were expected any minute. Julian carried the empty silver tray toward the hall, ready to go greet them, when Jerome said, "You've done well, you know. You should be proud."

"Excuse me?"

"There's just one detail you've overlooked. I won't be in this study tonight."

That stopped him.

"Close the door a moment," Jerome said calmly. "Don't worry. You're safe."

Julian hardly remembered doing as he was told. Just as he had the day Richard had driven him to the cliff face at Camp Cleave, Julian suddenly found himself petrified with fear. He leaned against the closed door of the study, staring at Jerome as the man wrote a note on a piece of paper, folded it, and started on another. Folding the second note, he wrote a name atop one page, a different name on the other, held them out for Julian.

"Hurry now, they'll be here soon. This is the most important step, Julian. Everything depends on it. Toby and Alyssa must receive these notes."

Julian held out the silver tray. Jerome rested the two folded notes there, just so.

The old man looked Julian in the eye. He didn't look away. "My brother's shown me everything about you, Julian. All your life you've been trying to atone for a sin that wasn't yours to own. That's why the penance never worked. You've ruined everyone's hopes for you again and again so that you never had to disappoint another soul."

Julian wanted to hit Jerome. He wanted to scream. Never, in the last six months, had the old man given any hint that he remembered what had happened at Camp Cleave. That he'd even known of Julian's feelings for beautiful, broken William.

"But look what you've achieved this summer, Julian. Look at everything you've set in motion." Jerome smiled. "It's never too late to start again. To fix things. To move forward. It's never too late to stop letting people down and start surprising them."

Jerome's phone had pinged on his desk. He said, "Ah. They're here."

Julian didn't remember when he'd started to cry. He did remember, with a lurch of pain he'd never understand, the smile Jerome had given him then. The gentle, proud smile of a parent. Or a friend.

"We're all trapped in our orbits in this family. Maybe with some luck you can do something about that." Jerome nodded to the notes. "Get downstairs. They need those."

Now, almost exactly forty-eight hours later, Julian lay on top of Richard on the house's roof, wrapping him in his best bear hug, and listened as the skylights squeaked and moaned around them. Richard struggled, Richard screamed, but Julian only held him tighter. He had an idea how this was going to end, and he didn't mind.

It's never too late to stop letting people down and start surprising them.

Julian held fast to Richard as Toby got clear of the skylights and made it back to the catwalk. He felt Richard trying to pull his hand—and his gun—free. Julian gave him a hard twisting squeeze to keep his arms screwed against his sides and the gun pointed firmly away. He succeeded.

And still Richard did the stupidest thing he could.

Maybe it was an accident. Maybe it was panic. Maybe a deep broken piece of his cousin's soul simply wanted to end everything.

Whatever the reason, without a word, Richard fired the gun straight into the glass beneath them.

Judging by the way Richard screamed as he plummeted to the water, he probably hadn't wanted to die. He wailed as he fell, sounding like a child, a boy, as the green waves rose up to greet them.

Julian himself only felt a remarkable sense of ease, maybe the first moment of real peace he'd experienced in fifteen years. It was over for him, but he'd always known this show would end sooner rather than later. Maybe, with any luck, Julian could stay clean on the other side.

And if God was kind, maybe he could see William again.

MARIE

WATCHING HER BROTHER DIE once had been bad enough. Watching him vanish through the skylights as Richard screamed like a boy in his arms: that was an agony fit for the Old Testament.

Someone was shouting in her ear. "Come on! *Come on!*"

Toby was on the catwalk beside Marie, tugging her arm and pointing to the northern wall. Luca was already seated in the rowboat. Wind howled around the great iron cross.

"We've got to *move!*"

For a man with a bad knee and a black eye from Richard's fist and a bloody ear where the man's bullet had grazed him in the hall, Toby still had plenty of zest in him. He practically carried Marie halfway down the catwalk before she could get her feet under her. She was so stunned by what she'd just seen, she was climbing into the boat before she realized that the wet weight dragging on her shoulders was her backpack and not just the first heavy pounds of grief.

"Hurry!" Luca shouted. "The water's coming."

So it was: green waves were already creeping up the tilted roof to the east. Toby was in the boat, struggling with the wet rope that tethered the little craft to the iron cross. Marie climbed in behind him, dropped her backpack, and thrust her hand inside.

Earlier this morning, while Toby had spoken with Alyssa in the Ezekiel Suite, Marie had taken a quick detour down the hall, into Richard's rooms next door. Last night, Richard made Marie hand over the key to the roof and the bloody knife they'd found among Toby's belongings. Richard had told her he planned to lock the evidence away in a safe in his room.

That was all well and good. But you'd think Richard would have been smart enough to move the safe's spare key, the one he always left hidden beneath the potted palm that sat near his room's window. A palm that Marie had moved time and time again to vacuum his carpet, picking up and returning the key every danged time.

These Wrights: they thought the house cleaned itself. Just like Ginger, who used to leave a paper trail a mile long across her desk, itemizing in perfect detail all the steps of her financial crimes. You didn't have to be an expert to see the woman and her siblings had been up to no good.

Nor did it take an expert to snap a few innocent pictures.

In Marie's backpack, beneath the change of clothes Toby had packed for Luca, under a bundle of papers wrapped in Saran Wrap and a simple plastic bag, her hand found a bundle of towels. She withdrew the bundle, threw the towels overboard and revealed the grisly blade Richard had planted in Toby's room last night.

"What?" she said to an astonished Toby, here in the little boat on the house's roof. "You thought I'd let him get away with this? Hold the rope taut."

Toby did as he was told. Luca stared at the water creeping up through the skylights.

Marie swung the blade down, severing the rope a moment before a great wave washed over the roof and carried them away.

———

By the time the rain ended, the only illumination in the wet, black world was a few distant flashes of lightning calming themselves on the horizon. There was still no sun. When a strange form bobbed past them in the water, Marie reached out and pulled it very close before she realized it was

Ginger, bloated with lake water, one pale hand still clutched to that awful journal. With a grunt of revulsion, Marie pushed the drowned woman away and watched them both sink, Ginger and the journal both, into the new lake. She wondered if Ginger had even had the chance to read that awful thing.

Marie let a few more things sink as well. Mechanically she dropped the knife into the water, followed by the key to the roof that she'd swiped along with it from Richard's safe. They both sank without a sound. *Where are you going? Where have you been?*

Lastly, Marie withdrew Jerome's torn scrap of a note from her pocket, the one that Luca had folded into a rose. Marie read it one last time in the glow of the far lightning.

> I know why
> Meet me o
> Midnig
> Don't be la
> Remember Matth

She crumpled up the note and tossed it, too, into the lake. She had the distinct feeling she was *still* looking at it from the wrong angle, but what did it matter? Marie was sick to death thinking about this place. These people. This weekend. All this violence and scheming and pain. Nothing could fix those boys from Camp Cleave. Nothing could fix her brother anymore. Marie had thought he was turning a corner this year, working here at Ramorah with such discipline and sober focus. So much for that.

Julian was dead. She used to imagine (with a shame so private she never acknowledged it even to herself) that whenever her brother finally passed on, she would feel free. Free from all the fear and worry he'd inflicted on her through the years. Maybe she wouldn't be happy, but she'd be liberated.

If only. Marie felt nothing now but a horrible mad ache, like God had reached into her chest and wrenched out half her heart. Had Toby felt this same way when his sister died?

What could a pain like this motivate a man to do?

Marie was watching the green water, too numb even to weep, when she realized there was someone else in the boat with them. A chill settled on her neck. A tingling silence smothered the lapping of the waves.

Risking a glance over her shoulder, she saw the shape of a tall man, a thin, dark shade, seated weightlessly on the boat's prow.

"I thought you'd gone," Luca said casually to the shadow. The boy was curled in Toby's lap on the floor of the boat, his head on Toby's chest, his smile easy and unafraid.

Marie heard a rush of whispered noise from the shade.

"Remember your promise," Luca said. "You're going to be friends with Tobias's sister. With my mom."

Toby was watching the shade carefully but without fear, the way you would a fire in its grate. A last gust of rain swept over them. The breeze died without a sound.

And then, when Toby spoke, Marie understood. She finally saw what Richard must have recognized a moment before Julian grabbed him on the skylight. What Sarah Nella had needed to talk to Toby about yesterday morning. What Corah had said at dinner Friday night.

Mother of God: Richard had been right from the start. A coincidence really is just God's way of tipping his hand.

"His mother's name is Willow," Toby said to the shade. "But sometimes she still goes by William."

VII

ASK AND YOU WILL RECEIVE

Toby

HE HAD KNOWN ABOUT his sister before anyone, maybe even before Willow herself. One Sunday when Toby was nine and Willow was eleven (back when she was still called William, of course), they'd filed out of the living room after their mandatory four hours of instruction and prophecy from Jerome Jeremiah Wright and dawdled in the back room of their uncle's house. Toby caught Willow fussing with the shoulders of her T-shirt in the glass of an empty picture frame, squirming in her jeans, pushing her hair around.

"What's wrong?"

"I can't get it right."

"Your clothes?"

"My skin."

Toby had understood. Even as a young orphan in the wilds of rural Texas, long before he ever knew what it meant to be *transgender* or *gender queer* or any of the other words Willow eventually taught him, Toby had known that it was more than his sister's clothes that didn't fit right.

There were plenty of fine young boys named William. She simply wasn't one of them.

When Toby was fifteen and Willow was seventeen, their uncle took a rare trip out of the house for the day. Toby couldn't remember why. Toby just remembered the way he'd stepped into their greasy kitchen that morning, rubbing sleep from his eyes, and found Willow dressed in pumps and a sundress and a perfect blond wig, smiling like a housewife from the fifties as she scrambled him a plate of eggs. Toby remembered the way the sunlight fell through the grimy windows to glint off her hair. He remembered the way Willow watched him, wordless, too afraid to even risk a smile.

He remembered the terror in her eyes. The joy.

Toby's heart had burst with happiness. Why not? It was the first time his sister had ever truly looked like herself. The first time in years she'd looked happy. Toby smiled.

"Do you think, from now on, when he's not around—you could call me Willow?" she said.

"Of course," Toby said.

And then their uncle's voice had sounded in the hall. He'd come home early. "Call you *what*?"

Silence had all but smothered them for the next two days. At the end of it, their uncle dropped a printed reservation on the kitchen table and said to Willow, "If you're staying in this house, you're going to this camp."

It was the place Jerome Jeremiah Wright promoted on his show every summer. Camp Cleave.

Willow gave Toby two great gifts in her life. One was Luca. The other gift came many years earlier, a few weeks after she returned from Camp Cleave. She'd come home a quiet, haunted shell of a thing, utterly unlike the girl who'd left (it was the first time she'd reverted to calling herself William, for one thing), and one day Toby caught his sister sitting in the backyard, her back against a tree, staring at the moldering fence with eyes so dead Toby feared, for a moment, that she'd done something drastic.

When Willow blinked, Toby said with relief, "What are you doing?"

"I'm building a palace."

"A what?"

Apparently someone *out there*—somewhere in the direction of Camp Cleave, that is—had taught her the trick. "Build a palace in your mind, the nicest place you can imagine," Willow told him that afternoon in the yard. "See the color of the walls, the texture of the floors. What color is the ceiling? Now imagine a door inside the palace. What material is it made of? What about the knobs and hinges? Look at the keyhole. Remember it well.

"Now open the door and see the empty room inside. See the walls and the ceiling. Check it for cracks. Make sure there's no escape."

Toby sat next to her, his eyes on the fence, and listened.

"Now, you can do one of two things. You can fill this room with details from a memory you want to keep forever. Maybe even reassemble something you've forgotten, a few details at a time.. Or you can take a terrible memory, something you can't bear to remember again, and toss it in the room. Quick, before it can escape, *slam* the door shut and turn the key. Hear it *click*. Make sure there's none of the memory still puddled in the hallway—they do that sometimes. Check the seals. Make sure none of it can slip through the cracks."

Willow took a shaky breath. "And then leave it there. Sealed away. Build another hallway with more doors so you can never find it again. Forget it. Leave that memory sealed up so tight that even God himself couldn't find it if he looked inside your head."

Toby used to wonder who had taught Willow this trick. Now, of course, it was easy to guess. Willow, for her part, had never been very good at maintaining her own palace. "Sometimes all the doors start opening and the only thing that keeps them closed are pills. Or heroin. Or both."

Toby could relate now. Being here, around these horrible people, in this horrible house, in this God-blighted state, had simply been too much for his own palace to handle. Toby couldn't keep the truth locked up anymore, not even to himself. He'd thought that with the help of his palace, he could make himself forget the truth of what he'd done—and what he'd spent the last six months *planning* to do at this very house—and seal it all up so tight that when the police arrived, he wouldn't have to risk getting caught up in his deceit.

That was another trick Willow had taught him, an old addict's tactic: if you forget the truth, you'll never tell a bad lie.

Not that Toby had wound up needing it. In spite of all his preparations, he hadn't spoken a single lie all weekend long.

Over the years, that memory of Willow in her sundress and pumps, that glittering moment of happy honesty between them, had taken up residence at the heart of Toby's memory palace. As Willow grew worse and worse after her time at Camp Cleave (and then worse still), Toby had sealed the memory away behind more and more halls and doors. It had simply been too painful to recall so much thwarted joy.

It was joined, at the beginning of this year, by a second memory. They were very similar, those memories, both in their shapes and their horror. The two memories had spent the last ten months together, sealed up behind a single terrible door in the pit of Toby's mind. It was the bad door. The worst door.

And it was opening at last.

Imagine Toby's surprise, shortly after this past New Year's, when he and Luca had returned home from a lean trip to the grocery store in California and discovered Willow in the kitchen, abruptly returned from one of her disappearing acts, clad in a sundress and pumps, scrambling them a plate of eggs in their tiny apartment on the fringes of LA.

"Mommy!" Luca had shouted. Toby set down his groceries and the mail he'd brought from downstairs and stared at his sister. He almost refused to believe how healthy she seemed. How happy.

Rehab, she mouthed over Luca's head, and for a brief golden moment, Toby allowed himself to imagine a happy future with his sister. He saw the three of them like this forever: happy, quiet, content. A family.

A home. After years in the desert, Toby and Luca and Willow might finally make themselves a home.

Toby was so pleased with the thought, he hardly noticed the envelope addressed to Willow in the pile of mail. He passed it to her after they'd eaten their eggs. Glancing at her as she read the letter inside, he caught the faintest shadow wash over his sister's face. "Everything okay?" Toby asked.

Willow laughed, tucked the letter back into its envelope, helped him sort the canned goods. "Just an old bill I never paid off."

After the groceries were put away and the dishes cleaned, Willow said she'd take a bath, if that was all right, and Toby said of course it was all right, and she went into the apartment's sole bedroom and emerged a few minutes later wrapped in a towel. He listened to the sound of the water filling the bath, he listened to the sound of his sister climbing in, the sound of something babbling at a low volume on her phone. Toby helped Luca with his math homework. He released a breath he felt like he'd been holding for ages.

After an hour, Luca turned away from his paper, looking suddenly very afraid. "She's been in there a long time."

He was right.

"Willow?" Toby knocked at the bathroom door. Knocked again. "Willow, are you all right?"

When she didn't answer, he sent Luca to his room. He broke the door open with his shoulder.

She'd swallowed a full bottle of Benadryl and climbed into a warm bath and let the pills drag her under. "Mostly painless," the police said later. *Mostly.* When Toby found her, his sister had looked like a drowned spider, the top of her head bobbing in water that had long since gone cold, an arm and a leg thrown over the rim of the small tub. Water fell from the faucet and struck her hair in a steady *drip.*

Drip.

Drip.

She'd left a video playing on her phone. It was *The Prophecy Hour*'s Christmas bonanza.

Toby had calmly closed the bathroom door. Sat on the toilet. Bundled up a towel and pressed it to his mouth and screamed until a blood vessel burst in his eye. "The Lord wants to give us all the good things of this earth," Jerome said from Willow's phone. "We just have to give. To give and live the way he demands. It's not so hard, is it?"

In the bedroom Toby discovered a bag containing twenty-four thousand dollars in dusty bills. After doing the math, he realized that after all the surprise contributions Willow had made to the family's finances through the years, the bag must once have held close to fifty grand. *You don't want to know what I did for that money.*

Along with the money there was a note. *As a friend of the family, we hope you can depend on us for any further assistance.*

Next to this was the envelope Toby had handed Willow that afternoon from out of the morning's mail. Inside it, Toby found a single sheet of paper. In a cramped, rushed hand, a man had written:

You did nothing to deserve it.

7:2

NOW, IN TEXAS, TOBY stirred from a wet doze, slumped against the rowboat's back seat, and found Marie staring over the side, tears glazing her cheeks.

She didn't look back at him. "You lied to me."

"No," he said truthfully. "I haven't lied once this entire weekend. I never had to."

They were drifting, alone and exhausted, over Lake Hebron. The rain had finally stopped. The flood had finally finished rising. Luca snored softly, curled up at Toby's feet, his head propped against Marie's backpack. Toby wondered if he would ever recover from the incredible guilt he felt in bringing Luca here. The agony of losing him, the relief at finding him safe, the horror that he might ever lose his boy again.

Here was another door unlocking, the shape of another memory filling itself in. Toby had never believed for a second that Alyssa's family's bigotry was simply *branding*, the way she'd always insisted, nor could he have predicted the plans the family had for the boy, but Toby had never figured out a way to come to this house and do what he needed to do without bringing his son along with him. It had always been the one flaw in the plan, the liability he could never square away.

Or, at least, the only flaw he'd seen in advance.

Toby had been worried for Luca the moment they hit the road. Maybe that anxiety had been what started it all, the disturbances in the palace that had haunted him from the moment he saw Lake Hebron.

Slam. Click.

Here on Sunday, the sky was still black, the lake endless. It was as if they'd drifted not out of Ramorah but out of their old plane of reality entirely. Toby and Marie and Luca might have been the last three people in the world: three souls drifting out of place, out of time.

Toby had told Kassandra the truth earlier this morning: he never read for pleasure. But he wasn't illiterate. He'd once read, for instance, that water is the greatest danger to any subterranean structure, which was

373

certainly true for the underground palace he'd built below the basement of his mind. When Toby stirred in the rowboat, he saw that the marble halls were in ruins, every door broken open, all of it sunk in the same black, glassy water that stretched around their little boat. A sunken labyrinth. A drowned tomb.

Toby would have to rebuild it soon (the police couldn't be avoided forever), but he could take an inventory for Marie of everything he'd kept sealed away all weekend. It seemed like the least he could do to repay her for her help.

"If you want to ask me anything," Toby said, "now's the time."

———————————

She didn't hesitate; clearly Marie had prepared a few questions while he was dozing. "Richard seemed to recognize you there at the end, but you said you'd never met him before. Where did he know you from?"

"I don't think he really recognized me. Maybe he saw some family resemblance, but I think Richard recognized *Luca* from when Richard knew Willow at Camp Cleave. I didn't realize until this weekend how much the boy takes after his mother."

"That must have been what Sarah Nella realized yesterday, too. What she wanted to talk to you about before the party."

"Probably so. According to Hugo, the family kept a list of all the friends of the family Jerome abused at the camp—not that I knew that when I came here. She must have recognized my last name from the list. It's probably why she kept calling me 'Mister Tucker.'"

"I know this is tacky, but I'm still so confused. Your sister started life as a boy, and then she became a girl. But how did she have Luca at all?"

"She never had any surgery or hormone therapy—we could never afford it. She lived as a woman, but sometimes she detransitioned when she fell off the wagon. I don't think she enjoyed it much. In a way I've always wondered if forcing herself back into a boy's life was some sort of self-punishment. It's how Luca happened. During one of those stretches,

Willow knocked up some girl to prove her masculinity or something. At least that's what she said."

"That sounds awful."

"It was. The girl, the one who carried Luca, she OD'd not long after the birth. It's why Willow came home with him. It's sort of a relief, honestly—it meant I was Luca's only next of kin after Willow died."

Marie chewed the shredded remains of a nail. "Jules . . . Jules once told me about a boy he'd fallen in love with out there when he got sent to Camp Cleave. A boy named William."

"Yes. That was her." It was a thrill to finally speak plainly. "And Willow mentioned Julian once to me too. I tracked him down after my sister killed herself."

7:3

FOR FIFTEEN YEARS AFTER Willow taught Toby how to build himself a memory palace, she never breathed another word about what happened to her at Camp Cleave. The closest she ever came was on a night, maybe the winter after her return, when she and Toby had gotten drunk off a bottle of Everclear she'd found in a trash can near their school and wandered the woods outside of town. "That whole family's fucked, you know," she'd said. "All the Wrights. The other guy in my cabin, he was some cousin they sent there before they'd give him a dime of his inheritance."

Toby had held on to this memory for years. (He'd already learned that with the right tricks, a palace could be as useful for holding on to things as it was for burying them.) A few years later, when Toby and Willow were leaving their first apartment in Los Angeles, Toby had finally learned the name of this distant Wright cousin when he discovered a letter Willow had started and then discarded behind the TV. *To Julian,* it began. *The only roommate I've ever been able to stand.* Toby would never know why Willow hadn't finished the letter. Probably because an addict never finishes anything.

He'd remembered these two stray details earlier this year, a few months after his sister's death, when a black Mercedes S-class had pulled up outside the school where he worked. If a coincidence really was God's way of showing his hand, then he'd tipped Toby a full house at that moment: a radiant young woman with blue-black eyes rolled down the window of the S-class to smile at Toby. "I'm Alyssa Wright. You've been expecting me."

Toby's first reaction had been absolute, blind shock. He'd seen this same Alyssa Wright on his sister's phone in the bathroom, smiling from the pews as Jerome delivered his Christmas sermon, and cold water *drip—drip—dripped* onto Willow's hair. That memory—the worst, the most dangerous memory—had burst open, right there in the school parking lot.

Alyssa had tilted her head. "Are you all right?"

Slam. Click. "Yes, sorry. I'm Toby. Good to meet you."

Julian hadn't been hard to find after that. Toby liked to think that on the afternoon when he'd first messaged the man, he'd just wanted to finally answer a few questions about Willow's time at Camp Cleave. Two questions, really. First, why had his sister left home a tender, placid soul and returned with a permanent storm in her heart?

And why had the letter that came for her shortly after New Year's driven Willow to end everything?

You did nothing to deserve it.

Toby liked to think he'd had no plans to kill anyone when he first messaged Julian. But if that was the case, why had Toby messaged him from a library computer with a fake Facebook account tied to a disposable email that could never be traced back to him?

JULIAN HADN'T JUST BEEN eager to talk: he'd been desperate to, like he'd wanted to talk to Toby his entire life. By the end of their first true conversation (conducted on burner phones, of course, bought from a convenience store with cash), Toby had learned almost more than he'd ever wanted to know about his sister's trauma. "The old man scooped William up and took him away. Sorry. I mean Willow. They never mentioned going by any other name."

"I think she was trying to live as a boy again when you knew her. It happened sometimes." Toby struggled to ask what he needed to ask. "What do you mean, that Jerome 'scooped her up'?"

Julian had explained to Toby that he and Richard Wright had *both* been fascinated with Willow at Camp Cleave. Maybe even in love. Richard had devised some challenge involving a rock wall to torment Julian, allegedly as part of a scheme to save Willow from Jerome's infamous behavior (behavior that no one who worked at the camp ever spoke about outright but that they all seemed to know), and when Julian had failed to satisfy Richard's demands, the little tyrant had made good on his threat.

"I don't know much about what happened to William those three days Jerome had them. Nothing good. But I know this: William, Willow—they weren't the only one. Jerome's been doing this for years. I think he's still doing it."

Toby hadn't said a word. He'd waited, breathless, as Julian finally proposed the idea they'd both known was coming.

"Someone should stop him, don't you think?"

7:5

"**I'd been trying to** persuade Jules for months that we needed to come to Ramorah and beg for work," Marie said in the rowboat. "We were beyond broke. Julian was taking a lot of pills. Then out of nowhere, this past April he said yes. Cleaned up his act. Packed his bags and moved into the house and put on a uniform for the first time in his life. I didn't second-guess it, you know. I thought Jesus had finally answered my prayers."

"Maybe he had."

"I doubt Jesus has a high opinion of murder."

"If he did, everything would have worked the way it was supposed to this weekend." Toby looked out at the water. They'd been drifting so long it was impossible to know where Ramorah had ever stood at all. "Sarah Nella is the only person who was actually murdered. Julian and I, we had the perfect crime planned. God just had other ideas."

Toby and Julian had budgeted for all sorts of contingencies, planned out every step of Friday night, but after that, nothing had gone quite right. Who could have predicted a rainstorm would hit the house the moment Jerome fell bleeding to the roof, that the storm would cut off the roads and kill the internet?

It was why Toby had spent much of Saturday *playing detective*: when it became obvious that the Wrights were more than happy to wait to call the police—when they seemed ready to brush the entire thing under the rug or, worse, to pin the murder on him—Toby had sealed up the memory palace as tight as he could and started gathering his own evidence. He'd made himself forget the horrible truth of what had happened on the roof Friday night. He'd made himself forget everything that had led him here, or at least buried it all so deep he could function without revealing himself or falling into a ball of nerves on the floor.

The pills helped. Until they didn't.

"Y'all planted the knife, didn't you?" Marie said. "The one Kassandra found in Richard's closet."

"Julian did. It even had Richard's fingerprints on it. After Richard finished chopping the salad on Friday night—the same as he did every night—he left the knife in the sink for Julian to deal with. Your brother wrapped the handle in Saran Wrap and hid it behind some cans in the kitchen pantry. Later, before Julian went upstairs to change everyone's linens for bed, he grabbed the knife, took it with him in his little trolley, and left it for me in the big umbrella stand in the dead-end hall where Jerome kept his spare canes. Julian even left it with some shopping bags and a spare pillowcase so we wouldn't leave blood in the stand itself."

"And after you killed the old man, you just had to take the Saran Wrap off the handle and voila—a murder weapon with fingerprints and everything."

Toby nodded. "After I was done on the roof, I left the knife in the umbrella stand for Julian to collect when he gathered up the laundry on Saturday morning. All Julian had to do was tuck the knife and pillowcase into his silver trolley and squirrel it away in Richard's closet as he made his rounds. The Saran Wrap dissolved in one of the cans of acetone the Wrights started keeping in all the service closets after the red paint turned up at the beginning of the year. The shopping bags went into the trash downstairs with all the bloody junk left behind after the family's chef sectioned the duck on Friday."

Marie leaned back, looking almost impressed in spite of herself. "He left the wire transfer in Alyssa's closet, too, didn't he? When he went to collect y'all's laundry."

"Yes. We didn't just want Jerome to die. Julian wanted Richard to suffer. We wanted the whole family ruined. And I wanted a way out of the marriage."

"Right. Because if Alyssa was indicted for fraud, you could terminate the prenup."

"And collect a massive penalty fee. Even after giving half of it to Julian, Luca and I could have lived comfortably for a very long time."

"It all sounds perfect, then. Except when the roads flooded, none of it could happen."

"Not just that. There were a couple things we didn't know. We didn't realize that Ginger had bled the family totally dry, meaning I might have never collected that penalty, and Richard had no hope of an inheritance."

"And no obvious motive. What else?"

Toby hesitated. Even now, even with the entire estate sunk to the floor of the lake, the memory of what had happened on Friday night scared him so badly he almost couldn't repeat it. "We . . . we had no idea Jerome went out onto the roof late at night. We assumed I'd find him in his study because he was always there when Julian went to change the man's sheets before bed. I think Corah's the only person in the family who knew Jerome went out to the roof."

"Behind a door with only one key."

7:6

FRIDAY NIGHT, NOT LONG after that ghastly dinner—*Oh, yes. I know a thing or two about sin*—Toby had stepped out onto the roof of Ramorah and stared, stunned, at the brilliant expanse of stars overhead. It was midnight: the appointed time. The witching hour.

"Remarkable, isn't it?" Jerome said.

Toby's palm sweated over the Saran Wrap that clung to the handle of the knife. His heart was in his throat. He didn't have long. An hour ago, a little before eleven, Alyssa had sat up in bed and whispered his name. When Toby didn't move, when he didn't answer her, he'd listened as his wife gathered up a few clothes and slipped from the bedroom without another word. Toby heard the suite's main door click open. Click shut.

He had no idea when Alyssa would be back. If she found their bed empty upon her return, tomorrow would get much more complicated.

"You can talk, you know," Jerome said, there on the roof of Ramorah. "No one will hear us."

"I didn't come here to talk," Toby said.

"Maybe not. But there's something you need to hear."

The old man crossed the roof of the west wing with the help of a cane, his white sweater gleaming in the starlight. He guided Toby past the A/C compressors and up the main wing before coming to a stop near the skylights. There they found a folding chair, a cooler, a massive black telescope. Peering into the telescope, Jerome swiveled it carefully on its legs, adjusted a dial, stepped away. "There. Look. It won't hurt you."

Confused (and more than a little unnerved), Toby peered into the lens. "It's a bunch of white dots."

"In the upper-right quadrant, past the constellation that looks like a snake, do you see the nine small stars that form a little jagged half-loop?"

"Yes. I think."

"Don't they look familiar?"

As if Jerome had spoken the words of a spell, Toby flinched away from the glass. He looked at the long scar on his forearm. He looked back into the lens.

"That's fucking crazy."

"The fishhook. It's not always visible—it vanished behind a chunk of space debris for a few thousand years, you know. The Babylonians were the last to see it. They said its appearance always foretold revenge."

Toby took a step away from the telescope. He didn't want to see any more.

"I know why you're here, Tobias. Billions upon billions of years ago, the Lord scattered those stars across the firmament to tell us secrets—all kinds of secrets. He lit them all, one by one, so that here, now, on this tiny speck of rock and hydrogen, I can look you in the eye and apologize for what I did to your sister."

Toby edged away. "Julian told you I was coming, didn't he?"

"I just told you who told me. The stars."

"That's fucking bullshit. Someone warned you. Someone told you who I am."

A draft of air, cool and quick as mercury, slipped past Toby's cheek. It left behind a rush of whispered sounds: *eeahsumdelptoebeyes*. At the time, Toby had disregarded the sound as a trick of his mind.

Now he understood what it meant:

He had some help, Tobias.

"You're going to waste a great deal of time looking for the answer I'm about to give you." Jerome sighed. He stared at the sky. "Your secret is safe. Your friend Julian never breathed a word of your plan to me, even when he had the chance."

Every door of the palace flew open at once. Rage blinded Toby. Rage and fear out of all control.

He raised the knife.

"Wait!" Jerome stumbled away. "For God's sake, wait. For your *son's* sake."

Toby hesitated. "What does Luca have to do with this?"

"Everything! You've done all of this for him, haven't you? You wanted revenge for what I did to your family. You wanted money to give the boy a better future. But listen, Toby, please." Jerome took a careful step backward, jogging the telescope with his elbow. Neither of them watched it fall. "Do you know how a star is made?"

Toby stopped. He said nothing.

"Pressure. An immense amount of pressure. You take a small clump of atoms drifting through the void, minding their own business, and you crush them and crush them until they ignite. Until they burn. Until they become something else entirely." Jerome watched him steadily. "All that pain—all that heat—it changes everything around it. It becomes heavy, dense, traps motes of dust in its orbit. It sends them spinning on courses they never wanted for themselves. Things start repeating. Over and over, the same pain. The same horror. Endlessly."

Above them, the stars burned.

In a smaller voice, so unlike his own, Jerome said, "Do you know how hard it is for a young man to lose the most important thing in his life right when he started to understand it? Do you know the damage it does to his entire family?"

"Yes. Yes, I do."

Jerome held out a hand. "Then give me the knife."

"Are you crazy?"

"Listen to me, Tobias—you don't have to do this. Taking a life, it's a terrible thing. Possibly the worst. It generates an immense amount of pain. It ruins everything around it. It sets a pattern in motion that can be impossible to stop. Killing me—it could create a new star in you. In your family. Don't do it to yourself. Don't do it to your son."

"Is this your way of begging for mercy?"

"Yes. But not mercy for myself. Didn't you hear the warning I gave you on last week's broadcast? God is real, Toby. And he is . . . terrifying." Jerome fixed him with those immense blue-black eyes. "The Lord has a great judgment coming for my family. Don't you *dare* do anything to endanger yourself now that his rage has reached its breaking point. Don't you dare risk losing yourself when Luca needs you most."

Of all people, it was the thought of the strange old woman he'd met at the Cracker Barrel that made Toby hesitate. She'd seemed so sincere. So terrified on Toby's behalf.

"Tobias, listen, we don't have long now. I've been shown the horror of what I've done. It's all up there in the sky if you just know where to look." Jerome's eyes traced the firmament. Even he seemed afraid to say what came next. "That's why I wrote that note to your sister. I wanted to apologize. To remove some of the guilt, to let her know she'd done nothing to deserve . . . to deserve what I did to her. But I had no idea the effect that letter would have on her. I didn't see it in the stars until it was too late."

The first booms of thunder echoed through the night. Overhead, a comet began its slow fall, a phosphorous needle threading its way through blackest velvet.

Jerome swallowed. "I still need to atone, Tobias. For everything."

Toby looked as deep into the old man's eyes as he dared. In spite of his rage, in spite of his fear, in spite of everything he'd done all summer to prepare for this moment, Toby finally asked himself a question he'd avoided every minute of every day.

Did Luca deserve to have a murderer for a father?

Jerome held out his hand. "There's only one way to break a star's orbit. Please. Let me fix this, if nothing else."

Toby held his breath.

He handed Jerome the knife.

"Thank you, son. Good luck."

The old man lowered himself, very carefully, to his knees, took a long breath, ran the point of the blade up and down his chest in search of a spot he'd clearly studied in advance. Jerome took a deep breath. He looked strangely at peace.

Not for long. He made a sound as the blade sank in—something between a moan and a child's startled yelp of pain—that made the bile rise in Toby's throat. Nothing could have prepared Toby for the astonishing amount of blood such a wound would produce. Jerome, too, seemed surprised. He gawped in shock and pain as it spurted across the roof, landing inches from Toby's shoes, and started spreading like a great lake across Jerome's white sweater. The old man toppled backward, landing on a skylight with a loud *thwack*. Toby wondered, now, if Jerome's skull hadn't cracked the glass.

The old man was still breathing—barely—when Toby withdrew the knife. The blade scraped across a rib on the way out with a sensation that made Toby shiver to the root of his spine.

He wiped as much blood as he could on a dry patch of Jerome's sweater and hurried away. He hesitated a moment in the doorway, turning back like he was afraid the old man might recover from the wound, and saw Jerome watching the stars. The first drops of rain started to fall.

Toby stepped inside. The door clicked shut behind him as he headed down the concrete stairs. He buried the knife in the shopping bags and pillowcase Julian had left in the umbrella stand, careful not to get any blood on his hands, took the service elevator to the second floor, and followed one of the many routes through the west wing that Julian had mapped for him. By the time he returned to his own suite—it only took a few minutes if you knew what you were doing—he was so frightened, he imagined he'd shed a trail of hair and sweat that would lead the police from Jerome's corpse straight to his door. What if Alyssa was already back in bed? What if she heard him come inside?

But there was no one in the suite but Luca, murmuring to himself in his sleep.

Toby lay in bed as the storm rolled in and the stars vanished behind great walls of black cloud. His heart thudded in his ears, louder than the thunder. His stomach was so light he could feel it falling through the bed, through the floor, through the earth.

All of Toby's defenses were failing him. He kept trying and trying—*Slam! Click!*—to seal away the memories of what had happened on the roof, what had brought him here, what he'd just heard, but his palace refused to comply. Doors kept bursting open. The entire marble labyrinth was threatening to cave in.

All because of a single, awful question:

How had Jerome known he was coming?

Now, today, Sunday, after everything he'd seen and heard, Toby found a certain peace in the knowledge that the world of logic and order waited on the far side of the estate's two creeks. He understood, now, that he'd crossed into a house with stranger rules than those that governed normal life. Jerome Jeremiah Wright, with the help of his dead brother—a brother who could read his prophecies in the stars—really had known ahead of time that all of this was coming.

But on Friday night, lying in his bed in the Ezekiel Suite, Toby couldn't believe anything so absurd. At the same time, he couldn't imagine that Julian had ratted him out: Julian had nothing to gain from such a betrayal. Nothing made sense. Nothing made sense.

Deep inside his mind, Toby had heard the faint low *creak-k-k* of a door swinging open. A bad door. The worst door. He heard a slow shuffle of feet, a wet *drip*.

Drip.

Drip.

He saw a pale, drowned Willow standing at the foot of his bed, dripping water onto the floor of the Ezekiel Suite as she asked, *What the fuck have you gotten yourself into?*

On Friday night, Toby had relented moments before his mind caved in entirely. He'd thrown his legs over the side of the bed, stepped into the closet, and dug open Alyssa's purse. He found the amber vial of anxiety tablets tucked into a pocket. He shook two into his palm and swallowed them dry.

We who are about to die salute you.

It worked. Toby took the memory of what had happened on the roof, the memory of all his many plans, and tossed it all behind the bad door. The worst door. He'd sealed the memory away in the same room where he'd stowed the memory of those few moments, earlier this year, when

Willow had returned from rehab and smiled in her sundress and heels and made Toby think that maybe, just *maybe*, she and Luca and he himself could finally be a family. A family with a home.

And then Toby buried all of it in the heart of the palace. He erased his tracks. He created so many doors and hallways he thought he would never find those awful memories again.

Slam. Click.

Slam. Click.

Slam. Click.

With just a little effort, there was no way back. No road home.

IT HAD BEEN SO long since they'd seen the sun, neither Toby nor Marie quite recognized its light. Suddenly, the lake had a horizon, a subtle warm line in the dark.

"Are you proud of it?" Marie said. "What you and my brother accomplished this weekend?"

Toby watched his son's sleeping face. *Pride* wasn't quite the word for what he felt. *Accomplished*, maybe. *Spent.* Months ago, when Julian had spelled out the first vague shapes of what would eventually become their plan to kill a multimillionaire minister, make themselves rich, and ruin the family in the process—"Think of the opportunity you have, Toby," Julian had said. "Alyssa's desperate to marry someone. *Anyone.* She'll turn thirty any day now"—Toby had put down the burner phone and backed away from it, terrified. A line in the sand had just been drawn. A lethal creek to cross.

But that evening at bedtime, Toby had walked into the bathroom and discovered Luca tugging at the shoulders of his shirt in the mirror. "I can't make it fit right."

Marie seemed finished with her questions. A long silence settled, a perfect dark stillness like the bottom of the ocean.

"What will you do now?" Toby finally said.

She shrugged. "I knew Ginger was stealing money from everyone—she left the paperwork lying around all over the place. I mentioned it to Julian, too, of course. That must be how he got the copy of the wire transfer to stick in Alyssa's purse."

"Yes. It was."

"Well, I made my own copies. And took pictures. I've got all of Ginger's bank information, even her log-in details. I figure if I move quick enough, I can drain some of the money she's got squirreled away." Marie gave Toby a dubious look. "I'm sure I could use your help with the rest of it, though. Legally speaking, you're her next of kin. Whatever's left of the estate, it's yours."

"My pleasure. Whatever money we make, we'll split it down the middle. That was the deal I made with your brother. In the meantime, you're welcome to stay at one of Alyssa's many properties. I hear the south of France is lovely this time of year."

Marie didn't smile, but she shook his hand. "Sounds like a deal."

"In the meantime, I'll teach you how to lock up a few memories," Toby said. "It'll make the rest of this easier."

Marie let out a long sigh, as if depressed at her own curiosity. "Before that, though, I have to ask one more thing—how did you know to go to the roof? How did you even get a key?"

In the distance, almost at the edge of sound, there came a dull *thump-thump-thump*. It could only be a helicopter's wings. It made Luca stir. The boy rose and blinked, the sun lingering on his wet lashes, dancing in the beads in his hair. He smiled at Marie, at Toby, at something past Toby's shoulder. "What's that?"

They turned and saw a shape that must have been bobbing for ages, unseen, in the gloom a few yards behind them. Something was slumped over a length of broken lumber. It wore a dark uniform. It had a head of black curls.

The moment they saw him, the man stirred.

On Friday afternoon, as Toby and the family stepped into the echoing marble foyer of Ramorah, Julian had awaited them with a silver serving tray bearing two folded notes. One was addressed to Alyssa. The other to Toby.

It had taken everything in Toby's power not to scream when he saw what Jerome had written to him. It was nothing like the note Jerome had written to Alyssa, though of course Toby had had no choice but to act as if the two notes were identical. Toby forced a smile as Alyssa read her own note aloud—"'My apologies, but I will be unable to see you until dinner. Welcome home, J.'"—and casually tucked his note into his pocket and said, "I'm sorry we won't be meeting him any sooner."

As everyone headed to the sun lounge for lunch, Toby had rushed into the bathroom under the stairs. He'd ripped his name off the top of his note and torn the rest of it down the middle, intending to flush each piece down the toilet one at a time.

The plumbing had other ideas. The toilet swallowed his name fine, but it choked and gurgled on the note's first half, the water rising nearly to the rim of the bowl before it sucked the paper away, and after recovering from a near heart attack, Toby had decided not to risk flushing the second half.

That didn't mean he wanted to leave it on his person. He'd folded the final portion of the note into a small square and tucked it under the potted orchid on the bathroom's vanity, telling himself he'd come back for it another time.

Later that evening, Toby's mind had been so taut with anxiety he'd never thought to worry when Luca used that same bathroom before dinner. Never even considered the way his son loved to look in trash cans and under containers, always on the hunt for scraps of paper he could fold into art.

Toby recalled what the note had read before he'd torn it down the middle:

> I know why you've come
> Meet me on the roof
> Midnight tonight
> Don't be late
> Remember Matthew 7:7
> -J

While Luca used the bathroom before dinner on Friday night, Toby had flipped open the grand Bible in the house's foyer to look up Matthew 7:7. "I can't remember the last time anyone read that thing," Ginger had said a moment later, descending the stairs like a lynx.

Toby had turned the page. No sense leaving anything to chance.

Matthew 7:7 reads:

Ask and you will receive. Search and you will find.
Knock, and the door will be opened to you.

Here, now, their boat drew up alongside the man in the water. Luca scooted aside to make room. The thudding of the helicopters wings grew louder. Toby helped Marie heave her brother aboard. Julian opened his eyes, took in the lake, and started to laugh.

Toby smiled to Marie.

"I never needed a key," he said. "Jerome let me in."

AUTHOR'S NOTE

IN THE FALL OF 2021, in the cautious final days of the pandemic, my life caved in. I'd spent three years working on a novel that succeeded at nothing but bankrupting me. I lost my apartment, my furniture, and a good deal of dignity. Seemingly overnight, I was suddenly sleeping on my parents' couch, back in my bigoted hometown, broke and scared with no future in sight.

But something amazing happened in that time. I didn't merely reconnect with my parents. I saw sides of them that I'd never appreciated as a child. I saw, for instance, that my father is a generous soul who was still working full-time, well past retirement age, to ensure he and my mother (and, for a while, me) were able to live securely. He was patient, forgiving, and kind. He was a fundamentally decent man, and I realized one day that there are far too few fictional heroes like my father: good men who love their families and will do anything for them.

In that moment, it was like two people walked through the door of my mind. One was Toby, a single father, poor and anxious and decent to the core. Holding his hand was Luca, his young queer son, a boy that Toby is determined to protect from the bigotry of the world and the horrors of poverty. I knew that Toby would do anything for Luca. Anything.

The moment I had these two characters, a whole book sprang up around them. I saw Toby and Luca walking into the home of a wealthy televangelist and finding a family that's rotten to the core. I saw just how dangerous Toby could be if his son was ever put in danger.

And I saw the twist in the book's last line that would turn the entire story on its head.

As dark as their story became, it was always a joy to write, thanks in large part to the bond between Toby and Luca. They're unlike any characters I've ever seen in a thriller, and they'll always have a piece of my heart. I hope, once you've finished reading *No Road Home,* that they'll be a part of yours.

ACKNOWLEDGMENTS

THIS NOVEL IS DEDICATED to my father, but both my parents deserve the book's first and loudest acknowledgment. They know what they did, and they know why I'm so grateful. Suffice it to say, my mother deserves a book of her own. I'll get right on that.

Many, many people read this novel through various stages of its development, some more than once. Stacey Armand read the book three times, in three different drafts, and is a saint incarnate. Andy, Colin, Hunter, Ross, Carter, Ian, David, and Jordy also read the book and offered invaluable feedback.

On the publishing side, I've lost count of the number of rewrites my agent, Melissa Danaczko, has endured with grace and endless insight. Loan Le saw the book—and saw all that she could bring to its story—and pounced on the title right when I was getting afraid no one would. My thanks to everyone at Atria, including (but not limited to!) Lindsay Sagnette, Elizabeth Hitti, Liz Byer, and all the dozens upon dozens of people who improve a book without the author ever even knowing it.

And finally, my thanks to all the readers who kept googling "John Fram new book" in the four years between this novel and my debut. I promise not to take so long with the next one. I'll get right on that, too.

ABOUT THE AUTHOR

JOHN FRAM IS AN author from Texas. His critically acclaimed debut, *The Bright Lands*, was named a Best Book of 2020 by Crimereads, Bookpage, and elsewhere. He lives between Waco and Austin.